by molly booth

HYPERION

Los Angeles   New York

First Edition, November 2016
10 9 8 7 6 5 4 3 2 1
FAC-020093-16260
Printed in the United States of America

Library of Congress Cataloging-in-Publication Data

Names: Booth, Molly, author.
Title: Saving Hamlet / Molly Booth.
Description: First edition. | Los Angeles ; New York : Hyperion, [2016] | Summary: "Fifteen-year-old Emma is acting as stage manager for her school's production of Hamlet when she finds herself transported to the original staging of Hamlet in Shakespearean England"—Provided by publisher.
Identifiers: LCCN 2015045426| ISBN 9781484752746 (hardcover) | ISBN 1484752740 (hardcover)
Subjects: LCSH: Shakespeare, William, 1564-1616 Hamlet—Fiction. | CYAC: Shakespeare, William, 1564-1616 Hamlet—Fiction. | Theater—Fiction. | Time travel—Fiction.
Classification: LCC PZ7.1.B668 Sav 2016 | DDC [Fic]—dc23
LC record available at https://lccn.loc.gov/2015045426
ISBN 978-1-4847-5274-6
Reinforced binding

Visit www.hyperionteens.com

For Nellie

1

I have a theory that the haircut started all of this.

It was three days before my sophomore year of high school started, and I remember everything: my hand shaking as I pushed open the door to the salon, the AC sending chills up and down my arms.

"Have a seat. Someone can take you in a minute."

I took a magazine and flipped through, not looking at the shiny-mirror half of the room. I hadn't had a real *hair-cut* haircut since we had moved to Massachusetts. But with everything that had happened in the last year, I desperately wanted a change. Needed a change.

I put down the magazine and pulled out the picture— some model I found when searching online. The cut was chin-length and feathery: supercool, supernew, superchic.

It'll be a miracle if it turns out like that, though, I had thought. *"Chic" isn't a word I can even say out loud.*

"Emma?"

I stood and blurted out:

"Hi!"

A twenty-something woman with short, spiky, purple hair raised her eyebrows at my too-enthusiastic greeting. She was curvy, with all kinds of piercings and dark, thick makeup. She looked like a gothic princess, or Queen Mab.

I didn't know how to wear makeup. I had slim hips, slim-to-none boobs, and my almost-butt-length hair was in a scraggly ponytail.

"So what are we doing today?" Purple Girl asked as I sat down in the metal spinny chair.

"I think . . . I want to cut it off."

"Awesome." She grinned. "How 'off' are we talking?"

I showed her my model picture. "Like this . . . but more like a fairy?"

Out loud, it sounded like something a kindergartner would say. I waited for her to smirk or laugh at me. Instead, her eyes lit up and she spun me away from the mirror.

"Let's do this."

Just one small snip. That's all it took. And then a long red ponytail landed in my lap. *That can't really be my hair,* I reasoned. *My hair is on my head.* But the hair was held together with an eerily familiar pink elastic.

Suddenly, I couldn't hear the noises of the salon. My heart pounded against my ribs. Bubbles of anxiety formed in my chest. Pop pop pop. *Deep breaths, Emma. Close your eyes. Make this positive.*

I pictured that with every snip, some stress from freshman year was being cut away, too: moving, quitting soccer, Lulu and Megan's kiss, The Horrible Party, and The Fog Machine Incident. I was leaving it all behind on the tiled floor, memories and worries tumbling away like leaves in the fall.

I began to calm down, and the bubbles popped slower and

sank lower in my chest. A new school year, a fresh start. The second year of high school had to be better than the first.

"What made you want to cut your hair?"

"I just, um . . ." I almost whispered. "I really need a change." I nearly said something about Brandon, but I stopped myself. *Don't go there, Emma. She's your hairdresser, not your diary.*

She *mmm*ed in response. Then her scissors sped up: *snip-snip-snip-snip-snip-snip-snip.*

"We're getting there—almost done!"

It felt like it had been ten minutes! The bubbles came back full force, boiling inside me. She whipped out a razor and started slicing the hair right above my eyes. I fought the urge to yank my head away. Or run. *This girl has purple hair; why did I trust her?*

"There!"

I didn't feel ready, but she spun me around. I cringed in anticipation of cringing.

The mirror.

"Don't you look great? I'm so happy with how it turned out!"

Did I look great? I didn't know. The girl in the mirror looked amazing, but I wasn't sure who it was. It was like someone had recast the role of me. The freshman-in-high-school Emma was gone, and a glamorous sophomore had replaced her.

I touched it gently. No more than a couple inches long on top and less than that on the sides and the back—way shorter than the model's hair. My bangs had been cut stylishly small and jagged. Little pieces near my ears were longer, and wispy. Suddenly, my freckles and slightly upturned nose worked: I looked like a supermodel. A fairy supermodel—Puck in *A Midsummer Night's Dream.* It was a terrifyingly great haircut.

I slid my vision to the left and eyed the scissors: *normal scissors couldn't have done this.* But they had black handles and pointy ends. Nothing mysterious about them.

"What do you think?"

We made eye contact in the mirror. Instinctively, I tried to sink back into the folds of my hair, but realized that wasn't an option anymore. Human interaction was going to change for me, clearly—this haircut meant no way to hide.

"I love it."

Last year, my wardrobe had slowly transitioned to all black. Not glamorous black, but normal black. Theatre techies were required to wear black for the shows so the audience couldn't see us working behind-the-scenes magic. Thanks to my theatre work, I had learned to be invisible: techies were swift, dark, silent.

My new hair wasn't silent—it shouted. Or screamed. So when I picked my first-day-of-school outfit, the black jeans and T-shirt were comforting. Even if my hair was loud, the rest of me would be quiet. Only one part of my outfit really made a fashion statement, and the one it made was the ultimate whisper:

Shoes. They were *the* shoes: black-on-black high-top sneakers, the supreme theatre-techie footwear. I had wanted them since last year when I joined stage crew, but I hadn't felt qualified. After my epic backstage blunder over the summer, I still didn't feel qualified, but I had bought them with my *Oklahoma!* stipend to console myself.

Monday morning, I took my time putting them on, and when I finished I admired my feet, wholly satisfied. *Hot damn*, I thought. *These shoes are the complete and total essence of cool.* A quick glance in the mirror made me grin: I looked nothing like First-Day-of-School Emma from last year.

I grabbed my backpack (carefully organized the night before) and thumped down into the kitchen. My cell phone buzzed with a text from Lulu:

> Be there in 5

I exhaled a whoosh of relief. Lulu had been on lockdown for weeks—no friends, no phone, no computer. About a month ago, after the opening-night performance of *Oklahoma!*, Lulu's girlfriend, Megan—one of the actors from the chorus—had kissed Lulu when she came out of the dressing room. Lulu's parents saw, and all hell broke loose. The Parkses were strict and narrow-minded, and not knowing what to do with their recently outed bisexual teenage daughter, their obvious solution was to cut her off from her friends and keep her from leaving the house.

I was looking forward to school starting for lots of reasons: not being the weird new freshman anymore, assistant stage-managing the fall production of *Hamlet*, seeing Brandon, and a class schedule that included Pre-Calc and Honors English II. But I was *really* looking forward to seeing my best friend every day again.

I grabbed a banana and was about to leave when Mom appeared.

"You look great, sweetie!" She set her briefcase on the island and fastened an earring.

"Thanks," I paused at the doorway. "So do you."

Mom was dressed all professor-y. Which made sense, because she was a professor. That's why we'd moved to Mass right before my freshman year: she had been offered a tenure track position at the local state college.

"Do you need a ride?"

"Lulu's picking me up," I said. "Any minute now, actually. I'll see you tonight."

"Emma-bo-bemma!"

Dad had developed an unnamed sense that recognized when important moments were happening in our house, so he emerged on cue from his home office in the basement. He spent his entire life down there, doing software and graphics. He also spent a lot of time shepherding my little sister, Abby, to her various prestigious activities. She was one of *those* seven-year-olds.

"Have a great first day!" Dad said from the top of the basement stairs, with his signature slicing wave. "And don't let anyone call you a boy! It's what's inside that counts!"

"Thanks, Dad!"

Gee, thanks, Dad.

And with that, I was set free.

They were still adjusting. It wasn't a surprise that my parents had freaked out about the hair. When I quit soccer mid-season last year, neither of them had understood. They still didn't. To be fair, that was partly because I had lied and told them I'd just suddenly lost interest, which didn't make a whole lot of sense given that I'd played soccer my entire life. Dad used to call my right foot "The Boot" and claim it was a "gift from the gods." No idea which gods he was referencing; we were the least religious family I knew. There was no way I could ever play soccer again. I'd quit overnight and ruined my team's season-long winning streak— without their star sweeper, they'd lost five games in a row and blown their chance at last year's playoffs. Everyone kind of hated me after that. No more soccer.

But I knew my parents had been secretly hoping I would return to her—that whole varsity, popular-high-school-athlete person. I could imagine them labeling freshman year as a Thing Emma Was Going Through. But the short hair must have confirmed their worst fears: I had officially become a weird theatre kid. The hair made it permanent.

Lulu's little red car pulled up.

"Em!"

She didn't even bother to close the car door, just sprinted across the lawn. I ran to meet her halfway, and we slammed into each other for the most epic of epic hugs. After a tight squeeze, I felt her sigh into my shoulder, her whole body collapsing just the smallest bit. We finally pulled back and considered each other after weeks of separation.

"Babe, your hair is *perfect*." She reached up and touched my bangs.

I laughed. "Really?"

"Really. Supercool, supernew, superchic."

See? Lulu pulls off the word "chic."

Even after a year, it was hard to believe she was my best friend. I looked her over for changes, but found none. She was still gorgeous—tall and willowy and intense, with slate-colored eyes and silky white-blond hair that cascaded down her back. That morning she was wearing a white sundress and strappy sandals. Not typical Lulu-wear—more like her mom had dressed her. I cringed inwardly, but it was a huge relief to see her.

Then came the hard part: We needed to *say* something. We hadn't really talked about what had happened with Megan, and I wasn't sure where to begin.

"How are you?" It felt like a lame question.

"I'm doing okay," she replied, giving me another quick squeeze before leading the way back to the car. "Better now." She flashed a small smile.

I dropped into the passenger seat, Lulu slid on big, dark sunglasses, and we eased onto the road.

"Lockdown has been lifted, tentatively," she continued. "We had a long talk yesterday, and they said I can try out for *Hamlet* as long as I come straight home after rehearsals. I played up the college angle."

"That was smart." Even with the rigid rules, Lulu's parents could never keep her from acting. Her talent was too undeniable.

"Yeah. I haven't told them what part I'm trying out for, though."

"That was smart, too."

We turned into the Belleport High School parking lot and sat in the car, watching the bustle outside the big brick building. Everything was made of brick or granite in Massachusetts—they liked their mud and rocks. Lulu pushed her sunglasses up onto the top of her head and revealed red and watery eyes.

"How am I going to get through this?" she stared at the school entrance. "What if everyone's talking about me? I don't want things to be different."

The only people at school who knew about Lulu and Megan were the drama kids who'd done *Oklahoma!* with us over the summer at Possum Community Playhouse. I was pretty sure they wouldn't spread rumors—drama geeks look out for each other 'cause we're all weird. I wanted to assure her that it didn't need to be different, that nobody else needed to know unless she wanted them to know, but I wasn't sure if that was an okay thing to say.

"Hey," I grabbed her hand. "It'll be fine. We're doing *Hamlet*, how could it be a bad year?"

Lulu and I had become friends because of Shakespeare; any references to the Bard could usually inspire her. She nodded and took a deep breath. Then she was out of the car, bag over her shoulder and sunglasses back on. I fumbled out the door to keep up with her.

She stopped in front of the double doors at the main school entrance and took a breath.

"All right, let's do this," she announced. "We at least have to show everyone how hot you look."

I beamed, and then immediately felt an unaccountable blush spread across my nose and cheeks. I turned away.

"Stop it, Em."

Lulu leaned in, her arms crossed.

"Let's get this straight," she said, keeping her voice low. "I'm not attracted to you, okay? You're my best friend, and you like boys."

My face was on fire. "You're right, I'm so sorry, I just—"

"Don't worry about it, babe." She ruffled my hair and then linked her arm around mine. Relief flooded through me: Lulu was changing, but our friendship wasn't. As we entered the school, I finally felt ready for sophomore year. But more than that, I felt ready for anything.

Lulu headed off to the junior wing, and I waded through the polo-clad crowd to get to my new locker. After arranging my things, I decided I would take the long way to homeroom, through the junior/senior territory, just on the off chance I would run into—

"Emma?"

I turned, feigning bewilderment.

Was it really possible for a guy to get four times cuter in three months?

His black eyes pinned me in place, and his triangular, dimply smile nearly knocked me over. He looked good: His shaggy dark curls had grown out a little, and he was more tan, and more . . . muscular. His biceps stretched the sleeves of his white T-shirt. One time last year, I'd seen him shirtless backstage. It was still my number one daydream.

"Brandon!" I smiled. "Did you have a good summer?"

"There's something I need to talk to you about." His smile morphed into a strangely serious expression. "Wait, something's different about you."

I was slightly annoyed that he had ignored the question I'd practiced the entire month of August, but happy he had noticed my hair.

"Yeah!" My smile brightened. "Do you like—"

"Here, come with me."

Flustered, I stumbled behind him until we ducked into a side stairwell. Blood rushed into my ears—was this it? Was something finally going to happen between us? And on the first day of school?

My Brandon Aiello crush had begun last year, when Lulu started bringing me to her *A Midsummer Night's Dream* rehearsals. I had looked up onto the stage, and there stood a *guy*—not a boy—with real stubble, in a soft, black leather jacket, laughing easily. I hadn't kissed anyone before, and I'd never really wanted to. But with Brandon . . . my feelings hit me straight in the gut, winding me, and I'd never recovered. Almost a year later, I felt like I'd made zero headway in the Brandon department—still no first kiss, nowhere close to a date.

But now we were alone. In a stairwell. And I was pretty sure my hair looked amazing.

"It's Janet," he said.

"What?" I replied with half a hiccup.

"Janet Shepard? The stage manager?" He had pulled out his phone and was scrolling through it.

"Oh, right, of course," I collected myself. Janet was my theatre mentor—a senior. I had worked on her crew all last year, and for *Oklahoma!* over the summer. She was the stage manager for *Hamlet*, and I was going to be her assistant. She was training me to take over when she graduated. "What about her?"

"Well . . ." Brandon held out his phone. "She sent me this email over the weekend. Her family decided to move to Australia."

I blinked at the phone, not seeing it. The emotions that had risen up when Brandon was pulling me into a stairwell for possibly romantic reasons plateaued before crashing down on me.

Janet. Australia. Hamlet. Koalas?

"So it looks like you're up!"

I stared at him. He gave me a pat on the shoulder. I couldn't even enjoy it. The bell rang.

"Welp! We should get to class."

"Yeah." I nodded robotically. "Class."

The next thing I knew I was sitting in homeroom.

Breathe in. Breathe out. Breathe in. Breathe out. Try to remember how to spell "breathe". Is it "b-r-e-a-t-h" or "b-r-e-a-t-h-e"?

It felt like a dream. One of those first-day-of-school nightmares that my brain concocted to make me grind my teeth at night. The rest of the morning blurred by as I waited to wake up. I barely noticed the senior varsity soccer girls snickering at my new hair.

Barely.

As I headed into the cafeteria, my sneakers squeaking on the linoleum, Brandon stopped me again, right inside the double doors.

"Emma, there you are! I forgot to mention . . ."

I braced myself for more.

"Auditions are tomorrow. Can you come help out?" he handed me a flyer with a skull on it.

Are you kidding? I thought. *Is Shakespeare the greatest playwright of all time?*

"Yeah, of course!"

"Excellent!" As he walked away to go sit with the computer club, I focused on a table behind him where Ashlee, Ashley, and Jennifer, my ex-teammates and ex-friends, were whispering, gaping in Brandon's direction and then back at me.

Yeah, that's right, a cute senior was totally talking to me.

As soon as I sat down next to Lulu, she looked at me seriously and said:

"I think the hair is working."

I relayed the morning's events, Lulu providing the appropriate amount of gasps and votes of confidence. As we speculated about auditions, I snuck a few looks across the room: Is this what being Brandon's stage manager would be like? Would he be stopping me in public, so the whole world could see a senior guy talking to me? Were we a team now?

I can do this. I can totally do this.

👑

The next day I was disappointed when I discovered "helping out" at auditions meant handing out paperwork and numbers, and then ushering people into the auditorium when it was their turn. I had been daydreaming of getting to sit in with Brandon and give my opinion of the performances. But that's not what a theatre techie does.

Brandon's role as student director was announced last year. It was always a senior, and once our drama director picked someone, there were only two requirements: 1. Put on a play. 2. Put on a *Shakespeare* play.

After being selected, Brandon had announced his choice: *Hamlet.* I had been surprised—Brandon was so good as Bottom in *Midsummer* I was sure he would pick a comedy. But Lulu's eyes had immediately lit up like steely fire. Knowing we didn't have many experienced guy actors for the fall, she had spent the entire summer learning the part of Hamlet. During *Oklahoma!* rehearsals she would balance both scripts on her lap.

"Wouldn't it be kind of weird for a girl to play Hamlet?" I had asked one summer night on the way home.

"Lots of women have played Hamlet," she scoffed. "He's considered a very feminine role."

I looked it up later, and she was totally right. But I still couldn't picture it being better than a guy doing it, since it was a guy's part and all.

Most of the students auditioning had chosen the "To be or not to be" speech. Lulu had anticipated this, and prepared instead Hamlet's first soliloquy, "O, that this too too sallied flesh would melt." I held one of the doors to the auditorium open just a crack so I could watch her.

"Lulu Parks, auditioning for the role of Hamlet."

She wore a thick-strapped white tank top with jeans and sneakers. Her hair was pulled back in a severe ponytail. This was Actor Lulu. She stood center stage and dropped her head. Her chest gave a subtle rise and fall, and then she began.

"O God, God, how weary, stale, flat, and unprofitable seem to me all the uses of this world!"

Lulu pouted, looking utterly, dramatically depressed. I almost laughed out loud. But then she quickly backed up as she pointed passionately at Hamlet's invisible mom, seething—

"Why, she would hang on him as if increase of appetite had grown by what it fed on. And yet, within a month (Let me not think on't—Frailty, thy name is woman). . . ."

I cringed. I never knew what to make of that line; I tried to ignore people when they told me Shakespeare was sexist, but sometimes it felt hard to deny.

I fought the urge to clap when she finished. She bounded out, and I gave her a big hug. She was beaming and flushed.

"It went well, I think."

"You were amazing!" I said, and I meant it. If any girl could pull off the role, it was her.

Lulu left after her audition to appease her parents. We had only a few more people waiting to take the stage, and I was working on my homework when a nervous voice asked:

"Can I get a form?"

I looked up. *What. The. What.*

"Oh, hey, Emma!" Josh Jackson nodded at me. "Cool hair."

"Thanks," I said and handed him a clipboard and a pen, trying to hide my shaking hands. "You're number forty-three. I'll call you when you're up."

"Great, thanks."

He picked a spot opposite from me in the auditorium lobby and sat, legs spread out, twiddling his thumbs. He went in ten minutes later, and I was left alone in the lobby under the fluorescent lights.

Fuzzy, lukewarm memories spilled on top of each other, all from The Horrible Party last Halloween. My sparkly orange top, a red Solo cup, a dark basement, my chest tightening . . . and Josh's big brown eyes, filled with sympathy and apologies. He had helped me escape that night; I don't think I could have left on my own. We hadn't spoken since.

What is he doing at the auditions for Hamlet?

I listened to him bumble through: "To be, or, not, to be . . . ?"

Oh, he's terrible, I realized, a bit relieved. *He doesn't have a shot at getting cast as a sentinel.*

It wasn't that I didn't like Josh. I did, actually; I liked him better than any of the other soccer guys. He was always really focused on his goalie game. But Josh didn't belong in my new, mostly comfortable theatre world. He inhabited the more normalverse of the rest of the school. Josh was on Earth, and I had made it out to Jupiter at least, maybe Saturn.

He finished and barreled out of the auditorium, both doors flying open at once. He dove straight into a corner of the lobby and bent over.

"Um, how did it go?" I asked, because it would be more awkward not to.

"Terrible," he replied, breath rushing out of him. "Remind me to never do that again."

"Why *did* you do that?" I asked before I could stop myself.

He didn't seem to care. "I've always wanted to try out for a play, but—" He took a raspy breath. "Sorry. It feels like I couldn't get my hands out in time and the ball hit me right in the chest."

I knew that feeling.

"Close your eyes," I instructed. "And list everything you've eaten today."

"Yogurt, granola, breakfast burrito, Fruit Roll-Up, three slices of pineapple pizza—"

"You don't have to say it out loud." I tried not to laugh.

He nodded, his eyes still closed. A few moments later he opened them and stood up, his body noticeably more relaxed.

"How did you know what to do?"

"I feel like that sometimes. Panicky."

His eyes focused on me intently. I looked away.

"Gotcha," he said quickly. "Well, thanks. See you around?"

He jogged out the lobby door into the parking lot.

At least I feel like I've helped him now, I thought, shoving my things into my bag. *We're even. That's the end of that.*

3

"**M**ama, you look amazing!"

Stanley White, the reigning Theatre Design King of BHS, paraded down the center aisle the following afternoon, grinning from ear to ear. Nerves shot through me, and I smiled back weakly. Stanley was a big deal in every way—six feet and solid, with big hair and big talent.

The Whites vacationed every August, and Stanley claimed he had never made it back in time for the first day of school. It was a point of pride for him—Stanley was a firm believer in fashionable lateness, except when it came to theatre.

He was also Lulu's other best friend. I would say he was my friend, too, except that he wasn't, really. Everyone thought we were a trio, but he and Lulu had been best friends since middle school, and I had only been Lulu's friend since last year. It was a strange dynamic. Mostly he just said things to embarrass me, and I got embarrassed.

"Where did my sweet little Jersey bumpkin go?" he said, and ran his fingers through my hair. "She's been replaced by redheaded Emma Watson."

"Really? You think so?"

Stanley was really good at flattery. And even though I knew that, it still worked on me every time.

"And I'm glad you didn't dye it," he continued. "We gingers have to stick together and reclaim the word."

Stanley's hair was *really* red: bright orange with teeny light-blond streaks, down to his shoulders. Most girls in the school would've killed for hair like his.

"Anyway, here we go," he sighed, taking out his design binders. "Another September, another student-directed nightmare. I honestly don't know why Gretchen keeps entrusting nearly half our season to amateurs."

"Come on," I said, taking my own black binder from my backpack. "It can't be a nightmare; Brandon's directing it."

"Honey bear, not all of us have such faith in your Brandon."

"My Brandon?" I hissed. "Keep your voice down! We're in the auditorium!"

"Why? Brandon isn't dating anyone, is he?" he said, hopping up onto the stage. "Who cares if you want to make out with his face?"

"Stanley, shhh!"

"This is going to have to be a complete overhaul." He wandered toward the wings, peering up into the lighting grid. "All I have up there are blue and green gels."

I swiveled and surveyed the auditorium.

Nobody's here. Nobody heard Stanley shooting his mouth off. Calm down.

"Well, it worked for *Wizard of Oz*." Our last show in here—the spring musical.

"Mama, this is *Hamlet* we're doing!" Stanley scoffed, motioning me to come over. "I need pallid and murky hues."

"And it needs to be pretty spectacular," I said, taking color gels and frames from him as we moved along the wing. "For your portfolio?"

"Yes," Stanley conceded, pausing to inspect a sidelight. "Perhaps my motivations for designing this show aren't entirely selfless. There's a lot riding on this for us seniors. I'm sure your Brandon feels the same way."

In all his talk about applying to schools, I hadn't realized Stanley was actually worried about getting in. Before I could come up with an adequate reassurance, he turned to me:

"How did Lu's audition go yesterday?"

Ah, good. Our favorite subject.

"I think it went really well!" I took another cut of green R88 from him. "From what I heard she totally nailed it."

"Good, good. That girl needs an ego boost like no other. She's been through a lot, and she needs our support."

Trying not to sound defensive, I said: "I was here all summer, Stanley."

"Of course, but you're new to Lulu's parents, and the stuff they've pulled in the past . . ."

Oh, fine. If this is a who-knows-Lulu-better contest, he's got seven years on me.

"Right. You're right. Okay."

We worked in silence for a few moments, until I remembered something that Stanley, who was additionally the Gossip King, would find *really* interesting:

"Hey! You'll never guess who was at auditions yesterday!"

His eyes lit up, intrigued, but just then someone burst out of the stage-right wing behind us.

"And here's a marvelous convenient place for our rehearsal!"

Every hair on my skin stood on end, and I felt a flush go

straight to my cheeks. *Brandon. My Brandon.* My Midsummer Night's Dream–*quoting, adorable director Brandon.*

Sigh.

"Emma! Stanley! Already getting started? Excellent!" he marched over to us. "I posted the list nigh ten minutes ago. Soon our actors will come flooding in!"

"May I?" Stanley prompted, holding out a hand.

Brandon retrieved a sheet of paper from his orange messenger bag. Stanley whisked it from his grasp and then paced forward and sat at the front of the stage. I set the gels and frames by Stanley's things and took the opportunity with Brandon to cough nervously and mutter something about the dust in the theatre. Before conversation could sparkle from there—

"What the hell is this?" Stanley demanded.

"The cast for *Hamlet*," Brandon replied evenly, walking over and standing at Stanley's side. I followed and looked over Stanley's shoulder.

My eyes landed on Lulu's part first, and then jumped around, taking in the rest of the cast. *No no no.* I leaned back not wanting to see the words anymore. My stomach sank through the stage's floorboards.

"But this is a joke, right?" Stanley shoved the list in Brandon's face. "Josh Jackson as Hamlet instead of Lulu? That's hysterical."

It was anything but, and Stanley and I both knew it. This would do major damage.

"Lulu is amazing," Brandon assured us as he grabbed the list and tucked it back into his bag. "But I needed her to play Ophelia. And Josh gave a good reading! Especially considering—"

"Considering he's a homophobic douche-bag soccer player?" finished Stanley.

The Horrible Party played in my mind's eye: I knew Josh wasn't the worst guy at our school, but Stanley didn't. The need to defend him, and Brandon, caused me to say something stupid:

"He's not so bad."

Stanley shot me a death glare before launching into an interrogation.

"Why did he even try out? Since when does he do drama?" Stanley stood up, pulling his intimidating size on Brandon's adorably average height.

"Oh, come on, don't you know that jocks secretly have the best singing voices?" Brandon said. "I mean, there's no singing in *Hamlet*. Yet, anyway. I think my interpretation calls for some contemporary musical numbers."

I suppressed a smile as Stanley fumed. "Do you think you're being funny? You're giving me a heart attack right now."

I tried to picture Josh as Hamlet, but the only image I could conjure up was him standing between the goalposts, crouched like a cat. Josh was a great goalie, but trying to imagine him in tights holding a skull kind of made my brain break.

"He doesn't care about Shakespeare or art; he's clearly only doing this as a résumé builder!"

"Look, let's just calm down, Stan." Stanley hated being called Stan. "I'm the director. This is my decision, and if you disagree with my casting choices, that's your problem, not mine."

The conversation had crossed over from amusing to distressing. Brandon stood inches away from Stanley's face, looking up at him, his gaze steady. Neither of them said anything for a moment, and then Brandon spoke again, his voice a little smaller:

"Well, it's actually kind of my problem," he admitted. "Are you still interested in designing for me? Because I'm a little screwed if you're not."

Stanley sighed and slapped his binder shut for emphasis. "Fine, fine. It's your grave, I suppose. I can light a douche bag just as well as I can light anyone else."

"Your skill knows no bounds," Brandon quipped.

Stanley whipped out his phone and disappeared into the stage-right wings.

"Now. Emma," Brandon turned to me. "Are you ready to be my stage manager? Even with Josh as Hamlet?"

I beamed like a dork, and for a moment forgot the sinking feeling. "Yes! Well, I'm gonna try—"

"Love the new hair, by the way. Have I already said that?"

"No, but thanks—"

"Josh Jackson? *Josh Jackson* instead of *me?!*"

At the top of the auditorium, illuminated by the fluorescent light from the lobby, stood my best friend, steam pouring out her ears and nose. Her graceful figure paused a moment before descending upon us. Stanley reappeared next to Brandon, watching smugly as Lulu continued to shout, careening down the aisle.

"By the pricking of my thumbs, something pissed off this way comes . . ." murmured Stanley. I jumped off the edge of the stage and started up the aisle toward Lulu.

"If I wasn't playing Hamlet because you found someone better, that would be one thing, but of all the sexist stunts to pull, Brandon! You can't honestly think that *Josh Jackson*—"

"Lulu, you need to—" Brandon called from the stage, trying to shout over her rant.

"Lulu Parks!"

Another voice cut through the chaos like a knife: our seventy-year-old drama director, Gretchen Terry, had materialized in the opposite aisle. Lulu's hands flew over her mouth immediately.

"If you want to be a part of this cast"—Gretchen held out a cautioning hand—"you need to cool it. Mr. Director, the rest of your players are waiting out in the hall. Perhaps a little scared of our Ophelia."

"Emma, can you go get them?" Brandon inched toward Gretchen, away from Lulu.

"Oh, I'd forgotten—" Gretchen eyed me. "Our new stage manager. Brandon, you don't plan on using a fog machine in this production, do you?"

Behind Gretchen, I saw Stanley's mouth drop open. Anxiety dragons rumbled in my chest. I gritted my teeth, shot an apologetic look at silent Lulu, and tried not to stomp into the hallway. At least my frustration with the situation (well, *Gretchen*), overrode some of my first-rehearsal-as-stage-manager stress.

"Um, hey! Everyone!"

I corralled the cast onto the stage. We had roughly thirty people. And I was in charge of them all. *Fantastic.*

"All right, circle up!" Brandon called.

While the cast tried to organize themselves into a basic shape, I pulled Lulu into the wings for a quick hug. Her arms were trembling.

"I'm so sorry you didn't get Hamlet," I whispered. "It really sucks."

"Thanks, babe," she whispered back. "But the show is going to suck more."

Then she flipped her almost-white hair over her shoulder and flounced back out onto the stage, greeting the freshmen with a smile. Theatre Queen once more.

We were mostly assembled, in a circle-ish-type way, so I grabbed my backpack to look for a spot—and found Brandon had saved me a seat.

"You good?" he whispered as I plunked down to his left.

"Oh, yeah, I'm totally fine."

Fine, that is, except for now that I was sitting next to him I wasn't sure I could move my legs. Josh sat three people away, shifting back and forth nervously. With his buzz cut and shiny track pants, he looked like he'd wandered into the wrong section of the yearbook.

Lulu was the last cast member to sit down. Gretchen had obviously given her a speech. Our theatre director was old and looked it, but she was also kind of a badass. She always wore a slim black turtleneck, which contrasted with her short white hair and big, clear glasses. She also had those magical theatre powers needed to calm down a drama queen or scare away stage fright: she was terrifying and comforting at the same time. She took theatre seriously, and if you messed up, there wasn't much you could do but take the backlash and cry. I figured that out firsthand over the summer, with The Fog Machine Incident. I was relieved she was more hands-off for the student-directed productions.

"Hamlet is my favorite play," Gretchen proclaimed, interrupting the flipping scripts. "It should be everyone's favorite play. That being said, it's a toughie. Five acts. If you don't cut a few scenes, or at least some lines, it will take over four hours to perform. If you're good."

Lots of eyes widening. Josh's big eyes got the widest.

"My advice"—Gretchen turned her large glasses toward Brandon—"is to cut things."

"Oh, I'm planning on cutting a lot of things," Brandon replied. "For instance, if anyone forgets their blocking, I'll be cutting off their feet."

That got a laugh out of everyone, including Gretchen, but I noticed Brandon had dodged actually responding to her advice, which probably meant he wasn't planning on cutting anything.

He respects Shakespeare too much to make cuts, I thought. *What a devoted artist.* And then I realized that meant I would be stage-managing an over-four-hour performance two weekends in a row. *I can do this, I can do this, I can do this . . .*

"Shakespeare is easier to read than it is to speak, and it isn't easy to read," Gretchen continued. "I'll be available throughout the semester for dialect coaching, so sign up for some time and take advantage of that. Those who were in *Midsummer* last year can attest it was useful."

Lulu and the other veteran actors nodded emphatically.

"And so, without much ado," Gretchen finished, standing up. "I'll hand this thing over to Brandon. First, though, a small piece of advice: 'Suit the action to the word, the word to the action.' "

Everyone applauded as Gretchen gave Brandon's shoulder a pat, then exited stage right, easing down the house stairs toward the basement rehearsal space, the Black Box, for the after-school kids theatre program she ran in the fall.

Theatre must be pretty easy when you're eight, I thought.

After Gretchen left, Brandon talked: about how *Hamlet* was the greatest play in the Western canon, how honored he was to direct it, etc. I tried to listen, but my attention kept wandering to Lulu, who was giggling with Kelly, another junior theatre kid, who would be playing Hamlet's mom, Gertrude. It wasn't like Lulu to talk during a rehearsal.

As Brandon's speech died down, I mouthed *Are you okay?* at her. Lulu shrugged and smiled at me too brightly.

So . . . no.

". . . so what is *Hamlet* about?" Brandon finished. The question seemed to freeze everyone at once, then blank stares or nervous glances ensued. Lulu, who would normally be all over that question, had now opened her script and was highlighting her lines with savage precision.

"Well, it's about a prince named Hamlet."

We all turned to stare at Josh, who was sitting wrong, with his legs splayed out into the middle of the circle. "And his mom marries his uncle, and then his dead dad, who's a ghost, tells him that his uncle murdered his dad, and that he has to avenge him. So then Hamlet has to sort of prove to himself that his uncle *did* kill his dad. And, you know, his girlfriend goes crazy and drowns in a river."

Nobody said anything for a moment. Lulu stared at her script as if doing so were the only thing keeping her from leaping across the circle and knocking Josh off the stage.

"Good!" Brandon smiled patiently. "That's a pretty good summary."

Despite the fact that the theatre dorks were appalled, I had to agree with Brandon: I'd assumed Josh didn't even know that much about the play.

"But what is it *about*?" Brandon pushed.

"Death?" said Rosie/Bernardo.

"Bros!" Greg/Horatio called out.

"Acting?" offered Tadas/Player One.

"Sexism," Kelly/Gertrude said, flatly.

"And a thousand other things." Brandon nodded. He seemed a little uncomfortable with the last suggestion.

My phone lit up in my pocket—a text from Stanley, to me and Lulu:

Outerspace Cafe after rehearsal?

As I read, I was vaguely aware of Brandon's voice saying, "Good. So. Let's begin. Emma?"

I shoved my phone in my pocket, quickly looked up, and realized I had the attention of the entire room. "Oh, um, what?"

Giggles. Deep, deep blushing. Brandon tried to hide a smile, but a dimple gave him away.

"Could you please read the opening stage directions?"

I had forgotten this was standard stage manager protocol.

I gulped like a cartoon character, but Lulu caught my eye from across the circle and nodded her head with solemn trust. I made myself focus on the line in front of me.

" 'Act one, scene one.' " My voice shook only a little. " 'A platform before the castle. Enter Bernardo and Francisco, two sentinels. . . . ' "

More hours than necessary later, Lulu and I trudged down the Foot—the long stretch of land in Belleport that sticks out into the harbor and leads to the lighthouse. Sandwiched between a seashell art studio and a penny candy shop was our little private universe.

The inside of the Outerspace Café was just as tackymagical as the outside. It was like stepping into the center of the nerd Milky Way, with walls painted an inky blue-black with great nova waves of purple and silver sparkles flowing all over them. Stanley had already ordered us astronaut ice cream, and was stationed at our usual booth with a misbehaving space cowboy painted on the table.

"So, do I want to know how the read-through was?" Stanley asked. I bit my lip—Lulu and I hadn't really talked on the way over.

"A nightmare," she replied firmly as we slid in. "If that's how the play is going to sound, we're in for a terrible run."

"Well, it wouldn't have been so bad," I ventured, tossing my math book up on the table, "if you hadn't 'accidentally' said half of Josh's lines before he did, or hadn't read Ophelia's part in that creepy, mannish voice."

"Did you really?" Stanley was delighted. "How could you do that to our new star?"

Lulu waved a hand as if her antics hadn't derailed whole scenes. "I was just trying to show Brandon that he could've cast a guy in my role instead."

"A male Ophelia?!" I laughed, erasing a step in the equation I was working on. "That doesn't make any sense. Effeminate Hamlet, yes. Dude Ophelia, no."

I thought they would laugh, too, but when I looked up, Stanley just raised his eyebrows. Lulu sighed and said in her serious voice, "This whole thing is just wrong. I'm sorry, Em, I know Brandon is your mega-crush, but he's a little sexist."

Lulu thought everything was sexist—she was a total feminist. *I mean, I'm a feminist, too,* I thought, *but I wouldn't accuse any of Lulu's crushes of being sexist.*

"I just can't believe he did that to me." Lulu viciously opened a menu and glared at the sandwich options. "Brandon knew I wanted to play Hamlet. I told him at the end of last year."

"But, um . . . he never guaranteed you the part, did he?" I asked.

"Okay, you." Stanley pointed a finger at me. "I hereby revoke all your talking rights on the grounds of your mushy feelings for that dimpled idiot."

"Well then," I retorted, "I guess Lulu isn't allowed to talk, either, on the grounds of the *ginormous crush* she had on Brandon in seventh grade!"

Stanley was stumped; Lulu hid her face in her hands, but I could tell she was smiling, just a little: "Oh my God! No! I always forget I told you that!"

I grinned into my ice cream.

"Anyway, that crush doesn't count," Stanley said, wiping his mouth. "Lulu has left boys far behind her."

"No, I haven't!" Lulu smacked the table. "I just like girls now, too. Don't put me in a box."

"Honey, we all know bisexual is a stepping-stone on the way to the glorious Temple of Gay."

"No. It's. Not."

They were starting to get loud. People were looking at us. This wasn't awkward at all. I stared at my homework, trying to appear studious.

"You know I'm just kidding," Stanley said. "But really, you haven't mentioned any guys since you and Megan—"

"That's because I'm in love with her," Lulu snapped. "I haven't mentioned any other girls either, have I?"

I became aware of the familiar playlist Outerspace kept on a loop: "*Ground Control to Major Tom . . .*"

I crunched a chocolate space-junk chip.

"Well, anyway," Lulu sighed. "I'm just disappointed. I wanted to try playing something new, and instead I'm stuck in the most stereotypical girl role of all time."

"You'll do something cool with it, though," I said. "And it will be a great show."

"Thanks, but I'm not expecting much." She looked sadly into her bowl, and then brightened in my direction. "But I do know that it's going to be the best stage-managed show ever."

"Oh, right! Janet's disappearance into a kangaroo pouch." Stanley grabbed my forearm. "I can't believe you didn't say anything before. We're going to have a blast working together! Are you nervous?"

"Yeah, of course," I said, extracting my arm. "I mean, I was expecting to be Janet's assistant again, and after what happened this summer . . ."

"One mess-up doesn't make you a bad techie, babe," Lulu said patiently. "I keep telling you that."

"Even if it was the most spectacular mess-up I've ever witnessed," Stanley added for support. "Remember all that fog billowing into the audience? I've never seen anything like it."

I dug my pencil into the math problem, trying to keep a shudder from noticeably going through me.

"That's not true!" Lulu jabbed her fork at him. "Remember when Derek directed *Merchant of Venice?*"

Stanley threw both his hands down on the table and cried, "The monkey! The monkey! I still can't believe he got a real monkey!"

"And the dress rehearsal when Kelly's mom brought her dog in—"

"And Max forgot to double-check that the carrier was locked—"

They collapsed into a fit of giggles. I tried not to feel jealous of their history, but sometimes it felt like I would never catch up.

"Well, at least you could applaud Derek for his commitment to authenticity." Stanley wiped tears from his cheeks. "It was a disaster, but Shakespeare probably would have used a real monkey. They had all kinds of weird animals imported to England back then. . . ."

As he trailed off, Stanley's beady eyes snapped into some sort of trance. He stared off into the walls, his mouth gaping, like he was really looking into space. And then a lightbulb clicked on over his head.

Literally. The barista had switched on the extra lights.

"Guys . . . guys . . . *guys!*" Stanley pulled out his notebook and quickly flipped to a blank page.

"I don't know who he's referring to," Lulu looked at me. "We're women."

"Fine, whatever, *women!* I just had a fantastic idea." Stanley began to scribble a diagram of our auditorium. I abandoned my homework and watched as his hand moved in swift, jerky movements across the page, adding details and smoothing edges.

"I'm going to design this show à la early sixteen hundreds. À la Shakespeare's time. À la Elizabethan England." He continued to scribble notes. I realized I didn't know the actual definition of "à la."

"It'll be like *Hamlet* would have been done way back when. Old-school *Hamlet*. Willy Shakes–style *Hamlet*."

"And, naturally, you'll need a trapdoor?" Lulu said, smiling at him.

"Oh, naturally, naturally," he said innocently. "Good point, Lu. Totally necessary for Ophelia's funeral scene."

I watched as he added a little rectangle center stage. As far as I could tell, Stanley had been forever pleading with

Gretchen to build a trapdoor into the BHS stage. And she had been forever explaining to him how it was a dangerous idea, and there were these tiny details called *building codes* and *the school board.*

"You know she'll never agree to it." Lulu stood. "I better get home. My parents aren't going to buy that a first rehearsal went all night."

Before the kissing incident, before Megan, Lulu would've been torn up about lying to her parents.

"You coming?" She looked at me.

"Yeah, great," I said, although part of me wanted to stay and watch Stanley. He barely noticed us paying and leaving; he was in the zone.

"He's a genius," Lulu said, turning the key in the ignition.

"A twisted, ginger genius," I agreed.

When we pulled up at my house, I paused and asked: "Hey, are you okay? I know getting cast as Ophelia was pretty crappy."

Lulu sighed and crossed her arms. "Yeah, well, that's just how things are going. I come out by accident, my parents hate me, I can't see my girlfriend. Why would I get the part I want? That wouldn't even make sense."

I reached for her. "Lu—"

She collapsed into my shoulder; I wrapped my arms around her.

"It's just too much," she whispered, voice thick. "It's *too much.* And I miss her *so much.*"

Megan attended Ralley, the private school two towns over, and with the summer grounding, it had been weeks since Lulu had laid eyes on her. I could still remember how my best friend had come home from an early *Oklahoma!* rehearsal bub- bling—it was a practice for learning the music, which didn't really require an assistant stage manager, so I hadn't been there. Lulu called me after and said she'd met *the coolest girl* from the chorus.

"She's, like, *so colorful*," Lulu had gushed over the phone. "She's got this crazy loud laugh, and she's a drama nerd like us. And her clothes are insanely bright. I think we all need to be friends—you'd love her."

The excitement in her voice had made me feel nervous, like she was going to ditch our best friendship for one with this new, colorful girl. I was old news at that point, *and* I only wore black. But then Lulu introduced us—Megan really was the coolest, and besides, it quickly became obvious they had something different. I remembered their heads pressed together in rehearsal; Lulu's long blond hair mixing with Megan's short, shiny black.

One night, Lulu had announced (quite dramatically) that when she and Megan had met, she could hear the stars begin to sing. I had no idea what she meant, but it sounded bigger, more romantic, than anything I'd ever felt for someone, so I didn't know how it felt to lose that, how to make her feel better.

I whispered to her as she shook. What could I possibly do to fix all of it? To erase the summer and save her from those months of pain?

I kissed her forehead, like I did with Abby when she got a cut or scrape.

And then I squeezed her tighter and held on.

4

The next day was our first real rehearsal. Brandon's schedule said we would be blocking the first two scenes of the play that day, and the cast was supposed to meet outside the school at the south entrance. When Lulu and I arrived, Brandon pulled me aside. (Actually pulled. He touched my bare arm and everything.)

"Emma, I'm going to take the actors on a walk for a character exercise. You can just meet us in the auditorium, okay? I won't need you to take notes."

"Of course! Cool!" I blurted, deflating inside.

"Excellent!" Brandon turned and addressed the cast: "My beloved actors: To begin our journey as our characters, we must first learn to walk like our characters. I hope you all wore sneakers, as instructed."

Brandon explained the exercise while walking backward, motioning for everyone to follow him around the building. Lulu crossed her eyes at me before putting on her Actor Face and joining the rest of the cast. Josh trailed behind, like a shy little kid, and tripped around the corner.

That's our Hamlet, I mentally sighed on my way back in. As I approached the right-wing entrance, I heard raised voices.

"What were you thinking?"

Gretchen and Stanley stood center stage, on either side of a big black shape on the floor. Gretchen was not happy.

"I was thinking: *How can we have Joshy jump into Lulu's grave if there's no grave to jump into?*" Stanley's words echoed in the almost empty auditorium. I wandered out onto the stage and then stopped dead in my tracks.

"There's a . . . hole . . . in the stage?" I asked.

Gretchen and Stanley noticed me for the first time.

"Yes, thank you, Emma, I hadn't realized," she snapped.

I startled and looked right at her. Her gaze was cold and hard. Her lips stretched into a thin line. The crinkles around her eyes had disappeared; her whole face was flat. It was a look that could decapitate.

Luckily, this time it wasn't me on the chopping block.

"Stanley, why don't you explain to me, and Emma, what made you think you could cut a hole into the school's stage?"

I didn't like being included in this. It felt as if I had walked right into a really uncomfortable one-act play.

"First, it's not a hole. I'm building a trapdoor." Stanley planted his hands on his hips. "Which, as you know, was a traditional part of English outdoor playhouses, and since my concept is taking this production back to Queen Lizzie, we really had to have it. As I've argued before, it was embarrassing we didn't have one already, really, considering the culture and tradition."

He looked so sure and sounded so convincing that I almost agreed with him. I glanced at Gretchen: not so much.

"And second, I don't think you understand the amount of pressure I'm under as the designer for this play, Gretch. It's *Hamlet*, and it has to be amazing for my portfolio—"

"Stanley, stop." Gretchen held up a hand, silencing him like a magic trick. "I know you're feeling pressure. You're a talented kid, and I've always let you do what you want within reason. This"—she gestured to the stage floor again—"is entirely out of the scope of reason. You've completely overstepped your bounds here."

Her voice sliced. Stanley's face was almost expressionless, but I think he was surprised at her anger. He wasn't talking his way out of this one.

Gretchen held out a worn hand: "I'll take your keys."

Without a word, he reached into his jeans pocket, extracted his keys, and dropped them in her palm.

"Keys to the auditorium are a privilege." Gretchen slid them onto the key ring she kept dangling off her belt loop. "One that I felt you deserved. You've broken my trust, and that changes things."

Stanley said nothing, just stared at the floor. Gretchen removed her glasses, rubbed her eyes, and took a deep breath.

"Now," she said, replacing her glasses, "we are going to my office."

Somebody gulped—I'm not sure if it was me or Stanley. He followed her off the stage and down into the aisle. Suddenly, Gretchen turned back.

"Emma."

I stood to attention and fought the urge to salute.

"Cover that up." She jabbed a finger toward the hole. "There's some cardboard and gaff tape downstairs. Put a sign on it marking it dangerous, and have *Hamlet* rehearse in the

Black Box. If Brandon sees the hole and asks, tell him we're not keeping it. I don't want him getting any ideas."

"Okay, I'll do that. All of that."

Up the aisle they went.

I grabbed an old, refrigerator-size folded box from the pile of cardboard in the basement and, armed with a big roll of black gaff tape, I approached the hole. It was big: rectangular, and about two and a half feet on the long sides. I kneeled down and stuck my head out over the opening.

It felt like I was looking down into nothingness. Dark space—an abyss that just kept going and going. . . . My head began to spin. . . .

And then I realized that it was just the Black Box. The lights weren't on, so it looked like a black hole, but in reality it was just a ten-foot drop to a black cement floor.

Gretchen has a point with the whole "dangerous" thing.

I ripped the cardboard box down the center and crossed one piece over the other, turning it into two layers. I taped all around the edges, then grabbed a Sharpie from my backpack and wrote on the cardboard:

DANGER: THIS IS A HOLE!! DON'T STEP ON IT!! YOU MIGHT FALL THROUGH IT AND DIE!!!

A little wordy, but I felt it conveyed what was needed.

As I admired my work, the cast came roaring into the auditorium. I intercepted Brandon and whispered that there was a "situation with the stage" and we needed to use the Black Box. He nodded, didn't ask questions, and smoothly told the actors that we would begin our rehearsal process downstairs.

Lulu looked at me with question marks instead of eyeballs, and I couldn't resist pulling her aside as the rest of the cast proceeded downstairs.

"What's going on, Em?"

"So you remember Stanley's whole trapdoor idea?"

"Duh?" She narrowed her eyes at me. I looked pointedly at the stage. Her gaze followed mine.

"What?! Oh my God. Stanley!"

"He's in Gretchen's office."

She laughed and shook her head. "I can't believe him. This show is so out of control already. You have to tell me every-thing later."

She squeezed my arm before following the cast into the basement. I checked the hole one more time, then went down myself. My pulse quickened as I approached the Black Box door—I felt a little panicked as I realized Lulu might be right.

We might be in for a rough afternoon.

👑

"Peace, break thee off. Look, where it comes again?"

"In the same figure like the—"

"Hold! Okay, Amelia? No pause after 'look.' Like this: 'break thee off. Look where it comes again.' Greg, move more stage left."

Brandon's directing style, so far, seemed to be interrupt-ing actors mid-scene and feeding them their lines the way he wanted to hear them said. Even when he was in character in his role as the Ghost, he would stop mid–ghostly turn and say "Hold!" scaring the crap out of everyone. The actors diligently repeated the lines back, but they were underclassmen and newer to theatre, so they weren't annoyed by how controlling he was being. I was dreading the next scene, when Lulu and the rest of the cast took the stage.

Sometimes that feeling of dread is overdramatic and unfounded, and the situation is much better than you thought it was going to be, and you think, *Why did I feel all dread-y? This is fine!*

But this wasn't one of those times. This was one of those times when your director *keeps* interrupting people, causing your lead actor to get lost in his speeches, prompting your best friend to recite half of his lines for him, *from memory*, inviting other cast members to exchange glances and whispers, which results in an *edgy* director and, ultimately, the rehearsal running over, which makes everyone, including the stage manager, feel tired, inattentive, and just generally pissed off.

I furiously scribbled blocking into my script while trying to keep up with the non-Shakespeare drama. Wiping a bead of sweat from my forehead, I realized for the first time just how doomed I was. Maybe I knew how to organize a show, but how did you keep everyone happy?

Please come back, Janet. I can't do this. I can't do this.

Being in the Black Box made this even more of a nightmare—it was hot and claustrophobic. I kept wanting to call a five-minute break, but the first and only time I tried:

"Not right now, okay, Emma? Good suggestion though."

It wasn't mean; he was just on a roll.

What he was rolling toward, I wasn't entirely sure. I just hoped the destination was planned.

Lulu had taken it suspiciously well the first time Brandon interrupted her, but a few minutes later, I saw why: She used it as a license to interrupt people herself. And by people, I mean Josh. She kept commenting whenever she felt like it, asking innocent questions like: "Is it 'sullied flesh,' Josh? Wow, I always thought it was '*sallied* flesh.'"

As bad as all of this was, it wasn't the worst part of rehearsal.

To me, the worst part was when Kelly, the junior playing Hamlet's mom, asked Brandon a series of thoughtful questions: "Brandon, what is Gertrude like in this scene? Is she cold? Does she actually care about Hamlet? Does she know that Claudius killed Hamlet's father?"

"*Hey! Spoilers!*" yelped Greg, covering his ears.

"Well, what do you think?" Brandon asked Kelly.

"I think a million things." Kelly threw her hands up. "But I want to know how *you* see my character." Kelly may have been a little frustrated with her casting. If Lulu had been Hamlet, she totally would have been Ophelia.

He paused a moment before ushering her back to her starting point.

"We're going to discover the answers together," Brandon said vaguely. "Let's go from the top!"

As Kelly grumbled, I jotted down more blocking notes, glad the questions I would be asked were more along the lines of: "How many people do we need to move the thrones?" or "Staple gun or gaff tape?"

But Brandon's lack of response worried me—he hadn't actually answered Kelly's questions. Questions I could have answered off the top of my head, just from reading the play. Was this some kind of director technique? Or did he actually not know the answers?

When we finally finished, Lulu came up to me: "I'm

staying late for language practice with Gretchen. Stanley's in the woodshop—he can probably give you a ride home. Is that okay?"

"Of course! Have fun!" I bit out a smile, anticipating a prickly ride with Stanley.

She dashed out the door of the Black Box, gleeful about her one-on-one Gretchen time. The rest of the cast thanked me as they left, which though nice, was a little alarming. *Actors actually acknowledging my presence. Another stage manager thing to get used to.*

"Hey, Emma."

I looked up quickly. The thing about Josh Jackson was that he was hot. Not in a theatre-dork-hot way, but a mainstream-hot way. Tall, wiry muscles, strong jawline . . . that kind of thing. I took a few seconds to speak.

"Hey, Josh."

"Did you have a good summer?"

I nodded enthusiastically. "Sure! Lots of theatre. I worked for Gretchen at Possum Community Playhouse."

"Really? That's so cool." He actually seemed to think it was.

"How about you?" I asked, very normally.

"Soccer camp, mostly. I worked at one in New Hampshire, and trained with the other counselors in our downtime. The kids were crazy, but awesome."

"That sounds great!" *He worked with kids?*

"Yeah, yeah, it was. Do you play anymore?"

I froze. His face fell.

"Sorry, I didn't mean—"

"No, no, it's okay," I said in a rush. "I don't, actually. I'm kind of done with soccer."

"Right, right." He scratched the back of his neck. "Well, if you ever want to kick the ball around, I could use the practice. I remember your foot."

We both looked down at my right foot. The way he'd said it, I kind of expected it not to be there anymore.

"Right." I looked back up at him. "But, umm . . . thanks. I'll keep that in mind if I feel the urge. To play."

"Cool. I'll see you tomorrow?"

"Four thirty in the auditorium."

It was hands down the longest conversation we'd ever had. As I watched him jog out of the Black Box, I wondered if Josh had always been that cool. Maybe I would've liked talking to him on the bus rides to away games.

"Hey, stage manager!" Brandon tapped me on the shoulder, and I spun around to face him.

"Hi, director!" We were the only ones left.

"Was that exhausting or what?" He slung his orange bag over his shoulder. "Maybe this is how jocks feel after practice."

"My hand's cramping a little," I offered. I couldn't believe he seemed so cheerful after that Shakespeare massacre.

He flicked off the light switch on the way out. "You need to do some finger weight lifting. Get in shape for the season." He winked.

I tripped on the stair and knocked my right shin hard against the step.

He should not be allowed to wink at me, I decided.

"Whoa, Emma! Are you all right?"

"Yeah, I guess I'm more tired than I thought."

Ow ow ow ow ow. I sat and rolled up my skinny-jean leg as far as I could get it. Brandon knelt down and we examined the small, acute scrape on my shin. A bruise was already starting to appear behind it.

This is going to kill in soccer practice tomorrow, I thought, without thinking.

"We're going to have to amputate." Brandon examined my wound, face serious and determined. I burst out laughing and he cracked a grin. "But seriously I think there's an ice pack in the fridge in Gretchen's office. I can— What's that?"

He interrupted himself and hopped up onto the stage. I followed, limping a little, as he easily ripped up one of the edges of the cardboard cover I had created.

"Whose grave's this, sirrah?" he quoted *Hamlet* as he knelt and peered down into the hole.

"Nobody's, according to Gretchen," I said, and then added, "It might be Stanley's."

Brandon laughed a big laugh, like a happy thunderstorm—a great boom and then a cascade of heavy chuckles.

I smiled, because I hadn't even meant to make him laugh. *Maybe I'm just funny. Maybe Brandon and I—*

"So our brilliant designer did this?" He stood up, admiring it.

"Yeah, but Gretchen said it's not going to be part of the set. She's going to fix it." I was relieved I had remembered to tell him, what with the wink and all.

"It's a shame." He sighed. "It's a great idea. It would really give our production an edge."

As I *mmm*ed an agreement, Brandon turned abruptly toward me and fired a question: "What do you think of the play?"

"Ummm . . ." I scuffed my right sneaker on the floor for a moment. I couldn't tell what he was asking, but then all at once thoughts flooded in—like that moment when you stare at a test, petrified, and then suddenly realize you know all the material. "I love *Hamlet*. It was the first Shakespeare I ever read. Hamlet's struggle is the most real, human thing I've ever encountered in a book—"

"Play," Brandon corrected.

"Yeah, play," I agreed. "Anyway, he's so caught up in his own mind that he can't actually *do* anything. I relate to that so much. I think a lot of people do."

Brandon nodded, his eyes cast down in concentration, his hand hovering over his mouth. He didn't say anything for a moment and then murmured: "How do I show that, though? How do I get the audience to see what's written on the page?"

I opened my mouth to answer him, but nothing came out. *Emma, you're smarter than this,* I reasoned. *Say something! You know Hamlet, you love Hamlet, you must know how to—*

"Yeah, I'm not sure, either." Brandon broke my silence. "A *Midsummer Night's Dream* was so much more straightforward, and Victoria was such a good director. She really knew her stuff. I mean, I've read *Hamlet*, but I'm realizing that I don't know how to . . ." He sighed again, and his body stayed in the sigh, sagged and heavy. I wanted to hug him.

"Well, I'm sure you'll figure it out." I sounded reassuring. "It was only our first rehearsal. We have a whole three months before showtime."

"Right, right." Brandon rubbed his hand over his face. "I just . . . I need a scholarship if I want to go to Julliard. My parents won't pay for me to be an acting major; they want me to do computer science. I'm good at that—really good—but I don't love it."

Information overload!

He looked straight at me then, and I must have appeared horrified, because he quickly smiled and touched my shoulder.

"Not your problem, though, Emma." He turned to leave. "It'll all be fine. So send the cast a reminder about rehearsal time for tomorrow? I think we'll probably be in the Black Box again."

"Sure," I said. "See you tomorrow." I watched him walk up the center aisle of the auditorium, the weight of his world on his shoulders. He closed the door quietly behind him.

Brandon didn't have it all together. He didn't know how to direct *Hamlet*. He was nervous about college. His parents didn't support his goals.

I tried to process all of this—everything I'd assumed about Brandon's life was wrong. Or maybe I hadn't thought about it that hard?

I sighed and sank down on the stage floor, took out my phone, and sent Stanley a text:

> Hey, can you give me a ride home when you're done? I'm waiting on the stage, next to your hole.

I attempted to do science homework, but how could I care about the planet melting when Brandon was in trouble? If you liked someone, you were supposed to care about the things they were dealing with, right? Right. So what would I do if I were Brandon's girlfriend?

I pulled at my black shoelace, imagining the hand holding and . . . other things that would take place. My pulse beat into my wrists as I pictured . . . almost felt—

Concentrate, Emma, concentrate!

Right. I blushed, even sitting alone on the stage.

How could I help Brandon? I couldn't make his parents

support his dream of going to Julliard. I didn't know his parents, and that would be weird. Anyway, I couldn't make an admissions committee accept him with a full scholarship. I felt useless. Stanley had left a few lights on, almost center stage, exactly where I sat. They seemed to shine on my thoughts and problems, making everything a little bigger and worse. I shivered—coming from the stuffy Black Box, the auditorium now felt chilly.

I opened my backpack to grab my hoodie and a handful of scripts flapped out. They had been scattered around the Black Box at the end of rehearsal; some of the actors were not working on their lines that night, and I totally had proof. Janet would have called them out on it in front of everyone. I would probably just find them at school tomorrow, give them their scripts back, and remind them when they needed to be off book—

Scripts. Hamlet. You can help Brandon with Hamlet. Durrr, Emma.

If I helped him with the show, there would be less overall stress in his life. Right? I pulled open one of the small red booklets. I'd read *Hamlet* three times completely through and seen it live once at a community theatre when I was in fifth grade. I felt I knew it pretty well—as well as I could know Shakespeare, anyway. Whenever I read one of his plays, I always found lines and metaphors I could've sworn weren't there before.

But this time was different. This time I couldn't just enjoy the text. This time I had a real purpose—I needed to be able to see Hamlet, to watch him in my own mind. That was the only way I could help Brandon *show* the parts of the play he wanted to.

I pulled out my black hoodie and shrugged it on, pushing the sleeves up to the big freckles on my elbows. I switched my phone to vibrate and stuck it in my front pocket. I ran my fingers through the strange, spiky hair on the back of my head. I closed my eyes, inhaled, exhaled, opened them.

I began to read.

5

BERNARDO
    Who's there?
FRANCISCO
    Nay, answer me. Stand and unfold yourself.

The opening lines jumped out at me—not just Bernardo,
but someone else, demanding to know: "Who are you, Emma?
Unfold yourself."
I'm working on that, okay? Check out the new hair.

KING
    But now, my cousin Hamlet, and my son—
HAMLET
    A little more than kin, and less than kind.
KING
    How is it that the clouds still hang on you?
HAMLET
    Not so much, my lord. I am too much in the sun.

As I read, Hamlet appeared in my mind as he usually does: not as a person, but as the abstract concept "Hamlet" that formed whenever I read the play. A swirl of adjectives: sullen, angry, passionate, frightened. Maybe a little dark hair and a black cloak. But I needed more than that to help Brandon; I needed a body, a voice, a solid manifestation of the Hamlet concept.

Where do I find that—where do I find him? Does he exist somewhere in my mind?

GHOST
    Adieu, adieu, adieu. Remember me.
HAMLET
    . . . Remember thee?
    Ay, thou poor ghost, whiles memory holds a seat
    In this distracted globe.

And then he was suddenly there: as Hamlet saw the Ghost, I saw Hamlet. As a real person. He stood on the stage in his inky black cloak, hair askew, crying out to his father, his face pained and filled with wonder. The Ghost disappears and Hamlet falls to his knees, his tear-filled eyes lingering where his father was.

I can see him.

    To be, or not to be—that is the question;
    Whether 'tis nobler in the mind to suffer
    The slings and arrows of outrageous fortune
    Or to take arms against a sea of troubles
    And by opposing end them. . . .

Hamlet takes out a dagger. He plays with it in his hands. He touches his face, his neck, showing the audience what might come if he decided to end the sea of troubles. His eyes search the blackness of the audience for answers.

I yanked my head out of the script, suddenly aware my heart was pounding. I looked out. The faint light of the auditorium illuminated the empty rows of red seats. Almost unconsciously, I launched myself off the floor toward the front of the stage, where Hamlet had been in my mind. I stepped into his place and immediately felt his words burning in my chest, moving up my throat, hot and urgent to get out.

"And thus the native hue of resolution is sicklied o'er with the pale cast of thought," I said, the words rushing past my lips. "Soft you now, the fair Ophelia!" I whirled around, expecting to see a glowing girl behind me.

But Ophelia wasn't there, of course, and for a moment it all stopped, and I laughed at myself, realizing how ridiculous I would have looked if someone from the cast had walked in. A techie, in her techie sneakers, shouting Shakespeare. And of course they would assume I have secret dreams of acting, because every techie must have secret dreams of acting. But I didn't, and that wasn't what was going on—although something definitely *was* going on. Here I was, planted at the front of the stage, reciting Hamlet's lines to an empty house. Something was happening to me. Something was happening to *Hamlet*.

I stepped back from the edge, shaking my head to refocus. But I couldn't sit down again. I began to pace back and forth across the front of the stage.

I nearly ripped the paper as I turned the pages of the script and stopped right before the climax, when Hamlet receives his challenge from Laertes. This scene was always strange to me because it was weirdly funny, even though it was almost the end and things were about to get serious and bloody. But you could see that Hamlet was finally going to take action—the scene ended with his famous lines:

```
If it be not now, yet it will come.
The readiness is all. . . .
```

The readiness is all.

In that moment there was a shift: subtle yet phenomenal. I blinked, and when I opened my eyes, something had changed.

I was Hamlet, too.

I stood on the stage and looked around—the other characters were up there with me: Horatio, my best friend, with kind, concerned eyes. My mother, elegant, wearing a deep crimson dress, entered behind me with Claudius, the striking murderer king, wearing my crown. Lords and ladies entered, swords were prepared for the duel. I hefted a few foils as I felt Laertes's glare from across the stage. I glanced at Claudius, who was accepting a goblet while whispering to my pretty mother. I smiled at her, and she smiled back weakly, nervous for me. Or maybe terrified of me.

She should be terrified of the man sitting next to her, not me. Laertes should be challenging Claudius, not me. My father, Ophelia—no, no. Don't think of them now.

I brushed Horatio's hand off my shoulder, walked toward the center of the stage, and faced away from Laertes. The murmur of the court died away as I closed my eyes and let my hands fall to my sides. The dark was calming. I knew the dark, and I knew we would soon know each other better. This is the way it would be, the way it was always going to be.

The readiness is all.

A whistle sounded. I opened my eyes, turned, and strode forward. My feet moved into a stance automatically; Laertes mirrored me. The whistle blew again. Laertes lunged and the crowd gasped—

I was already falling by the time I felt my right sneaker step onto the thin cardboard. My elbow cracked on the side of the hole. My hands flew up, grasping for the edge. I was suspended in the air. And I wasn't Hamlet, Prince of Denmark, falling into Ophelia's grave—I was Emma, and I was falling through the stupid hole Stanley had cut into the stage.

The Black Box is underneath the stage.

I'm going to hit cement.

I'm going to break my legs.

I'm going to die.

I'm not ready.

6

What I hit was strangely soft.

Cement is not soft.

My skin felt rough fabric underneath me, like canvas. I lay there, facedown, on something uneven and puffy.

A bed? No. More like a gym mat. Did Gretchen put a gym mat in the Black Box?

It was dark. My ankle throbbed, and my ears rang.

Did I hit my head?

I looked up. The hole was closed. Brightness leaked through cracks in the stage floorboards, making blurry rainbow spots.

The ringing in my ears softened into a buzz, as if they'd been clogged with water. *Mom's cure for watery ears: hop on one foot, shake your head.* I decided to try this, but when I stood up—

Crack! My head hit the underside of the stage. I rebounded from the wood and fell backward on the mat, faceup this time. I lay there, dazed.

Why is it so close? Where did ten feet go?

I took in a shuddery breath, wheezing a little.

Don't panic; ground yourself. Where are you?

I stretched my hands out to either side, skimming the floor. My fingers closed around small sticks. *No . . . straw.* I grabbed handfuls of the gritty stuff and sat up, holding it close to my eyes, trying to see it.

I don't think I'm in the Black Box. There's straw here. I'm not in the Black Box. But how was that even possible?

The buzzing got louder until it hurt. I shut my eyes and I clutched my head, mashing straw into my scalp. Something burst in my ears, and suddenly: roaring, laughter, footsteps overhead, music. A blast of noise. It was deafening. Was there a volume button somewhere?

I need to get out of here, wherever here is.

I opened my eyes and saw a large, soft light on the other end of the space. Now that my eyes were adjusting, I could see a stepladder to my right, and a maze of wooden foundation beams between me and the light. Afraid of bumping my head again, I dropped down and crawled clumsily through the labyrinth. My knees rubbed into the dirt as I shuffled along the ground.

My jeans will never be the same.

Another roar. Then shouting voices. More laughter. A creak. Then a louder crack. I paused, waiting for the ceiling to cave in. It held, and I shuffled forward quickly. The noises above me changed every few seconds, and each new blast sent my pulse pounding.

One more turn to the left, and then a set of stairs appeared in front of me. My hands slapped the first wooden step, and I crawled up into the light.

At the top, I was blinded once again and hit full-on with the stench of garlic.

7

I paused near the top of the stairs to take a deep breath. Bad decision. The air was damp, and when I inhaled deeply, my nose seemed to wince. Multiple, horrible smells attacked my nostrils: garlic, beer, smoke, and bad armpit smell. *Really bad* armpit smell, like a middle school locker room—if the middle schoolers were smoking drunks who had a serious garlic addiction, anyway.

My breathing, weirdly, eased, and then my eyes began to adjust. Up here, it seemed to be light outside, somewhere, even if the room itself was a bit dim. To my left, there was a wooden door with an iron handle; to my right and in front of me, a room full of shadowy figures that paced in silence, like ghosts. The front wall of the room had three archways, and light seeped through the dark cloth covering them. I watched as a quiet figure walked through the right archway, sweeping the cloth aside and stepping out into the light, vanishing as the cloth fell back into place. I heard noises and realized where the deafening sound was coming from: Something loud was happening on the other side of the arches.

You must know what's happening; you must know where you are, I tried to reason. *Figure it out, figure it out.* I whirled around, looking for something familiar. *If I could just take a minute and—*

"Boy!" a voice hissed at me.

Someone was standing over me. I clambered up the last few steps and stood to attention. Face-to-face with him, I saw he was wearing some kind of a helmet. The visor cast a shadow over his face, making it hard to look him in the eye.

"Put this away, and hence thee over to Master Wick."

He pushed a pile of metal into my arms, and I scrambled to hold on to all of it. He strode away to a clothing rack on the right side of the room, and I stood there, dumbstruck. *Who's Master Wick? What am I supposed to do with all of this junk?*

"The armor tub's over there," whispered a light voice in my ear, at the very moment a soft touch alighted on my arm. I turned back to my left: a girl, about my age, wearing a long, sparkly white dress and pounds of silly makeup. Pasty white foundation, bright pink blush. Her hair was curly blond, piled up on her head. It didn't match her black eyebrows, so I guessed she was wearing a wig. She gestured toward a big metal tub next to the clothing rack, squeezed my arm, then floated over to the left arch.

"Thanks," I whispered at her back. I wanted to call out to her, *Hey, wait! Can you tell me where I am?* But for reasons I couldn't yet grasp, it seemed important to stay silent.

I tiptoed over—my ankle twinging but apparently okay—and placed each piece of armor into the tub. It was lined with wool, making my work easy and quiet.

As I finished, an invisible string in my chest drew me forward to the closest arch. Suddenly, I stood at the opening, a hanging cloth blocking whatever was out there, the great light people kept disappearing into. I reached forward—

"Boy!" A gruff voice stopped my hand.

Is that my new name? The call came from a man I hadn't noticed before. He sat on a wooden chair, hunched over a little table in the space between the center and left arch. He waved me over as he coughed quietly into a handkerchief.

"Yes? Me?" I whispered.

"O' course thee," he croaked.

"Wick, when shall I exit?" Another man stepped in between us. *So the old, croaky man is Master Wick.* The interrupting man was younger than Wick, but older than me—thirty or forty or fifty. His brown hair, mustache, and small beard were greasy, and he was dressed in an elaborate jacket with a ruffled collar; bulgy, balloon-like shorts; tights; and shoes with heels. Plus a hat. With a feather.

"Exit at 'You shall keep the key of it,'" Wick said, pointing at a manuscript on the table in front of him. "And enter . . . now."

He gently shoved Greasy Interrupting Man toward the right arch. G.I.M. smiled at me as he brushed past. I instantly wished he hadn't. *Ew. Ew. Ew. Ew. Ew. Ew!* His teeth were so yellow, and there were little holes in some of them.

I shuddered and turned back to Master Wick. *Or maybe just Wick?* He was older, maybe sixty, pale, and a little sweaty. His skin was wrinkled deeply, like tree bark. He wore a floppy hat, a plain shirt and vest, and those balloon-y shorts. All of it was a dusty, dark blue. His left eye looked bigger than his right, and he was eyeing me with it.

"Boy, wave at the keepers." He pointed to a pair of gawky teenage boys, a little younger than me, standing at the left arch. They were dressed in similar worn blue coats and trouser pants.

The keepers? I did as I was told and waved at them. On my cue, they ducked their heads, hefted a bench between them, and went through the arch.

Okaaaaay . . .

I peered over Wick's shoulder: In one hand he clutched the handkerchief near his mouth, and with the other he ran a finger down the top manuscript page. I tried to make out what the writing said, but the words were written in ink. Not typed, but *written*, all blotchy and swirly. Something about the words seemed familiar; it looked like English, kind of, but it was hard to read.

There was one thing I could decipher though: Wick was reading a script. The format was all there on the delicate, brown paper—character names and dialogue beneath them. In the margins, there were scribbled but neat notes.

Suddenly, I knew exactly where I was: *backstage.* Wick was the stage manager, and the men in fancy clothes asking him questions were the actors. The "keeper" boys were part of his crew, and they had minded my cue. Which meant . . .

I'm Wick's assistant?

I looked around the room and saw it for real: The actors were pacing and fiddling with their props. Nobody was speaking above a whisper. The costume rack, the crates and table for props . . . this was exactly what backstage looked like.

I let out a mental sigh of relief. I had no idea what had happened to me, but if I was in a theatre, how bad could it be?

Except . . . this theatre was unlike any other I had worked in. There weren't any wings, or lights, or sound boards, or mics. What did the stage look like? Could I peek—

"Got a name, boy?"

Me. My name. Can't use my real name; they think I'm a boy.

"Umm, Em, sir," I said smoothly.

"Em? Is that for Emanuel, boy?"

"Yes," I agreed. *That was a freebie.* "Emanuel Allen."

"Thou art an Allen? In sooth?" Wick looked up from his script. "Is Edward thy kinsman?"

Who's Edward? Should I want to be related to him?

I decided to play it safe, and shook my head no as Wick's large eye searched me up and down. I stiffened from nerves—what if it was a magical eye that could see through lies?

"Is this the new assistant?"

Another greasy man had just come offstage. Not just greasy, though—he was striking. His forehead was unusually high, and his hair was blondish red and curly. He was dressed in all black, but an extravagant black—costume black. A black meant to stand out, not the hazy black of stage crew.

"Yes," Wick replied, turning a page. "He says he goes by Em."

"Emanuel Allen," I repeated, because I didn't know what else to say.

The actor grasped my hand in his big, hairy-yet-elegant one. "Well met, Master Allen. Richard Burbage. Or, today"—he gestured to his costume—"Prince of Denmark."

I gaped. *Prince of Denmark?*

"Thou may be Prince of Denmark, but thou art wearing the wrong doublet," Wick nodded at him. "I prithee: Change and get thee to the stage, Highness."

Burbage winked at me and went to the costume rack.

"Sit." Wick lightly kicked the stool next to him. I sat. "Now, Master Allen, this is a new play, so 'tis fitting for thy first day," he whispered, turning the page and cueing a few more actors onto the stage. "Most of the players are bumblin' 'round like newborn foals. Except for Master Shakespeare: 'Tis his play."

Shakespeare.

"'Tis a good one, too," Wick said, scanning another page.

"What's it called?" I asked, breathless.

"The Tragedy o' Hamlet," Wick replied, turning a page. I chomped down on my bottom lip, fighting the urge to squeal. "But it'll be the tragedy o' *nobody* if Burbage forgets to enter." Wick turned. "Master Burbage! Stop lookin' at thyself! Play a prince *on the stage!*"

Burbage looked up from a small mirror hanging on the back wall. He snatched up a book from a prop table and strode to the precipice of the stage-left arch. There, he paused.

He took a deep breath, and with that deep breath his body transformed—his posture and stance were more upright; his face became a blank slate, wiped clean of expression. I recognized what he was doing—I'd seen Lulu do it a hundred times before going onstage. I didn't know quite what it was, but it looked as if the actor was becoming empty somehow, before filling up with someone else. I watched Burbage become empty, then open his book and assume a look of perfected interest in the page, hunching his shoulders slightly. *Becoming Hamlet.* He strode onto the stage with his nose almost pressed into the binding.

As I stared after him, Wick interrupted my awe:

"Want to know what a book-keeper's job is, boy?" he muttered. "We keep the actors from ruinin' the play."

8

I wanted sophomore year to be different, but this was a little much.

I knew I needed to get back to the basement. I had to try and figure out how I'd gotten here and how the heck I could get back. But this was *Hamlet*—there was so much to do. Every time I took a step in the direction of the stairs, Wick barked a new order at me. I tried to check my phone at one point, to see if it still worked. But it was frozen from when I had left my own time—7:29 p.m. It was kind of eerie.

But I decided I'd worry about all of that later. Better to focus on my work, running around at Wick's command: prompting actors, cueing the stage-keepers, and handing off/receiving props or costume pieces. It was strange, but the actors didn't seem to know the whole story of *Hamlet*. They knew their parts, but were fuzzy about the overall plot (maybe because of all the ale they kept backstage). They were constantly checking in with Wick, who referred to his "Plot," which was a breakdown of *Hamlet* into entrances, exits, and scene changes.

They called their small backstage area the "tiring-house." Which was funny, because it was practically buzzing with energy. At first it seemed chaotic, but I quickly realized Wick had it under control. He directed the play from his chair like an orchestra conductor: He knew just how to time entrances, set-moves, and costume changes. Instead of sheet music, he had a chart of all the movements needed to run the show, called the "Properties List." But more than what was written down, Wick seemed to feel a natural rhythm with his actors. He knew which actors needed more time to change and which ones could remember their own props. His stage directions were so well organized it was almost artistic.

As actors came and went, swords gleaming at their sides, I tried to guess which one was Shakespeare. Though I had known Shakespeare was an actor, truthfully, I had always imagined him in an attic room, bent over a table, scribbling by candlelight. Not onstage, reciting his own lines to a noisy crowd. So I was curious to spot him, but with everyone in costume it was impossible. Plus, most of them had the same beard. . . .

During Ophelia's grave scene, I could just see through a gap in the curtain. I knew it wasn't right to peek, but I was too curious. The glare from the sun made it hard to see past the edge of the wooden stage, so I could only glimpse a few actors.

"Lay her i' th' earth, and from her fair and unpolluted flesh may violets spring!"

I watched Laertes help two of the teenage-boy actors lower Ophelia into her grave: the trapdoor. Watching her body disappear, I felt a shiver on the back of my neck. She was really dead and being buried in the ground.

A thought jolted me out of *Hamlet*: If I had traveled here through the trapdoor, did that mean Ophelia was going to ... ?

I held my breath and listened for footsteps on the basement stairs—nothing, no sound. My imagination quickly pulled up an image of the Ophelia girl on the floor of the Black Box, confused and terrified.

But then, as if from a puff of smoke, she appeared at the top of the steps, grinning from ear to ear. She smiled at me, one side of her mouth smirking slightly, and floated back to the prop table to dispose of her flowers. I marveled at her noiseless footsteps.

Why had I traveled through the trapdoor, but she hadn't? It kind of seemed like dream logic, so maybe I *was* asleep. But was I ever going to wake up? I tried to put those thoughts aside, so I would be useful to Wick, even if he was a grumpy old stage manager my dream-brain had concocted.

Soon we were at the end of the play—too soon, it felt—and the younger cast members, teenage boys dressed as pages, carried on the swords for the final duel scene.

"Sly, thou shouldst be onstage as Horatio finishes," whispered Wick to the crowned man playing Fortinbras. "Enter just at, 'Good night, sweet prince.'" Sly nodded briskly, jumped to the stage-left arch, and stood on the balls of his feet, waiting for his cue.

"There we are—all done." Wick turned the final page. "Everyone's either onstage or ready for their last entrance—now they just need to murder each other." I held back a giggle at his matter-of-factness. "Hast thou ever seen a play at the Globe, boy?"

The Globe. I shook my head. My English teachers had

passed out pictures of Shakespeare's famous theatre over the years, and I was aware of a re-created Globe theatre in London. I vaguely recalled Stanley bragging that he had been there once as a kid with his parents.

"Well, we cannot have that"—Wick paused to cough into his sleeve—"can we?"

Without another word, he scrambled off his chair and up a ladder at the back of the room. I followed him up, ignoring my ankle's protests.

We emerged on another wooden floor, turned a corner, and came out on a balcony full of audience. Wick put a finger to his lips—"shhh"—and we shuffled, standing in the aisle next to the last row of seating.

Golden afternoon sunlight poured in through the open rooftop of the circular theatre, illuminating the bright colors that took me by surprise. The pictures I'd seen had made me imagine the Globe with plain wooden seats and pillars, but this space was a coloring-book nightmare. Deep blue, red, and green colored every post, mast, and beam. Intricate, mechanical golden designs wound their way up the balconies. It was way too much—hideous and beautiful at the same time. Only the stage floor was plain wood. I could see the faint outline of the trapdoor at the center.

We were on the third balcony, the highest level of seating, and our view of the stage showed us the back of the actors' heads. The Globe was at once huge and somehow smaller than I'd imagined. The distance from the stage to our level at the top was only about the distance from midfield to the goal. The three floors of balcony seating went all the way around, and the rectangular stage jutted into the middle of the open space at the bottom. It was a tall, theatrical donut.

I realized that it wasn't only the space that made the Globe seem so big: It was the thousands of people watching breathlessly as Hamlet and Laertes matched each other point for point in their duel. Well, almost breathlessly—the audience certainly had enough breath to smoke pipes and shout at the actors. Food and drink sellers made their way through the crowd, like at our big home soccer games at BHS. Only instead of popcorn and sodas, they were selling apples, nuts, and ale in ceramic bottles.

All three floors of balconies were packed, while the people standing in the yard were practically on top of one another. Kids and adults alike leaned their elbows on the front lip of the stage, gaping up at the actors. The whole yard squirmed and cried out whenever Hamlet or Laertes landed a blow.

The balcony crowd was more restrained. Up at the top, we were among men and women dressed in silk and feathered hats. Everyone wore something on their head, even the people in the standing crowd. A woman sitting on the end of the row in front of me wore a deep crimson gown, her shiny blond hair swept up into her matching silk hat. I felt self-conscious of my own bare head.

Wick's total concentration on the stage turned my attention to it: Gertrude was drinking out of the poison cup. The stage was very bare—two chairs as thrones for Gertrude and Claudius, and nothing else for the set. Two red marble pillars towered at the front, holding up the triangular thatched cover that made a roof just for the stage. Two of the actors hid behind the pillars to watch the duel. About a dozen actors were onstage, either playing a specific role or as part of the general court watching the duel. The costumes were as bright as the theatre itself—intricate and rich, as if they'd been taken straight off the lords and ladies in the high balconies. In the sunlight, the colors dazzled.

Gertrude fell, and the whole audience gasped. A few people even cried out for her. *Why is the audience being so disrespectful? Can they please shut up?* I thought, but then I realized I could clearly hear the lines—

"O, villainy! Ho! let the door be locked. Treachery! seek it out."

Hamlet landed his final blow on Claudius and put the poison cup to his uncle's lips. Gasps rippled through the balcony crowd, while the standing audience below gave a great cheer. I glanced at Wick: His eyes were bugging out of his head, like if he opened them wider he could see the stage more clearly. Where could I apply to get magical stage manager eyes?

I couldn't see the actors that well. But their voices were loud and clear. If these guys could teach a voice-projection workshop at BHS, we wouldn't need mics.

As Burbage died, I felt his final words deep in my heart:

"The rest . . . is silence."

Hamlet went limp in Horatio's arms. As Horatio bowed his head and clung to his friend, I was surprised to feel tears in my eyes, and audible sobs came from every corner of the theatre. I tried to wipe my eyes discreetly, but found Wick looking straight at me as I did. I expected him to be smug and gloating. Instead, I saw he was misting up, too. His big eye twinkled at me, and if I wasn't hallucinating, he even nodded his head.

"Back down the ladder, boy." The moment was gone; Wick shoved me toward the opening. "They need their cue for the dancin'!"

Dancing?

I crept down into the darkness of backstage, too carefully for Wick, who crashed into me on his way down. He leapt off the ladder and hopped into his chair in a blur. The old man could really move.

I took my place on my stool beside him as he pointed at actors, lining them up.

Fortinbras finished his last speech, and thunderous applause shook the entire theatre. The newly dead actors rushed offstage and lined up as Wick directed. The man playing one of the gravediggers, called Armin, went to the front of the line and whipped out a flute. Wick gestured to him, and he began to jig and play merrily. The actors followed him through the center arch onto the stage, smiling and stomping as they went. The clapping evolved from a messy roar to a steady, pulsing beat.

It's the end of Hamlet *and they're doing a dance?!* I imagined what would happen if we ended our BHS production with a jig, and almost laughed out loud picturing the confusion on our parents' faces.

"Now, Master Allen, stand just there," Wick gestured to a spot next to the center-arch entrance. "And extend thy arms just so."

I quickly stood and copied his example, holding out both my arms as if to receive something. He nodded and then turned back to his desk, not giving me further instruction.

"Is this some kind of . . . test of the will?" My muscles had already begun to ache.

"Nay, boy, 'tis more of a test of the snout," he chuckled.

A few moments later it was quite obvious what he meant, when fifteen or so actors came crashing backstage, stripping off their clothes. They smiled, thanked me, and dumped beautiful costumes into my arms.

Beautiful costumes that reeked so strongly I almost reeled backward. I stumbled to the wooden costume rack and began hanging furiously, trying to distract myself from more than a dozen hairy chests.

As I hung up Claudius's purple robe, I sensed a patient presence hovering behind me. I turned—there stood a boy, a little older than me, shirtless. He held a familiar sparkly white dress. He was pale, with short black hair and blue eyes. He had some blush streaked down one side of his face, and white makeup only halfway rubbed off. His features were soft and delicate: his nose dainty, his lips small yet full and the color of bubblegum. Three dark chest hairs spiraled just under his collarbone, and he had no facial hair whatsoever. With his small ears that stuck out ever so slightly, he looked like an elf. He gently handed me the dress.

"Many thanks for taking this." His voice was airy. "I think it would look better on thee, anyway."

I froze. He knew I was a girl? How could he tell? What did they do to women who tried to pass as men around here?

A million possible punishments spun in my mind: They could put me in the stocks, or behead me, or even just banish me from the theatre and the trapdoor, so I'd never get home or see this amazing place ever, ever again—

Then he winked at me and fluttered away.

I felt my jaw drop. Our eyes met again across the room, and he smiled, satisfied. I bit my lip—was he really not going to tell anyone?

I shook my head and turned back to my task. The dress was beautiful but scratchy, and I got it on the hanger as quickly as

I could. As I held it up to place it on the rack, I recognized it: The boy had given me Ophelia's dress. I snuck another look at him—he was shrugging on a loose linen shirt as he laughed at something Burbage was saying. His laugh was sweet and sounded like falling flower petals.

Ophelia. Of course. The women's parts were played by men. Or, in this case, a beautiful teenage boy. I took a quick survey of the room: Yup, I was surrounded by dudes. I had known somewhere in the back of my mind, in the English-information vault, that there were no women actors in Shakespeare's time: I'd heard it a dozen times in class, and from Gretchen, *and* from Lulu . . . but I had never been able to imagine how that would work. Looking at the boy Ophelia, though, I realized there was a lot I couldn't have ever imagined before.

There are more things in heaven and earth, Horatio, than are dreamt of in your philosophy. . . .

Suddenly, his gesture felt more sincere. Maybe I could trust him not to tell anyone. Maybe he got it, since he played Ophelia and wore that sparkly dress.

As I was hanging up the last pair of bubble shorts, Wick announced:

"Chamberlain's Men! When our crowd has all departed, Master Shakespeare requests a meeting onstage, all company present."

My hands paused in their work, and my legs shook down to my sneakers. The Chamberlain's Men were grumbling to one another as they shrugged on their clothes, but I couldn't move or speak or breathe.

I'm going to meet William Shakespeare.

9

I *thought he was going to be taller.*

We were assembling for our meeting in a loose semicircle on the stage, and there he was: standing in front of the center curtain, wiping white powder off his cheeks as the rest of the Chamberlain's Men trickled out from backstage. I now understood why I couldn't pick him out before: He had played the Ghost, Hamlet's dead dad, Hamlet Sr.

The same role as Brandon, I realized. Does Brandon still exist somewhere? Do I still exist?

I had no hope of identifying Shakespeare backstage, with his face caked in otherworldly white like that, but as he smeared it off his face and onto a few handkerchiefs, I had slowly begun to recognize him—the long, dark brown hair flowing away from his balding patch, the little pointy beard and mustache. The very Shakespeareness of him. He was slim, and not very tall—maybe five foot five or so—wearing a white shirt, blue vest, those poofy shorts, tights, and heeled black shoes.

Wick was quietly conversing with Master Shakespeare, but I couldn't hear them above the general hubbub of the other actors and stage-keeper boys.

I sat with my back to one of the big marble pillars, half-hidden, starting to feel the effects of the last few hours. Every fiber in my muscles strained whenever I moved. My shin still hurt from the results of Brandon's wink, the skin on my elbow stung, my ankle twinged, and my brain pounded and pulsed in my skull. I was always exhausted after a first run-through, but this was worse.

And as my physical exhaustion started to sink in, panic rose to the top: Wait, wait, wait, what was I doing? Why was I here? How was I going to get home?

Shhh, I'm waiting for notes from the director.

I wanted to close my eyes, but that didn't feel like a good idea. I forced myself to look around, to stay conscious.

From this angle, I could see more details of the stage. It had pictures painted on the back wall, lots of mythology. Hercules shouldering the world, Poseidon parting the sea—all in vivid color. I looked up slowly, and my gaze got caught at the top of the theatre. The underside of the stage roof was painted the brightest blue I had ever seen, with shining gold stars.

Suddenly, I realized: The Globe was a new theatre. I knew what a worn-out theatre looked like, and this wasn't it.

If the Globe had been built recently, I was probably about four hundred years in the past. Or in an alternate dimension? How was any of this possible?

As my fuzzy brain grappled with perplexing time-things, the boy who played Ophelia sat down next to me. His left cheek was still smudged with a little white and bright pink. He must've noticed me staring, because when our eyes met he rubbed at his face with his sleeve and smiled at me sheepishly.

His smile was *whoa*. Dimple in one cheek, long lashes batting at me. Nothing wrong with *his* teeth. I turned and leaned slightly away from him, afraid that if we touched I might burst into confetti.

Oh, calm down, Emma. He's beautiful, he wears makeup, he plays women. Gay. Gay. Gay. Definitely gay.

Shakespeare (!!!) took a step forward, drawing my attention back to center stage.

"All here? Good."

William Shakespeare just said something. I just heard Shakespeare talk.

"Men, today the audience rejoiced in our tale." His voice was deep and sounded like smooth, warm glass. He paced as he spoke, gesturing with his handkerchief.

"Lords, ladies, and groundlings alike assured me they will be back for the next performance of our *Hamlet*. The day will be called naught but a monetary success."

The actors' faces lit up, and whoops and cheers erupted. Perhaps this wasn't the disaster meeting they had anticipated.

"But while our audience is willing to forgive any number of mistakes and incompetencies for the sake of the story—"

Oh no.

"—I am not."

Their faces dropped at once. Wick stood with his back against the other pillar, puffing on a pipe, expressionless.

"I have counted," Shakespeare said, pulling a piece of paper from his vest, "the number of lines that were cast into the abyss of the unspoken, the number of times your steps weaved a tangled web upon the stage, the number of ways your faces betrayed your characters. What could possibly be the excuse?"

Silence. Wick wheezed, then coughed into his sleeve.

"Before I continue, we must acknowledge the good work of our book-keeper." Shakespeare nodded at the recovering Wick. "The timing of the entrances and the set changes were the most theatrical parts of the play, and that falls on him, and our stage-keepers."

Shakespeare bowed his head in thanks at Wick, and the rest of the cast murmured their "many good thanks." Wick nodded in return. He kept a straight face, but his chest puffed up with pride. I knew it was a good feeling when the technical stuff went right, even if the performance was kind of bad. It meant that you'd done *your* job well, at least.

"And now for more notes."

"Will—" Burbage stood up.

"Wouldst thou have thine, Burbage? First of all, 'tis 'solid' flesh, not 'sallied.' A distinct difference—"

Oops. Shakespeare would be pretty pissed to know everyone's been messing up that line for four hundred years.

"Master Shakespeare," Ophelia-boy cut in, raising a small hand. All eyes turned to him, and by association, me. I kept my head down and hunched my shoulders.

"Master Cooke," Shakespeare replied evenly.

"Well, sir." Master Cooke was hesitant. "And I know I am a new player, sir, but it seems to me every performance has its flaws, and today's performance was not worse than the day before, or the one before that."

There was a murmur of agreement in the company. I couldn't believe this guy. Who back-talks Shakespeare?

"That may be true, Cooke." Shakespeare cracked all of the

knuckles on his right hand at once. *Yuck.* "But *Hamlet* is not the play from the day before, or the one before that. *Hamlet* is a great tragedy, a tragedy of the mind, and we must rise to meet the words I have written. Men, this performance needs one simple thing: more rehearsal."

A collective sigh. This group was really good at synchronized dramatic reactions. But I kind of got it—rehearsals after opening night were always difficult to get through.

"Will"—Burbage rubbed the bridge of his nose—"we already *had* a rehearsal for *Hamlet*."

A *rehearsal? As in* one?

"Yes, Richard, but we need another one. Probably at least two more. We've begun a habit of little rehearsal, and it shows on our stage."

They had *one* rehearsal? How did they even make it through the play? How did they memorize their lines? This was madness.

Another man stood up.

"Shakespeare, we have *Satiromastix* to learn for next week, and we must review *Henry V* for Saturday. We've no time to rehearse *Hamlet* again."

Two new plays in two weeks?! How was that *possible?*

"Sly," Shakespeare hissed through his teeth, "dost thou wish to hear the number of times thy words deviated from my script? Indeed, it would be quicker to count the times thou wast correct."

"Untrue, Will! I spent the entire morning—"

"Enough," Shakespeare snapped, silencing Sly. "This is a matter for the shareholders. Thou must remember thy place."

Sly sighed and sat heavily as six other actors stood. All of them were older—around Shakespeare's and Burbage's age.

Shakespeare shot Burbage a pointed look. Burbage cast a handful of questioning glances at the other standing actors—the "shareholders," apparently—and they all nodded reluctantly in response. Burbage strode to the back of the stage and stood beside Shakespeare.

"Will is our playwright." Burbage placed an elegant hand on Shakespeare's shoulder. "And our playwright says there is more work to be done. He sees what we cannot—therefore we must follow him."

The silence in response was different this time: resigned, grudging. It seemed like everyone knew that what Burbage said was true, however much they might have resented it.

"We will set aside time to rehearse on Monday. 'Tis settled, no more gibberish. I want to go home before we have to come back again."

Burbage was clearly in charge in some way, because this sent everyone in different directions. Many clumped up to chat, and some grabbed their things, crossed the yard, and left through one of the house entrances. I stood slowly, trying not to lean much weight onto my twingey ankle. I placed my hand on the pillar for support and felt a sharp pain in my index finger.

A *splinter?*

A sliver of wood had embedded itself, striking through the spiral of my fingerprint.

"'Tis oak," Cooke/Ophelia sang at me, his face suddenly very close to mine.

"It's made of wood? But it looks like marble," I replied, like an idiot.

Cooke nodded at me, eyes wide, and reached out and held the pillar in his hands. I watched as he swung his body around—he disappeared for a moment, then his head popped out on the other side of the pillar.

"I reckon thou know'st, as thy trade is in the playhouse, looks can be deceiving," he said, his voice light but low. He then grinned and sprang off the pillar into the yard, landing lightly on his feet. It was a five-foot drop, and he made it seem like a hop off the sidewalk curb.

I stared as he almost skipped to one of the side doors on the ground near the stage. He grasped the big black iron handle, then turned and aimed a wave at me, wiggling his fingers.

And with that he vanished into the outside world. Most of the actors had already gone—the stage had thinned out. Only Shakespeare and Burbage were left at the back. Shakespeare was smiling and laughing at something Burbage said.

Getting what he wants must put him in a good mood, I thought. The two of them sauntered backstage into the tiring-house.

If everyone left, I could try the trapdoor and see if I could get home, or end the dream or whatever. I looked at the paintings, the intricate designs, the wooden stage. This theatre was so beautiful.

Wick appeared at my left.

"Come, Master Allen, we have chores."

Thank goodness.

Part of me didn't want to wake up just yet.

10

I followed Wick backstage, where the stage-keepers were wait-ing for us—six pimply, awkward boys a few years younger than me. They were clearly intimidated (maybe frightened) by Wick.

He instructed us to put away props, straighten up the tiring-house, and empty the "piss pail" out back. Luckily, that task did not fall to me, as the assistant book-keeper.

I supervised and helped three keepers clean up the house, which included the balconies and the yard. We picked up apple cores and bottles and gathered up spongy red cushions from the benches, then we stuffed them into a long, narrow cupboard cut into the side of the first row of seating. For an extra penny, you could rent one of these cushions for the performance to make your seat more comfortable. Not a bad idea. Our auditorium seats were getting flat.

By the time we were through, the sun was starting to set, and there were no houselights to flick on. I had thrown myself into the familiar techie work, but now worries started to creep in: *It'll be dark soon . . . Will the trapdoor work? What if this dream doesn't end? Where am I going to go?*

Before long, the other stage-keepers were dismissed, and it was just me scuffing my sneakers on the dusty floorboards, and Wick carefully laying out tomorrow's script. All of the scripts were kept in a locked chest at the back of the tiring-house.

Wick was reviewing for the next day, scanning the pages by the light of a small candle. After the first few scenes, he seemed to recover his bearings, and grunted in satisfaction before setting the pages right again.

"All right, boy, I'll be seeing thee soon enough." He clapped a hand on my shoulder. "Before thou goest, look to the under-stage. I forgot Yorick's skull has likely been abandoned down there in Hell, and he doth not deserve such a fate."

He shoved the candle's metal holder at me. It had a little hook, which I clumsily slid a finger into.

"Don't drop it, boy. The Globe's made o' wood and horse-hair plaster. It'll burn and it'll stink."

"Right, of course." I gulped.

"Canst thou get home?"

That's a loaded question, I thought. But I said: "Don't worry about me!"

"Not worried," Wick grumbled. "Just askin'."

"Umm, right. Then yeah, I'm fine."

Wick hopped to the back of the tiring-house and paused at the door.

"Thou did a fine job today, Master Allen," he called. "Much better than I thought."

"Thank you!" I was surprised.

"Just one thing: Get thyself some clothes in London. I cannot guess what logic goes into what thou wearest in the country, but in London we wear doublets"—he gestured to his vesty thing—"and slops"—he gestured to his poofy shorts. "Best to fit in."

I looked down at my black hoodie, skinny jeans, and black high-tops. My carefully chosen outfit had been deemed uncool by a sixty-year-old man wearing blue velvet shorts.

"I'll try."

"Till tomorrow. I shall see thee anon."

He sprang through the back door and disappeared. I could hear his cough echoing into the night.

I realized then that although he was a little grouchy, I really liked Wick. He was like a sea urchin: spiny on the outside and soft on the inside. I wished I could stay and work and learn more from him, and then I realized what I was wishing.

I'm alone, in the dark, in a world I don't know. My hand grasping the candleholder shook. My heart thumped loudly. *Thanks a lot, heart, you're making this so much less scary.*

I descended the little staircase into Hell—the cast and crew's affectionate name for the basement. I crouched down and navigated the maze to the mat where I had fallen hours before. Yorick was waiting for me there, and I heaved him up with one hand and almost dropped him when I realized it was a real human skull. My fingers felt grime and smooth bone underneath. I used the candle to look at the empty eye sockets, the long teeth. It was almost gross, and yet strangely comforting—I wasn't quite alone.

I hurried up the stairs, holding him (or her?) close to my chest. I wrapped the skull in a piece of cloth and placed the bundle carefully on the props table. Then I stepped out onto the stage. It was startlingly bright: the sky was lit up with thousands of stars, and a beaming sliver of the moon shone onto the stage like a half spotlight.

Noises from the outside world floated in through the open top of the theatre—a rushing wind, and street sounds like laughing, screaming and shouting, growling . . . *growling? Did I just hear growling?* This was not helping.

The trapdoor sat center stage, between the two pillars and back a few feet. I knelt and blew out the candle. The trapdoor didn't have a handle, and it took me a moment to figure out what to do. Maybe time travel made your brain a little wonky.

Wait, how wonky? Would I still be able to do pre-calc?

The tips of my fingers gripped the edge of the trapdoor and lifted up one side. There were no hinges; it was just a heavy board, held up by a rim around and just under the hole's edge. I lifted up the side just enough for me to squeeze through, took a deep breath, and slid into the hole. The lid fell closed after me with a bang—

Oof.

It was just a normal fall. I was back on the mat in the straw. If my calculations had been correct, I should have fallen onto the cement floor in the Black Box. Which would have hurt—a lot. Obviously I hadn't thought that through. It was a good thing my plan hadn't worked.

No, no, no. Not a good thing. What am I going to do?

Get out of Hell first, then panic, I told myself.

I couldn't see my hand in front of me. Without the moon or my candle, there was no way I was going to be able to get through the maze and find the staircase to the tiring-house. The only way out was up.

My flailing hands found the stepladder to my right. I placed it in the center of the mat, crouched over the first step, and crawled up. On the third step, I was able to give the trapdoor board a nice big push. It flew backward and clattered, landing somewhere out of sight. Grabbing the back edge of the hole, I heaved myself up onto the stage.

I lay there for a moment, taking labored breaths. Stage crew doesn't keep you in shape like soccer does.

All at once, I realized the moon and the stars were gone, and the darkness felt different. It was quieter, but somehow less expansive. There was no noise but a low hum.

Wait, there's a light.

There were actually three lights, looming in the near distance.

E X I T   **E X I T**   **E X I T**

11

"You ready to go, Mama?"

The overhead lights came on. Stanley was standing at the right-side audience exit. I rubbed my eyes.

"What time is it?"

"Seven thirty. Were you waiting long? I just got your text message. Signal in the workshop sucks. Why were you sitting in the dark?"

I checked my phone and watched the clock change to 7:30. A minute had passed. A *minute*? I couldn't have dreamed that much in a minute-long nap.

"Mama, were you asleep? You look like hell."

I turned to Stanley, who was wearing shop overalls and an old white T-shirt. His hair was pulled back into a tight bun. He appraised me curiously.

"Yeah." I hopped off the stage. "I fell asleep. You know how these big blocking rehearsals are."

"Hmmm."

He didn't believe me. I wasn't sure if I did, either. I wanted to act normal and tell him, *I had the craziest dream!* If it was a dream, it was the kind of dream Stanley would probably really appreciate.

But something held my tongue.

On the way home in his big black SUV, Stanley kept asking questions I didn't know the answers to: How did rehearsal go? What scenes did you do? Did Lulu seem okay?

I could hardly remember anything that had happened during rehearsal. It felt like hours and hours and far away ago.

"How shitty was Josh?" Stanley tried again.

"Oh, give Josh a break," I mumbled. "It's not his fault he got cast. And it must be really weird for him, since he doesn't hang out with anyone in the drama department."

"I know he's your best soccer friend." He clicked his tongue. "But your defending him is starting to get old. It's no fun, and it's not very loyal to Lu."

I sighed. *Maybe he's right, but I can't let him trash Josh after what Josh did for me.*

"But, by the way"—Stanley turned down my street—"you were right about Gretch. She's scarier than Maleficent when she's mad."

I nodded faintly in agreement, half smiling, but inside my brain a phrase scrolled across in big bright letters:

I'm going insane, I'm going insane, I'm going insane!

When we pulled up outside my house, Stanley stopped me as I tried to get out. "Mama, I think you're hiding something from me." He drummed the steering wheel.

"I think I'm not." I clutched the door handle. "Thanks for the ride—"

"Did you and Brandon make out or something?"

At that moment, the idea of anything happening with

Brandon was so distant, and so not the point. "Yeah, right. As if that would ever happen. Can I go now, Stanley? I'm exhausted and I just want to—"

"Methinks the lady doth protest too much."

"Oh, *shut. Up.*"

I jumped out of the car before he could stop me, and trudged up to my room. It was a Wednesday night, so the house was empty—Mom's night class was Wednesdays, and Dad would be with Abby at her evening swim lesson. Good. No one to pretend I was fine for. I shut the light off and toppled onto my bed. Here, the darkness was small and calming. I knew everything around me by heart.

My phone lit up. *A text from Brandon?!*

> Hey, I know rehearsal was rough. Thanks for listening to me whine. You're doing a great job, kiddo.

Kiddo?! What does that mean?

I sighed and rolled over to face the wall. I didn't have the mental capacity to overanalyze that at the moment.

As I snuggled under the covers, I wished for my usual dreams: all my teeth falling out, poisonous fog monsters, that one about Lulu as an action-movie star . . .

Drifting off, I felt cozy and comforted and normal. All the weirdness of the night started to fade away. It had probably just been a product of my drama-nerd imagination.

Maybe you're just a little too excited by Shakespeare, Emma. . . .

"Emma?"

For the second time that night I was surprised by someone turning on a light. I sat up to see Dad standing in my doorway.

"Were you asleep? It's only eight fifteen."

"It was a long day." I wiped the sleep scum out of the corners of my mouth.

"You were out late partying last night, weren't you?"

I rolled my eyes. *Sure—that's clearly something I would do.*

"We picked up a pizza on the way home. We got you sausage."

My stomach growled. Dad chuckled as he turned to leave. "Hey, take your sneaks off before going down. You know how Mom gets about shoes in the house."

"Right."

"That hair is looking better and better, Emma-bo-bemma."

He grinned at me and left. I opened the closet door and checked out my hair in the mirror on the inside: one giant swoop, like a wave breaking on the side of my head. Excellent. My phone lit up in my pocket—a text message from Lulu:

> So Stanley just told me you hooked up with Brandon tonight?!

Oh God. I texted her back quickly.

> Ha-ha, I wish. No, just Stanley being creative. If that ever happens you'll be the first to know. I'll text you WHILE Brandon's kissing me. xoxo

I set my phone down. *Okay, next: pizza, send out the Rehearsal Report, one chapter of bio, two for history, and a response for English . . . look up time traveling on the internet?*

Yeah right, Emma. You did not time travel. You had a dream. A cool dream. Nothing more.

I pulled a sweatshirt and flannel bottoms from my dresser, then flopped on the floor to take off my sneakers. But as I went to unlace them, I felt a chill on the back of my neck.

My new, shiny, all-black sneakers were smudged around the edges and on the toes with an orangey dirt. This wasn't normal black New England dirt from my backyard. It was dirt from the basement of a theatre that existed in the *real* England, four hundred years ago.

I sat staring at my shoes, dumbfounded. My eyes unfocused and refocused on them at will. My stomach growled again, interrupting my aching, dizzy mind.

I numbly unlaced my sneakers and threw them in the closet.

Calm down, calm down, I ordered the anxiety dragons. I had probably just stepped in something earlier and not noticed. That was the only reasonable explanation.

Shaking slightly, I changed into my pajamas, then lay down on the bed just for a moment, to try to regain my sanity. The top of my head throbbed. I had to take an ibuprofen. Ibuprofen would make everything better. . . .

I woke up six hours later and heated up my pizza. As I typed my report on *Dracula*, I noticed my index finger pinching in pain with every tap of the keys. Finally I paused and held my hand under my desk lamp. My throat closed.

A splinter.

Oh. My. God.

12

In movies or books, the main character always decides that they just hit their head, or they were asleep.

But my trip wasn't like a dream, where the details begin to fade as time goes on; it was a memory that sharpened with each passing day. I tried to ignore it, but they all became clearer: *Wick. Shakespeare. Burbage. Cooke. The Globe.* Sometimes during these memories, a stray, disturbing thought hovered in my mind's peripheral vision: *I want to go back.*

Three weeks later, our auditorium's stage still wasn't fixed. Right after my trip, maintenance had boarded up the hole, and it had been that way since. We had to work around it in rehearsals. I tried to give it a wide berth, never getting too close. What if the boards broke and I fell in again and disappeared? In front of *everyone*?

That Friday, Stanley and I sat in Gretchen's office for the first *Hamlet* production meeting. I'd never been in a production meeting before. Stanley had explained to me that Gretchen liked to hold them so we could practice for our "future careers." Production meetings like this happened all the time in real, non-high-school theatre. Plus, they were useful for the show, and all that.

I was there to run the meeting and take notes. Stanley was there to present his progress on the lighting and the set. Gretchen was there to present her producer progress and to be presented to. Brandon had yet to show up.

Stanley wore hot pink, his hair in a ponytail. I wore skinny jeans and a black Henley with my scrubbed-clean black sneakers. While we waited, Gretchen used the time to call some parents from the children's theatre.

"And last, Bobby will need a pair of black ballet slippers and black tights. No, it's his costume. I'm not implying anything about your son, Mr. Walker, but he's playing a fairy. . . ."

Stanley caught my eye, and we grinned at each other and shook our heads.

I'd never been in Gretchen's office before, and I had thought it would be cleaner. Every surface was stacked with haphazard paperwork. Colorful show programs and posters hung everywhere, some of them faded from the sunlight streaming through the line of windows at the top of the wall.

I was nervous, and wishing Janet was still here for me to shadow. I opened my binder and flipped through it. That didn't help, though. I just ended up cringing at the last few scenes we'd blocked. My notes were sloppy, my handwriting loopy, like Mom's, instead of my usual precise-and-straight. My stage-managing had obviously suffered from my lingering brain fog.

"Sorry, everyone. Mr. Stratton kept me after class."

Brandon creaked into the office, looking adorable in his leather jacket and dark-washed jeans. Gretchen held up a finger to her lips and motioned for him to sit.

He slid into the chair next to me, and our knees touched. It would have been exciting, but I don't think he noticed at all. He stared at the floor with glassy and listless eyes. He had been tired lately, and a little erratic in rehearsals—stopping midway to do a trust exercise, or to question the meaning of the text without coming to any conclusive answers. Things were going pretty well, though, apart from that. The show was moving along.

Stanley glanced pointedly at Brandon, then back to me. I tapped Brandon's shoulder. He looked up, so startled I felt like I must have been wearing a *Scream* mask.

"You okay?" I whispered.

He smiled at me faintly, his dimples not even dimpling, then he opened his notebook and stared into it with the same apathetic expression. I shrugged at Stanley, who rolled his eyes. Gretchen threw down the phone and crossed a name off her list before looking up.

"So nice of you to join us, Brandon. Let's get started. Madame Stage Manager"—Gretchen yanked a notebook from under a towering stack of papers—"you have the floor." Her eyes met mine in a challenge. The floor I supposedly had began to sink beneath my chair.

Stop. You can do this. You can run a meeting.

"First up, let's have a report from the director." I said it too quickly, but I got it out. I turned to Brandon, who snapped to attention.

"Yes, thanks, Emma," he said to a page in his notebook. "Everything is going well on my end. We'll be finished blocking after next week."

I scribbled that in my production meeting report. Shakespeare's men had one rehearsal, and it was going to take us a month to just finish the blocking. Mind officially boggled.

"Next week I'm cracking down on the actors being off book for act two, especially the leads: Josh, Greg, Marcus, Kelly, and Lulu. Well"—Brandon smiled wryly—"Lulu's already off book. On multiple parts."

Last week, when Josh had missed rehearsal for an away game, Lulu had stepped in as Hamlet and nailed all the lines without her script. She'd even learned all the blocking for the duel at the end, and the cast whispered about how much better she was than Josh. In retrospect, Brandon probably should have just read Hamlet's lines himself.

"Have you cut anything?" Gretchen asked. "That would make things easier."

"No," Brandon replied. "Not yet, anyway."

Gretchen said nothing, but gave him a look that said loud and clear: *Explain yourself.*

"I thought I'd get the whole thing blocked and then cut what was weakest," Brandon elaborated.

"Well, it doesn't seem like that would be a prudent or popular technique." Gretchen leaned forward. "A careful read of the play would point out some obvious edits for a high school production."

Stanley clearly loved this drama, and was looking back and forth between them gleefully, as if watching a soap-opera tennis match.

"I *have* read the play carefully," Brandon insisted. "And right now I can't see myself cutting anything, actually."

"Fine," Gretchen raised her eyebrows. "It's your decision"

Brandon's face fell. I could almost see the words being stamped onto his forehead: *your decision.* It *was* his decision, though, and I didn't get why Gretchen was giving him such a hard time. Awkward, tension-filled silence ensued, and I wondered if all production meetings were like this.

You're the stage manager! Step in and say something.

"Brandon, if you're done with your *director's* report, Gretchen, could you give us your *producer's* report?"

I tried to remind everyone what their job was.

"Sure thing." She opened her notebook and peered at the page. "I've bought the paint Stanley asked for, and we'll be taking a trip to get the hardware store this weekend. Stanley knows he's allowed to work only in the wood shop from now on, and won't have access to the theatre after hours until late November, before and during tech week. And he'll be supervised then."

Stanley snorted a teeny snort.

I made a note. "Who will be supervising him?"

"The stage manager, of course."

Stanley didn't look at me, but his eyes flared wide at the floor.

"Great," I said, strained.

"Possum Community Playhouse has agreed to lend us anything we want from their costume barn, provided they aren't using it for their fall production. Brandon, you and I can go pick some things out when we get closer to tech week. Start thinking about what you want, if you haven't already decided."

"I have some ideas!" Stanley declared, suddenly animated again.

"That's fine, Stanley," Brandon said, cutting him off, "but I think I've got the costumes under control."

Stanley opened his mouth to reply, but Gretchen's look shut it. He crossed his arms.

"Lastly, I want to report on who has come for dialect coaching." Gretchen passed out a sign-in sheet with names scribbled on it. Lulu's name was first on the list, of course. I was surprised by how many people had seen Gretchen for help, including—

"Joshy?" Stanley raised his eyebrows. "He's been to see you? Could've fooled me."

Gretchen took back the list. "He's seen me a few times since rehearsals started. Josh is . . . trying. But he has a lot of work to do, and he's not great at staying focused. This stuff doesn't come easily for him."

"Understatement of the century," muttered Stanley.

Not focused? That description of Josh sounded off to me. I remembered watching the boys practice last year: Josh was the most intense guy on the field. At Stanley's comment, Brandon's brow furrowed, and he opened his mouth to say something, but I interrupted:

"All right, then, how about the report from our designer?"

Stanley brightened. "I thought you'd never ask." From behind his chair, he pulled out a big piece of blue poster board and set it on a music stand.

"As you can see," Stanley said with a sweep of his hand, "my designs are inspired by the productions that took place at the Globe."

A shiver went up my spine. The poster board was littered with old drawings of the Globe. None of them got it exactly right, though.

"And I'm staying pretty much true to original production conditions, sans the trapdoor, which was cut due to . . ." Stanley paused, perhaps on the brink of a rant, but finished instead with, "Which was cut."

We all oohed and ahhed at Stanley's board. In between the pictures of the Globe, Stanley's own drawings and concept art stood out as breathtakingly beautiful: a simple set like at the real Globe, but with purple, blue, and green lights, and candles everywhere. There was a full drawing of the gravedigger scene, the dark purples and blues casting inky color onto the characters.

Wait a minute.

"This production is supposed to be a re-creation of the original Shakespeare plays?" I asked.

"Yes, Emma, that's what I said," Stanley said patiently.

"Then why are you lighting it like that?" I asked, pointing to the gravedigger drawing.

"Like *what?*" Stanley fired back. He obviously didn't like being questioned, but I couldn't keep my mouth shut.

"Like, with colors. And so dark," I could feel Brandon's and Gretchen's stares. "The original production wouldn't have had colored lights or candles, and it would have been performed during the day, so it wouldn't have been this dark."

"She has a point. . . ." Brandon mused.

"This isn't an outdoor theatre," Stanley rebutted through clenched teeth.

"Regardless," I continued, despite my heart practically pounding out of my chest, "if you're going for accuracy, you should make it brighter. Oooh!" I jumped up in excitement, my binder falling to the ground, as ideas popped into my brain and out of my mouth. "You could keep the houselights on so the actors can see the audience, like they used to be able to. And, instead of doing traditional lighting for every scene, you could begin the play with a really bright light coming from the front, and program the lights to slowly fade over time, like the sun slowly sinking. *That* would be accurate *and* cool."

"Whoa!" Brandon stared, agog.

Hell yeah!

"Emma, a stage manager does not interrupt the designer." Gretchen's eyebrows were raised, and she looked at me pointedly. I froze, mid-high.

"I didn't interrupt him. . . ." I mumbled, and then sat back down slowly.

"But those were some good ideas. Stanley, I hope you took notes."

Stanley's mouth gaped like a fish. He closed it, and then began to scribble furiously.

Sparklers went off in my head, and my hands trembled as I picked up my binder. *I had some good ideas!*

I nervously stole a look at Brandon, and found he was grinning at me. A real grin, with the corners of his mouth digging into his cheeks. It gave me the confidence to say one more thing.

"Oh, and I think we need to keep the trapdoor." My voice was surprisingly firm.

"That's not something we're going to discuss." Gretchen's firmness outdid mine. It was the tone that normally struck terror into my veins, but I knew I was right about this. Time to be honest with myself: I had been to the Globe, I had seen Ophelia lowered into her grave. I knew the trapdoor was important.

"But the hole is already there," I reasoned, unreasonably. "And it is a piece of important theatre history. Think of everything we could use it for! It would make us a popular spot for the drama festival competition. And you could require the student directors to research how the trapdoor would have been incorporated into their Shakespeare plays. Plus, I mean . . ."

Gretchen stared at me, hard.

"The hole is already there," I repeated, gulping.

Gretchen turned away and thought for a moment, drumming her fingers on the desk. The three of us held our breaths.

"All right," she said finally. "You've made some good points, Emma. Stanley: work on it with Zoe, and finish it quickly. We'll need to get it inspected and approved."

Zoe was Ms. Holloway, the BHS shop teacher who helped out with bigger set projects. She adored working with Stanley, and vice versa.

"I'll find her right after the meeting," Stanley said, his voice calm. But his eyes were practically bugging out of his head, and his face was turning red with excitement, almost matching his hair. Brandon gave me a thumbs-up, and I beamed. Until Gretchen said what she said next:

"Now your report, Emma."

"My report?"

"Yes, your stage manager report."

I looked down at my notes and flipped back into my binder. I landed on a page of star doodles and Brandon's name written over and over and over. I shut it quickly. I had nothing.

"I didn't realize I needed to report," I admitted. Gretchen seemed to take a little too much pleasure in this.

"Of course. We need to know how the preparation for tech week is coming along."

"Tech week? We've got seven weeks till tech week," I sputtered, and checked the calendar on my phone, just to be sure.

"Yes," Gretchen said, "but by then you need to have recruited the crew, created set-change and prop-flow sheets, a game plan for the cue-to-cue, etcetera."

She was right. I had so much to do and I'd barely started.

"This is all new for Emma," Brandon interjected, his voice warm and forgiving. "But she's doing a great job with rehearsals. I'm sure she'll have everything together for tech week."

I stared at Brandon. Stanley gave me a subtle kick.

"Well, we'll do this again in a few weeks, Emma," said Gretchen, wrapping things up. "Have a report by then. I think we're done for now."

I was pretty sure closing the meeting was my job, but I really needed to get out of that office and breathe. Stanley squeezed my hand as I left.

"I'll see you later, Mama," he said. "I've got work to do. Lu was staying to do homework in the lab—she should be around to give you a ride." He quickly typed and sent off a text.

"Thanks!" I smiled.

Using my powers to save the trapdoor had appeased him. Without another word, he tore out of the office in the direction of the auditorium. Gretchen turned back to her call list, and I scooted after Brandon, who was lingering in the hallway outside.

"Where did all that come from?" He was staring at me hard, his face so close to mine. I felt a blush begin.

"What?"

"All of those ideas." His eyes seemed to be searching mine. "Have you ever done lighting design before?"

"No. Well, a little." I fumbled with the binder in my hands. "I helped Janet and Stanley set up the lights for *Oklahoma!* over the summer."

Brandon nodded enthusiastically. "That's really cool; I didn't know you did that. Hey, do you want to get coffee

Monday after school? We'll have some time before rehearsal, and I'd like to hear more of your thoughts on the play."

What? With him? Yes. Of course he means with him. But can he really? Is this a date? What do I say? Do I tell him I don't drink coffee because it's disgusting? No. Just say yes. YES!

"Yeah! Um, yes, I'd like that."

"Good," he said, very businesslike. He turned to go, but I suddenly felt bold and stopped him with a timid tap on the shoulder. He turned back.

"Thanks, by the way," I said, my blush deepening. "For, um, bailing me out in there. I didn't know I needed to do a report—Janet never mentioned reporting—and it was really nice of you to say what you said. How you think I'm going to do it all okay."

He chuckled. "Well, I know you will. Stage-managing is just organizing, and you're so organized. It's not that hard. You'll be fine."

The blush drained right out of my face. A strange, prickly feeling started at the base of my neck and made its way down my shoulders and arms.

What do you mean it's not that hard?

"Emma!"

I turned to see Lulu approaching. Before I could think of how to set Brandon straight, he was leaving again.

"Coffee after school on Monday, then?" he called to me.

"Yeah!"

He trotted away down the hall as if he was scared of Lulu. I was torn between running after Brandon to explain that my job was important and mentally running through my coffee-date-worthy wardrobe choices in my head.

Leggings, black collared dress?

"Hey, babe." Lulu watched Brandon leave. She looked at me, puzzled for a beat, but then asked: "How did your production meeting go?"

"Kind of weird, but overall good. How are you?"

"Oh, you know." She tucked a strand of white-blond hair behind her ear. "Bad. My mother overheard me on the phone with Megan last night. She didn't know who it was for sure, because I don't keep Megan's name in the phone, but I think she knew anyway. I'm on lockdown through the weekend."

"I'm so sorry." I touched her shoulder. "Is there anything I can do?"

"Thanks, I wish." She rubbed her eyes. "I just feel suffocated at home. I called Chip on Stanley's phone during study period, but he's so busy. He said he can't come home. Too many credits this semester, along with his research job."

Lulu's brother, Chip, was in his senior year of college two states away. When Lulu had first come out to Chip, he hadn't reacted the way Lulu had hoped. But when things got bad with their parents, he had pulled himself together, and now he was supportive.

In the brief moment that we separated to get into her car, I made a wish that Lulu and I were sisters and I could just bring her home with me forever.

"By the way, did I just hear that right?"

"Huh?" I clicked in my seat belt.

"Brandon, asking you out."

"Do you really think that's what it was?" I gushed, in spite of myself and her serious face. "I mean, maybe it's just a meeting. But that's not what it sounded like, is it?"

"No," she said. "It sounded like kind of a date."

I felt my face light up.

"But," she continued, her voice lacking emotion, "I don't understand why you'd want to date the jerk who's ruining our school's production."

"What?" I sputtered.

"Come on, Emma." Her tone was condescending. "He's a bad director."

"Lulu, that's not fair—"

"No, it's totally fair. His rehearsals are a mess."

I felt my face burn. "Well, if the rehearsals are messy, that's my fault, too."

She paused for a second. "No, I mean, it's really his responsibility. And besides, he chose Josh over me for Hamlet. I don't understand how you can like someone who did that to me."

Our eyes met, hers full of hurt. I felt blindsided, trying to grasp at a defense.

"Lulu, I've liked Brandon for *a year* and he's actually *asked me out*." I hated how desperate my voice sounded.

"Right," she fired back. "He hasn't shown any interest in you before. Why now?"

It was like a punch in the gut. Lulu had never said anything like that to me. Ever. I felt emotionally winded. Lulu waited for a response, and when she didn't get one, she turned the car on and began to drive.

"I can't think of a single reason," I whispered finally. But actually, I could think of a few: my new hair, my new look, my new, itty-bitty amount of confidence. Maybe the plan had worked and Brandon was really into New Emma.

Which was great. That's what I had wanted to happen. So why was my stomach sinking? Was I really okay with a guy liking me because I had changed my appearance? Was this *Grease* or something? I was never really okay with the ending of *Grease*. Sandy shouldn't have had to change for Danny. But this was different, because I'd changed for myself. Or had I?

I melted into the passenger seat and was silent for the rest of the ride. My thoughts were a swirling, negative mess. I resented Lulu for ruining this. Why couldn't she just be happy for me? I felt frightened and small—was I really being a bad friend? But it felt like she was being a bad friend, too.

As we pulled up in front of my house, she picked up the conversation where we'd left off, and it was clear she had been simmering the whole five minutes.

"Whatever the reason he asked"—she jammed the car into park and looked at me, her eyes narrowing—"it doesn't matter. The Emma I know wouldn't *want* to date the guy who's ruining her show. And who denied her *best friend* the role she deserves. If you were really my friend, you wouldn't do this."

I let her angry words batter at my chest. But inside I was screaming, *screaming* at her to be reasonable. What came out instead surprised both of us.

"Lulu." I heard my voice go hard and cold, like Gretchen's when she was angry. "If you were really *my* friend, you'd put aside your petty grudge and be happy for me. Who knows if you could even pull off Hamlet? You probably make a better Ophelia anyway."

My words visibly stung her, and I wished instantly I could take them back. *Oh, crap.* Her face crumpled.

"Lulu, wait, oh my God, I'm so—"

"*Get. Out.*"

I fumbled out of the car as she burst into tears and began to shriek. Which only proved my point about her being a good Ophelia, but that wasn't a very helpful thought in the moment.

She sped away. I ran up to my house, crashed through the door, and let myself fall facedown into the living room carpet.

What just happened?!

Why had I flipped out at her? Why wasn't she happy for me? What had I done that made her so mad? Was she just being a buttface?

No. That's not Lulu.

Or maybe it was. As much as I resented Stanley whenever he brought it up, I hadn't known her as long as he had. But I knew—felt in my heart—she wasn't *trying* to be mean. Just like I hadn't been trying to be mean, either.

Did she really hate Brandon so much? They used to be theatre friends; they were perfect together playing Titania and Bottom in *Midsummer*. Brandon was just hilarious, and Lulu . . . Lulu had been amazing. She took whatever Brandon gave her and spun it around to suit herself, while being generous with his big moments, too. But she was the one who had really shone—she'd brought out all the different facets of Titania's character, nailing every line. Just like when she had stepped in as Hamlet at last week's rehearsal.

Oh.

How could you be so stupid, Emma?

Lulu was a dedicated actor stuck in a role she was unhappy with. But more than that, Lulu had proved she was good, the best, at the role she wanted—twice—and it didn't matter. She could prove she was good again and again, and it wouldn't matter. It was all out of her control. Maybe, to her, this was all connected to what was happening with her parents and with Megan?

Uhhh, yup.

And here I was, being giggly about my date in front of her.

I groaned and rolled over on my side, all curled up.

"Emma? Are you home?" Mom's voice floated down from upstairs.

I set my shoes by the door and grabbed my phone out of my backpack. No texts from anyone. Big surprise. Stanley probably knew about the fight by now and already hated my guts. I opened the calendar on my phone and entered for Monday:

Coffee date (?) with Brandon

"Mom?" I called, sliding my phone into my sweatshirt pocket. "Can I talk to you?"

13

Rehearsal on Monday was scheduled for 5:30 p.m.—later than usual, because of the big home game.

I was antsy all morning. I had spent the weekend cooped up doing homework, trying not to look at my dormant phone, which hadn't rung, beeped, or buzzed since Friday. So when it lit up during third-period study hall in the library, I freaked a little and yelped in surprise, earning a glance from the librarian. I sheepishly picked it up and tiptoed into the magazine section to check it. Brandon.

> Hey, Emma—can I get a rain check on coffee? I'm swamped with college applications. I need to use the time before rehearsal to work on them.

Ugh. The very date that had inspired the biggest fight my best friend and I had ever had was now called off. *Figures.* I sighed heavily, pretty dramatically I guess, because I got a look from a senior guy who was trying to read *Gossip Girl*.

I smiled apologetically and then typed back:

> No problem, of course! Whenever you're free!

I made my way back to my seat, feeling completely rejected by the entire world. And, of course, as soon as I sat down, the bell rang. A stab of terror went straight through my chest.

I had to go to lunch.

Mom had told me to talk to Lulu at lunch: to apologize, to point out that we were both under stress from the production, and to say that things had gotten out of hand. To assure her that I loved and supported her, no matter who I might want to have coffee with. Excellent advice, which, at the time it was dispensed, seemed very simple to carry out.

A timid survey of the cafeteria brought the realization that following Mom's instructions would be impossible: Lulu and Stanley were nowhere to be seen. No blond or bright-red heads stood out in the crowd. No curly-black-haired Brandon, either. Maybe he was working on his college apps through lunch. I wasn't sure if I'd have the courage to sit with him anyway.

I backed out of the cafeteria doorway and stood against the paste-colored wall, trying not to look like a total creep as people passed me on the way in. My heart pounded in my ears: Not only was my best friend avoiding me, but I didn't have *anyone* to sit with. It was like November of freshman year all over again, when I was alone, and a soccer disgrace, and during lunch the whole school leered at me, and I could feel myself disintegrating into dust.

No, I told myself. *That was last-year Emma. This-year Emma can sit by herself in the cafeteria and be okay. It won't be the end of the world.*

Oh, but it felt like it. I sat at a too-large table, my *Hamlet* binder open in front of me to create the illusion I was busy. It wasn't working, though, and I felt the gleeful stares of the soccer girls from across the room.

Emma, you can't hang out with us if you're going to freak out. Emma, if you were actually cool you could handle this. Emma, if you were really our friend . . .

My throat got all lumpy. I couldn't eat. After a few minutes, I started planning my escape, but then a tray slid in next to mine. A tray stacked with pizza, cheesy fries, Fruit Roll-Ups, and an alien-green sports drink.

"Game-day food?" I asked, my voice sounding choked as Josh Jackson plunked down next to me. He wore his infamous pale-pink goalie shirt. (When Stanley wore pink, Josh's friends whistled at him in the hallway. When Josh wore pink, they all agreed: "Real men wear pink.")

"Yeah," he sighed. "I'm kinda nauseous, so I tried to pick food that I couldn't not eat."

Cheesy fries had never helped me with nausea.

"Are you nervous?" I asked, peeling the cling wrap off my sandwich carefully.

"I'm always nervous before a game." Josh cracked open the sports drink. "You know? I'm used to it."

I did know, but I was never really used to it. My throat opened up a little, enough for me to actually eat. Josh shoveled fries into his mouth and jiggled one leg. I glanced around the room and was met with curious, disturbed looks. We were sitting in a fish bowl. It was a good thing

Lulu wasn't around—if she didn't want me dating Brandon, she definitely wouldn't want me sitting with the guy who stole her part.

Neither of us said anything else for a good five minutes, which made the conspicuousness worse. As the seconds passed, the silence between us got bigger and bigger, like an awkward bubble being slowly filled with air. And then I couldn't take it anymore: I popped it.

"Hey, Josh." My voice was surprisingly clear. "Why are you sitting with me?"

I looked directly at him. His sandy-blond hair had grown out of its buzz cut and was a little shaggy and unkempt. He nodded, acknowledging the question, and ate a few more fries before replying.

"A few reasons." He turned to face me, his expression friendly but serious. I noticed a collection of pimples breaking out on his forehead. "Number one: You were sitting alone. Last year, after you quit the team, you sat alone for a while. I've always felt bad I didn't sit with you then."

I felt my eyes widen. "Josh, you didn't have to—"

"Number two." He clenched and unclenched his jaw. "My team is giving me crap for doing the play, and they think I'm going to screw up in the game today. I'd rather not be around that when I'm trying to get in the zone."

"Makes sense," I croaked.

"And number three." He wiped his hands on his pants and then reached forward for my script. "You're cool, and I thought maybe you could help me."

I nodded but didn't say anything for a minute. I needed to process the amount of honesty that Josh had just thrown up onto the table. I finished off the last bite of my sandwich and started in on a pudding cup. Josh didn't seem to care that I was silent. He was clearly content flipping through my script. For a half-second heartbeat, I was afraid he would find the doodles of Brandon's name. But then I realized that I trusted Josh. If he saw them, he wouldn't tell anyone.

"So, what's this?"

I froze, my mouth full of chocolate wigglyness. *He found them already?* Josh shoved the binder under my nose. I pushed it back to get a good look at the page. It was act three, a scene we were going to rehearse that afternoon.

"It's the scene where Hamlet confronts Gertrude, and the Ghost comes back and tells Hamlet to stop harassing Gertrude," I explained.

Josh nodded and set the script down in between us on the table. "Yeah, I know. But you know Shakespeare, right?"

A complicated question. I went with: "Yeah."

"I need to know—is the Ghost really there?" Josh's eyes searched the page intently. "Can Gertrude see it, or is Hamlet just hallucinating? Or did the Ghost, like, 'magically' make it so only Hamlet can see him? I asked Brandon, and he told me I have to decide for myself." He leaned back in his chair and scratched his head, like a cartoon character. "But I don't . . . I don't really know how to do that."

Seriously, why did Brandon cast him again? I wondered, and then instantly felt bad: He was being so nice to me, after all. And I could see he was trying.

I chided myself and thought about how athletes at BHS aren't encouraged to pursue their academics as seriously as the other students. Josh had probably dribbled his way through *Hamlet* in English class, and the teacher had let him get away with it.

"Well, I think there's evidence to support all of those theories. But since Gertrude never acknowledges the Ghost, I see it as Hamlet actually going crazy and hallucinating—like his conscience conjures up the Ghost again to keep him from hurting Gertrude."

"That makes so much sense!" Josh cried out, completely oblivious to the startled looks he got. "Great, I can play it like that. If it's cool with you, I have a few more questions. . . ."

As he turned back to act two, I let out a small, happy sigh—slowly, so it didn't make any noise. My best friends weren't speaking to me and my date was canceled, but I was back in Shakespeare World.

Toward the end of lunch, Josh explained that he couldn't memorize his lines until he knew what was going on. It took a minute to sink in, but then I realized what that meant:

He hasn't learned his lines.

Six weeks away from tech week on a full-scale production of *Hamlet*, and Josh knew *nothing*. He wanted to really *understand* his lines and what they meant, so he could memorize how to say them. I saw the logic, but I also didn't want my director to have a heart attack.

So I agreed to help Josh figure out how to be Hamlet. Memorizing, text analysis, whatever. He was clearly desperate if he was coming to me, and I couldn't let the play fall apart. Plus, I mean . . . no one else wanted to hang out with me, even if it was just for my help.

The bell rang. I gave him my number, and we made plans to make plans to meet sometime that week.

"I'll see you later at rehearsal?" He stood and picked up his tray.

"Yeah, break a leg at your game!"

"Not really hoping for that."

We parted ways. The whole school let out a breath of relief that they no longer had to witness such a baffling pair. But I found I was already hoping he would sit with me the next day, too.

👑

After school, I slunk out of the library and into the auditorium. As I tried to close the door quietly behind me, Stanley bellowed:

"Mama! Get your cute butt over here and look at this beautiful piece of majesty!"

Doesn't he hate me?

But without hesitation I hopped down the aisle and up onto the stage, stopping right before the center, where there was now a perfect outline with a flat board over it. No knobs or hinges or anything.

Exactly like the trapdoor at the Globe.

I knelt down and felt the smooth edges. My fingers tingled, and I felt that want at the back of my mind. *Go back, go back, go back . . .*

"Wow," I breathed. "It's perfect. Is it safe?"

"Of course it's safe!" Stanley retorted.

I looked up at him.

"Okay, yeah, that was a valid question," he conceded, squatting down beside me. "But it is safe. Zoe helped me construct the bottom of it so it's good to stand on. You 'can't' use it for rehearsal until we get an inspector in here, but I won't tell if you won't."

"Sounds like a plan." I smiled.

"An illegal plan, technically," Stanley quipped. "But I wanted to thank you—you really had my back in that production meeting. This"—he said, gesturing to the trapdoor—"couldn't have happened without you. You're the best, Mama."

I threw my arms around him. We were both pretty surprised—his big torso was stiff at first, and I almost lost my nerve and took back the hug—but then he softened. His arms wound their way under my backpack, around me.

"It was just a dumb fight," I said, still hanging on for dear life. "I didn't really understand what was going on."

"I know, Mama," Stanley said simply, and then pulled back. "And I know you, and I know you're not a self-centered jerk."

I winced, picturing those words coming out of Lulu's mouth.

"Can you talk to her for me?"

"I'll try my best, Mama." He stood, too. "Now I've got to go find Zoe—she's disappeared, and that means she's doing something fun without me. Enjoy my masterpiece, I'll be back in a few."

"I will. Okay."

He turned to go, then paused. "Wait—how was your date?"

"Oh, Brandon canceled." I blushed. "He has college applications to work on before rehearsal."

"That's probably for the best."

"Umm, thanks?" I said.

"No, I don't mean it like that," he assured me. "I just mean something's up with that boy. Well, gotta go! See you in a few, sweetie." He ruffled my hair and was gone.

I smiled and ran my fingers through my hair, pulling it back into place. Stanley and I had totally just had a friendship breakthrough. I felt good, but also wary of the rectangle to my left that wanted to suck me in.

Just a quick trip, the mischievous voice whispered.

Stanley and I might finally be friends, I hissed back. *Why would I go anywhere?*

I needed a distraction. I set my backpack down, then fake dribbled around the front of the stage, pretending a break-away. A small part of me had always dreamed of being center forward.

I imagined the seats in the theatre were bleachers—it was a Friday-night home game and everyone was here to watch. Lights beamed down, the fans called out, the stage melted into green grass with clear, white lines. Just my teammates, cleats, and the ball. It had all been so simple back then.

That is, until it all became *incredibly complicated* because of that stupid Halloween party. If it wasn't for that night, I would be on my way to captaining the team. I closed my eyes and pictured it, then kicked the invisible ball as hard as I could into the left wing.

Goal!

As the crowd cheered, I noticed a costume rack in the wing, filled with a crazy assortment of clothes. I riffled through them—some were punk, some were Elizabethan-esque, some were fake medieval. Brandon was clearly trying a few things out.

The erratic-ness continues.

My fingers gravitated toward a shirt/vest combo and a pair of trouser-ish pants. Dark blue, made of heavy material, they could almost pass for the clothes the stage-keepers wore at the Globe. I felt an urge to try them on, just for fun.

Sure. Just for fun.

My phone buzzed. I hopped over to my bag and pulled it out. Lulu!

> Hope you're having a good time on your date.

It was the most passive-aggressive text I'd ever received. My hands shook violently as I deleted it and shoved the phone into my pocket. The warmth of hugging Stanley disappeared instantly.

Things were no longer better. They were bad, bad, bad. Maybe Stanley and I were friends—*actually friends?*—but Lulu and I were still on the rocks. Not just on the rocks: A tidal wave had crashed us onto a jagged beach and we were broken bodies slowly bleeding to death. The anxiety dragons began to bellow in my chest.

The trapdoor drew me toward it. I was caught in its force. I blinked, and then I was kneeling in front of it again, my hands reaching out and lifting off the board. I paused and checked: no sign of Stanley or Zoe or Gretchen in the auditorium. I looked down into the darkness and found it was looking back at me. It wasn't the emptiness of the ten-foot drop into the Black Box. This darkness was full.

I reached my right hand tentatively down into the inky black and almost cried out. It was thick, like soft, dry fog. I moved my hand in slow circles, and the darkness began to crackle like static. I reached deeper in, and my hand disappeared. When I pulled it out, I half expected to not have a hand anymore, but it was still there. It tingled.

This is real.

I ran to the costume rack, pulled the pants on over my leggings, slipped off my dress, and slipped the shirt and vest over my tank top.

Then quickly, calmly, I stepped into the darkness.

14

I had been afraid that if I tried to go to the Globe intentionally, the trapdoor might drop me down into the Black Box, or in some other theatre four hundred years in the future instead.

But somehow it worked, and the darkness spit me out into the basement of the Globe. The transition was a little easier the second time around: I was expecting the dusty mat, and I avoided smacking my head on the low ceiling. The basement maze was easier to navigate, and I only bumped one knee on the way to the stairs.

My ears were ringing just a little as I stepped up into the tiring-house. I shrank back from the intense light like a vampire—all the archways were open, their curtains pulled aside. Backstage was deserted. Wick's chair was empty.

"Again!"

Shakespeare's glassy-smooth voice echoed from the stage. I tiptoed to the right arch and peeked out: it was a sunny morning at the Globe, and a little chillier than I expected. At first I couldn't see much—it was all bright light—but when my eyes could focus I saw that Cooke and Burbage were onstage, with Shakespeare standing at the front, directing. They were doing the "Get thee to a nunnery" scene. Cooke was in a simple blue dress. Burbage wore a handsome deep-garnet doublet with bloomers and tights to match, while Shakespeare wore a similar outfit, shiny and dark green, made of silk. The Chamberlain's Men were an inattentive audience, scattered throughout the galleries, all bent over, studying their scripts. I had come during *Hamlet* rehearsal, not a show.

"Master Allen," a voice growled, "get off the stage!"

Wick sat in the first row of gallery seating to the right. I quickly retreated out of the archway and used the door at the back of the tiring-house to slide in beside him in the gallery.

I felt the firm wooden bench beneath me and the heat from the sun beating down through the top of the O. The sense evidence raised goose bumps on the backs of my arms.

I can feel all of this—it has to be real.

I also couldn't remember a dream where my stage manager smelled so . . . unbathed.

Wick looked about as good as he smelled. He was peaked, and wrinklier than the last time. A stack of cloths near him served as coughing rags, and he hacked into one quietly before he finally turned to me.

"How now, Master Allen? Thou dost not look quite so country today."

"I managed to find some things," I replied.

"Thou needst not have come for our rehearsal, though— but I suppose thou wish't to watch?" he asked hopefully.

"Yes." Sure I did. Or maybe the mysterious mechanism by which I was time traveling had fantastically placed me down in time for a rehearsal that was supposed to have happened a month ago. I decided then that if this was a dream, it was the coolest dream my brain had ever come up with.

Wick smiled his approval and coughed again, this time into his sleeve. I inched a little away on the bench. I wasn't sure if modern cold medicine could cure Elizabethan germs, and the last thing the BHS *Hamlet* needed was four-hundred-year-old sniffles.

Shakespeare was methodically working through the scene with Cooke and Burbage. Cooke was in his dress but wasn't wearing his makeup or wig, and at first I wanted to giggle watching him, but I held it back. *The assistant book-keeper mustn't giggle during rehearsal,* I told myself. Shakespeare stopped the scene again and gave thorough notes on their performances:

". . . and thou must be *frightened*, Master Cooke. Burbage is a scary man, thou hardly needst play at all."

Chuckles and cheers arose from the small audience of players. Burbage bared his teeth at Cooke, and Cooke squealed in feigned terror—more laughter.

"'Tis the first good-natured thing Master Shakespeare has said all morning," Wick whispered to me. "Before now he has put on an antic disposition."

"Enough, gentlemen! Again, from where we started last."

Shakespeare returned to his spot at the edge of center stage and motioned for the action to begin again.

"Why art he so . . . um . . . antic-y?" I whispered back.

Wick eyed me, his big eye getting all red and veiny as it searched me up and down. He then seemed to decide I was worthy of the answer.

"Well," he rasped, "if thou must know, Master Shakespeare's wife and his little ones will be a-comin' to London next week. To see his new play. I believe he wants to impress them."

"Oooh." I nodded and turned back to the stage. It was hard to imagine William Shakespeare anxious to impress anybody.

But that would account for his intensity. Shakespeare's bulging, dark eyes moved quickly around the stage, flickering between the actors. He pursed his lips on some lines, and smiled, rapt, at others. I found myself fascinated—*What is he thinking?* I'd never seen someone so in the theatre moment. Except maybe Lulu or Brandon, but both of them lacked something that Shakespeare had. Or maybe it was the other way around: maybe Shakespeare lacked uncertainty.

Suddenly, Burbage and Cooke were circling center stage saying their lines.

"I loved you not," Burbage/Hamlet teased Cooke/Ophelia. He said the line with mischief and flair—it wasn't obvious if he meant it or not. Lulu's Ophelia usually responded to this line with a flash of anger, but instead, Cooke let his face fall just the tiniest bit before stage whispering back as he turned away from Burbage, but toward me:

"I was the more deceived."

A lump formed in my throat. I knew what it was like to have someone you trusted betray you. *That's probably how Lulu is thinking of me right now.* I forced the lump down and tried to watch the show objectively.

Cooke's Ophelia was fragile, but firm in her perception of things. It was such a strong, feminine take on the character. I wondered how he got in her head so easily.

It's probably because he's gay. I wonder what it's like to be gay in the 1600s.

The scene ended, and Shakespeare actually smiled.

"We're done with that for now. Many good thanks, Master Cooke. Now, Burbage, off with thy madcap—time for the Player scene."

"Master Shakespeare likes to do that," Wick whispered, making a note.

"Do what?"

"Make new words," Wick explains, holding out a piece of paper with a list on it. If I concentrated really hard, I could read what it said: a list of words, with "Madcap" now at the bottom. *"Gossip"? "Moonbeam"? "Puking"? Did Shakespeare really make all of these up?*

"The way I see it," Wick said, his big eye thoughtful, "is he's got more imagination than words can say. He needs more, so he makes 'em."

"Very sensible." I thought about how fun life would be if I just started making up words whenever I needed a new one. *Shakespeare might be onto something.*

I was watching him again as he lightly darted around the wooden stage, among the actors he had assembled. His thin frame made for agile movement. I leaned forward in my seat as he stopped to adjust poses, explain dialogue, or sweep one actor into the center and then exchange them for another. I was starting to get it—Shakespeare saw the scene as one big picture, and each line, each hand gesture, each movement across the stage affected the composition. In this scene, Hamlet was excited and passionate, but also spinning and shaky. Every person onstage had to contribute to getting Hamlet's state of mind across to the audience.

I tried not to think about our BHS production and how much it paled in comparison to what was being created in front of me.

"Master Wick!" Shakespeare snapped his fingers. "Where's the pipe?"

Wick jumped up—apparently he forgot I existed, or thought me incapable of fetching a pipe for Shakespeare. I wasn't complaining, though—the sun was warming up the theatre, and the wooden bench was oddly comfortable.

"Pssst . . . assistant book-keeper!"

I startled and turned. Cooke had appeared behind me, in the last row of seating. Wick looked preoccupied—he had stationed himself at the front of the stage next to Shakespeare, puffed up with importance. So I slunk to the back row and slid in next to Cooke, who smiled like we were already the best of friends. In his hands, he held a scroll of brown paper with inky, flourishing writing.

"How's it going?" I whispered, then realized how modern that sounded. With Wick I was careful not to say much, but with Cooke, my guard went down. Probably since he looked around my age. He tilted his head and stared at me. *Here comes the blush.* "I mean, how now, Master Cooke?"

"I have been wondering, Master Allen . . . I prithee, what part of the 'country' art thou from?"

"Umm . . ."

I realized I knew absolutely no Elizabethan England geography. *Quick, change the subject!*

"Do you want help running your lines?" I pointed to the script.

"I know them by my heart, but many good thanks for thy offer," Cooke's smile never seemed to leave his face. "Wouldst thou like to see?"

It was like he read my mind. I accepted the scroll from him and unrolled it to the beginning, but the beginning wasn't act one. This script began with Ophelia's first lines in act two. I scanned through the scene and realized a lot was missing.

"Where's the rest of it?"

"'Tis my part," Cooke explained, unrolling the scroll to demonstrate. "Just the cues and lines for the lady Ophelia."

"Why don't you have the whole script?" I asked, appalled. Then suddenly it all made sense: During that first performance of *Hamlet*, the actors didn't know the whole story because they didn't *have* the whole story.

"The parts are easier to learn like this." Cooke shrugged. "No distraction of the other lines. And 'tis less coin to have the scribe make parts instead of whole scripts for the company."

"That . . . makes sense, I guess."

"Thou guessest right," Cooke quipped. "Anyway, Master Shakespeare told us all the story of *Hamlet* before our rehearsal. That's how the company knows the play before we perform it. But we must remember many plays, and after a while they blend together, like a great painting of plots."

He gestured before him like he was showing me the painting. I watched his hands swirl the clouds of glittery dust, like he was a wizard and the air was seeping magic. Then he placed his hands in his lap carefully, one on top of the other, and turned to me, his eyes catching mine. I sputtered and looked away.

"And who chooses the plays?" I asked.

"The shareholders," Cooke said, sounding a little bored. "Shakespeare, Burbage, Condell . . . the senior actors. They own the theatre."

I nodded and bit my lip. *So that's why Burbage, Shakespeare, and all of them make the decisions. They actually own the place, like the board at Possum Community Playhouse.*

"Master Allen, how many sun spots dost thou have?"

Cooke's delicate nose was suddenly inches from mine, his eyes counting my freckles. I leaned backward, dizzy.

"Umm, a lot. So, Master Cooke, how do you remember so many plays at once?"

He laughed his light, flowery laugh. "My part is always the same, Master Allen. I play the young woman. Master Burbage is always the hero. Armin plays the fool. Heminges is always the Horatio, and Shakespeare plays whatever he likes."

So they all have roles they specialize in. That makes sense.

"But how do you memorize all the lines?" I didn't even want to count how many lines of dialogue they must learn per week.

"The rhythm," Cooke tapped his lines in the script. "The playwrights take care of everything for us players—all we need is in the rhythm of the lines. The words can be anything, if thou hast the rhythm."

He said all of this like it was obvious. I knew about iambic pentameter, the rhythm of Shakespeare's poetry—*da-dum da-dum da-dum da-dum da-dum*—but I didn't know that it could help you memorize.

Maybe this could help Josh?

"And how dost thou remember all the cues, the ons and the offs?" Cooke scooted forward eagerly, his knee touching mine. "How didst thou learn to be 'keeper of the book'?"

We're not going there.

"This is a nice dress!" I touched the skirt that came away from his leg.

"Oh, yes! Pretty, isn't it?" he singsonged in his Ophelia voice. He was easily distracted, I was finding. "Almost as pretty as our assistant book-keeper," Cooke finished, his voice dropping to his high-but-normal tone.

"Shhh," I hushed him. "I don't want anyone suspecting anything."

"Oh, thou needst not worry," Cooke whispered low. "No player in our company has ever seen a woman with locks like a man."

I pictured the ladies sitting in the gallery during *Hamlet*, with their beautiful updos. He was probably right.

"Then how did you figure it out?" I asked. Much to my embarrassment, no one else in the company batted an eye at me playing a boy.

Cooke's pale pink lips parted into a dazzling smile.

If only I were as pretty as he is, I thought, I'm sure my coffee date with Brandon would end in a full-on make-out session. With tongues and everything. Although the thought of that was almost more terrifying than appealing. . . .

"'Twas very simple," Cooke said. "The moment I saw thee, I felt a song on my lips and a flutter in my heart."

I froze. *What?*

"And despite what thou, and all of Denmark, may think," he continued, waving a hand toward the rest of the cast. "Ophelia's heart would not flutter for a man."

He turned and stared deeply into my eyes. *Blue blue blue.*

Then Cooke kissed my left cheek. I had never been kissed before, not even on the cheek. Not like that. His lips were soft. My skin burned, and my stomach felt as though someone had physically flipped it upside down. Or shoved a live duck in there.

He quickly pulled away, but the kiss still seemed to be playing on his lips as he grinned at me.

"'Till we meet again, Master Allen."

"Ngughhhh," I replied daintily.

He rose, and floated into the tiring-house. I thunked down the gallery stairs, back to my bench in the front row. A few moments later, Wick sat down beside me and clapped me on the back.

"Don't mind him, Master Allen." Wick shook his head. "He's a silly one, that Master Cooke. I reckon he'll never play a man as well as he plays the women."

I smiled weakly in agreement.

With the dazzling Cooke gone, the sun began to make me sleepy, and I realized it was probably time to get back home and get ready for my own *Hamlet* rehearsal. A few minutes later Wick called a break, and I snuck into Hell and pushed my way up through the trapdoor again.

When I climbed out onto my own stage, static sparking off my clothes, I realized that my left cheek was still tingling.

15

"Get . . . thee . . . to . . . a . . . nunnery! Why wouldst thou be a breeder of sinners? I am myself indifferent honest, but yet I could accuse me of such things that it were better my mother had not borne me. . . ."

Suddenly, Josh snapped out of character and threw up his hands. "Okay. Can someone tell me what I just said?"

I almost spit my sip of soda all over the stage. Lulu sighed, rolled her eyes, jutted out one hip, and crossed her arms, embodying exasperation. I couldn't blame her—this was the third time Josh had stopped their scene. I tried to make eye contact with her, to share our frustration in a subtle kind of way, but if she noticed, she ignored me.

It was only Josh, Brandon, Lulu and I working on this one bit—rehearsal had gone late and we'd sent everyone else home. Josh needed my help more than I had realized. As frustrated as Lulu and I might've been, he felt worse.

"Why am I telling her to get to a nunnery?" he demanded of Brandon. "Aren't I in love with her?"

The scene I had watched acted to perfection at the Globe earlier in the day was a train wreck four hundred years later. Josh didn't know what he was saying, so he didn't know how to act, and Lulu was phoning it in, big time. Her Ophelia gave a simpering reply to whatever Hamlet said. I, personally, was exhausted, and listening to it all was just painful.

I miss the Globe already.

And it was weird, and sad, being in rehearsal with cold-shoulder Lulu. It seemed like her grudge was just getting bigger, taking up this whole space around her that I wasn't allowed in. I kept wanting to make a silly face at her, or send her a private, telepathic message. Stuff we would normally do to get through a long rehearsal together. Apparently Stanley hadn't been able to convince her to talk to me. She would barely even look at me, except for all the glaring.

"No, you're not in love with her. At this point, you can't trust her," Brandon explained, gesturing at Lulu. "Her dad is closely tied to Claudius. You hate her now."

"I hate her," Josh repeated, deadpan, staring at the script.

"The feeling's mutual," Lulu muttered.

"Hey," Brandon pointed at her with his pencil. "Enough talking, woman."

Lulu's eyes burned red, and then she used them as lasers to disintegrate Brandon. I knew he had been joking, but he couldn't have made a worse joke if he tried. I stood up suddenly, instinct telling me to keep her from exploding.

"Does he really hate her?" I asked.

Brandon turned to me, a quizzical expression on his face. He was wearing a denim button-up today, and his hair was loose, curling down a little past his jaw. Maybe he would want to go for coffee tonight if I said something smart.

"Yeah, do I?" Josh couldn't keep the frustration out of his tone. He shifted from sneaker to sneaker, his shiny track pants bouncing light into my eyes.

"What do you mean?" Brandon's eyebrows bunched. "Yes, he hates her. He's certainly not in love with her right now. You've read the play, Emma."

"I have read the play." I indicated my copy of the script. "And I don't think he exactly *hates* her, do you?"

Three different mouths opened to reply, but I barreled onward, picturing Cooke and Burbage doing the scene.

"I think it's more like they're both feeling betrayed in this moment. You know, Hamlet feels betrayed by his mother, and therefore women in general, and therefore Ophelia."

"Yes, thanks, Emma." Brandon's voice was tight.

I paused. No one said anything else or moved. I continued.

"So I don't think he *actually* wants her to be a nun, because I think deep down he does still love her, as we see in act five. I think he's telling her not to become corrupt. So maybe act it with more disappointment, and desperation?"

Josh nodded at the script but didn't look at me. Lulu smirked to herself. Brandon stared at the ceiling.

"Like, you could maybe touch her face on this line—"

"All right!" Brandon raised his voice and cut me off. "We need to continue rehearsing; no more chatting about the text. Go from 'I did love you once.' And, Josh, remember: You hate and distrust her right now. You're disgusted with her and her family."

Josh's eyes slid from Brandon to me, then back to Brandon. He rubbed the back of his neck, then turned around and walked toward the back of the stage. He called:

"Where am I, Emma?"

"Huh?"

"I don't really know where I'm standing." He searched his script, his forehead pinched. "Sorry, I forgot to ask before."

I looked down at my script. My handwriting was sloppy, and I couldn't tell if the note said to start stage R or stage L.

"Umm . . . hold on . . ."

"I got it." Brandon held out his script to Josh to show him. "Upstage right, traveling down left."

"Great, thanks." Josh glanced at me before heading to the back of the stage.

My face flushed like a bad sunburn. My notes should have been clearer. I should have known Josh's blocking instantly. I could feel a wave of annoyance coming off Brandon, crashing in my direction.

They started the scene again. I sat back down at the front of the stage, feeling like a two-year-old. My eyes burned now, and I couldn't tell if I was just tired or about to cry. I sipped my soda again, letting the caffeine bubble up through my nose and into my brain. I took a deep breath and corrected the blocking, erasing the old, indecipherable note.

Brandon was wound up—that was why he'd snapped at me. He was under a lot of pressure. It didn't mean he hated me. But if he wanted my opinion so badly, wanted to go to coffee, why did he shut me up in front of everyone?

Brandon changed the blocking I had just fixed and ordered me to note it in the script, as if I hadn't already started doing that. As I viciously erased, I kissed my coffee date good-bye.

Rehearsal ended. Instead of relieved, I felt like someone had stuffed rocks in my backpack. As I turned to book it up the aisle, I felt someone's eyes on me—Lulu. She was a few feet away, putting her coat on, glaring, but only half glaring.

Something else seemed to flicker in her eyes. Maybe she missed me, too?

"Lulu." I peeked at Brandon and Josh. They weren't paying attention. "I'm really, *really* sorry about our fight."

She kept her eyes down, zipped herself in.

"How much longer are you—" I began. She glanced at me. I rephrased. "Are you going to stay mad at me forever?"

Lulu picked up her bag and walked past me down the aisle. She looked back over her shoulder, my heart jumped—

"Yeah, that sounds about right."

Tears filled my eyes as she whipped around and marched out of the auditorium. I ducked out a side door before Brandon or Josh could notice.

When Mom picked me up, she saw my face and hugged me. I told her about what happened.

"I'm so sorry she hurt your feelings, sweetie." We sat in front of the house in the driveway. She ran a hand over my head—the first time she'd done that since I cut my hair.

"Thanks."

"But remember"—she looked me in the eyes—"if that's what Lulu is saying out loud, she must feel pretty rotten inside."

I nodded. I knew that was true, though it was hard to remember in the moment.

I fell straight into bed. I'd never felt so tired before in my life—maybe only after a soccer doubleheader. As I burrowed under the covers, I calculated. Because of my detour to the Globe, it felt like midnight to me, even though it was only 7:30 p.m. Time-travel jet lag was definitely a thing.

I shut my eyes, and both rehearsals immediately began to play back, alternating memories, and I felt relieved whenever

I found myself back in the Globe. But then I would jolt back to the modern-day *Hamlet*, with Brandon snapping at me and putting me in my place as stage manager (and a bad one, at that).

No creative input for you, Emma.

I cringed, and my chest caved in. Just as it felt like it might be too much, another memory played instead. Every part of me relaxed, and sleep began to overtake me. I reached up and placed the tips of my fingers on a certain spot on my left cheek. It still felt warmer, and somehow sparklier than the rest of my face.

I felt myself smiling as I dozed off.

16

After Monday's disaster, I kept my head down for the rest of the week—did my homework, took clear notes in rehearsals, didn't interrupt to "chat about the text." Instead, I watched Brandon bumble through scenes giving confusing, and often contradictory, direction. A little part of my soul died, but I didn't say a thing. What could I do? He was the director, and I was still kind of hoping . . . but the opportunity for a date seemed more lost with every passing day. Every time I began to swoon over him, I tried to stop myself: *It's not gonna happen.*

True to her word, Lulu hadn't spoken to me since the whole "mad at me forever" conversation. She was nothing if not thorough. So I avoided the cafeteria completely, because I was afraid Josh would want to sit with me again, and then Lulu would see and get even more mad, and then we would never, ever get back to being best friends.

Truthfully, it was kind of annoying. I really wanted to sit with Josh; I had liked talking to him. When Lulu glared, or flat-out ignored me in rehearsal, it was hard not to go to a bad place: *I'm missing lunch with Josh because of her?!* Josh was funny, and nice, and he sat with me when nobody else would. He'd even wanted to sit with me last year, when I was alone. Why was I passing that up for Lulu?

But I knew why.

Josh isn't the only one who's rescued you, remember?

After The Horrible Party, my world became dark. I sat by myself at lunch, and wore my hair down, a curtain to hide behind. After a few weeks of this, Lulu had appeared out of the shadows, like a bright, powerful light.

"Emma. You like Shakespeare." She had cornered me one day after my favorite elective, Dramatic Literature. We had been doing *Macbeth*.

I nodded, because it was true. I did like Shakespeare. I guess she could tell by how I spoke in class. It was the one class at school where I still felt comfortable. No soccer girls in English for Nerds.

"Good." Lulu had nodded back. "We're doing *A Midsummer Night's Dream* right now in the drama department. I play Titania."

I had known that. Everybody knew who the theatre dorks were, and everyone especially knew Lulu, with all the white-blond hair and the narrowing eyes.

"Anyway, come to the auditorium after school. We need more stage crew."

She stared at me, hard and gray. At the time, Lulu really scared me—her intensity in class was intimidating. But no one else was asking me to be part of something; no one else seemed to care that I existed anymore.

"Okay, I'll be there."

Her smile back had surprised me—it was radiant and kind.

Sitting in the corner of the library, quietly munching a peanut-butter sandwich, that memory was the only thing keeping me from tearing my hair out. So I continued to lunch in the magazine section, day after day, hoping for a reprieve from my best friend. Having no life can do wonders for getting your homework done. All of the homework. For that week and the next. I spent a lot of time touching a certain spot on my cheek, too.

Trips to the Globe were tiring—my body had to deal with extra hours every day. I had friend drama, stage manager duties, and honors classes . . . but how long was this magic trapdoor going to last?

So I made a pact with myself:

If you can make it through the week, you are allowed to visit Cooke—err, the Globe—on Friday afternoon.

Friday afternoon, Friday afternoon, Friday afternoon became my mantra.

That's why Thursday night snuck up on me—I hadn't considered that anything vaguely interesting could happen before Friday afternoon. I was sending out some e-mails to potential crew members, while snuggling with Abby as she watched her favorite pony TV show, when my phone lit up. I expected it to be Stanley, but it was a number I didn't have saved in my phone:

> Hey, Emma. it's Josh. Are you free for Hamlet help after school tomorrow? The Outerspace Cafe downtown, maybe?

He must've got my number from the *Hamlet* contact sheet. I squinted at the phone and bit my lip as ponies, and Abby, started to dance in front of me. I felt conflicted—Josh needed help, badly, and although rehearsals were depressing and awkward now, part of me didn't want our *Hamlet* to let down the original production so terribly. Plus, I mean, I'd told him I would. But what if Lulu found out I was helping him? She would be so angry and hurt.

An evil, over-the-top version of Lulu's voice played in my head: *You're only helping Josh so Brandon will think you saved the show, and like you, and finally ask you out to coffee again (and you hate coffee, so that's stupid).*

Wow, I thought. *Good point, Imaginary Evil Lulu.* Maybe Brandon would finally go out on a date with me if I could get his Hamlet in working order. And I *did* have all that advice from Cooke on poetry beats and memorizing lines. . . . I could do this. I replied, all smooth:

> Hey, Josh! Sounds good. Meet there after school?

Ten seconds after I sent it, my phone beeped again:

> Will do. Looking forward to it.

And then I got to work.

Despite my ulterior motives for helping Josh, I was excited to hang out with him: Every girl in school wanted to hang out with Josh Jackson, and here I was, about to casually go downtown with him. Last-year Emma would have never believed it. I selected an outfit: black high-tops as usual, black tights, short skirt, flattering black turtleneck, and my favorite gray jacket. A little hair gel and my gold hoop earrings. It wasn't like I was going on a date with Josh or anything, but he was hot, and I wanted to look cute going out into space with him.

Salty wind whipped at my cheeks as I hurried down the Foot—the first days of October had brought the New England chill. Josh was waiting outside when I got to the café, but it took me a second to recognize him. He wore normal, albeit preppy, clothes. Jeans with a leather belt, a blue collared shirt with a gray sweater over it. He looked smaller somehow. He was pacing back and forth on the sidewalk out front, the red *Hamlet* script clutched tightly in one hand.

"Hey, Josh!"

"Hey!" He smiled.

The Outerspace Café twinkled, inviting us in. I wanted to sit at our usual booth. I checked myself, though, and led Josh to a booth at the back where we'd have a little more privacy.

Josh gestured at the art on the wall next to us. "You into this show?" he asked as he sat down across from me. The framed Time Lord stared at me, seemingly asking the same question.

"Oh . . . no, not really," I admitted. "I've only seen a few episodes."

"Did you know that this guy"—he gestured to the picture on the wall—"played Hamlet for that Royal Shakespeare place in London? There's a DVD of it."

"I've heard of that," I said, surprised. "But I've never seen it."

"It's good."

He's watched it?

"I really liked Kenneth Branagh's *Hamlet*, too," he continued all nonchalantly. "I don't know which one I like more. I'm not sure I would know how to choose."

I stared at him. He flipped open the menu, smiling to himself.

"Do you want to order?"

We got hot chocolates and a plate of raspberry-filled Mars cookies to split.

"So let's get down to business." I opened my binder. "I made something for you."

I pulled out the script I had created the night before and slid it across the table to him. Josh shoved the rest of a cookie in his mouth and leaned forward to examine the text.

"What's this?" His mouth was still slightly full of cookie.

"Your new script," I explained. "It's only your part, not anyone else's."

He flipped through it, his forehead wrinkled.

"Thanks," he said, finally. "But why should I use this?" It wasn't mean: He was really asking.

"Because"—I held it up against his old copy—"this one has a bunch of stuff you don't need to be worrying about. You know the play, so you should just be focusing on *your* part, on *your* lines. This is Hamlet's story you're trying to tell; you don't need to tell the rest of it, too. The other actors will take care of that, in their own way."

"That's so smart." Josh took the script back. "That's the most helpful thing anyone's said to me this entire time."

"Great." I grabbed a cookie as he looked through his new text. "So Gretchen must have already talked to you about iambic pentameter, right?"

Josh wrinkled his nose like a kid being offered Brussels sprouts. "Yeah, she mentioned it, but I don't think I really get it. It's hard for me to concentrate sitting across from her. I feel like she's going to yell at me when I mess up."

I know that feeling.

So it was up to me. I wasn't entirely sure I got iambic pentameter, either, but Cooke said it was supposed to help with memorization, and I trusted Cooke, so I had looked it up and reviewed it the night before. It was worth a shot, right?

"Well, let's try 'To be or not to be.'" I took out an enlarged copy of the speech I had printed out, with space in between the lines. As I started to place it on the table sideways, so we could both see, I felt Josh slide in next to me, looking down eagerly at the paper.

I cleared my throat and took a sip of cocoa.

"So, umm . . ." I grabbed a pencil from my backpack. "Iambic pentameter is a rhythm."

"Right," Josh nodded. "Like . . . *DA-dum DA-dum DA-dum?*"

"Close. It's actually *da-DUM da-DUM da-DUM da-DUM da-DUM.*" I pulled the speech toward us and scribbled underneath each word of the first few lines. I had seen a few examples of this online. "So, you see, some words have more of an emphasis. That's the rhythm of most Shakespearean verse."

Josh took the speech and studied what I had written underneath.

"Try it," I ordered.

He sat up straighter and read: "To BE, or NOT to BE, that IS the QUES . . . TION?" He ended the last part on a bit of a strange squeak. I didn't want to make fun of him, but then he looked at me and we both cracked up. I expected Josh's laugh to be deeper and more reserved, but it was a noisy, dry chuckle.

"Okay, yeah, there's a bit of a cheat at the end of the line." I giggled. "But that's basically it. Try the next line."

We went through the whole speech like that, Josh's voice popping with squeaks and strange punctuation.

"I sound so idiotic," Josh said mournfully when we finished.

"You're just getting used to it," I assured him.

"Or maybe I just can't get it," he said, his brown eyes flickering up at me. "Maybe this is a waste of your time."

"No, it's not!" I said, although that really remained to be seen. I flattened the creases in the paper. *How do I make him get this?* "It's really easy, it's just like . . ."

I felt him staring at me as I stared off into space, trying to pull something useful from an asteroid cluster on the back wall.

"Ground Control to Major Tom . . ."

"Like a song? Or a rhyming game?" I scrunched up my face.

"Okay, kind of like something you'd sing at camp? We had to sing all these songs at soccer camp with the kids, where you had to clap your hands and all that."

"That's perfect!" I bounced on the seat. "Yeah! Just like that. It's like a summer-camp song that you know really well."

"So if I do this enough"—Josh looked at the paper, raising his eyebrows—"it'll be as easy as 'The Wormy Song'?"

I laughed. "That's the theory!"

"Then let's go again."

So we did. We worked through the speech again. And then

again. And a few more times. Sometimes I clapped the DUMs for him. We got more hot chocolate and raspberry cookies. And then I made him say a few lines without looking at the page, and in what seemed like no time at all, he could say the whole speech from memory. He spoke it in monotone, staring at the table like a creepy robot, but he could do it.

"It's so weird!" Josh burst out after finishing it a third time. "I don't know why the *da-DUM* helps, but it works. It's like my brain already knows what's coming next or something? I don't know, it's so weird."

I felt so proud of him, and me, that I almost hugged him. The urge was strong, and he was so sincerely happy, but my arms didn't dare. What if Lulu walked in right at that moment? Or the varsity soccer girls? I shook off the fuzzy feelings and went on to the next logical step.

"Great! So let's do it again." I crumpled up the paper and threw it at the other side of the booth, to Josh's alarm. "But this time, think about what the words *mean*."

"Okay." He closed his eyes, rubbed his hands over his face, and sighed. "But what *do* they mean?"

"What do you think they mean?" I asked, genuinely curious.

"Who are you, Brandon?" Josh demanded, throwing his hands down. I wasn't sure how to respond to that, so I didn't say anything.

"Sorry, I'm just—I don't have the answers to those questions most of the time," he said. "And he keeps putting me on the spot in rehearsal, and it's so . . ."

"Embarrassing?" I finished.

"Yeah. Embarrassing. Almost as embarrassing as when Lulu says my lines five thousand times better."

Her name sounded awkward coming out of his mouth.

"Can I ask you something? Why does she hate me so much? Is it just because I got Hamlet?"

I nibbled a cookie, stalling. "Well, Lulu hates a lot of people right now," I managed. "She's going through a lot. She has a tough time . . . at home."

This seemed to sink in with him. "I didn't know that."

"Not your fault; how could you know something like that?"

He shrugged. "Everybody's got their stuff to deal with. I could've given her the benefit of the doubt."

Like I didn't.

"Anyway," I flipped the pages. "This speech is mostly about Hamlet deciding whether or not to commit suicide."

"Really?" Josh leaned on one elbow. "I mean, sure. Let's do it."

"No, no, no," I shoved the script at him. "What do you mean, 'really'? Do you think it's about something else?"

"Well, I'm sure it's kind of about that." He pressed the script open flat and stared at it. "But Hamlet doesn't seem like he wants to commit suicide to me. He's got a real mission here. He has to kill Claudius."

"Of course, but he's also—"

"So how could this speech really be about *actually* killing himself, then? According to this play, he would just go to purgatory with his dad, and what good would that do?"

I hadn't thought about that before.

"So I was thinking"—Josh cocked his head to one side, as if changing position would change the meaning of the text—"maybe this speech is about being stuck in a weird place. Knowing that you have to do this *thing*, but not being brave enough to do it. Being too much in your head. 'The native hue of resolution is sicklied o'er with the pale cast of thought.' Doesn't that sound like being scared to do something, not suicidal?"

"Yeah," I said, faintly. "Yeah, it does."

I'd always thought this speech was about suicide. Maybe it still was? But clearly it was about this, too.

Josh leaned forward in his seat and brought the script up right to his nose:

"Okay, let me go from the beginning again."

As he started the speech, his eyes fixed on the wall of stars this time, I finally understood why Brandon had cast him: It wasn't that Josh was an amazing actor, and it wasn't that he knew Shakespeare really well. It was the opposite of those two things: Josh was discovering the stage and these words for the first time in his life. He was curious and eager, but stuck in the role our high school put him in. He was recognizing himself in Hamlet, and unearthing things about both of them as he puzzled through acting and Shakespeare. It was a pretty cool thing to watch.

And if I was being totally honest, it was hard not to find it hot, too.

17

When we finished, Josh and I took separate buses—he went home, and I went back to the school. It was a little late, but I was hoping the auditorium would still be open. I hadn't waited all week to spend an afternoon with Josh Jackson.

Though now I'll be waiting until the next *afternoon with him.*

It had been great, surprisingly great, to have someone to talk to; I missed having actual friends. But I was still determined to get my time-travel fix.

The doors opened—no sign of Stanley. Which was good, but I also felt a tiny pinch of disappointment. I wanted to brag to someone about my success with Josh . . . but could he keep it from Lulu?

I changed quickly into my stage-keeper blues and lifted the lid off the trapdoor, setting it down on the stage as quietly as possible, just in case. The black hole beckoned, and I lowered myself in, sneakers first, relishing the feeling of falling.

Only slightly dizzy, and seeing only a few spots, I climbed

the stairs into the tiring-house, which was warmer than usual. Not yet at the top, I heard Burbage:

"... we cannot keep rehearsing *Hamlet*," he said, his voice firm. "We have Dekker's play to learn by next week."

"Damn Dekker!" Shakespeare hissed.

I could see them now—they were alone backstage, Burbage in red, Shakespeare in mustard yellow. I stayed down a few steps, hiding out of sight. From this angle, a gold hoop earring glinted at me, dangling from Shakespeare's left ear.

We have matching earrings.

"Damn thyself, Will." Burbage shook his head. "'Tis a brilliant play, but we shall be better by *playing* it for the people."

"I am the playwright." Shakespeare slammed his fist on Wick's table. The ink pot rattled. "And I say we must rehearse again. And yet again, if need be."

Burbage took in Shakespeare's miniature tantrum and crossed his arms.

"Richard," Shakespeare tried again, "hast thou lost thy sense of *art?*"

I nearly burst out laughing—he sounded so much like Stanley.

"Oh, thou needst not worry, 'tis safe intact." Burbage placed a hand over his heart. "But I fear thou hast lost thy *sense*, Will. And no one would blame thee, after what thou hast endured—"

"'Tis naught to do with that." Shakespeare waved a hand, silencing him. "I merely want the play to achieve its promise."

"My dearest playwright, thou must see the truth," Burbage sighed. "We cannot continue to rehearse a play, to push our good company to the brink of insanity, because of what has passed."

"Burbage, if thou speakest to this once more"—Shakespeare drew an alarmingly large knife from his belt—"I shall cut thy throat and use thy blood to scatter the fields of Agincourt—"

I couldn't help it: I gasped.

"How now, Master Allen!" Burbage cut him off cheerfully, obviously not particularly worried by Shakespeare's whole blood-scattering knife threat. "Did Lucifer release thy soul?"

"And his body, it seems." Shakespeare re-sheathed his dagger and glared at me as I stumbled up the stairs into the room.

That angry face rivals Gretchen's, I thought. Not sure who would win a stare-down, though.

"Oh, yeah." I smiled past Shakespeare's dirty looks. "No more Hell for me, thank goodness. Although it's no less hot up here . . ."

Burbage laughed, full in the belly. "'Tis true, 'tis true. 'Hell itself breathes out contagion to this world.'"

He nudged Shakespeare, who smiled a little in reply and then turned to me.

"If you'll excuse us, Master Allen." Shakespeare waved a dismissive hand. "Master Burbage and I must discuss shareholder business. Get you into the yard—we'll need you today."

"You"? Why did he use *"you"?* Everyone else at the Globe said "thou."

"We have no business to discuss," Burbage corrected him, placing a hand on his shoulder. "We must rehearse *Hamlet* now, Master Shakespeare."

Shakespeare looked up, surprised, and a smile began to form on his pouty lips.

"I know thou thinkest thy play is perfect and done," Burbage continued innocently. "But I insist it is a travesty, and

I am especially dreadful in it. We must practice again. Come now." He shot a big fat wink at me. I grinned back at him.

He then pushed a pleased-as-punch Shakespeare through the left arch.

Burbage made as if to follow, but then made a loop and spun around to face me.

"Master Allen, Master Shakespeare hath reminded me," he said, his voice low, "I have been thinking of thee, young and new to our fair city of London."

"Umm," I said, unsure of where this was going. He strode over to the props table, bent down, and picked up something from underneath it.

"Here." Burbage presented me with a brown leather sheath and belt. "In these times, thou must learn to protect thyself."

I lifted it carefully from Burbage's palms and pulled on the handle—a gleaming dagger, about seven inches long, slipped out. It was heavy and sharp and beautiful. I shuddered, thinking of the damage it could do.

"I cannot accept this." I kind of wanted it, but it seemed too expensive a gift. "Many good thanks, Master Burbage—"

"Thou shalt keep it," Burbage said firmly. "I cannot have thy head on my conscience, Master Allen. Thou art small, and a dagger wilt do thee good."

He said this kindly, as if my smallness were embarrassing. I didn't know what to say, so I clipped the belt around my waist, slid the knife into its sheath, and then smiled back at him.

"Good man!" Burbage clapped my back, and I stumbled forward. "Let us attend to the most dramatic playwright of our time."

I laughed, and he smiled a warm yellowish smile before marching out onto the stage. I went to the right-side arch, the dagger tapping my thigh as I walked. I liked the feel of it. Though it was a giant, sharp weapon that I didn't know how to use, it was comforting to know I had it. Just in case a war started while I was here, or something.

I peered into the center of the Globe. Shakespeare was assembling a scene, and Burbage stood behind him, smiling assuringly at the skeptical company. How was Burbage so tolerant of his hissy fits? And what had he been talking about—what had Shakespeare "endured"?

Just then, I caught sight of Cooke in the yard.

Maybe he'll kiss my other cheek today. I brightened at the idea, but then I immediately began to wonder: *Should I want Cooke to kiss me again? What about Brandon? What about*—

". . . sick this morning."

I realized I had wandered off the stage, and someone was talking to me. Shakespeare was talking to me.

I blinked and looked around. Who was sick? Cooke, Heminges, Sly, Armin—

Wait—

"Wick's out sick?"

"Dost thou keep wool in thine ears?" Shakespeare said irritably. "Clear thy head: Master Wick shall return this afternoon, but you shall run the rehearsal till then, assistant book-keeper."

He shoved his *Hamlet* script into my hands, a mess of loose leaves of paper. I took it and bounced the bottom against my stomach, straightening it out.

Okay, run the rehearsal, I told myself. *You run rehearsals all the time. This can't be any worse.*

Famous last thoughts.

Shakespeare's happiness at getting his rehearsal time quickly gave way to his trademark intensity, complemented with annoyance at Wick's absence. All morning, we drilled scenes over and over. He was never satisfied, and would run one section of one scene ten times over, making small changes to the lines or blocking. He seemed frustrated that the actors didn't know the story as well as he did and couldn't immediately do what he wanted. By the time I called a break, Burbage's face was long, Heminges was kicking the columns in frustration, and the rest of the company was one big mutter of discontent. Everyone was being driven crazy.

Except for Cooke, who, no matter how many times Shakespeare snapped at him to *go again*, seemed mystifyingly, constantly cheerful.

At the break, Shakespeare sent me backstage to get an additional prop torch for the next scene. I bent my head and jogged back into the tiring-house, where I found Cooke sitting in a corner, his hands over his face, quietly sobbing. Even his crying sounded pretty, like singing. I ran over to him and knelt at his side.

"What's wrong, Master Cooke?" Our joke had become to address each other formally.

"Oh, Master Allen." He sniffled, wiped at his nose, and tried to blink back the tears. "'Tis nothing." He stood up and handed me the torch from the props table, having read my mind somehow.

"If it's nothing, it's a big nothing," I pointed out. He laughed sadly.

"Yes, well." He rubbed at his eyes. "When one has waited one's entire life to be an actor for the Chamberlain's Men, one would hope that the experience would live up to expectations. And if it does not, one feels quite a large nothing sitting upon one's chest."

"You aren't—" I began, and then caught myself. "*Thou* art unhappy working here?" I'd liked the only jobs I'd ever had: babysitting or working in the theatre. But I was fifteen, and I certainly didn't have to worry about any permanent work situations. At sixteen-ish, Cooke was crying over his.

"No, no," he assured me quickly, dabbing at his eyes. "The Globe is everything I dreamed. But alas, it seems waking dreams come with fears, and I am grieved to disappoint Master Shakespeare. It seems 'tis all I do."

I bit my lip. He was so sad in his pretty blue dress, his shoulders hunched. I took a step toward him and gave him a gentle, timid hug.

"He's disappointed in everything right now, Cooke." I pulled back and tried to look him in the eyes, but he was still wiping at them. "His wife and kids are coming soon to see the show, and I guess he's freaked out about it. I mean, he's nervous about it."

Cooke's red and bleary eyes widened at the information, and probably my choice of words. "Oh . . . I had not known."

"So don't worry!" I said. "He's just determined to get it perfect. It's not about thee personally, Master Cooke, or thy performance."

"No, clearly not." Cooke brushed off his dress and stood. "But it shall be about thee, Master Allen, if thou art not swift with that light."

Crap!

"Oh, right!" I turned to go, but before I could, Cooke took my hand and squeezed.

"Many good thanks, dearest."

A shock went up my arm. I seemed to pop up into the

air and land five feet away from him. He laughed, happy this time, and I blushed and rushed out into the yard again.

Smooth, Emma, very smooth.

I tiptoed to the left of Shakespeare and slid the torch into his hand. He immediately handed it to one of the actors and waved me away. He wasn't the most appreciative director, but he hadn't yelled at me yet. Just at my friend, whom I was beginning to develop a *bit* of a massive crush on.

The sun sank lower in the sky, and soon Wick was walking through the front doors of the Globe. He looked *dreadful* but insisted he was fine. We positioned ourselves in our usual spots in the gallery.

"Many thanks for thy help," Wick acknowledged, wiping his nose. "More rehearsal for *Hamlet?*"

"Is that a bad thing?" I asked, putting my feet up on the bench in front of us. Wick smacked them back down, and I jumped and sat up straight.

"We have many other plays that need work," Wick sighed. "My books, but *Hamlet*, go unused."

"How many different plays do we perform?" I asked.

Wick coughed, and then wheezed: "In what length of time, boy?"

"A summer?"

I assumed they didn't perform here when it got cold.

"About three dozen. A little more."

Wick smiled smugly at my gaping reaction. *More than thirty-six plays?* How was it possible for the cast, the crew, to remember everything that came before, while learning the next play? I mean, I could faintly remember some of my cues from *Oklahoma!*, but if I had to remember that, and *Wizard*, and *Midsummer* at the same time . . .

"Master Wick." Cooke floated over, eyes dry. "Couldst thou study me for Ophelia? I have my part." He had his scroll tucked under an arm.

"Yes, one moment, Master Cooke." Wick stood, his knees cracking. "Let me fetch my book."

"Many thanks." Cooke nodded.

In spite of his wheezing, Wick sprang out of the gallery. Cooke leaned his elbows over the riser in front of my bench.

"Does Master Wick help you memorize your lines?" I asked.

"Nay." Cooke shook his head. "Master Wick teaches me how to *say* my lines. And with all of Master Shakespeare's corrections, I need study."

"The book-keeper *teaches* you?!"

"Of course!" Cooke laughed at my surprise. "Dost thou not agree that Master Wick knows the plays best?"

"Yeah, he does," I agreed, but I was still perplexed. Josh was the first actor who had ever asked me for help on analyzing text or learning how to act. Lulu worked with Gretchen, and nobody else in the cast had ever approached me. That wasn't what being a modern stage manager was about. I loved helping Josh, and was instantly envious that Wick got to be a teacher, too.

"One day"—Cooke tapped my shoulder—"thou shalt teach me my lines."

"Oh, I doubt that."

"O, verily thou shalt." He smiled. "When thou art the keeper of the Globe."

I smiled back, then quickly looked down at my hands.

I'm not who you think I am.

"Em," Wick affectionately called me by my first name. "Get thee into the tiring-house, boy. Thou must learn to affect the sound. The stage-keepers will show thee."

"Great." I hesitated before standing up. As much as I was curious what "affecting the sound" entailed, I was reluctant to leave Cooke. He always had so much to teach me.

The stage-keeper boys showed me how to create sound effects out of Elizabethan resources. Mostly pewter mugs, pipes, and branches rustled together. At first it seemed silly compared to the BHS sound system and the easily edited audio files we used. But as I tried out different ways of creating the noises, I got into it—the branches could sound like the wind, or the roar of a wave. The pewter mugs banged together sounded like someone crashing over, or struck together quickly, like swords clashing. The noises weren't actually that realistic-sounding, but somehow they seemed more authentic. I couldn't play the pipes, but the boys could, and I imagined how they would add sound for the supernatural plays, like *Macbeth*. I wanted to ask about that, until I realized I didn't know if *Macbeth* had been written yet.

When we were through, I thanked them and went out into the yard. Wick and Cooke were still working, heads bent over Cooke's part.

Maybe if I didn't have to take care of all of our silly technology, I could do what Wick does, and coach the actors. I was falling in love with theatre at the Globe, fueled by passion, where the effects relied on the words of the actors and the performance itself.

This is what my job was supposed to be, I realized. *Somewhere it all got lost along the way.*

I was beginning to feel exhausted—it was evening in my time, and the end of a long week. As the players got ready for a new performance, Wick sensed my draining energy and insisted on sending me home, though he was the one who needed more sleep. I was tired, but hesitant to leave.

Wick will be fine, and you'll be back next Friday, I told myself as I headed down into the basement of the Globe for my journey back. Cooke caught me on the stairs.

"Didst thou forget something in Hell?"

"Um, yes, yes I did." I twisted the end of my shirt in my hands.

He considered me, his fingers elegantly cupping either elbow. "Well, I hope thou findst it." He smirked and strutted away.

He knows, I thought as I crouched down and made my way toward the light at the end of the maze. *I don't know how, but Cooke sees right through me.*

When I pulled myself out of the trapdoor and onto my own stage, I almost felt contempt for the lights, the booth, the speakers. Weeks ago, it seemed impossible to imagine putting on a show without them.

And now I felt myself waiting—waiting for next Friday, when I would allow myself to return to Elizabethan England, where theatre was simply better.

If I did become the book-keeper for the Globe, I thought on my bus ride home, *I could teach the actors how to say the lines. They would want me to use my analytical brain.*

Whoa, there! I chided myself. *I'm drawing a line here: The Globe is amazing, but you can't abandon your life.*

I stepped off the bus and made my way down my street. Working at the Globe was only a fantasy, I knew. And besides, I wouldn't leave my family, or Stanley, or Lulu. . . .

I reached into my backpack and checked my phone for texts: still nothing.

Maybe Lulu had already left *me.*

18

On Thursday of the following week, we had the next production meeting after rehearsal. Stanley and I huddled together in Gretchen's office—we were approaching mid-October, and it was starting to get freezing. Brandon was sitting in the corner, his leather jacket zipped all the way up, typing furiously on his laptop. Stanley wore a black pea coat and turquoise scarf, and I was tucked into a long black cable-knit sweater. Gretchen was running late, but had left a note for us to wait in her office.

"Whatcha doin', Brando?" Stanley reached over and poked him with a pencil.

"Stanford application," Brandon muttered at his screen.

"Odd choice for a theatre program," Stanley quipped.

"It's for computer science," Brandon said irritably. "I'm applying to a few schools as a CS major. Just in case."

"Probably smart," Stanley said to me. "But I'm only applying to conservatories. If I don't get in where I want to go, I'm not going to college: I'm going straight to Broadway."

He flicked his hair, which seemed more like a nervous gesture this time. But I knew Stanley would get in exactly where he wanted to go: He was the kind of person those things happened to.

Brandon seemed like that kind of person, too, though. I wanted to tell him that, but I knew if I tried now, Stanley would roll his eyes at me and/or crack up.

"Sorry, kiddos." Gretchen appeared in the doorway, and we all sat up straighter. She brushed past us to her desk. "Kids-theatre crisis."

Stanley smirked. "Those babies don't know what a real theatre crisis is."

Gretchen opened her notebook. "George threw up mid-monologue, and Anya slipped in it and fell on her wrist."

"Ah," Stanley offered. "Well, maybe they do."

I couldn't help a giggle.

"Let's get started." Gretchen nodded at me.

"Right. Brandon, could we have your director's report?"

He kept typing and didn't look up from his laptop. Stanley shrugged. I looked to Gretchen, who looked pointedly back at me.

Yikes. Okay.

"Brandon!" I raised my voice, making it sharper.

"What!" Brandon looked up.

Gretchen tapped her pencil on her notebook.

"Your director's report," I prompted.

"Right, right, of course," Brandon set down his laptop, picked up his notebook, and flipped to the middle. "We've blocked the whole show—we just need to keep working through the scenes. I would say the cast is doing pretty well. Except for Josh—"

I looked up from taking notes.

"—who is doing great, actually, compared to before,"

Brandon finished, brushing his hair out of his face and smiling his real, dimply smile. "Josh has really turned a corner. He's still nervous, but he's remembering most of his lines now."

It was true. Josh and I had been working in the library during lunch every day that week. I was still in friendship banishment, and I was too anxious to eat in the cafeteria. I had drafted an e-mail to Lulu a couple times, but couldn't bring myself to send it.

Dear Buttface, please talk to me again. . . .

So when Josh asked me to work on his part during lunch, I didn't want to chance her seeing us together and using that as more ammo against me.

"So you're ashamed to be seen with me?" Josh had raised an eyebrow when I first explained the situation in the auditorium before school Monday morning.

"No!" I almost yelled. "Well, kind of. Not ashamed, I just . . . can't be seen with you."

I expected some kind of hurt reaction, but he just chuckled his dry chuckle and shook his head.

"I know, it's so silly," I agreed. "*Me* being scared of being seen with *you*."

He stopped laughing. "What?"

"Oh, you know." I smiled ruefully. "You're the popular goalie, and I'm the theatre dork now."

His forehead wrinkled and his large brown eyes questioned me. I bit my lip.

Did I say something wrong? Isn't that the truth?

"I guess." He finally shrugged. "But I don't think of myself like that. I know it's there, but . . . And I don't think of you like that, either—"

"It doesn't matter." I cut him off, pulling my backpack over my shoulder. "If you want to work, just meet me in the library for lunch."

"Will do." He looked at me thoughtfully and then followed me up the auditorium aisle.

Every day during lunch period, we met in the library and drilled his lines from his "part." He asked loads of questions about Hamlet's motivations, and grew more comfortable with the language as we talked it through. I was starting to see his soccer intensity in his memorization, his thinking. He wasn't perfect, by any means, but each day I was more impressed.

So the past week had been cool to watch. With every rehearsal, Josh began to move into the role. Instead of confused and slow, now he was excited and jittery onstage, bouncing around with his athletic energy. It was kind of manic, but his lines came out right. Brandon noticed the change, and his rehearsal mood had improved significantly.

It was working. I was helping Brandon by helping Josh. And when Brandon found out, he was totally going to kiss my face and stuff.

"I've noticed Josh's progress." Gretchen nodded. "He came to see me this week and there was definite improvement."

"I wonder how *that* happened," Stanley muttered bitterly.

I smiled, seeing my opening, but Brandon burst in—

"I think I've finally gotten through to him." He leaned forward and bobbed his head, black curls bouncing. "It feels like he's just going to keep getting better."

Gretchen agreed. I shut my mouth. Brandon seemed so happy to take credit for Josh's new skills. And as excited as I was about working with Josh, and as much as I wanted to impress Brandon, it suddenly occurred to me that my director might not be happy that his stage manager was working with his star outside of rehearsal. What if he thought I was trying to undermine him?

Just keep quiet for now, I told myself. *You can tell him when the time is right.*

Brandon was energized now. "Aside from that, the rehearsals are going to be longer from here on out, and I've been selecting costumes."

Stanley perked up at that. "What have you decided? Something extravagant, I hope."

"Yes, actually." Brandon pointed at Stanley. "I'm giving each character their own distinct look."

"Cohesively, of course." Stanley nodded.

"Cohesive in its variety," Brandon corrected.

"Or, cohesive in its cohesiveness," Stanley suggested.

Gretchen looked between them and clicked her tongue, but said nothing.

"Let's move on," I said. "Anything else, Brandon?"

"I'm all set," he said tightly, and shut his notebook. Stanley's nagging hadn't gone over well.

"Well, in that case . . ." Stanley pulled a poster board out from behind him and showed his new set designs: three arches and plain wooden furniture, and bright sunlight like at the Globe. The drawings of the stage seemed to be missing something, but I couldn't figure out what it was.

"Zoe and I just finished the thrones," he explained. "And we'll be working on the curtains for the arches next week."

"Very good." Gretchen made a note. "Do you need more fabric?"

"I found some in the supply shed."

"Thrifty. That's what I like to hear." Gretchen nodded.

"I'm also gathering sound effects for the show," Stanley explained, and pressed a button on his phone: Eerie, howling wind played. I pictured the beginning of the show, when the guards were shaking in the cold on the battlements.

"Excellent!" Brandon said. "That sounds perfect!"

"I know," Stanley said smugly.

"If you're done," Gretchen cut him off good-naturedly, "I'll do my report—if that's all right with you, Emma."

"Oh, yeah," I nearly choked on my spit. "Please, uh, proceed with the producer's report."

Gretchen explained that things with our show seemed on track, and she was swamped with the children's theatre show, which would go up on the cafeteria's stage a few weeks before ours.

"So as long as *Hamlet* is going smoothly, which it seems to be"—she looked at her notebook over the top of her glasses—"in the coming weeks, I'll be turning my attention primarily toward *The Duck Witch of Duckville*."

Everyone looked at her at once.

"They wrote the play," she explained.

"Ohhh," we chorused.

"It's a doozy," she chuckled. "Now, Emma—"

I was way ahead of her. "I will now proceed with the stage manager's report." I opened up my binder to my carefully typed outline.

"I've posted crew sign-up sheets in the hallways at school and already have four people ready to go." I stared down at the words, hard. "And Yohan, who you all may remember from the stage crew of *Wizard*, told me he's interested in assistant stage-managing."

"Great!" Gretchen put in.

"I've made a new copy of the script and written clear blocking notes for the light-board operator"—I gestured toward Stanley, who took a bow—"and the sound-board operator, whom I've yet to assign."

"Lastly, I've created a *Hamlet* scene-flow of entrances, exits, scene changes, and props."

I reached into the front of my binder and pulled out the stapled copies to pass around. Technically, it was a properties list, just like Wick's at the Globe. Stanley, Brandon, and Gretchen all took a moment to flip through them.

"This is very thorough," Gretchen said, sounding surprised. "Well done."

"Excellent job," Brandon murmured into the paper.

"Thank you!" I beamed.

It had been a pain in the butt, too, but working with Wick had taught me that it was the most useful document a book-keeper could have.

"So, that's it! Except . . ." I bit my lip. I wanted to make a suggestion, but those usually got me in trouble. "Um, never mind. If there aren't any questions, let's wrap this up."

"Good!" Gretchen slapped her desk. "All of you, out of my office. I have disgruntled parents to call."

Stanley and Brandon pushed out of their chairs and quickly filed out. A thought occurred to me, and I stayed behind, moving to the front of Gretchen's desk.

"Um, Gretchen?"

She was already sifting through forms. "Yes, what?"

"Why in Shakespeare do characters sometimes address other characters as 'you,' and then sometimes they use 'thou'?"

She set the forms down. "'You' was the formal second-person form when Shakespeare was alive," she said. "'Thou' was informal—something you would use with your friends or family, people you were familiar with."

"So was 'you,' like . . . mean?"

"Not exactly, no. It was a sign that someone was a stranger, or a higher rank than you," she explained. "But in Shakespeare's plays, it is sometimes used to insult someone. Like when Hamlet uses 'you' toward Gertrude in the bedchamber scene."

"And that's an insult . . ." I scrunched up my face in thought. "Because he's using 'you' to his mother, like to say she's not his family?"

"Exactly!" Gretchen smiled warmly at me for the first time in months.

So Shakespeare was probably annoyed with me. I frowned. *Or skeptical of me, or something.* I'd never heard anyone, from the stage-keepers to the lead actors, call each other anything but "thou." Everyone was equal in the theatre—except me, apparently.

"Anything else?" She sounded curious.

"No, that's it. Thank you, see you next week."

"See thee next week, Emma."

I threw my backpack over my shoulder, and when I turned to give her an awkward wave as I left, she was staring after me, smiling slightly.

Maybe one day she'll forgive me for The Fog Machine Incident. Maybe one day she'll think I'm legitimate.

As I rounded the corner, a big arm reached out and pulled me against the wall.

"Mama!"

"Crap!" I yelled. "Stanley, don't *do* that!"

"Just wanted to surprise you." He grinned. "Now tell me: What were you going to say in the meeting but then stopped? Also, do you want a ride home?"

I accepted his offer, and we made our way to the north exit.

"Oh, it wasn't anything," I said. "I just lost my train of thought."

"Lies!" Stanley announced. "You had an idea for the show, didn't you?"

"Well, yeah," I admitted as I braced for the chilly air on the other side of the doors. "But when I tried to say my ideas in rehearsal, I was kind of shut down."

"By Brandon." Stanley shook his head. "Because he's an egomaniac."

I stopped walking and gave Stanley a *look*.

"Okay, okay." He held up his hands. "I may have egotistical tendencies, too. I'm not so big that I can't admit that. But I want to hear your ideas. I like ideas."

I avoided his gaze as we made our way to the car.

"I'm just a stage manager," I reminded him. "I'm not supposed to have ideas about the set, or the acting. My ideas are supposed to be about break times, or binders, or—"

"Who cares?" Stanley opened the door and slid down into his car. I opened mine and followed him. "Not all stage managers have creative ideas about the show, but you do. And we're in high school. No one's, like, *paying you* to keep your mouth shut."

I considered this as we pulled out of the parking lot.

"Okay, well," I said in a rush, "I just had this idea that we could make the sound effects sound more old-fashioned. Not so high tech. More like they would've sounded back then."

"That is *brilliant*," Stanley breathed. "See? You need to tell me all your ideas, so I can take credit for them."

I laughed nervously. *And I'm taking credit for ideas I got from the stage-keepers.* But it felt so good to have Stanley curious and complimenting my ideas.

"But, honey." He pulled down a street. "Why are you suddenly so full of inspiration?"

"What?"

"Where did all of this come from? You barely spoke in the theatre last year, and now you've got all these master-y Shakespeare ideas. Where are you getting them?"

We sat at a red light. Stanley tapped on the steering wheel.

"Umm . . . from my brain?" I said indignantly, even though I was kind of lying. He wouldn't believe me if I told him the truth.

"All right." We pulled out into the intersection and turned left onto my street. "If you say so."

I could hear him saying *Lies!* again in his head. He was clearly suspicious but letting it drop, for now. We pulled up in front of my house. I didn't move to get out right away, and he raised his eyebrows at me.

"So how's Lulu doing?" I asked tentatively, knocking my knees together.

Stanley's whole body sagged: He leaned forward and let his forehead drop onto the steering wheel. "Oh, Mama, not good."

"How not good?"

"'I Dreamed a Dream' not good." He sighed. "I shouldn't be telling you this—she told me not to tell you anything, actually, the little duck witch. But it's gotten worse. Her parents took her phone away, for good. She's not allowed to use the internet at home. They wanted to yank her from the play, but instead they set up this thing with Gretchen so that they know when rehearsals start and finish, so Lulu can't lie about that anymore. She's shut away in her house all the time, like the beautifully tragic Rapunzel she is."

I was stunned. All of that in a couple weeks of us not speaking. I felt numb and heavy all at once.

"That's horrible." I rubbed my hands up my face, through my spiky hair. "What can we do?"

"You can't do anything," Stanley groaned, "but wait for her grudginess to subside. She's always been like this, but I think with everything that's happened in the past couple months, it's worse."

I sighed. "Okay."

"I'm there for her as much as possible," he continued. "At school she uses my phone to call Chip, who's trying to help her through it. I just can't . . ." He trailed off, staring out his window. "Sometimes I can't get through to her. Sometimes she's fine; it's just there are these moments now where she seems so . . . It's like she's checked out. Like she's not really here."

Stanley looked like he might cry. I'd never seen him cry before.

"Hey." I touched his shoulder. "It's gonna be okay." There was no promise behind the words, but they seemed to help. He looked over at me hopefully. "Once her parents stop being so stupid, or she gets out of that house, she's going to be herself again."

He took a deep, shuddery breath and nodded. "You're right, of course; she just needs to get away from them. Or they need to step up."

We both stared out the window for a moment, into the October dark.

"I'm so lucky I got my parents," Stanley whispered.

"I'm lucky, too," I agreed.

19

The bell rang for lunch, and I grabbed my books and headed to the library. Josh was sitting outside the doors in a lightning-bolt goalie shirt and track pants. He had worn the same shirt when the boys won against Billerica last year—he'd made at least eight great saves.

"Hey!" I smiled, fighting the urge to smooth my shirt and run my fingers through my hair. "You ready for 'Tis now the very witching time'?"

"You know it." He smiled back and stood up. "But I'm starving and I forgot to bring lunch. Let's do this in the cafeteria."

"Josh, you know that I can't." I started to panic. "If Lulu sees us—"

"Will that really matter?" He put a hand on my shoulder blade and started to walk me down the hall. "She still won't talk to you; I've seen how she acts at rehearsals. Being seen with me isn't going to make it *worse* at this point. And I think the librarians are starting to hate us."

I didn't agree with him about Lulu—if she saw us together, she would probably take it personally. But how long was I supposed to hide? It had been almost a month now. How long did I let this dictate my life?

"*. . . forever?*"

"*Yeah, that sounds about right.*"

I stopped in the hallway, ignoring Josh's lead. I hadn't even considered that before. *What if this is actually over?* Maybe Lulu and I were never going to be friends again. Maybe things were broken beyond repair.

The thought splintered me into a million little pieces, like the wood chips in the yard at the Globe. Sad, sad, wood chips. I wished with all of my heart that none of this had happened. If Lulu hadn't fallen in love with Megan, if her parents hadn't freaked out . . . if Josh hadn't auditioned for the show . . .

Would I still be here? Best-friend-less?

But, I thought, *if Lulu could just forgive me for this stupid fight . . .*

Suddenly, the me-pile of wood chips was sad, but also kind of fed up.

"Emma?"

"Okay," I said. "Let's go."

He smiled so big he practically bared his square, handsome teeth. I turned my head away and wiped a few stray tears at the corners of my eyes.

Can teeth be handsome? You're such a weirdo, Emma.

I grew more nervous as we got closer. But, I reasoned, the librarians really *were* starting to get annoyed with Josh and me for working on *Hamlet,* and even more for occasionally laughing a whole bunch when we were *supposed* to be working on *Hamlet*. And I liked the librarians. They, at least, would talk to me.

Josh's hand steered us into the cafeteria. I pretended to read as we moved through the line, but actually glanced nervously around the room. We were getting all kinds of looks: curious stares and bug eyes. Plus whispers so loud they might as well have been shouted.

Josh seemed oblivious, and piled his tray with pizza, yogurts, a peanut-butter sandwich, cashews, and a slush drink. At the last second, he bought two Fruit Roll-Ups. We made it out of the line alive. He shoved a handful of cashews in his mouth as he asked: "Where do you want to sit?"

An open table in the far corner, near the windows. Separated, but with a straight shot to the door. The second I sat down, my phone beeped with a text from Stanley:

Really, Mama? You're not making this easy for me.

I nearly jumped out of my seat. I looked up and spied Stanley's brilliant hair. He was sitting with Lulu at the opposite end of the cafeteria. His head was tilted and his eyebrows were raised. Lulu looked over, met my eyes for a second, and then sat back in her chair and crossed her arms.

"I don't think this was a good idea," I murmured to Josh, and passed him my phone. He read the text, then glanced up to where Stanley and Lulu were sitting. He tapped my phone, closing the message.

"I think they're being kind of dramatic."

"We're theatre people," I pointed out. "We live for drama."

"You don't." Josh passed me his script and a Fruit Roll-Up. "You live for this."

"I live for . . . watermelon-strawberry-fusion bombs?" I peered at the label.

He smiled, the corners of his eyes crinkling. "Have you had one before?"

"Nope."

"Well, now you're gonna live for them."

I bit into it.

"Well?"

"It is indeed a bomb of watermelon-strawberry fusion."

"I knew you'd like it," Josh said, happily taking a bite that consumed approximately three-quarters of the piece of pizza. I stuffed another piece of the pink-and-red, slightly slimy food-thing in my mouth, and noticed Ashlee, Ashley, and Jennifer sitting at their table in the dead center of the room. Ashlee pointed a manicured fingernail at me, and then whispered to Jennifer and Ashley.

My chest tightened. I looked down at the table and closed my eyes. Bad idea. The noises of the cafeteria twisted until it sounded like the roar of music and voices in Ashlee's house last Halloween. The Horrible Party.

We were celebrating another win in an undefeated season. Ashlee had given me a Solo cup filled with some kind of orange punch. I drank it quickly, because I was nervous, and it was sugary, like an orange Popsicle. I'd already had two beers and was beginning to wobble as I walked. Ashlee laughed at me, tugged on my long ponytail, and told everyone how adorable I was. I smiled, adorably, and found an open chair. Jennifer passed by me and stopped to refill my cup with more punch. I drank that, too. It was delicious.

I tried to stand up a few minutes later, but the floor felt uneven. I was going to sit back down, but then Ashley grabbed me and pulled me through the basement door—walking down the stairs felt treacherous, and I leaned on her. She patted my head. The basement was dark, and some song I didn't know blasted out of large speakers: slow R & B, kind of sexy music. Tiny, twinkling lights from a small, whirling, multicolored disco ball reflected off my sparkly orange top. I watched the glittery spots swirl around the room. My head began to spin with them.

"Emma's here!" Ashley had squealed. "She's finally gonna have some fun."

"It's about time." Jennifer smiled.

"Bring her over! Max is lonely, and he thinks Emma's a cutie pie."

"Aw, shut up, Ashlee."

Ashley passed me off to Jennifer, who took me by the hand. I stumbled forward: There was Ashlee, sitting on Josh's lap, watching me like a cat. In the strange lighting, it had been hard to tell what was happening, but there were several couches, and people, my teammates, were moving all over them. Max, the sweeper and captain of the varsity boys team, was sitting next to Josh, looking me up and down. I liked Max—he'd always been so nice to me, giving me sweeper tips.

I had liked all of them. They were my friends; they took care of me. Now I was woozy, and they were looking at me funny. In a new way. Ashlee's eyes met mine, challenging me. My brain was full of punch—I didn't understand.

What do you want me to do?

Then Jennifer had pulled my hand, leading me toward Max. Ashley looked at me, then to Ashlee, uncertainly. I took a few steps, then it dawned on me:

Was I supposed to . . . *do stuff* with Max?

My legs stopped walking. I was stuck ten feet away from the couch. I couldn't move. Maybe I didn't want to move.

"What are you doing?" Jennifer asked.

"Guys, maybe we shouldn't—"

"She's such a baby," Ashlee laughed. "Come on, Emma."

I tried to answer, but my chest tightened. My rib cage was squeezing my lungs. I tried to gasp for breath in a really subtle way. Things were starting to get blurry. I wanted to jump out of my body.

My friends were all saying things I couldn't quite hear, and then I couldn't hear anything but the bass beat of the music. A burning sensation had started in my stomach, like the anxiety dragons were roasting my insides.

I just stood there, scorched, or maybe frozen. I was barely aware that Jennifer was trying to yank me forward, and Ashlee was saying something to me, something about being weird. But everything was flashing lights and vibrating noises, and I couldn't explain to them that I couldn't move even if I wanted to. That I could barely breathe. That I wanted to go home.

Suddenly, large brown eyes were close to mine:

"Emma, are you okay?"

I shook my head.

"Do you want to go home?"

I nodded. A callused hand grabbed mine.

"Emma? Are you okay?"

I mumbled something back. *Why is he asking again?*

"Open your eyes."

I was staring at a gray, speckled table. I looked up—Josh's eyes were close to mine again, but we were in the sunny cafeteria. He looked at me searchingly.

"Hey, you're white as a sheet."

"A ghost," I corrected.

"A ghost is just a sheet with eyeholes," he said, and smiled, waiting for me to laugh. I rubbed my cheeks with my hands, trying to get the paleness out of them.

Either beet red or sheet pale. Nowhere in between.

"But seriously." I could feel him watching me. "Are you feeling okay?"

"Yeah, let's just, um. . ." I muttered. "Let's just get started."

I pulled the script toward me, took a deep breath, and read the first few lines aloud:

"'Tis now the very witching time of night, when churchyards yawn, and hell itself breathes out contagion to this world. Now could I drink hot blood, and do such bitter business as the day would quake to look on—"

"Sounds good," Josh interjected. I punched him lightly in the shoulder—it almost hurt, because muscles—and we both laughed. For the rest of lunch, I didn't look up from my script, or away from Josh's face.

If I stay in this bubble, I'll be okay.

We made it through the speech just as the bell rang. I stood up, shaking slightly, and threw my trash away. Josh insisted we walk out of the cafeteria together, and I didn't argue. He buffered the glares I felt from Lulu on the back of my neck. I glanced back as we left. Bad idea. Ashlee was glaring, too. Her and Lulu's combined force shot daggers into my stomach.

"Can we work this weekend?" Josh asked, snapping me out of my daze. We were suddenly at my locker.

"Sure."

"Cool, I'll text you."

As he jogged away, I missed his happy, calming presence, but I also felt relieved as I walked, alone, to history. I liked the anonymity being a theatre kid gave me, and being friends with Josh meant I was on the radar again.

I really like Josh, I thought, plunking down into my seat. *If only he wasn't so popular.*

20

"To whom do you speak this?" Kelly asked.

Josh's brow furrowed. "Do you see nothing there?"

"Nothing at all, yet all that is I see."

"Nor did you nothing hear?" he asked her desperately.

Kelly's face flashed in surprise, out of character for just a moment, and I smiled and then felt the smile turn into an enormous yawn. Kelly was totally impressed: Josh not only knew the scene, he was *acting* it. He was nervous, but he knew what was happening; he knew how Hamlet felt.

"No, nothing but ourselves."

He turned back to watch Brandon—as the Ghost—slowly back offstage. Josh's breathing was heavy, and he, for the first time in that scene, seemed terrified.

"Why, look you there! Look how it steals away—my father in his habit as he lived. Look where he goes even now out at the portal!"

Kelly placed a gentle hand on Josh's shoulder. Josh turned and jumped. He was skittish, but much better than before.

It was Halloween. I had spent the majority of the last week, when I wasn't at rehearsal, asleep. My trips were starting to take their toll: I was tired all the time. Any spare moments I had were spent helping Josh in between naps.

We'd had lunch together every day, five days in a row: talking about the meaning of the text, writing out small iambic-pentameter reminders in his script, sometimes doing the scenes in silly voices. I never got sick of it—Josh was so focused and into the play, and his energy spread, warming my Shakespearean heart. Our work together kept me going. I always left Josh with a small burst of energy, feeling like I could do all my homework in an hour, run a mile, and maybe think of the magic words that would make this whole Lulu thing better.

"What if you, like, set us up?" I had asked Stanley during a set-building session earlier in the week.

He shook his head. "I can't bring it up again, Mama. She's too fragile."

Thinking of her as fragile made me want to talk to her all the more.

"O Hamlet, thou hast cleft my heart in twain!" Kelly cried, shoving Josh away as he tried, tentatively, to embrace her.

Even his blocking is correct!

I felt so proud; I wanted to tell everyone in the room that I had been helping him. But I was still waiting for the right moment, if there would ever be one.

The person I most wanted to tell was Lulu. Before the fall, she would have loved to help me teach Josh Shakespeare, if it had been for a class or something. Last year, our favorite best-friend Friday nights were spent reading plays aloud together. I felt the absence of her all the time.

Lulu wasn't there for rehearsal on Halloween; we weren't doing her scenes. That was probably a good thing. I'd watched her Ophelia wane every day, as she watched Josh's Hamlet get stronger. Her performance had become fickle—one moment she'd be angry, the next, demure and powerless. As Josh got even better, she seemed to care about the show less and less. I worried that I was hurting her even more by helping him. But why couldn't she just accept that this was the way things were? Maybe she could play Hamlet in some future production, but for right now, we all had to work on this Hamlet.

"I do repent." Josh crouched at Grant's/Polonius's body. "But heaven hath pleased it so, to punish me with this, and this with me, that I must be their scourge and minister."

I felt a smile trying to push its way onto my mouth. Watching him up there, excited about Hamlet, soothed my aching guilt a little.

Then a chorus of giggles erupted from the rear of the theatre, and all the warm-and-fuzzy emotions welling inside me stopped. I turned—everyone turned—and saw Ashlee, Ashley, and Jennifer, sitting in the back row. They all smiled and waved, ponytails bobbing. Josh waved back, uncertainly. I clutched my notebook, trying to hide the tremors in my hands.

"Should I ask them to go?" I whispered to Brandon.

"Why?" He bent over me and whispered back, "If they like it, they'll get more people to come for the shows. It's fine." He smiled his most dimpled smile and raised a hand at them. "Continue!" he called back to the cast.

For the rest of the scene it was hard to concentrate. I couldn't quite hear what the girls in the back row were whispering, but their mutters clawed at my ears. I stopped checking to see if Josh and Kelly had their blocking down. It looked okay—no one was falling off the stage. Instead, I bored inky spirals into my script, wishing the girls would go away.

"This counsellor is now most still, most secret, and most grave, who was in life a most foolish prating knave."

Greg *pfffff*ted in laughter. Josh had actually nailed the joke.

"Come, sir, to draw toward an end with you. Good night, mother." Josh grabbed ahold of Grant and started to drag him offstage.

"Am I going the right way?" Josh suddenly broke character. Grant opened his eyes and looked up at Josh.

I fumbled a moment, but found the note: "Yeah, it's exit stage left."

"And we'll end there!" Brandon hopped up out of his seat next to me in the front row. "Excellent job, everyone. Have a happy Halloween!"

Kelly grumbled, along with most of the cast. They had been miffed we had to come to rehearsal today. I wasn't too upset about it—everyone else went to a party or something, but I had learned my lesson. Before, I'd thought maybe Lulu, Stanley, and I would watch *Rocky Horror*, but clearly that wasn't an option. So rehearsal, then homework, and admiring Abby's warrior penguin costume.

As I shoved my own things into my backpack, a perfume wafted over me: cleat leather, shin-guard sweat, and strawberry lip gloss. I turned. Ashlee had come down the aisle with Ashley and Jennifer in tow, making a beeline for Josh, who had just jumped down off the stage. The rest of the cast scattered.

"Josh!" Ashlee jogged over to him, black shiny ponytail swinging. "I had no idea how *amazing* you are at acting."

"Thanks, Ash." Josh smiled a tentative, dopey grin. "That means a lot."

"You were totally great," Jennifer agreed, hovering behind Ashlee. "There's this whole other *actor* side that you've been hiding!"

"Ha-ha, yeah, well, I didn't really know about it." Josh relaxed and leaned back, his elbows resting against the edge of the stage in his I'm-the-coolest-guy-ever pose. I tried really hard not to roll my eyes, but it was too painful, so I turned away and indulged myself. Unfortunately, I had turned toward Brandon, who saw this. He eyed Josh and shook his head in annoyance. We were on the same page.

"When's your opening night? We'll have to come see you!" Ashlee announced, and the others cooed agreement.

"Umm . . . I don't know, actually." Josh looked sheepish, then glanced over and caught me bold-faced staring. "Hey, Emma, when's our opening night?"

"It's December second," Brandon answered for me. He sidled up to the group. "Did you girls like what you saw?"

"Oh, it was very cool," Jennifer assured him.

I tried to will myself into invisibility, but it was too late: They had all turned toward me now. I felt their eyes appraise me: not-quite-tight-enough skinny jeans, boring sneakers, lesbian haircut, awkward stance.

"Emma, I forgot you did this now." Ashley smiled at me. I almost winced from her sweetness. "You certainly look the part, don't you?"

"Sure," I muttered.

"Did it hurt to cut off all that beautiful hair?" Jennifer feigned concern. "Do you regret it?"

"No."

It felt like any second they were going to whip out vampire fangs to devour me.

"Careful with this one." Ashlee turned to Brandon, her tone light but menacing. "She has a tendency to ditch before the big game."

Brandon's brows pinched together. "Oh, well, Emma's a reliable—"

"We still can't believe she quit," added Jennifer. Ashlee and Ashley nodded in agreement.

"It's been a year," I said. "I think you can believe it by now."

"A year exactly," Josh amiably agreed with me. A second passed where I didn't understand what he was saying, and then I did: Halloween of last year. I quit the day after.

"Are you coming to the party tonight?" Ashley asked Josh. Ashlee affected disinterest, but I bet that she had orchestrated this whole thing.

"Yeah, yeah, I'll be there." Josh nodded. "I'm going to be tired, though—it's been a long day, with practice and rehearsal."

"We'll figure out some way to keep you awake." Ashlee smiled her cat smile. I waited for Josh to blow her off, but he scratched his head and looked at the floor bashfully.

"Oh . . ." Josh stuttered. "Ha-ha, okay."

I had had enough. I didn't need to witness this version of Josh. I hadn't seen him since last year, and I hadn't missed him. I was halfway up the aisle when Brandon called after me:

"Emma!"

I turned back around.

"Do you want to go get coffee?" he called loudly. Ashlee, Ashley, and Jennifer all froze and stared.

Happy-panic, like too much caffeine, spread through my chest. "Now?"

"Yes, now! Let's go!" Brandon grabbed his bag and was up the aisle and next to me in a flash. Ashlee and Ashley exchanged glances; Jennifer pouted. I didn't allow myself to look at Josh.

Forget them. You've got a date.

I cursed past-Emma for pulling on the boring black hoodie and jeans this morning, but followed Brandon to the top of the auditorium. As we walked through the hallway and out toward the parking lot, I noticed something shimmery and blond in the corner of my eye: Lulu was across the lot, watching me go to Brandon's car.

What is she still doing at school?

I paused before getting in and tried a halfhearted wave in her direction. She glowered for a moment, then got inside her car and slammed the door. My hand fell slowly, and I sighed.

"Everything good?"

"Oh yeah." I slid into the passenger seat and smiled. "Everything's great."

21

The ride over was a teensy bit awkward—I barely said anything, and I laughed too much at everything Brandon said. But he was relaxed, and it was starting to feel like it used to, before the play got so . . . *Hamlet*-y.

We parked in the big lot downtown. Halloween lights and decorations on the shops cast an orange glow all over the pier. Luckily it was busy and noisy, with everyone walking around in their costumes, so I didn't feel I needed to say anything. I went to open the door to the Outerspace Café, when I realized Brandon was still walking. I hurried to catch up with him as he opened the door to the other coffee shop a few stores down. Lulu, Stanley, and I avoided this place—the drinks came in sizes that we couldn't pronounce, and the color scheme was sophisticated and bland.

But there must be something good about it, I thought as I trailed after Brandon. *Or he wouldn't have brought us here.* A few tasteful green and yellow gourds were their only Halloween decorations.

"Why don't you grab a table by the window?" Brandon said. "And I'll get our drinks. What kind of coffee do you like?"

None. Because I'm a nine-year-old. "Um . . . I think maybe I'll just have tea?" I scanned the menu, but I was so nervous it might as well have been written in Elizabethan English. "Something black, but with a lot of sugar."

Brandon looked bemused. "Leafy sugar water, coming right up."

I laughed nervously, and then grabbed a table by the window. I hopped up onto the sleek, high silver chair. From my seat, I could see the Outerspace Café, sparkling with purple lights, a big, toothy jack-o'-lantern sitting on the stoop outside the door. I longed for a cushy booth and, if I was being totally honest, for someone I felt more comfortable talking to.

But I was with Brandon, who I had liked forever, who was buying me tea, whose butt I could check out as he stood in line.

This is actually finally happening. I forced myself to appear relaxed and smile as he brought over our drinks. He looked so good in his black V-neck, jacket, and tight jeans, his hair pulled back into a curly ponytail. With his overall cool factor and my short hair, I couldn't help thinking: *We probably totally look like a college couple.*

"Here you go, tea with extra sugar."

"That's a lot of tea," I said as Brandon set down a huge mauve mug in front of me.

"Yeah." Brandon slid onto the chair across from me. "This place recognizes the need for bowls of caffeinated beverages."

I laughed. He took a sip from his equally huge cappuccino, and when he brought the mug down, foam covered his top lip. I imagined kissing it off, like they do in the movies, and felt shivery, and then repulsed at my own cheesiness.

Okay, okay, now what?

Take a sip of your tea, Emma.

TOO HOT TOO HOT. NOT ENOUGH SUGAR. GROSS.

I managed to swallow without coughing.

Good. This is going to be fine. Stare off into space while he takes a sip. Now ask him a question.

"So . . . how are your college applications going?" I poured in a couple of the extra sugar packets Brandon had brought over.

"Oh, you know, fine." He waved a hand. "I've finished my applications for all the places my parents want me to apply to. I can't submit anything to conservatories till the play goes up—I'm filming *Hamlet* and sending it out as part of my portfolio."

"Oh, wow!"

"Yeah, it's all very time consuming." Brandon took another sip. "But don't you worry. You have a few years before you have to deal with all of this. You'll have grown so much more as a person by then."

"Right. Cool." I stared down at my black sneakers, which suddenly looked incredibly juvenile.

Why don't I own any chic boots or heels or something?

I set my mug down on the saucer and sloshed a little tea. My fingers got all sticky.

"So." Brandon's eyes leveled with mine. "I thought we should talk—"

Ahhh!

"—about the show," he continued. "I feel like things have been kind of off between us, and I don't like that."

"Me neither."

"I guess I was taken aback by how good you are at this stuff," Brandon said. "I didn't expect it, and I felt kind of threatened."

I burst out laughing. "What?"

"I know, I know." Brandon laughed, too. "You're not very threatening. Anyway, I realized that we should, you know, actually talk about this. Are we cool?"

"So cool!" I assured him, beaming, even though a tiny seed of doubt was sprouting in my stomach.

"Excellent." He sipped his cappuccino. "I was really impressed by your ideas in the first production meeting, by the way. It's good to keep Stanley on his toes—we don't want him getting too comfortable." He winked again. I was happy I was sitting down.

"Oh, well." I laughed a little. "I just had a brain blast all of a sudden, and I blurted it all out like an idiot."

"No, no!" Brandon leaned closer in. "It was great. You were so into it."

"I guess I've been feeling inspired lately," I said, and took another long sip of tea. The caffeine and sugar coursed through me.

"Yeah, I've noticed."

He sounded alarmingly bitter. *Wait, I thought we were cool?*

"So how do you think the production is going?"

"I think it's going as well as it can!" I chirped, instantly realizing that was the wrong thing to say.

"As well as it can?" Brandon said. "What do you mean by that?"

I considered this for a moment. What I really meant was that once you've seen Shakespeare's company, a high school cast can never truly measure up. I meant that while Josh was rapidly improving, he wasn't Richard Burbage, and checked-out Lulu/Ophelia was about as sympathetic as a floorboard—no match for Alexander Cooke. I meant that

Brandon was nowhere near the director Shakespeare was (however insane he seemed to be), and that we rehearsed, and made progress, at the pace of a snail with a sprained ankle.

"Oh, you know." I quickly backtracked. "Just that I'm sure it will live up to its potential."

"Yes, excellent." Brandon nodded, all suspicion gone. "With Josh doing so well, I think we're headed in the right direction. It's amazing how much he's improved, right?"

"Uh-huh." I couldn't look at him, or I might tell him the truth.

Which seems like a really bad idea now.

I forced myself to smile and drink more tea. I wasn't sure what to say next, and Brandon looked pensively into his cappuccino. We both drank in silence. I missed Cooke's soft laugh, and Josh's focus.

Of all the boys I could be spending time with, why I am here with Brandon? I was startled at the thought, and pushed it away. *Because he's gorgeous and funny and he asked you out. . . .*

I started to pay attention to the people around us—freshman girls from BHS giggling over their cell phones and iced coffees. Two women in their twenties, plugged into laptops, typing away furiously. A couple with tall sandwiches and big smiles. A sigh wanted to sneak out, but I didn't let it.

"Let's get down to it, shall we?" Brandon said, his voice cutting through the thick fog of coffee-shop noise. *Get down to it? What does that mean? Ba-bump. Ba-bump. Ba—*

A notebook hit the table in front of me. Brandon's hands flipped to a page titled *Act 4 Notes*.

Wait, what's happening?

"So I wanted to get your opinion on the Ophelia madness

scene," Brandon said, unaware of the confusion and devastation pouring out of my chest. "It's clear you know *Hamlet* really well, and I realized I should use all the resources I can. I was thinking you could be a bit of an assistant director. I didn't want one before, but this is different. I'll even credit you in the program!"

I should have been delighted. I wanted to contribute to *Hamlet* with my ideas, like Wick did, but I was completely caught off guard. This had quickly turned from a date into a business meeting. Or maybe it had been one all along.

"Brandon," I sputtered. "I'm the stage manager, not the assistant director."

"I know. But I realized you have more potential than just stage-managing."

Just stage-managing? I knew it was supposed to be a compliment, but suddenly I wasn't taking any of this as a compliment. I didn't feel good—everything was twisting inside of me.

"Thanks," I said, the word sounding hollow. "But . . ."

"So do you think Ophelia drowns?" Brandon pulled out his script. "Or does she really commit suicide? And any tips you could give me on handling Lulu would also be great. Something about her performance is off, and we need to fix it, but she's just so hostile."

Handling Lulu? He thought I could help rein her in, fix her Ophelia. He hadn't even noticed we weren't friends anymore. *I can't fix her, and neither can you.* Bubbles formed in my chest— not anxiety bubbles, but bubbles that released pockets of angry air when they burst.

It was one thing to not want to date me, but he couldn't use me, and he couldn't talk about Lulu like she was just a problem with his show.

I felt exhausted, and so frustrated, and one other thing I couldn't put my finger on. Brandon was oblivious; his eyes scanned the page, then looked up at me, hopeful for answers, but I couldn't hold his gaze. My sugar packets had been torn into teeny, teeny pieces. The table was littered with them.

"I have to go."

"What?" Brandon said. "Why? Are you okay?"

No. I feel nauseous, but I can't explain why. "I just need to go." I stood up.

"But, Emma," Brandon protested as I pushed my chair in. "I really need your help."

Too bad. "I forgot there's somewhere I need to be."

The coffee-shop bell rang cheerfully as I stumbled out onto the street. I didn't look back to see if he was following me. I stopped at the street corner.

Disrespected, I realized. That was the other thing I felt. Did Brandon actually value me, my feelings, my work, at all?

Deep breaths.

I closed my eyes and tried to picture a world where Brandon actually wanted to go on a date with me. Nothing happened. So I pictured a different world instead.

There's somewhere I need to be.

As if I had summoned it, the bus pulled up. I slumped into a seat and felt my stomach lurch as the bus jerked into motion again. I composed a text in my head:

Hi, Lulu. I miss you. Everything is weird/bad. Brandon doesn't like me like I liked him, and I think he might not be as great as I thought. . . . You've probably known that all along. Josh is cooler than I thought he was, but he's still kind of a jerk, maybe, and might be making out with Ashlee at a party right now. I have a crush on a guy hundreds of years older than me, which is perverted when you think about it. Oh yeah, and I've started time traveling on the regular now. Cool, right? But what do I do, Lulu? Why aren't we helping each other anymore?

I sighed and stared out the window, feeling my eyes begin to water. It was all too complicated for me to sort out, and for the first time since cutting my hair, I missed it. I wanted to sink back into the folds.

22

The auditorium doors were, thankfully, still unlocked, and though the lights were dimmed, there was evidence of Stanley's presence somewhere in the vicinity: The stage floor was covered with grid sketches and gels carefully lined up. Tricky Stanley. He wasn't supposed to be there without my supervision, but I found it hard to care at that moment.

I mean, what's he really going to do? Two trapdoors would be tacky.

I ducked into the girls' dressing room and shrugged on my blue Globe uniform. I paused in front of the mirror: My eyes were red, and the skin underneath was deep purple. It almost stopped me—I didn't want to look so awful in front of Cooke—but I couldn't bear being here a second longer.

My feet walked me up onto the stage, and the trapdoor edges seemed to glow. My fingertips traced the outline and gently lifted a corner. I placed the panel aside, scooted forward, and dangled my feet over the edge. The fog was warm this time, and enveloped my calves in calm. Just knowing that soon I would be a world away slowed my breathing, laid a blanket of powdered sugar over my mind.

It's all going to be fine. Cooke will kiss you again, and you'll get to watch grumpy William Shakespeare creating masterpieces, and Wick will tell you what to do, and you won't worry about anything happening or anyone alive past Queen Elizabeth's reign.

Wick!

I had forgotten I had made a plan. I grabbed my backpack and foraged in the bottom for the bag of cough drops I had picked up at the drugstore with Mom the night before. Strawberries and cream. (They didn't have ale-flavored.) I shoved the bag in one of my large pants pockets, took a step out, and dropped into the now-familiar black.

I hit the mat and planted my feet in a squat. It stuck.

I have mastered the dismount.

The light from the floorboard cracks illuminated two swords lying haphazardly in the dirt. I hefted them up, careful not to cut myself—the Globe didn't mess around with props. A thing was the thing it was: a sword, a sword; a skull, a skull. I liked that.

A shuffle of footsteps shook the stage above my head, and some loud gasping went with them.

A performance! I grinned. *At the Globe!*

Which meant I was supposed to be upstairs.

I hurried along the path—left, left, right—and up the stairs into the tiring-house, which felt cozy with its muffled daylight and strangely comforting ale/garlic/BO/smoke aroma. The first thing I saw was Wick's small frame hunched over the script. I deposited the swords carefully into the barrel and reached under the prop table to grab my dagger from where I'd hidden it—there was no way I could bring that back to the future with me. I buckled it into place, feeling stronger instantly. Then I tiptoed over to Wick's desk.

"Master Wick."

He turned. His eyes were watery—sick, not tearful watery—but he looked a little less yellow than the last time I'd seen him. He motioned for me to hurry up and speak.

"Um, Master Wick," I whisper-stammered (*whammered? stispered?*), "Dost thou . . . still contain a cough?"

It wasn't a perfect sentence, but he didn't seem fazed. "Just a tickle remains, Master Allen," he croak-whispered (definitely *croakspered*), his hand going to his throat. "Did thee gather the swords?"

"Oh, yes. But another matter . . ." I reached into my pocket. "I brought thee a remedy from home. Er, the country." I untwisted a cough drop from its casing and held it out to him.

Without missing a beat, he turned and hissed, "As Cooke exits, Sly." Sly nodded and stood at the ready by the left arch, a group of men behind him. Wick turned back to me, his eye suspiciously regarding the cough drop.

"'Tis pink." He palmed it.

"Put it in thy mouth," I instructed, with exaggerated pantomime. "And let it sit on thy tongue. It will calm the tickling."

He watched my gesturing dubiously. "Forsooth, I hope thou dost not intend to pursue the stage, Master Allen." He popped in the cough drop and turned back to the script.

"Well, um, I have more if thou requirest any." I plunked down onto the stool and awaited further orders. A few moments later I heard a noise from Wick:

"Mmmmmmm."

His eye twinkled down at me.

"Many good thanks, Em." He smiled, close-lipped, the cough drop rattling on his teeth. "This country cough remedy is much easier to bear than sucking a lemon."

At first I thought that meant he didn't really like it, but then I saw half a shriveled lemon sitting on his table near the quill stand. I had never appreciated modern medicine more. I gave him a gentle pat on the back, to which he grunted in reply.

The scene changed—Cooke blustered into the backstage area in a towering red wig and an extravagant purple velvet gown, accompanied by one of the younger apprentice actors in a simple black shift dress. They were barely backstage when two groups of armored actors poured onto the stage from either side arch.

Well, this isn't Hamlet.

Cooke went immediately to one of the mirrors and began to reapply his pasty white makeup and Fruit-Roll-Up-pink blush. Wick seemed to be all right, so I sidled up to Cooke and leaned on the table next to him.

"I love thy dress," I leaned in and whispered. It was maybe the boldest thing I'd ever done in my entire life.

What have I got to lose? Another guy rejecting me? So what?

His eyes didn't stray from the mirror, but he said: "Then I find myself envious of an article of clothing."

I stifled a giggle and was about to reply (with something equally witty, I'm sure), when I was called back.

"Take Master Haddock and get thee up to the cannon," Wick ordered. "I fear my lungs are too small to rise to the Heavens today."

"The cannon," I repeated, my skin suddenly prickling with cold. He had to be kidding.

"Dost thou have wool in thy brain?" Wick rasped. "For the final battle. Haddock has seen me load it—he can show thee the way of it."

Master Haddock, a red-faced boy with a mop of brown hair, smiled nervously at me from behind Wick. He looked like someone was threatening to smack him in the head with a frying pan and ordering him to *be happy about it.*

I bit my lip as Wick's eye leveled at mine. I couldn't explain to him that the last time I had been tasked with a major special effect I had blown it.

Not as much as you'll blow it this time.

"Master Allen: Thy book-keeper hast given thee an order," Wick said impatiently. "And Master Shakespeare's play needs a cannon."

"Of course," I said through gritted teeth. "We'll take care of it."

"Aye." Wick snorted and waved me away. "Get it a mug of ale and a wool blanket."

I was on edge, and fought the urge to snap at him: *Oh, shut up!* Instead, my wobbly legs followed Haddock toward the ladder that led to the stage attic, "the Heavens." But as I stepped onto the first rung, Wick called me back once again:

"Ahh, before thou goest to war, Master Allen, couldst thou spare another pink country lemon?"

I tossed another cough drop at him before hastening up the ladder to my doom.

I'd never been up to the Heavens before—it was the attic space in the hutch roof that covered the stage, held up by the big, red pillars. Wick had once quizzed me on what I thought the roof's purpose was:

"Umm . . . to shield the actors from the sun and rain?"

"No," he had answered smugly. "'Tis to shield the *costumes.* The costumes are more highly prized than the players, Master

Allen." He had then chortled quite a bit at his own joke. But I think he was partly serious.

Haddock and I emerged into a small room with slanted walls. We walked in the middle, toward the point of the gable and the little window that overlooked the audience. In the center of the floor was a square hole: another trapdoor, but without the door part and with a small pulley system. I tried to peek down at the stage, and my stomach immediately gave a lurch—it was a forty-foot drop. I knew some actors were lowered down through the hole for the God bits in plays.

What would happen to me if I went through that portal? Would I end up dangling in midair from the grid at BHS, hanging from a Fresnel light?

I moved to the small, triangular window on the front wall of the room. I mostly couldn't see the play, just the faces reacting to it, their mouths all agape, the balcony audience all sitting on the front of their benches in earnest. The clanging of swords, pounding steps, and agonized cries directly below cued me: We needed to hurry up.

The cannon was smaller than I expected: only about two feet long. It was kind of adorable, if it weren't for the fact that it might explode at any second.

"Where's the ball?" I whispered, looking around the floor. I then looked back at Haddock, who was staring at me like I'd grown another head.

"Pardon, Master Allen," he stammered, "but dost thou not know we shall be loading a blank shot?"

Oooh, we're not actually firing a cannon ball.

"Aye, of course." I nodded. "That makes sense. So we don't kill anyone."

Haddock nodded enthusiastically back. *Good.* We were on the same page about the whole no-actual-death thing.

He showed me how to look down the barrel of the cute-but-terrifying cannon and check for debris. Seeing none, we stuffed the charge—a small rag filled with gun powder—into the cannon, using a thick wooden stick to shove it in.

"Next, the fuse." Haddock took a small piece of wire and quickly inserted it into a hole at the base of the cannon shaft, and stabbed it up and down a few times. He then removed it and took a short cord from his pocket and inserted that into the hole instead. A great cheer erupted from the crowd, and we heard Burbage shout:

"Well have we done, thrice valiant countrymen!"

"We're close!" I whispered.

"Almost through," Haddock assured me. He took from behind him another balled-up rag and handed it to me, and indicated it should follow the charge. I had just finished ramming it down the barrel when he held out two small pieces of stone to me.

"Here. Master Wick said thou shouldst light it for practice. He said one day thou wilt need to run a show thyself."

I took the stones in my hands. I'd been a Girl Scout from third to eighth grade, and I was fairly confident of my fire-starting skills. But this seemed like neither the place nor time to be counting on Camp Runamook.

"No, no," I shoved it back at him. "Thou shouldst."

Haddock held up his hands and refused to take back the flint. "All due respect, Master Allen," he said, "but thou art a book-keeper, and I a stage-keeper."

He's right. You should know how to do this.

Right then, the second cue came in, Condell lamenting:

"But I had not so much of man in me, and all my mother came into mine eyes, and gave me up to tears!"

My hands shook, and the stones seemed to jump in my palms. Then in one swift movement I struck the flint hard and sure. The feeling of triumph lasted for a brief moment, as the sparks bounced into the air. . . .

And then they landed on the floor, which immediately began to smoke.

Time stood still.

Last summer, opening night, *Oklahoma!*, Possum Community Playhouse. Ten minutes till the top of the show. Stage crew and actors running in every direction.

"Crap. Emma. The fog machine!" Janet looked up from her pre-show checklist. "Can you go warm it up? I need it hot for act two."

"Got it!" I was already on my way.

"It's the red button!"

"Got it!"

I had slipped into the right wing, where the fog machine hung out at the back curtain, nozzle pointed at the stage. I pressed the red button. Job done. Next thing on the list.

Ten minutes later, the curtains opened and a twenty-foot wall of fog billowed into the theatre and onto the audience. The sprinklers went off and the music turned into a series of shrieks and blaring alarms.

"What *happened?*" Gretchen's voice cut through the noise and smelly smoke. Our full house was stampeding out of the auditorium.

"Emma!" Janet yelled. "Which red button did you press? 'Warm up' or 'On'?"

I had been helping to usher kids out of the wings. I froze.

There were *two* red buttons?

I blinked and watched my fingers brush the "On" button of the fog machine. I knew now it was the wrong button, and I tried to keep myself from pressing it, but I couldn't. I was stuck in the unchanging memory. My right pointer finger pressed it over and over and over and over. . .

"Not again!" I cried out, back at the Globe. Instinctively, I ripped my shirt over my head and grabbed the pee bucket from the corner. I sloshed the contents onto the spark, and used my shirt to smother it out.

"Go!"

I tossed the flint to the horrified Haddock, who calmly and expertly lit the fuse. We covered our ears and waited: The cord seemed to take forever to burn down—we had missed our final cue line, and each second was agonizing. I imagined the actors struggling to come up with filler lines. Shakespeare could make up something on the spot, couldn't he?

BANG!

The deafening blast shot the cannon back a few feet, and through the smoke I saw Haddock catch it as it rolled back toward the trap-hole. When the gray clouds faded, I found myself curled in the fetal position on the floor and strangely wet on one side.

Pee.

I looked down at myself: no shirt.

I was huddled in a puddle of Elizabethan urine in a rainbow-polka-dot bra.

I sat up and scooted back into the corner, my hands across my chest to cover myself. I met eyes with Haddock, who was sitting opposite, staring at me, aghast.

"Master Haddock!" I gasped. "Go down to the costume room and fetch me a change of clothes."

His eyes were locked onto my boobs.

"Now!"

He scrambled down the ladder and quickly returned with a light green garment. He passed it to me, his hand reaching as far away from his body as possible.

"A *dress?*" I hissed. "Does it look like I need a dress? Never mind, don't answer that. Get me a *shirt* and a *doublet*."

He mumbled an apology and scampered down and up the ladder once more. This time he passed me a slightly worn, but handsome, dark-blue doublet and a white shirt with billowy arms. He'd also brought the matching blue poofy shorts and a pair of lighter blue tights.

"Thank you." I took them from him. "And now hear this, Haddock: if thou tellst *anyone* what thou hast seen . . ."

I had no idea what threat would scare an Elizabethan boy. And then it came to me: I pulled my dagger from its sheath and pointed the tip at his face.

What am I going to do, cut off his nose?

I grappled for words, but Shakespeare supplied them: "I shall place a curse on thee and thy family: a plague on your house!"

"Understood, miss," Haddock stammered. "Master! Master Allen. Understood. I have seen nothing. No need for cursin' and the plague."

"Good." I lowered the dagger, placing it back in its sheath. "Then I won't have to kill thee." I sighed and then smiled at him. He looked relieved and smiled back crookedly.

I told him to get out so I could change, and back down the ladder he went. As soon as he was out of sight, I burst into silent tears of relief. My torso shook, all my muscles in my legs and arms tensed, my lips blubbed like I was a crying little kid. And then I heard the audience applauding: not just clapping, but great whoops and cheers from the yard to the top of the balconies.

You didn't ruin the show, I assured myself. *There's no fog filling the auditorium, no fire alarm going off, no sprinkler system starting. It was late, but the cannon went off and the show went on.*

I breathed a deep, shuddery breath and got to work: I unbuckled my dagger belt, then slid off my BHS trousers and used them to blot at the right side of my body, whisking away the drops of pee. Thank goodness none of it had gotten in my hair. I unlaced my sneakers and pulled on my new blue tights, which fit surprisingly well—Elizabethan men were kind of short. I popped into the bubble shorts. They were silly, but very comfortable. I slid on my belt, then turned to the back wall, just in case, to unhook my bra and flop the white shirt over my head. The material was softer than anything I'd ever worn, but smelled like my soccer bag on a hot September game day.

I picked up the doublet last: It felt more special than the rest of the outfit. One arm through, then the other, and I hooked the fasteners up the front. It fit like a glove—tight enough that my boobs weren't announcing themselves. They'd already done enough of that today. The sneakers went back on over my new blue feet. I straightened up the attic and made a mental note to return after the show to scrub the floor where the spark had been. Was there even any soap at the Globe, though?

I made my way down the ladder hesitantly; each rung seemed to shake beneath me. It was ironic. I'd escaped my own world to come here and de-stress. I hit the floor and paused to rub my eyes, which were still stinging a bit from the smoke. When I opened them, Cooke had appeared before me, his grin so wide and full of mischief it was almost unbefitting his refined clothing.

He curtsied low to the floor, bobbing his head down, but looked up at me with merry eyes: "My lord."

I laughed, which quickly solicited a round of glares from the actors, and a "Tut-tut" from Wick. It seemed the least of my worries, though, especially with the noisy crowd outside. I shrank back in apology, but then turned my attention to Cooke again, and bent one knee in my own deep bow:

"My lady," I whispered.

This was so amusing that we both bent over in silent hysterics. Maybe it was the massive panic attack I had just fought off, but I felt an urge to reach out and grab his curly orange wig, and bring my lips to his—

"Fancy boy!" Wick called. "Dost thou care to finish the show?"

Cooke's eyes held mine as I strutted in my funny shorts over to Wick's table.

"The cannon was eleven lines late," Wick rasped at me as I approached. My legs turned to lead, forcing me to stop mid-stride. "And seven of those were from an imaginary script."

"Yes, I . . . um . . ." I was too mentally exhausted to come up with a good excuse. "We had some trouble with the lighting of it. Haddock got it working, though."

He stared at me hard, his big eye squinting. Gretchen's angry face flashed in my mind.

"I'm very sorry, sir." My voice caught in my thickly coated throat. I felt the tears coming, was sure I was going to cry, when Wick did something completely unexpected: He shrugged.

"No one's died, Master Allen." He laid a hand on my shoulder. "And the playhouse is still standing."

I gulped. "It could have burned to the ground, though."

"But it did not," Wick said, and sat me down on my stool. "And thou learnt to fire the cannon. So all's well that ends well, eh, Master Allen?"

Is this a trick?

He sat back down in his own chair and deftly waved Cooke and a few more actors into their places.

"Ahh, but . . ." He turned back to me, and I braced myself for the real eruption: "Next time, thou shalt not be late on the cue."

He stared at me. I waited for him to finish my punishment. He said nothing more, and so I couldn't do anything but reply:

"No, I shalt not be late on the cue."

"Good."

We finished out the rest of the play in series of swift prompts, and soon Armin was leading the company out onto the stage for a jig, the majority of them smeared in blood. ("'Tis not human blood," Wick assured me. "Only goat blood." I felt only marginally better about that.)

The dance ended in a round of stomping, and afterward, as I hung up the bloody costumes, the itch I usually felt to return to my own time didn't come. *Disrespectful*

Brandon, vengeful Lulu, Ash's Josh—I don't want to deal with any of them.

I snuck a look at Cooke and glimpsed his pale, bony chest.

Him, I want to deal with.

I turned away, but it was too late—a blush burned across my face. That one glimpse gave me the warm dizzies.

"Are you going to come out, Master Allen?" Cooke called at my back.

I froze, holding the shoe I had been polishing furiously in an attempt to distract myself from Cooke's three dark spiral chest hairs.

"Come out about what?" I whirled around on the heels of my sneakers.

"Not *what*." Cooke smiled, shrugging on a shirt, thank goodness. "*Where*. Out into London. Tonight."

"Oh, I don't know . . ." I glanced at the arches, to the night outside.

"Thou must come into the city, to the tavern, with us," Cooke pressed, fastening his bloodred doublet. "That shoe beggeth for thy mercy."

I looked down: my hands were scrubbing the shoe into shiny oblivion. I quickly dropped it into the bucket.

"Only if Wick says—"

"Thou art going tonight," Wick growled, on cue as always, from across the room. "Thou finally lookst to be a city lad, and I will not have thee spoiling it on an empty, dirty playhouse."

I was touched, but cries of protest arose from the company.

"The Globe's not *dirty!*" Burbage feigned outrage. Shakespeare fastened his own doublet, looking peeved. Wick held up his hands in an apology:

"I love her, truly," he said. "But she's a dirty world we live in, lads."

"Not as dirty as the lads in it," Cooke quipped brightly. A good laugh was had by all, and then the company started to disappear through the arches, clapping each other on the shoulders and jingling their change purses.

I stayed behind, tidying things up, waiting for the rest of them to clear out. It felt like Cooke was doing the same; he kept fussing with his wig, arranging and rearranging it on its holder as actors passed him and made jokes about his hair. He took them all good-naturedly, and threw a few sly glances at me.

Wick left with the last group, and finally we were alone. Cooke set down his comb and walked toward me with a purpose. My heart couldn't beat.

Is he going to kiss me? Am I going to get my first real kiss tonight?

Another thought nagged me as he came closer: *Are you sure you want him to be your first kiss? Are you sure you don't want it to be with—*

"May I accompany thee, Lady Man, on this fine London evening?" He smiled. His eyes seemed to promise more than just an escort.

"Thou mayest, Sir Woman," I conceded. He slipped an arm around my waist and, naturally, one of my arms slid around his shoulders. Paired up like old friends, we walked through the center arch and out into the yard. The sun had just set, and the gathering night air was chilly—but my doublet and Cooke kept me warm.

We followed the rowdy parade of actors through the theatre, listening and laughing along with their complaints and anecdotes of the day's performance. Apparently

Shakespeare himself had messed up a line—this was obviously the most hilarious thing that had ever happened. My black sneakers crunched across the yard, in time with Cooke's light, floating footsteps.

The big door at the front of the yard, directly opposite the center arch onstage, loomed in front of me. There were three entrances to the yard of the Globe, but this one was the largest, where the majority of the groundlings would come pouring in for performances.

When it was our turn, I hesitated on the threshold; a shiver went up my spine. To be safely tucked into the Globe was one thing, but to be *out there*—the darkness through the doors was full of unknowns.

So I balked, but then felt Cooke's hand gently squeeze my side. His arm pressed into my back, propelling me forward, whisking me into the London night.

23

I had expected the Globe to be surrounded by a metropolitan London. We were a popular playhouse, after all, so I had pictured the outside world something like an Elizabethan Broadway. Instead, creaking tree branches blew in the wind, and green lawns sprawled across the landscape, with cobblestone streets worming through them.

The Globe is in the suburbs?

Outside smelled somehow worse, like a sewage plant, and the air was damp. The moon and stars had come out and were the only light to see by—no streetlamps yet, apparently. This made it more difficult to walk, as the streets weren't fake, yellow-brick-road cobblestone, but *actual* cobblestone. It felt like jumping from rock to rock in tide pools—I had to balance from step to step and move quickly. Cooke snickered at my shakiness, and I reached up and smacked him on the back of the head. *So romantic.*

I barely said two words the whole walk—I was too preoccupied with this new world to speak much. I let myself be led from one street to another until we popped out on the shore of an enormous river. I'd heard the cast call it the Thames before. Many of them had to cross this river to get to and from the theatre. The seventeenth-century commute.

There were shining lights scattered across the water, and I soon realized they were attached to ferry boats. On the other side of the river waited a softly glowing city—downtown Elizabethan London.

Burbage called over two boats and hustled all of us into them. In all my time in Belleport, I'd never actually been on a boat, and I hoped I wouldn't get seasick.

Cooke got in first and offered me a hand. I gracefully tripped into the boat, but somehow got seated and upright, with Cooke's arm around me. Our fellow passengers were Burbage, Shakespeare, and the other senior actor-shareholders. The ferryman, a spry man with a bushy, blond beard and gray cap, used a long pole to push us away from the shore.

The boat moved along steadily, the river slapping at the sides. I felt a little queasy, but tried to focus on what was waiting ahead.

To our right was an enormous bridge. *London Bridge*. It certainly wasn't falling down. From what I could see, there were buildings all along the sides of the bridge, like a regular street.

Maybe someday I'll live on London Bridge. I quickly shook that thought from my head. That was just a fantasy. A particularly nice fantasy, what with Cooke's arm draping behind my shoulders. *I wonder if the other actors think we're gay?*

About halfway across, sick of being teased for forgetting his line, Shakespeare threw another miniature tantrum.

"No more, Burbage, or my next tragedy will have no part for thee!"

"A tragedy without a hero?" scoffed Burbage. "That's near as silly as a playwright forgetting his own words!"

Cooke grinned at me, and I smiled back. Two huge egos clashing—it reminded me of Stanley and Brandon.

"Nay, it will not lack a hero," Shakespeare said, a smug look on his face. "But the hero shall be a sophisticated *woman*."

My head snapped to look at Cooke, who seemed calm, but his eyes grew even brighter than normal.

"And who will play this 'sophisticated' *woman*?" Burbage laughed. "Surely not Condell again—he was dreadful as Margaret in *Richard III*."

Condell opened his mouth to protest, then closed it and shrugged. The rest of the boat erupted in laughter.

"Master Cooke will play her, of course," Shakespeare replied evenly. "The most talented man in our company."

The other actors oohed. Burbage had no comeback for that, and his thick, orange eyebrows scowled at the bottom of the boat. *He must actually feel threatened by Cooke.* A tiny, fuzzy ball of pride formed in my chest, just like how I felt when Josh got his lines right.

"I would be honored!" Cooke called out from our place at the stern. "I feel ready for the challenge of the hero."

Some of the actors cheered, some looked back and forth between Cooke and Burbage nervously. I held my breath, waiting for a skirmish. But quick as wit, Cooke followed this statement with:

"And thou needst not worry: I am prepared for such a role. I would never forget the lines of the great Master Shakespeare."

I burst out laughing, and I wasn't the only one: hoots and howls roared up and down the boat. Shakespeare's face, formerly smiling approval, dropped, revealing how tired and fed up he was. He brought up his left hand and covered his face as he shook his head. *Did Shakespeare just face-palm?* I laughed all over again, my abs hurting and my eyes watering as we pulled into shore.

I hopped out of the boat first and offered my hand to Cooke this time: He alighted on the sand and entwined his fingers with mine. I blushed, and could barely look at him as we fell to the back of the pack. Cooke kept up with the company's conversation, laughing and contributing. I smiled small smiles and felt Cooke's dainty thumb rub along the base of mine. As we climbed up the steps and into the streets, I realized what was happening:

This is what a date is supposed to feel like.

Which made my smile fade, just a little. Not because I wasn't happy to be with Cooke, but because I realized I had never been anywhere close to feeling like that with Brandon. It was hard not to feel the sting of all the time I had lost pining after someone . . .

And then we rose up onto the street level, and my head emptied of Brandon and filled up with *London*.

Crowded, torchlit streets filled with people and horses pulling dark carriages through the narrow alleyways. I kept to the side, so as to not bump into anyone and have them get suspicious of my pectoral muscles. We made our way through the cobblestone streets filled with groundlings.

None of the buildings were very tall. I was used to Boston, or New York, where "city" meant skyscrapers. Nothing towered here, and it made me feel much bigger in this world. There were *real* towers, though—they just weren't very towering. And this London seemed completely devoid of the familiar big-city comfort of police officers. There wasn't a cop in sight.

Cooke helped me weave in and out. The Chamberlain's Men obviously knew the way to our destination by heart, and the windy night chill kept them speeding through the streets. As he pulled me around a corner, I noticed for the first time that Cooke was slightly taller than me: I had always felt we were the same height. Just as it began to drizzle, we ducked through a big wooden door.

My last cast party had been the summer before, for *Oklahoma!*, in the community center just around the corner from Possum Community Playhouse. Heartbroken Lulu had commandeered the karaoke machine and sung morbid show tunes all night. Stanley had brought perfect marble cupcakes and made sure only his favorite people in the cast got them. A few parents had put out a ginormous bowl of fruit punch that had dyed everyone's lips red for the night.

This party was already different: I was in a different country, in a different time, with a cast of men primarily in their late thirties/early forties. Obviously it was going to be different. But as Burbage led us into the Red Bull Tavern, I realized just *how* different.

I had vague pictures of what a bar might be like from the movies: swanky, glass tabletops, pink martinis made with shake-y bottles, caramel-colored alcohol poured over ice, men and women in glamorous after-work clothes, buying each other drinks and flirting from a script. The Red Bull was the opposite of everything I had pictured.

Stairs led us down into the smoky basement pub. A wooden bar littered with bottles and pewter mugs stood between us and the large barrels behind it. Tables adorned with drooping candles lined the walls, with hobbledy wooden chairs accompanying them. Patrons included slightly dirty men and women, sipping from pewter mugs and smoking pipes. The whole place smelled like the pee bucket from the Globe's attic. Coming down the steps, I felt like an alien descending off its ship onto a bizarre, ugly new planet. As soon as we walked in, the bar woman's smudged face lit up:

"How now, Master Burbage!" she cried. "Here to celebrate thy victory over France?"

"Didst thou see the play today, Marion?" Burbage grinned.

"Never miss a *Henry*," she proclaimed proudly, sticking out her chest a bit.

"Thou shouldst be at church, not the playhouse!" Condell called out from the back. "Thy soul will be damned, Marion."

"Aw, they would never let me through the gates anyway." Marion giggled, then turned to her patrons already seated in the chairs. "You lot! I got the handsomest men in all of England here, and you're spoilin' it with your sorry backsides."

The men groaned a bit but moved to the bar and made room for the Chamberlain's Men to sit.

"The Red Bull is our spot across the river," Cooke explained as we sat down at a smaller table off to the side. "Other days, we're at the Mermaid on the South Bank."

"The South Bank is where the Globe is?" I asked.

"Yes, Master Allen." Cooke leaned toward me. "Does not it seem odd to thee? Thou know'st so little of thine own life."

"Um, well, I—"

"A round of ale!" Heminges called out. "And bowls of tobacco!"

Ugh. I really hope I don't have to smoke.

"So, Em."

I turned to look at Cooke: he was lounging back in his chair, his legs sprawled out. It was startling—he wasn't sitting cross-legged with perfect posture. He looked almost like Josh, except for his dancing blue eyes.

"Never been to a tavern before?"

I kicked his shin under the table, and he laughed.

"I thought so!" he said, receiving the two pewter mugs the waitress brought us. "Thou look'st a bit pale. How much ale hast thou had today?"

He passed me the mug, and it dipped into my hands, heavier than I expected.

"Um, none?"

"Thou must be dry as a bone!" His eyes widened, and he pushed the other mug across the table. "Here, have both of these, and I shall have her send another one for me."

"No, no!" I said, reaching out and pulling down his already-signaling hand. "I'll just . . . I'll just start with one."

He conceded and grabbed his mug, slugging back half its contents in one go. I looked down into my own mug—swirling, bubbling liquid, with a layer of filmy foam on top. It looked like my mouth felt after going to sleep without brushing my teeth.

"Could I have a glass of water?" I asked, stalling. I'd only drunk alcohol once before, and I remembered how important it was to keep hydrated when drinking. I specifically remembered because I hadn't done that, and my head had pounded the entire weekend after. Cooke nearly choked on his drink and slammed the mug down on the table.

"Em, hast thou been drinking London's water?"

"Um . . . no . . . but why wouldn't I?" I whispered, hoping no one was listening.

"It'll sicken thee!" Cooke almost shouted. "'Tis sludge, London water. Turns insides out."

"Oh, yes, I had heard that."

*So they drink ale because the water is bad. Does that mean
everyone is drunk all the time?* I looked at the rest of the company, their cheeks red and their eyes filled with . . . mirth?
They sure do look drunk.

I was a little thirsty and a little curious, so I brought the
mug up to my lips and took a big gulp.

Too much. Too much!

Very carefully, I let the liquid fall out of my mouth right
back into the cup.

"Somefin' wrong with the brew, love?"

I thought nobody had noticed my subtle regurgitation, but
the female voice came from behind me. I turned—Marion
was standing there, her frizzy red hair piled on top of her
head, gaudy blush smeared down her cheeks, in clothes like
the groundlings wore at performances—dirty, whitish-gray-
brown. Her boobs were pushed up so high I found myself
wondering where her nipples were. She grinned at me.

Teeth. Teeth. Where are your teeth?

"I just needed to cough," I explained, and gave a completely unconvincing demonstration.

In response she gave me a good whack on the back, which
ironically made me choke on my own breath. Cooke snorted
into his mug. A couple good hacks later I was fine, but the
woman was still there.

"Art thou new to the Chamberlain's Men, boy?"

I nodded and took a smaller sip of ale, then remembered
that alcohol taste from the party last year. The watery beer
that Ashlee had pushed into my hands, insisting in front of
everyone that I drink.

"It's Emma's first beer! Isn't she the cutest?!"

Elizabethan ale was marginally better; it tasted like mold and sour flowers.

"To Master Allen!" Cooke announced, standing up on his chair light and airy. "Our good apprentice book-keeper!"

The whole company toasted me. Burbage glanced at Cooke and shot me a wink.

"Oh, how fanciful!" Marion squealed when the toast was over. "Let me introduce thee to my girls."

She called over to two teenage girls who had been handling the bar.

Why does she want me to meet her daughters? I wondered. Cooke's blue eyes mocked me from the other side of the table. *This can't be good.*

The girls approached our table and the woman introduced one as Grace and the other as Prudence. They didn't look anything alike but were also exactly the same: more frizzy red hair and yellow teeth. Their mother whispered in their ears and left us. Grace deposited herself into Cooke's lap and began fiddling with his doublet clasps. Condell and Heminges whistled from one table over. Burbage called out:

"Ladies, you should know he likes to wear dresses!"

This got a howl from the rest of the company. Cooke raised his mug at them and cheerfully took a swig. Prudence looked at my lap pointedly, but I didn't move—the last thing I needed was someone realizing I was *missing* something. I crossed my legs and smiled up at her, tight-lipped. I thought that would convey the message, but she pulled up a chair next to me.

"Art thou a player, Master Allen?" she asked, twirling one of the frizz-curls that hung next to her face.

"No," I said. "I work behind the stage."

"Ahh!" Prudence's eyes lit up. "So hast thou seen 'em all naked?"

Cooke, who had been easily chatting with Grace, suddenly took an interest in our conversation.

"N-no," I stammered. "I'm too busy working. That is, I don't mean to look at them when they're changing. I mean, I *don't* look at them. . . ."

My face felt like I had swallowed a handful of Red Hots. Cooke, Grace, and Prudence all laughed, confirming that I was blushing up a storm.

Where's the bathroom? I thought, desperately trying to think of a getaway. *Oh, never mind, it's probably a bucket in a corner.*

"Well, that is really lovely," said Grace. "You cannot find a man these days wit' any modesty."

"'Tis true," Cooke agreed. "I know I haven't got any."

She playfully hit him on the shoulder. Watching them together, I felt something hot and sick burning in my stomach, and I took another big swig of ale.

And then there was a hand on my thigh.

"I think 'tis very sweet," said Prudence, her voice low and husky.

I don't know what's happening.

Her hand started moving higher up my thigh; I pushed it down. I tried to catch Cooke's eye, but Grace was holding his mug out away from him, teasing him.

"Fine, fine." Prudence laughed at me blocking her advances. "But a nice boy, modest as thyself, deserves a proper kiss."

She dove onto me. Her lips felt like . . . skin. Her head bobbed around as her mouth moved all over mine. *It's like I've always worried—kissing isn't magical at all.* It was just lips pressed against other lips. *So awkward. Too much spit.* My lips stayed firmly shut as her tongue tried to pry at them. *This is my first kiss.*

This is my first kiss.

I grabbed her shoulders and shoved her away. She fell off me, and she and Grace erupted into giggles.

I stood up, knocking my mug onto the ground. My head felt too big for my body. The girls shrieked in laughter. My eyes found Cooke's. He winked. I glared. He looked confused, and then his face folded into some other emotion—maybe even concern.

Too late.

"Wait, Em—"

A wave of déjà vu washed over my head, nearly choking me. I had to get out.

I stumbled up the stairs and paused, my head tipping slightly to the right all on its own. The Chamberlain's Men, my genius actors, were all drunk. Grace was pinning down Cooke. Burbage, Condell, Heminges, Sly—everyone else was smoking, drinking, or fondling a woman. It was revolting.

They're all revolting.

I turned to go, but something caught my eye through the smoky haze: In the back, I saw a lone figure, his pen moving like lightning across a scroll. I watched Prudence approach him, but he waved her away with his unoccupied hand. In this chaotic nightmare of an evening, there seemed to be an aura of stillness around him that nobody dared interrupt. He didn't care about any of it.

And neither did I.

I spun around and ran up the stairs, bursting out the heavy door into the streets of London.

Alone.

24

Cooke didn't follow me. The air outside was wet and smelled like onions, urine, and mud. Shadowy people lurked in my peripheral vision. A big cat darted across the street in front of me, and I nearly screamed, but stopped myself. I didn't want to draw attention.

My head was full of ale, but my sneakers seemed to remember the way back to the bank of the Thames—one street to the right, one up, one to the left, straight shot to the end. Carriages thundered past me, and I pushed myself up against walls to avoid getting smooshed. I was vaguely aware of women standing on corners. Big men smoking pipes. Large rats scuttling by my feet. I could see just enough to be terrified. My hand automatically rested on the hilt of my dagger—a dagger I didn't really know how to use.

The edge of the river felt scarier than before. Black ink slapped against the shore. Boats moved across the expanse, small spots of light. None near enough to pick me up, though.

My mind unhelpfully brought up an image of Josh, in a skeleton shirt, pulling me up the stairs into Ashlee's kitchen:

"Emma . . . do you want to go home?"

I had nodded back. He had pulled my jacket from the pile in the living room and ushered me outside, where he called a friend to come get us. I was more drunk then than now, but I remember suddenly feeling safe, safe, safe safe safe.

Why did I ever come here? Why am I hundreds of years away from Mom and Dad? From Josh? Who's going to save me now?

A big fat raindrop fell on my eyelid, breaking me out of my panicked swirling. I opened my eyes, and the first thing I saw became my new plan:

The bridge.

A boat ride would have been quicker, but I had no money anyway. I hurried up the stone stairwell and back up onto the street. My feet slipped and slid on the cobblestones; my sneakers gave me no traction.

Careful, Emma. You're buzzed.

My fingers pulled at my lips as I walked, as if they could pull that kiss out of them. I wanted a do-over. Did first kisses count if they happened while you were time traveling and pretending to be a boy?

You can't get unkissed, I told myself. *So yes, they count. That counted.*

Lulu had her first kiss in seventh grade playing spin-the-bottle at a party. That was normal. Why did the normal things never happen to me?

The entrance to the bridge towered over me. A big stone arch. Not big—*huge*—with flags whipping in the rainy wind. I took a few steps out into the misty bridge world—it took me a moment to realize how enormous it was. London Bridge was an entire city. Dozens of houses and shops lined each side, glowing with their own small lights that were dimmed by the black rain and fog.

The bridge seemed to stretch on forever. Dark figures stood between me and the other side, like one of those shooting games at the arcade. I didn't have a blue or red gun, though—and I didn't have the rape whistle Mom gave me for trips into the city. I took a step forward and my dagger tapped my leg. At least I had that.

"You'll make it to the other side," I whispered aloud to myself. *Because you have to.*

My feet moved along the slick stone. My sneakers squeaked too loud. Elizabethan shoes didn't squeak. Someone was going to find me out. Buildings passed by as the rain began to beat down. It didn't take long to soak through my clothes. At least it got rid of the shadowed people—they ran for cover and ducked into houses.

The wind blew harder and harder.

Cold. Very cold.

Squeak, squeak, squeak, squeak, squeak . . .

WHOOSH!

A harsh gust of wind knocked me over. The rubber tip of my right sneaker caught in a space between two cobblestones, and my ankle wrenched as I fell. Sharp pain, like the game where that right-forward girl tackled me.

I pushed myself up and continued on, limping and slipping all over the street. The rain blew horizontally now, soaking me from every angle. My doublet and shorts grew waterlogged, heavy. I stumbled from one side of the bridge to the other, making forward progress in diagonals.

Suddenly, another arch loomed ahead of me, and another gust of wind from behind carried me through the threshold to the other side. I was so relieved I fell to my knees, panting as water dropped off my forehead. I looked up, just as a cloud moved and the moon shone down, and there, decorating the arch like flags were—

Heads.

Heads on spikes.

Maybe twenty of them. Bloated, deformed human heads stared down at me from the archway. Their eyes were white. On some, the skin had worn away to patches of decaying flesh and bone. Others were fresher.

Lightning flashed behind them. I heard someone screaming—

I'm screaming.

I screamed and I screamed and I screamed, and then I puked.

And then darkness.

25

I woke up cold and heavy on hard wood. It was still dark out, still smelled Elizabethan-y. I sat up with a jolt and promptly tipped to the side and fell smack down onto the floor.

"Master Allen!" Cooke's voice to my right.

I groaned and pushed myself up onto all fours, then tipped back onto my hip.

"Where . . . ?" I began, but quickly recognized the benches and blank stage. The Globe. First-floor gallery.

"I found thee at the edge of the bridge."

I turned to look at Cooke. He sat on the bench, illuminated by the bright moonlight, all innocent in his red poofy shorts.

"Thou wast in distress." He leaned toward me. I cringed, remembering the vomit. "I carried thee here . . . I don't know where thou livest."

No, you really, really don't.

He looked at me, blue eyes wide with concern, lashes batting rapidly. Was he expecting a thank-you? After he had let that terrifying girl kiss me? When he laughed at it? When he was a part of that whole piggish, sexist scene?

"I have to go." I stood up and promptly tripped. The gallery railing caught me. I wasn't sure which part of my body wasn't working.

"Em—" Cooke stood and reached out a hand to help me. I ignored it.

"Have a good night." I gathered my strength and walked down the gallery stairs into the yard. I felt like I was floating, like I wasn't really there. I hoped it just looked like I was going out the back door, not about to sneak down into the basement and travel four hundred years into the future. Would it still work when I was this messed up? What if it spit me back out here?

As I started up the stairs to go backstage, I looked over my shoulder. Cooke hadn't moved.

"Master Allen," he called, "I feel as though I have offended thee."

"Yes!" I called back. "You did!"

"How . . . ?"

I wanted Cooke to go away. I felt like I'd vomited up every soft, warm feeling I'd felt for him.

"I thought you were my friend," I called, projecting my voice clearly. "Friends help each other. They don't laugh at each other when they're scared."

He took this in, his face turning slightly yellow. Or maybe that was the light of the moon.

"Scared?"

"Whatever." I didn't have the energy to explain. I didn't want any of this anymore—Elizabethan England was supposed to be my escape, but everything had become so complicated here, too.

"Thanks for the lift," I waved at Cooke. "Bye."

He threw up his hands, reminding me for a second of frustrated Hamlet/Josh. Then he turned and walked out of the theatre the other way, toward the Thames. His head drooped. I would've felt bad if I hadn't already had way too much bad to feel that night.

When he was gone, I painfully made my way into the basement, too tired to light a candle, too fried to care about the dark or bumping my head a dozen times. I pulled myself up onto the BHS stage and passed out.

26

The next thing I heard was a tapping noise.

A familiar tapping noise.

I realized the world was only dark because my eyes were closed. I slowly drew my eyelids open, half a millimeter at a time. My brain pounded against my skull. My eyes opened all the way to find the source of the tapping—a foot on the floor next to me. I jerked backward, my right hamstring tightened. I felt myself almost hissing, and then I looked up in the dim light and saw whom the foot belonged to.

"Stanley!" I stood up, and a blanket fell off me. I had been on a bed. I tried to throw my arms around him.

"Mama, don't touch me! You're soaked!" Stanley pushed me back down onto the bed, and I let out a hysterical laugh. He reached over and flicked on the overhead light. I flinched as my eyes adjusted.

Stanley, wearing a lilac polo and khaki jacket with faded jeans, stood in a turquoise room. A gigantic dry erase calendar hung on the wall across from me. A laptop in a bright red case pulsed softly on a desk under the window. The bed covers were a graphic black-and-white swirly pattern. A stuffed elephant with yellow plaid ears gazed at me adoringly from the head of the bed.

We're in my room.

"How did I get here?" I sputtered.

Stanley raised his eyebrows. He had moved and was sitting in my fuzzy black butterfly chair with his legs crossed.

"I hardly think it's your turn to be asking questions, honey."

I stared at him, waiting for more. He sighed, crossing his arms, too.

"Do you want to tell me why I found you half-drowned and feverish sleeping on my stage tonight?"

What is he talking about?

"Wearing, admittedly, the most put-together outfit I've ever seen you in."

I grabbed at my clothes—damp blue velvet. *A doublet.* I reached toward my waist—*my dagger.* My brain flipped through the catalogue of the day's events: Ashlee and Josh, Brandon, a tearful bus ride, the cannon, the boat ride, the tavern, the ale, Cooke, Prudence, the kiss—

The kiss. I've been kissed.

No. I didn't want to think about it.

Instead, I remembered the last, worst part of the day: the bridge. The heads. I shuddered. Those bloated eyes, and the dripping blood, and the gaping warped mouths—I felt Stanley drape the blanket around my shoulders again. I looked at him; his eyes were filled with worry and impatience. How was I ever going to explain this?

"Are my parents . . . ?"

Stanley shook his head.

"They aren't here."

"What time is it?"

"Eight."

They must still be out trick-or-treating. "Okay," I croaked, my throat clogged with phlegm. I could already feel a cold coming on.

"Emma, did he hurt you?"

"Who?"

"Brandon," Stanley said patiently. "Lulu stayed late to do lab work, and she said she saw you two leaving rehearsal together."

The coffee not-date. It had been earlier that day, but it felt like hundreds of years ago.

"Yeah," I sighed. "He did hurt me."

Stanley's eyes turned into fireballs.

"But he didn't mean to!" I finished quickly, surprised by his fierce reaction. "It just . . . It wasn't a date. I wanted it to be, but he just wanted to pick my brain for *Hamlet* ideas. That's what hurt."

Stanley cooled off and sat down next to me on the bed. He gave my wet arm a small, reluctant pat.

"I'm sorry, Mama," he said, voice sympathetic. "But you know, it really wasn't meant to be. I mean, you two aren't a good fit."

I smiled sadly. "That's what someone says to you when the person you're obsessed with doesn't obsess you back."

"No." Stanley leaned forward. "I mean, yes. But it's also what someone says when one of their best friends is obsessed with a boy who couldn't possibly obsess her back."

Ouch.

"Thanks for the clarification," I said sarcastically. "But I think that's what I just said."

"Ahh!" Stanley stood up, and pulled his hair back. "You're right, but what I mean is . . . Mama, Brandon is totally gay."

I stared at him. *Is he speaking English?* "What?"

"Very gay." Stanley nodded. "I didn't realize it till, like, a month ago. But it's there. It's a thing."

"And you know this how?" I demanded.

"Oh, come on." He rolled his eyes. "*I know.*"

"Okay." I folded my arms. "If you *know*, then why didn't you tell me before?"

"Duh." Stanley mirrored me, crossing his arms. "Because I thought you were totally into Joshy now. You're with him, like, all the time."

The small amount of energy I had left went to blistering my ears bright pink. I stood up.

"I think I need a shower."

Stanley stood up, too, and put a condescending hand on my shoulder. He closed his eyes and nodded. "Don't think, honey. Know."

That got a tired laugh out of me, my throat aching with it. I removed my soggy sneakers; my right ankle twanged in pain. I tossed the shoes in the direction of the closet and paused in the doorway to look back at Stanley, who had sat back down in the butterfly chair and was browsing through an old Girl Scout magazine.

"So, I'll see you tomorrow?"

"Mama." Stanley's eyes locked with mine over the top of the magazine. "I recognize that you absolutely stink and badly need some tropically scented body wash—"

But.

"—but I'm not letting you off that easy. Whatever the hell's going on with you, we're going to talk about it. I'll see you in a few minutes, when you smell better."

He went back to reading the magazine. Too tired to argue, I sagged into the hallway and practically fell through the bathroom door.

I wanted to get the dagger off first. I unbuckled the clasp and shoved it into the highest bathroom cupboard, out of Abby's reach. Then I unhooked the doublet carefully, and somehow got out of the bubble shorts. I peeled off my see-through, soaked shirt and tights.

In the shower, I forgot about everything except hot water. The coconut shampoo washed the Elizabethan rain out of my hair. Pink, rosy soap on a purple loofa scrubbed away the grimy sexism from the bar. I turned up the pressure and the heat, and let it pound onto my back, into my skin.

When it got so hot I felt nauseous, I turned it down again and took my time: I painstakingly shaved my legs. I brushed my teeth for two whole minutes (I counted). I opened my mouth into the shower spray, gargled, and spat, clearing my throat. When the bathroom door opened, I poked my head out from behind the shower curtain.

"Bemma, dinner is ready!" Abby shouted at me over the shower. "And there's a boy eating with us. And he's got *fire hair.*"

I laughed. "Thanks, baby penguin, I'll be down soon."

Though I wanted to stand under the water forever, I made my hand reach out and push the faucet handle down. I couldn't leave Stanley alone with my family for too long—who knew what he'd say to them. I pushed back the curtain and stepped onto the bathmat, my toes grateful for the soft fuzziness. I dried off and threw my wet, possibly ruined Elizabethan clothing into the hamper. I heard Wick's words in my mind's ears: "The costumes are more highly prized than the actors."

Crap. How much would it cost to replace this? Then I remembered that it cost a penny to see a show at the Globe. I could probably afford it.

I shook the thought away. *No more Elizabethan England. I belong there less than I belong here, which isn't saying much.*

Towel wrapped around me, I dashed into my bedroom and pulled on sweatpants and a sweatshirt. I scrubbed the wet from my hair, opened my closet door to find my slippers, and caught myself in the mirror again: my hair was matted down, I looked paler than a ghost, my freckles barely visible, and a scrape on my left temple pulsed.

But I was clean.

As I reached into the bottom of the closet, my hand knocked into my old soccer bag, the cleats spilling out of it. They smelled terrible, but kind of like home too. I couldn't remember the last time I felt like that. Maybe theatre wasn't where I belonged after all.

I slammed the door shut, put on my thickest socks, and the slippers over them.

I grabbed my pre-calc textbook and made for the stairs. Standing at the top, I could see Stanley helping Dad divide up Chinese food into our big wooden bowls. Abby sat on the stool, in her penguin costume, organizing her piles of candy. She giggled at something Stanley said, and he gave her a poke in the dimple.

Safe, safe, safe.

"There she is!" Mom called from the living room as I descended the stairs. "You look awful, sweetie. Long day?"

"Thanks. And you have no idea," I assured her as I dropped down on the other end of the couch.

Stanley swooped in from the kitchen, Dad and Abby trailing behind, and delivered bowls of food. "We'll talk after dinner," he whispered to me.

"No, we won't."

"He's great!" Dad whispered and winked while Stanley chatted with Abby. "Are you done with that Brayden guy?"

I didn't deign to answer. I was too busy staring at the pink-red sweet-and-sour sauce dripping into the white rice just like—

No. Definitely not like blood dripping from severed human heads.

A sound suddenly echoed throughout the house:

DIIIIIIING!

"Can you get that, Em? The candy's on the counter."

I sighed, shoved myself up, and grabbed the witch's cauldron full of candy. When I opened the door, I was already bending over to address—

Someone a lot shorter than Lulu.

She was on my front stoop, under our porch light, wearing jeans and her pink fleece jacket, backpack on, cheeks flushed and stained with tears. She said nothing at first, just clutched her backpack straps, her upper body and arms stiff. It took me a minute to realize what was different: her white-blond hair had been chopped into an uneven chin-length cut. It looked like it had been done with a pair of kiddie scissors.

"Lulu?"

She glanced inside my house, and then gestured for me to come outside. *I must be dreaming.* I set the candy down, stepped outside, and closed the door behind me, as silently as I could.

We stood a foot apart. The gusty Halloween wind blew

around us, nipping our skin. I couldn't remember a time in the course of our friendship, even with everything that had happened, when we had both looked this terrible at once. Lulu wiped her face, and then looked up at me with those gray, brimming eyes.

"Is Stanley here?" she asked, her voice raspy. "His parents didn't know where he was."

My heart sank. She wasn't here to see me.

"Oh, yeah he is, I'll go get him." I turned, only to feel a gentle, insistent tug on my sweatshirt. I turned back. She was worse: Big tears ran down the already set tracks on her cheeks, her mouth quivered and opened slightly.

"My parents kicked me out," she whispered. "They went through my room during rehearsal and found a love letter from Megan. They told me I could be 'an abomination' or live in their house. Not both."

"Oh, Lu—" I reached out, but she stepped back away from me and muttered to herself, wiping furiously at her cheeks and eyes.

"They don't want me anymore. What am I going to do? I have to go to school tomorrow. I have a test. I have to go to rehearsal. I don't want anybody to know about this. They can't know that I'm . . . I can't—I can't—" She doubled over, clutching her stomach.

Out of everything that had happened to me that day, nothing was worse than seeing her like that. To feel it sink in. To realize she had been dealing with this without me. It felt physically painful, like someone had slipped a dagger into my side.

I folded my body over hers, wrapping my arms around her. She jerked away, I let go. Then she curled into me and let me hold her.

"Hey." I took her face in my hands. "Everything's going to be okay. We love you the way you are."

Her face crumpled. "You shouldn't." She pushed herself into my neck. "I'm rotten. I'm in love with Megan, I'm a terrible actor and a terrible friend and daughter, and nobody wants me anymore."

"That's not true!" I nearly yelled, pulling back and putting my hands on her shoulders. "Lulu, I'm so sorry you feel like this. But none of that is true." I felt desperate. This was really bad.

"It *is* true." Lulu insisted. Her eyes were blank, staring into her own darkness. "Nobody wants me. I'm—I'm *wrong*, and I've never felt so, so, so . . . I wish that I wasn't—"

"Shut up."

We both looked up, but it was too late: We were hit full-force with the impact of Stanley's ferocious hug.

"Shut. Up." He repeated, and through all the tangled arms, I could see tears in his eyes, too.

"None of us are wrong," he said, his voice firm. "And you the least of us, honey."

"And *we* want you," I added, and felt Stanley's hand squeeze mine. "We want you more than anything in the world."

In any world, I added to myself.

Her whole body shuddered as she collapsed into us. Our tears smeared in with our hair, our clothes, and for a moment all three of us were connected in an impossible closeness. I scrunched my eyes closed and pictured my heart pouring love into Lulu's.

We love you. We'll help. It's going to be okay. You're good, you're good, you're good.

"Lulu!" We all startled and jumped apart. Mom's smiling

face appeared around the door. She stepped out and wrapped Lulu in a hug. "Sweetheart, we've missed you. Are you here for dinner? There's extra."

"That would be great," Lulu replied. I could tell she was trying to sound normal. "Thanks, Doctor Allen."

Mom pulled back, and I could see her register Lulu's face, then Stanley's and mine.

"All riiiight . . ." Her brow furrowed. "Let's go inside. We'll eat. And talk."

She kept one arm around Lulu, took her backpack with the other, and ushered her inside. Stanley followed right behind, but I stayed outside and plunked down on the stoop, next to Abby's tiny jack-o'-lantern. The candle inside it flickered.

I needed to breathe, so I took a moment to look up at the stars. It was a clear night, and my eyes jumped from one group to the next. I thought about how Lulu said the stars sang for her and Megan. And I realized that, maybe, they had sung for Cooke and me, too. I was glad to have finally felt a little bit of what that was like. But I knew our star-song had already ended. Even though an hour ago I was sure I wasn't ever going back, this felt like the final decision, and in light of how my evening in London had gone, it was surprisingly hard to make. I gathered my courage.

"Good-bye," I whispered, finally, to the stars. To Cooke, to the Globe, to Shakespeare and Burbage, to Wick. "I'm sorry. I need to stay here. I can't be selfish anymore."

I got no answer, no protest from the sky, and took that as my cue to go inside. As I stood in the entryway, closing the door behind me, I heard Stanley:

"And we'll get someone to even it out and layer it, don't worry."

27

"Three flying saucers, two black hole coffees, and . . ."

"A large Orion's Belt," I finished, rubbing my face.

"What's large is what's under his belt." Stanley nudged me.

"It's too early for that," Lulu grumbled, batting at Stanley's face.

I had to agree. Eight a.m. on a Sunday was not the time for sexual puns about tea. Or at least not the time I would be awake enough to laugh.

"Emma, we're moving to the table now."

I blearily ordered one more coffee and a blueberry muffin, before lurching forward and following Lulu and Stanley to our booth. I slid in across from both of them. I wasn't really awake yet, which wasn't optimal, considering the secret plan I was currently carrying out.

"I'm glad you suggested this, Mama." Stanley reached over the table and snapped his fingers in my face. "Good coffee and a greasy breakfast is the only good way to start tech week."

"There's no good way to start tech week." Lulu let her forehead fall onto the table. Her new polished, silky bob fell forward, too, splashing across the night-sky table. I reached forward and sleepily rubbed her head.

"We're gonna have a good cue-to-cue," I said, my voice still a bit raw and scratchy from the vicious cold I'd brought back from my rainy night out in London. I'd searched *plague symptoms* online a couple times, but it didn't seem like I'd caught that, thank goodness.

"Absolutely! Our tech team is so ready." Stanley sipped his coffee. "A little caffeine and we'll all be ready. Even you"—he nudged the pile of hair next to him—"the fair Ophelia."

It was the first day of our weeklong race to a performance-ready *Hamlet*. We had an all-day cue-to-cue, or Q2Q, looming ahead of us. Stanley and I would be sitting in the control booth, going from one set, sound, or light change to the next, finalizing them in the fresh performance copies of the script I had made. The actors would be kind of like puppets, moving or speaking only when we needed them to. Although I was nervous, and still sleepy from prepping the night before, I was actually psyched to be running my first tech week. For the actors, it was Hell Week. For the techies, it was Awesome Week—we were in charge.

Our flying-saucer egg sandwiches came, which perked up Ophelia. I checked my phone: 8:13. We didn't need to be in the auditorium for about an hour, but I had something planned for 8:30.

"Well, you're all ready, and your crew seems ready." Lulu paused in devouring her sandwich. "But the show is so far away from ready."

"It's always like that," I reasoned, sipping my dark, highly caffeinated, and sugary tea. "Everything's a mess during tech week, but it all pulls together."

"Right." She nodded. "But it's usually the tech stuff that's a mess. Reorganizing and getting the cues straight and everything. It's not usually the performance itself that's bad."

She had me there. We had been working nonstop for the past three weeks, and it still felt like it wasn't enough. The show was long—too long—well over five hours. The material felt too expansive: The actors' performances would be great in some scenes, but other scenes were so unrehearsed that it seemed like a miracle if they got through them. Even I had sent out ten pages of line and blocking corrections after the latest run-through. I was worse than Shakespeare. Stanley and I were trying, Brandon was trying, the cast was trying, even Lulu was trying—but it felt like none of us were trying at the same thing.

If I said this was all strictly due to the difficulty of the material and Brandon's directing choices, I would be lying. Things were weird in the theatre—very weird. Better than before, obviously, because Lulu and I had made up, and in fact, she was staying with my family while her older brother and her uncle Seth—who seemed to have the most level head in the family—had long talks with her parents. So I had my best friend back, and I spent all my waking moments with her.

But now there was new tension. Brandon and I were professional, but standoffish. The only way I could see to recover from the coffee disaster, and my yearlong crush, was to disengage entirely. I wasn't sure if Stanley was right about Brandon being gay, but now I *was* sure that he didn't like me like that. In fact, recently, it didn't seem like he liked me at all.

So I stuck to getting my part of the show in order: recruiting crew members, training my assistant stage manager, and supporting Stanley in whatever he needed. I told myself that all that mattered was that Lulu was okay, and that the show would actually happen.

To add another layer, I had a problem I'd never experienced before: I had too many friends. Three friends may not seem like a lot, but when two were skeptical of the other one, it felt like way too many. After Halloween weekend, Lulu, Stanley, and I were back to sitting with each other at lunch. That next Monday Josh had approached to sit with us, and I had shaken my head behind Lulu's back and sent him away. He shrugged it off, and later I gave him a rough idea of the situation with Lulu, but I still felt bad. Not, like, *really* bad, though, because he seemed pretty cool with the one person in the school who delighted in making me feel like dirt—Ashlee.

But it didn't seem like they were back together. They didn't sit together or walk in the hallway holding hands or anything. Even so, Josh and I had been a little distant since my last foray to England—his Hamlet was passable now, my trio of friends was back together . . . We didn't really have an excuse to hang out anymore.

And then I realized I didn't want an excuse; I just liked being around him. My other friends didn't exactly feel the same way. Which meant I needed a plan.

I checked my phone again: 8:27. Lulu and Stanley were despairing about Kelly's dreadful costume. The caffeine was finally waking me up, but at the same time was also starting my jitters.

What if this is a really bad idea? What if Lulu hates me again?

"That dress does nothing for her curves, either," Stanley clucked. "Kelly's got it going on. She should not be wearing a sack."

"Exactly!" Lulu banged her coffee mug on the table. "Gertrude is supposed to be hot!"

"Yeah, totally." Josh slid into the booth next to me. "Because that would really play up the whole Oedipus angle, and I think that's something that's just kinda there, you know? So we should go ahead and deal with it."

Lulu sat bolt upright. Stanley leaned forward and looked back and forth from me to Josh, one eyebrow raised.

"Here," I passed Josh his plate and coffee. He nodded in thanks and popped a chunk of blueberry muffin into his mouth.

"So, we should probably get over to the theatre." Lulu nudged Stanley, but he didn't move.

"No way. This just got interesting."

She was stuck on the inside of the booth, so she sighed and crossed her arms, falling back against the seat. "Em, do you want to explain what's going on?"

I was kind of just hoping if we all sat at the same booth we would magically be friends?

"Um, well," I began, confidently.

"It's fine, I got this." Josh leaned forward, his elbows on the table, his hands clasped. "I asked Emma if we could find a time for all of us to meet. I have something I want to say to you." He looked at Stanley. "Both of you, actually."

"It would've been nice," Lulu said through gritted teeth, "if we had *known* we were being ambushed with some kind of ridiculous heart-to-heart at eight thirty in the morning."

"I'll pay for your breakfast?" I tried. She considered this for a moment, looked at Stanley, who nodded, and then nodded at Josh.

"You may proceed."

"Great, thanks," Josh said earnestly. He took a sip of his coffee. He was taking his time, and I liked that. I'd really missed hanging out with him.

"So, I wanted to apologize." Josh scratched the back of his head, like he did when he was thinking hard. "For a few reasons. Stanley: I'm sorry. My friends are jerks to you at school, and I've let them get away with it. That's messed up."

Stanley obviously wasn't expecting to be singled out first. He was speechless.

"Since joining the play, I've realized a lot of things about how I've been acting at school, and how I was affected by the people around me. I think you're a great designer, probably the best part of our show."

He said it so simply, so honestly. I was proud that he was my friend. I hoped Stanley saw him as worthy of being one of his, too.

"Thank you." Stanley glanced up at Josh. He wasn't crying, but his voice was heavy with emotion. For once, he didn't have a comeback. He just half smiled and sipped on his coffee.

Then Josh turned to Lulu, who was biting her lip, looking at him nervously.

Please do a good job with her.

"And, Lulu: I just wanted to say that I think you're an amazing actress. And I'm sorry I'm playing Hamlet and you're not, and that must be really hard, and I don't really know *why* I got cast, but . . . I've learned a lot from you. I've watched you in the school plays since we were kids, and I could never keep my eyes off of you onstage. You're better than anyone I've ever seen. Part of why I wanted to try out was watching you all these years."

He paused and searched her face, trying to gauge whether or not this was going well. She smiled the tiniest smile, and said:

"No, no, don't stop there. Please go on."

Stanley, Josh, and I laughed. I felt a teeny bit of edginess soften at the table.

"Okay, I totally can." Josh nodded. "You're smart, and talented, and dedicated. That being said—"

Oh no.

"—I was hoping we could call a truce."

"A truce?" Lulu narrowed her eyes at him.

"Yeah," Josh pressed on. "You've kind of treated me like crap, and I'm not sure I deserved it. I understand *why* you felt the way you did—"

"Oh really, did you?" Lulu demanded. "You understand me, my life? You know what I've been going through? You get it?"

Josh froze.

"Lulu," I said, forcing my voice to sound calm, "you know he didn't mean it like that. He's trying to apologize."

"Did that sound like an apology to you?" Her glare turned on me.

"Yes," I said, not backing down. "And it also sounded like the truth. You have treated Josh like crap. It wasn't his fault he got cast as Hamlet. You know that's true."

Her bob shook with anger, and she stared at the ceiling, refusing to look at me.

"You need to let this go," I said gently. "We have so much to get done this week. We have a show to put on. You've got too much going on to be holding grudges."

Lulu didn't move. I bit my lip and looked at Stanley, who held up his hands: *Hey, I didn't do this, you did.* Josh shifted nervously in the booth, his right leg jiggling up and down. I felt him trying to catch my eye, but I couldn't offer him any comfort, so I turned back to Lulu. Our eyes met. We had a teeny, telepathic argument. I won.

"Fine." She sighed. "You're right. I'm sorry I treated you the way I did. I know it's not an excuse." She gulped and looked at the ceiling again. "But I had . . . *have* a lot going on in my life right now."

Josh was immediately grateful: "It's okay. Thanks."

"And thanks for apologizing for being Hamlet, although Emma's right—it wasn't your fault. And you're not bad at it. Anymore, anyway."

He smiled. "Yeah. Emma's been helping me with that for a while."

"*I knew it!*" Everyone looked at Stanley, who shrugged. "Well, I had a theory."

Josh burst into his dry laugh, I giggled, and Lulu smirked and took out her phone. The whole table seemed to lower itself three feet—the tension was no longer pushing us upward.

"So, yeah." Josh checked his watch. "We have about twenty minutes. I'll get us more coffee, if you all can give me the low-down on how to survive Hell Week."

"Done," Stanley said. "Two black holes and a—"

"A large Orion's Belt with a bucket of sugar," Josh finished. "I know her order." Lulu smiled at that. He jumped out of the booth and went to the counter.

"So, what?" Stanley demanded, as soon as Josh was out of earshot. "Are we all friends now?"

"I don't know." Lulu shook her head. "But I feel a lot better."

I gave her hand a quick squeeze. Josh came back and doled out our drinks in to-go cups.

"The first thing you should know about tech week"—Stanley stirred his coffee—"is that you have to do whatever the stage manager wants. Literally, anything."

"I'm cool with that." Josh grinned.

"What if she tells you to let me play Hamlet?" Lulu countered.

My phone beeped, and I checked it while they continued to torture him. It was a text from Lulu:

Lunch break. You're going to tell me everything.

Everything? I thought as I stuffed the phone back into my pocket. *We're going to need a three-hour lunch break.*

28

"**I** have a new interpretation of Ophelia's madness," Lulu announced. It was finally lunch break, and we'd snuck out to her car for some alone time. Nobody could find me there and ask me to change light cues, or locate the glow tape, or line the cast up in alphabetical order by favorite food.

"Oh?"

"Yes. She went insane because her father made her wear a twenty-pound marshmallow."

"Interesting." I nodded. "I don't think anyone's ever done that before."

"It'll get me a scholarship for sure." She munched a pretzel stick. "But all kidding aside, my dress is hideous and weighs more than Brandon's ego."

Despite his aura of superiority, I doubted Brandon's ego was in good shape at this point, but I believed her about the dress. The cast was putting the costumes on for the second half of the Q2Q rehearsal, and I'd been hearing dark rumblings from them all morning, ever since the fitting.

"But more importantly," Lulu continued, "you have to tell me: What's going on with you and Josh?"

"Erm." I swallowed my bite of sandwich. "Nothing?"

"Right." She poked me. "You sat together at lunch every day for a month."

I bit my lip. I still felt a little awkward when our time apart came up in conversation.

"Yeah, working on the show," I said.

"Babe, he clearly likes you."

My skin prickled. "No, obviously not."

"He looks at you like you're a big, shiny soccer ball."

I threw a crumpled napkin at her. She giggled.

"Okay, but even if he *did* like me, which is impossible . . ." I checked my watch: We needed to head back in. More fun! "That would never work. He's popular and I'm a theatre nerd."

I put my lunch things away and got out of the car, hoping that would end the conversation. It was fun to be gossiping with her again, but this subject made me uneasy.

"First of all, he *totally* likes you," Lulu said, following me back around to the auditorium entrance. "Second, this isn't *Romeo and Juliet*! People who like each other can date without dying! I mean, Megan and I—"

"—actually like each other!" I finished for her quickly. I didn't want her to think I thought her relationship was futile. "Unlike me and Josh."

We paused outside the entrance.

"Seriously?" Her eyes narrowed. "You don't like him, even a little?"

I really didn't know how to answer that.

"I just . . ." I said. "There's too much going on, and I just finally got over my Brandon obsession. . . ."

Lulu's face fell. I bit my lip and looked away. I hadn't meant to bring that up. I wanted things to be smooth between us. She reached out and took my hand.

"Em, I'm really sorry for how I acted about you and Brandon." Tears welled in her eyes, like they had so many times recently. "I was so angry, and it exploded all over. But I want to be supportive, and I want you to be with whoever makes you happy."

"I'm sorry, too," I managed, though my voice caught in my throat. "I shouldn't have said what I did."

She pulled me in for a hug. I nearly started crying again, just out of relief.

"So obviously the person who makes you happy is Josh, right?"

I groaned. "We're gonna drop this right now. I've got a job to do."

"Please, look at my costume."

We all turned to see Lulu, who had burst into the techie booth, wearing an enormous beaded white dress. Like a stupid bride version of Cooke's.

"We saw it onstage," I reminded her.

"It's worse up close." Stanley's nose wrinkled.

I spoke into my headset: "Sound cue forty-five, stand by . . . go."

Lily, our freshman soundboard operator, fumbled a few seconds before hitting the cue, as she had done for almost every cue. I noticed her staring at me anxiously, so I smiled, and her whole body relaxed. I made a note to go over the board with her again.

It was the end of our Q2Q—and honestly, eleven hours for a five-and-a-half-hour show was pretty good time. A sentiment, I found, that brought no comfort to anyone in the last painstaking hour. The entire cast and crew were coming unraveled.

At my command, the silly "palace noises" began playing over the speaker system. Brandon had shot down the old-fashioned-sound-effects backstage idea, on the grounds that we were using mics for the leads and he wanted all the sound to be glossy and consistent. It was strange that this idea didn't apply to his costume choices.

The actors hadn't appeared onstage on the cue. I took a breath and pressed another button, turning on my headset feature known as the God Mic:

"We're at act five, scene two, people," my voice boomed throughout the auditorium. **"If you're not dead, you should be onstage."**

"No one should give you that kind of power," Stanley muttered.

"How can he seriously expect me to wear this?" Lulu continued. "I look ridiculous. I can't even walk; I'm going crazy."

"Method acting." Stanley nodded, working at the light board. "Not the safest route, but if the dress helps you get into character . . ."

Lulu bopped him on the back of his head with her script. Lily looked frightened, so I smiled at her again before returning to the problem.

"Did you talk to Brandon about it?" I asked, though I could guess the answer.

"Why would I do that?" She crossed her arms. "It's not like he has any idea what this is supposed to look like. You've seen the rest of the costumes."

As she said this, the actors finally stepped into place for the last scene: Josh's costume was this long black steampunk jacket, while Greg looked like a rich preppy kid. Kelly was hidden in her huge tablecloth-patterned shift dress, and Marcus, playing Claudius, looked like he had just stepped out of a children's book, all red and yellow and gold, with a big shiny, fur-lined crown. It was like ten different Hamlet costume concepts smashed into one.

What kind of Hamlet *is taking place in Brandon's brain?!*

But I just shrugged, because as it was going, the BHS *Hamlet* would be as good as the average high school production.

And really, what are we aiming for here? I thought tiredly. *It's not like anyone will care about our show years from now.*

I flicked on the God Mic and blasted into the theatre:

"Act five, scene two, go."

"I'm sorry, sweetie." I turned back to Lulu. "I can't really talk about this right now. We're almost through; I'll see you after? Here—" I passed her one of the oranges I had brought. "You're done, so take that off and snack on this."

"Okay," she said glumly, and took the orange. "Thanks. I'll see you in a bit."

She got stuck in the doorway on her way out, and I nodded to Lily, who helped push her skirt through.

I explained that, given the time everyone had already spent in the theatre that day, I had made the executive decision to e-mail my notes out that night. A big cheer went up from the cast—and by big, I mean the limpest, lamest cheer ever. They had nothing left in them.

"So, um, that's all for today, then." I stood at the front of the stage, addressing the cast, who were sitting in the first few rows. "Please come tomorrow ready to start our run-through at five thirty. You're all doing great!"

I raised a rousing fist in the air. I got a few back in response.

"I have a few notes. . . ." Brandon stepped in front of me and droned on about everyone's personal responsibility to make the show great. I spaced out. When he was finished, he shot me a smile, and though my instinct was to grin back, I looked away.

"Anyway, see you tomorrow. Contact me with any questions." I held up my phone and waved it. "You're all done."

Suddenly, the cast woke up, grabbing their stuff and joking and laughing on their way out.

Oh good, they live.

The crew and I had a lot to do to finish up for the day— resetting the set pieces, sweeping the stage, tidying up backstage, combing the auditorium for trash, checking the trapdoor and underneath it. Just like at the Globe.

No, I stopped myself. *No thinking about the Globe. You've got more than enough to do here.*

Lulu and I were getting our ride home from Stanley, so they were both stuck helping me. I tasked my Assistant Stage Manager, Yohan, with the housekeeping, and asked Stanley to check the trapdoor, while Lulu and I headed down to assess the grossness in the dressing rooms and turn off the lights. She made for the girls', so she could grab her stuff. Thinking everyone else had left, I headed to the boys' dressing room.

I pushed open the heavy door and froze: Brandon was propped up against the wall, leaning into Josh, smiling and wearing only a white undershirt and blue plaid boxers.

Brandon laid a hand on Josh's shoulder, and then his face started to tilt in toward Josh's and—

"Oh, sorry!" I quickly closed the door and called back through the vent at the bottom. "I didn't realize anyone was still in there."

"Emma, it's okay, you can come back," Brandon's voice called.

I paused. My heart was beating fast. *Oh my God. Are they both gay and I never realized? Am I actually the worst at telling whether someone is gay or not?*

I slowly opened the door and poked my head back in. "Just wanted to check on the general cleanliness situation in here."

Brandon chuckled. He hadn't laughed with me in weeks. "The situation is under control, General Cleanliness."

"Excellent." I kept my eyes down. "Then, um . . . at ease."

As I pulled the door shut, I felt myself turn green. But I didn't like Brandon anymore. Was it just leftover jealousy? Why was my heart beating so hard against my chest? I wanted to run back in and shout or something. Anything to distract them.

I needed a distraction, too. I shook myself off and helped Lulu tidy the girls' dressing room. Before we went upstairs, I checked the boys' one last time—the lights were off. So they were either gone and nothing had happened, or . . . or something had happened, and *then* they had left. . . . Either way I didn't want to feel as disillusioned as I did.

We emerged in the auditorium to find Stanley sweeping the stage, chatting with Josh, who sat at the front. Brandon, and his orange messenger bag, were gone.

"Where's the crew?" I asked. I made eye contact with Josh and then quickly looked away.

"Sent them home," Stanley said, fussing the dirt into a pile center stage. "They were so worn out, the poor things."

I remembered my first Q2Q on *Midsummer* and how exhausted I felt at the end. But also happier than I had ever been at BHS.

"Hold this for me, Joshy?"

"Sure, Stan."

"Touché."

Lulu and I flopped into front-row seats. I felt funny every time I looked at Josh—that sick feeling again in my stomach. Was I jealous because of him, not Brandon?

No. I was going insane. I'd been in the theatre too long.

I checked my phone: 9:03 p.m. Almost twelve hours.

"You all set, Cinderellas?" Lulu yawned "You'll want to go to the ball tomorrow night."

"Only if you let me borrow that dress." Josh grinned, emptying the dustpan into the trash.

Lulu dove her head into her hands. "Yes, please, take it away forever. Wear it, burn it, I don't care."

"We *could* burn it," Stanley mused, throwing his bag over his shoulder.

"If you're going to burn it," I said as we all trooped up the aisle, "don't make plans to do it in front of the stage manager."

"Yeah, I wouldn't cross her," Josh agreed. "She seems kinda scary."

I laughed, softly punched his shoulder, and pretended I didn't notice Stanley's and Lulu's pointed looks at each other. We made our way into the chilly parking lot. I pulled my jacket in around me and tried not to feel warm and fuzzy sitting next to Josh in the backseat.

First Cooke, then Brandon, and now this. If he and Brandon are a thing, then I got this all wrong, again.

"Tomorrow, during lunch?" Lulu called back at Josh through the car window, as we were dropped off.

"You got it."

They'd made plans to work on their scenes together. *Success!*

We reheated the burgers and fries my parents had left us, and took them up to my room.

"Anything from Chip today?" I asked through a mouthful.

"Mhmmm," Lulu pulled out her prepaid phone Mom had given her so she could talk to her brother. "He says I might be able to move in with Uncle Seth over winter break."

I stifled a gasp. "Doesn't he live in—"

"Brooklyn."

Big waves of nausea hit me. I slowed down considerably, taking smaller bites.

"How do you feel about that?"

Lulu shrugged but looked away. "I like New York. I want to go to school there anyway, I guess."

She rubbed at her nose. I couldn't believe her parents would rather she move to New York than try to accept her identity.

"So, how's Ophelia?" I changed the subject—I didn't want to press her harder. *Don't burst into tears.* "Apart from the dress."

"Ophelia's completely crazy," Lulu sighed, and pushed her hair out of her face. "And I hate to say it, but I'm starting to relate to that."

"Lulu—"

"No, no, listen." She sat up on her knees. Her eyes were lit up—I had just become her audience. "I've always thought that

Ophelia was this throwaway character and that Shakespeare was a sexist pig for writing her so fragile. She's a woman, right? So she's weak and can't survive without men. Great."

I cringed inwardly. Before the Globe, I had thought of her like that, too.

Lulu held up her hands. "But lately I've been thinking: She's always been controlled, right? By her father, by her brother, by general sexism and the court."

"Right."

"But then she has this love," Lulu said, getting starry-eyed. "And nobody will ever convince me that Hamlet was a good boyfriend, but she had this love. And the first thing we see in the play is her father take that away and minimize her world so it's all about him and her brother and properness again."

"So." She stood up, bouncing on the balls of her feet. "She does what they say, and she follows their rules, and what happens? She loses not only Hamlet, but everyone in her life. She was brought up to rely on men, to be controlled by them. And then the one time she tries to get something for herself, the whole thing cracks and falls apart and she's just *so alone* and *so done* with living in this sexist world that doesn't make any sense. So she just lets it take over, and gives in, and lets herself drown in it."

Lulu wasn't looking at me anymore—she was gazing past me, out the window, or somewhere deep inside. In the last few weeks, I had worried that Lulu might have thought about killing herself. But to hear her talk about it, through Ophelia, as if drowning was the only option . . . the breath in my chest turned into a sharp pain, prompting me.

"Lu." I reached up and caught her hand, and she snapped out of it.

"She's not really a sexist character," Lulu said firmly. "It's actually showing the effects of sexism on somebody. The effects of devaluing somebody because of who they are, and not treating them like a person."

"Yeah, I think you're right."

"I can show that." Lulu smiled sadly.

"I never realized how much her situation was like yours," I said. "You've been through so much lately."

"Yup." Lulu sat back down and paused. "But even with all of this bad stuff that's happened . . . I realized recently that I can't regret any of it. If I did, I'd regret realizing who I am."

I gulped. "That makes sense." I'd spent so much time wishing these things hadn't happened to Lulu, it hadn't really occurred to me that she was grateful they had.

"Yeah. And I realized that playing Ophelia has been really good for me."

I raised my eyebrows.

"Don't tell Brandon."

We both erupted into exhausted giggles. It felt weird to laugh about something that had been such a big deal—something that had hurt us both a lot. But it felt good, too.

"It's a shame, though," Lulu said eventually. "If I had just waited and had my mental breakdown opening night, I could have cut my own hair during the show, before the madness scene. It would've only worked once, but it would've been totally dramatic."

I laughed and hugged her, pulling her close to me. She slept in my bed that night, and I drifted off holding her hand.

29

"This is a certified nightmare," Stanley declared.

It was 9:37 p.m. We'd started at 5:32 p.m. And prompted by Stanley's designs, Brandon had announced that, in keeping with Shakespearean tradition, we didn't need an intermission for the show. Like, at all. Out of all of the things Brandon could've cut, why did it have to be the intermission?!

So that was one of the problems.

"Light cue forty-six," I said into the headset. "Go."

Stanley went. The other, much bigger, problem was that we kept stopping. This was supposed to be our first shot at a straight run-through with tech. But it was less formal than a dress rehearsal, which apparently meant Brandon still got to stop whenever he wanted to tinker with things. "No, I don't think you're saying that right," he'd declare, bursting out of the wing. "Can we pause for a second? I just want to nail this down, while we're here."

He was trying to make up for the decisions he had never made, and pretty soon, all the actors wanted to kill him. During a break, encouraged by Lulu, I tried to confront him about it:

"Hey, Brandon?"

He turned, smiled. "Emma."

I almost swooned, out of habit. "Do you think, since you're kind of an actor now, it would be good for you to just concentrate on your acting during the run-through? And do notes at the end?"

"No." He was still smiling. "I think if I don't catch these things in the moment, they'll never get fixed. How can I make notes when I'm trying to stay in character?"

"Okay." I backed off, though he was making absolutely no sense. "I just think it's maybe slowing us down. And Gretchen's going to be here tomorrow."

"We can still go slow now," Brandon said patiently. "We're not performing yet."

And how are we going to learn to go faster if we don't practice? I wondered. But I just nodded and walked back to the booth to report to Lulu and Stanley. Ever since the coffee "date," I had cared less and less that Brandon was running his show into the ground. It wasn't worth it to do this with him anymore, and it wasn't my place, so I let it go.

The one true success of the evening came when Lulu nailed her madness scene. I watched, fascinated, as she became more and more distant as the scene progressed—her eyes were unseeing, her gestures faint. It was almost as if she were becoming a ghost. Was this what it felt like to be Lulu, growing more and more invisible?

"And will 'a not come again?" she sang softly. "And will 'a not come again? No, no, he is dead."

As she exited, she scattered the flowers in her hands across the stage listlessly—as if holding them had become too much of a burden. I shuddered. Stanley nodded silently in agreement.

And then, later, I found myself riveted as Josh delivered his speech:

"If it be now, 'tis not to come," Josh said somberly to Greg. "If it be not to come, it will be now; if it be not now, yet it will come. The readiness is all."

I sighed, remembering how those words had stung me the first night I time traveled. But they meant something different to me now: We were so far from ready; we were completely out of control.

"Light cue sixty-nine, go."

At 10:43 p.m., we were finally done. Lily let out an enormous sigh, and I couldn't tell if it was relief or despair. I met with the crew privately afterward and thanked them for a good run-through. I told them they could reset and then head home; we'd do my crew notes the next day. I had a bad feeling about the length of Brandon's notes for the actors, and that feeling was not unwarranted.

"So I hope all of you wrote down the corrections I gave you *during* the run." Brandon stood at the front of the stage. Lulu was falling asleep, curled up in her front-row seat, and Josh's head kept lolling back. "But I managed to jot down a few during breaks, too. First off, Kelly: Who is Gertrude? Did she help kill her husband? These choices need to be more obvious. Great. Next—"

I glanced at Kelly, whose face had gone stony and cold. This was not going well.

After Brandon's lengthy, broad notes, I gave my notes for the cast: messed-up blocking and lines that were dropped. I was too nervous to look directly at each actor while giving them, but the aura I felt from my audience was something like: *Yes, we know we suck, kindly shut up, please?*

"So in conclusion . . . everybody just read through your part and cues before tomorrow," I finished, closing the notebook. "Rehearsal starts directly after school. Let me know if you have any questions before then. You did a great job today!"

They stood like zombies and shuffled out of the auditorium.

"Good work," Brandon said, turning to me. "I think we'll be ready by Friday."

"Sure," I said, because there was nothing else to say. I knew Gretchen was going to tear us apart the following night.

"Do you need a ride?"

"No, Stanley's driving me—" I stopped, realizing Brandon wasn't talking to me.

"Yeah, man, thanks," Josh said. "Let me just grab my stuff."

"Could I get one, too?" Lulu asked Brandon.

"Of course," Brandon said, but his voice was tight.

"Great." Lulu hurried over to me. "I know you and Stanley have to stay later, but I really need sleep. I'll see you in the morning. Is that okay?"

"Of course," I said. The more sleep she got the better.

"You have to stay and work, huh?" Josh had changed out of his steampunk Hamlet garb and was sporting his normal preppy clothes. Soccer season was over now, so no more goalie shirts. He looked nice.

But did he look *gay* nice? Was that just a stereotype? And since when did I care so much if Josh was gay? With the show to run, and Lulu to take care of, and, yes, homework to do . . . I'd barely had time to register my feelings about Josh, much less organize them.

"Yeah." I yawned and leaned on the stage. "Stanley wants to adjust a few side lights, and I have to 'supervise' him."

"It's really late." Josh's brow furrowed.

"It's the life of a stage manager," I assured him. "We come in early, we stay late, we drink massive amounts of caffeinated beverages."

Josh smiled, but not with his eyes. "Well, take care of yourself." He took a few steps up the aisle, in Brandon's direction. "It can't be easy, holding up the whole show." He waved as he left.

"It's not," I said to nobody. I watched them leave, tried to discern anything between Brandon and Josh, anything that would clarify one way or the other. . . .

Stanley popped up behind me, pressing a wrench into my hands.

"Let's get started."

It was past midnight. We were still at school. I felt drunk from exhaustion.

"A little to the right, and forward," Stanley commanded. "Is that where Josh stands for ''Tis now the very witching time'?"

"Yeah," I mumbled.

I had been turned into an actor-puppet—Stanley needed to adjust the lights, and I was playing Hamlet, Ophelia, Claudius—whoever he needed. My interpretations of these characters were loosely based on slugs.

"Do you think Josh is gay?" I asked Stanley, more out of sheer boredom than anything else. At least that's what I told myself.

Stanley's gloved hands moved the light down about three hairs. "Why? Did he say something about me?"

"No reason. It's just I never considered it."

"I don't really get that from him." Stanley paused, focusing the light. It beamed down from overhead, like I was in an interrogation room. "Why do you want to know about Josh? Are you ready to admit you want to make out with *his* face now?"

"Oh, shut up," I sighed. "Never mind."

"Yes, let's not talk about boys. Boys are boring." Stanley hopped off his ladder, apparently satisfied with the top light. "Let's talk about you."

Not this again.

I'd dodged his inquisition about Halloween night—when he found me soaked and passed out on the stage—because of Lulu's sudden appearance. We'd been so busy with the show since, and I thought he might've let it go. So wishful.

"Stanley, no, I don't want to talk about it." I could hear the desperate want for sleep in my voice. "Besides, you really wouldn't believe me anyway."

"How do you know what I wouldn't believe?" He flashed the light directly into my eyes. "Try me."

I was just tired enough that telling Stanley didn't seem like an impossible idea. It might even feel good. I could just say it and then let him deal with it:

I time traveled to Elizabethan London and worked at the Globe and met Shakespeare and while I was there I liked a boy and then I went to a tavern and drank ale and had my first kiss with a strange woman and it was crap and then I ran through London in the rain and there were severed heads and then I fainted and ended up back here, soaked, unconscious, on the stage, wearing bubble shorts.

"No," I said finally, realizing he might think I needed hospitalization. "You wouldn't believe it, and I would really appreciate it if we could just drop it. At least until *Hamlet* is all over."

"*Hamlet* is never over," Stanley quipped. "And I'm never letting you off the hook. Back up a few steps, please."

I sighed again and did as I was told. Just as my sneaker hit the edge of the trapdoor, it exploded open.

BAM!

Stanley tripped, knocking the ladder off the stage. The ladder fell into the front row of seats with a series of terrifying crashes. I threw myself stage right for cover.

Silence. I slowly lifted my head and saw Stanley huddled stage left. I followed his openmouthed gaze to the trapdoor, where someone, a person, was climbing out. The visitor heaved himself up onto the stage, then collapsed, breathing heavily.

That sparkly white dress was very familiar.

"Cooke?" my voiced cracked.

"Master Allen!" He stood, the beads of his dress rattling. "How now! Thou art safe?"

"Yeah, I'm safe, I think." I stood up, my legs shaking. "How did you get here?"

He grinned. "Didst thou think I had not noticed how thou camest to the playhouse every day?" He crossed his arms, obviously pleased with himself.

"Um, yeah. I didst think that."

He laughed his soft laugh. In my peripheral vision, I could see Stanley gesturing wildly. But I couldn't tear my eyes off Cooke, who knelt in front of me. He took my right hand in his small ones. He seemed even more delicate and petite here, on my stage.

"I want to apologize to thee, Em." His cherry-pink mouth formed words that I hadn't known I really wanted to hear. "I behaved dreadfully at the tavern. I thought thou wouldst laugh when Prudence kissed thee. I prithee, canst thou forgive me, dearest?"

I blinked. More than anything else I had experienced in the last few months, this felt like a dream. In spite of myself, I felt the icy grudge toward Cooke begin to melt inside my chest.

That is, until Stanley stepped in beside me and whispered in my ear: "Is he actually straight?"

"What are you doing here?" I asked, ignoring Stanley. At this question, Cooke's face clouded over.

"I hate to tell thee, but thou must know: Master Wick is dead."

I yanked my hand from his grasp. "What?"

"He left us two nights ago." Cooke stood up and tried to take my hand again. I stepped back. "When Burbage told us, I tried to get to thee through the trapdoor. I must admit, I did not understand the way of it at first." He smiled briefly, then became serious once more. "He died in his bed. We had not realized he was so ill."

Stanley tried to put an arm around me, but I shrugged him off, walked to the front of the stage, and stared unseeing into the audience.

Cold washed over me. *It's not true.* Wick was my bookkeeper. Wick was my friend. He wasn't even that old. *People like Wick aren't supposed to die. They live in the theatre forever, running shows as long as there are writers to write and actors to act.* I fell to my knees and put my head in my hands. *If I had been there, I could have brought him antibiotics, or maybe I could've brought him here, to see a doctor—*

"Okay. You've upset my Mama. Who are you? Who's Master Wick?" I heard Stanley demand of Cooke.

"Master Wick was the good book-keeper for our Globe playhouse," Cooke replied softly. "Master Allen, Em, is—was—his apprentice. My name is Alexander Cooke." He paused. "I meant no offense to thy mother."

My eyes formed tears that dropped freely into my hands. Did he have a funeral? A grave? Did Elizabethans have graves, or did they just throw people into pits?

"So when you say 'Globe playhouse,' do you mean Shakespeare's theatre?"

"Thou hast heard of it?" Cooke was suddenly delighted. "'Tis a wonder, knowing how far away thou livest. Master Shakespeare writes and acts there, yes, but 'tis owned by Master Burbage and his brother—"

"Is this the only reason you came?" I stood and turned, not willing to listen to his adorable chatter. "I think you can go now, Cooke."

Cooke stopped, mid-gesture, in his sparkly dress. Stanley looked at me calmly, expressionless.

"I came for another reason," Cooke announced, clasping his hands together. "I came to fetch thee."

"Oh no." I wiped at my eyes. "I'm sorry you came all this way, but I will not be fetched."

I was never, ever, ever going back now, no matter what adorable boy burst through the floor and apologized to me next.

"Listen: I have just come from the morning's rehearsal," Cooke's voice became urgent, imploring. "*Hamlet* will play again today, but since Wick is gone, Master Shakespeare is keeping the book."

Stanley mouthed *Shakespeare* after Cooke said it.

"I'm sure he's very good at it, considering it's his play," I replied.

"No," Cooke said flatly. "He's terrible. 'Tis not his play in this way. His temper is short. He listens to the show and forgets to cue our stage-keepers. He is miserable that he cannot play the Ghost. He kept the book for yesterday's *Hamlet*, and I swear, Juno thundered from above and caused it to rain, 'twas so dreadfully done."

I pictured a wet, Wick-less Globe. Utter chaos.

"I don't care," I said tiredly. "You got through that one all right, so why should I come back now?"

"Dost thou recall that Master Shakespeare's wife and children are coming to London today?"

Today?! How was I supposed to keep all this time stuff straight? I panicked a little—*Hamlet* was supposed to be perfect today.

"'Tis a performance of great importance."

"Not more important than my own performance," I retorted halfheartedly.

"No, thou dost not understand me." Cooke was suddenly in front of me again. "I have discerned that this performance, this show, is a tribute to Master Shakespeare's son. I heard Heminges talking about it, when we heard of Wick's death. *Hamlet* is for Shakespeare's son that died, Em."

What Shakespeare had *endured*.

"Oh yes!" Stanley snapped his fingers. "His son's name was Ham*net*, and he died two years before the play was first performed. I think he was nine?"

Cooke and I turned and stared at Stanley.

"What?" Stanley said indignantly. "I read! So his wife and other kids are coming to the play, and it needs to be good."

"Yes," Cooke answered.

"And you need a stage manager?"

"A book-keeper," I corrected automatically.

"Yes," Cooke replied to me.

"Then it's settled," Stanley said, turning his gaze to me. "You need to go."

"I—" I stopped and let my hands fall to my sides.

"So how does this work?" Stanley pointed to his trapdoor. They both turned their attention to it. Neither noticed I wasn't following until they were standing over it. Cooke, statuesque in his sparkling gown, reached out a hand to me.

"Why should I go?" I asked, standing firm. "Shakespeare never did anything for me." I knew in my heart that might not exactly be true. *But he didn't do anything for me on purpose.*

"Em, dost thou have no compassion in thine heart?" Cooke stared me. "Is it not a noble thing to do, to aid a suffering man and his grieving family?"

His forehead bunched up in confusion. He expected better of me.

"Oh, yes, the greatest playwright ever is suffering *terribly.*" I rolled my eyes. Cooke's blue eyes flashed with hot anger, just for an instant. It was the first time I had ever seen him like that. I was suddenly aware of every hair on the back of my neck. I didn't want to disappoint him, but it felt like that was all I could do. Even if I went back, how could I run the whole show without Wick?

"Emma!" Stanley threw his hands in the air. "Don't you *care* that your show is going under? Wouldn't this Master Wick guy care?"

"Oh, shut up! You didn't even know him!" I yelled, and they both jumped. I wanted to storm out of the auditorium, but my sneakers felt cemented to the stage. A fresh round of tears poured down my cheeks; my hands shook as I tried in vain to wipe them away. They were coming down too fast.

But he was right. I squinted my eyes shut and tried to shake my own conscience from my head, but it kept coming: *Wick loved Shakespeare. Wick loved Hamlet. Wick loved theatre more than anything else. Wick would care.*

You loved Wick. Love Wick.

You care, Emma.

Without my express permission, my body reacted to my thoughts. Three seconds later I stood over the trapdoor, in between the boys. Cooke's eyes lit up.

Maybe I am who he thinks I am.

"Even if you don't care about *Shakespeare*, which I find incredibly hard to believe," Stanley said, grabbing my right hand, "I would never forgive you if you didn't take me to the Globe."

I took a deep breath. "Fine, let's go."

Cooke took my other hand, and an unwelcome shiver flew up between my shoulder blades.

"Whenever you're ready!" Stanley said gleefully.

Cooke whispered, his lips brushing my ear: "Emma is a lovely name."

I closed my eyes. Their hands clutched mine so tightly I could feel my bones crunching. I jumped, and they followed me into Hell.

30

We landed in a mess of arms and legs, all tangled together on the mat. Cooke and I led Stanley through the basement. As we ascended the stairs, Stanley coughed and covered his mouth and nose.

"Mama, this place smells like a garlicky armpit," he said, his words muffled through his shirt.

I turned on the stair: "You have to call me Em here, or Master Allen," I whispered, then stopped to think. "Better go with Master Allen, actually."

He rolled his eyes and gestured a hand: *Continue.* I hurried up the last few steps. The tiring-house was deserted.

"Rehearsal." Cooke nodded his head in the direction of the arches and the yard. He peeked out the right arch, and then turned back to me.

"'Tis a wonder," he said, his eyes wide. "They are all exactly where they were when I left. But I was in thy world for some time, at least."

I nodded. "You were probably there about fifteen minutes. But time isn't the same in your theatre and mine. I don't know how it works, but it's different. It seems like it works for me."

"As it should," he said with approval. "Is that why thy hair hast grown?" Cooke reached one hand and plucked at the hair on the top of my head. It had been over a month since I'd had it trimmed—it was a little shaggy now.

"Yes." I batted his hand away. "That's why."

He smiled sheepishly. I was here, at the Globe, to do whatever Wick would have wanted. But I still didn't know how I felt about Cooke, not with that horrible kiss lingering on my lips. I turned to find Stanley taking pictures of the prop tables and costumes with his phone.

"Hey!" I hurried over. "Cut it out!"

"Nobody's *looking*," he protested, taking another shot of a skull. But he was wrong. Cooke hovered behind us, fascinated by the flash. "Besides, is there some rule against it?"

"I can't believe your camera even works." I grabbed it from him and checked: no signal, just like mine. I handed it back to him. He was right, after all. There weren't any rules for my time traveling, necessarily. But taking pictures still somehow felt inherently wrong.

"Master Allen?" A deep, glassy voice came from behind me. I jumped—I hadn't heard anyone approach. I saw Stanley's jaw drop as his hand reached out and calmly snapped another photo. I pivoted, slowly.

"Master Shakespeare," I said, keeping my voice steady.

"Thou hast returned." He crossed his arms, but the "thou" was telling. Maybe he was a *teeny bit* happy to see me? Or at least recognized my potential usefulness?

Shakespeare was dressed in book-keeper blues. I suddenly realized I totally wasn't—Wick would've snickered at my embarrassing twenty-first-century crew outfit.

"Master Cooke told me that the Globe hath need of a book-keeper today," I replied. Cooke beamed. I could hear Stanley trying not to laugh at my Elizabethan English.

"Aye, verily. And who is thy friend?"

"Master White." I stepped back and put my hand on Stanley's shoulder. "He has come to see the show."

Shakespeare reached a hand forward and shook Stanley's. "Well met, Master White. Although," he said, eyeing Stanley's hair, "better if thou had been 'Master Red.'"

Stanley broke out into a series of awkward, astonished laughs: "Ha, ha, ha! Good one, Mister Shakespeare."

"*Master,*" I corrected through gritted teeth. "Shall we rehearse, then?" By the look of the sun, we had about two hours till performance time. Soon we'd have an impatient audience.

"Yes." Shakespeare let go of Stanley. "I will need to change first, but then, yes, we should rehearse."

He strode briskly over to the costume rack and began to strip. I dragged the shocked Stanley out into the yard, Cooke following. I seated Stanley in the first row of gallery seating and made him promise *no more pictures*, then ducked backstage again. I knew he would take them anyway.

Shakespeare was out in the yard now, and so I was alone in the tiring-house. They had at least prepped the show well: Everything was in place for act one. I double-checked anyway, running my fingers along the wooden prop table, pulling the swords out of the barrel to check for the one with the "poisoned" tip. It was all where it should be.

Reluctantly, I went to Wick's desk, between the left and the center arches, and carefully sat down. The chair was sturdy. On the desk was the manuscript for *Hamlet*, squarely in the middle, with the title page on top. There were no rags or cough-drop wrappers. Someone had cleaned up.

Wick had never asked me to turn the pages, nor required me to hold his script. I was scared to touch it. The paper looked so delicate, as if it might crumble to dust if my clumsy fingers brushed against it.

Thou cannot run the show if thou cannot handle the script.

I reached forward: It was softer than normal paper, but sturdy. I found the first page of the script looked eerily like my own *Hamlet* script: many notes in the margins. The handwriting was clear, but the spelling was all funny—I was glad I knew the show so well in my own English. I flipped through the pages to the last one, which had some kind of seal of approval from the "Master of the Revels." I made a mental note to look that up later.

I turned the script over to set it to the beginning again, then pulled the plot sheet from the small shelf, set it on top, and tried to read: This was more difficult. All the entrances, exits, and set changes were scribbled in Wick's shorthand. It looked like a more complicated cursive, and I could barely read it. I would have to rely very much on my knowledge of the play in my own time.

I sighed and let myself sink back into the chair. Wick's scripts and plots were all that was left of him in the playhouse, and I would have to stare at them for hours straight if I was going to run the show.

Could I do this? I'd have to prompt the actors and the stage-keepers, and somehow not fall apart while doing it.

Why are we even performing now? Shouldn't we be in mourning?

My throat began to burn in that about-to-cry way, when a large hand rested on my shoulder. I looked up: Burbage gazed down at me with his usually merry eyes, now serious and sad. He wore his shining black Hamlet costume.

"'All that lives must die, passing through nature to eternity,'" he said softly.

"I wish I had an inky cloak," I replied, wiping at my eyes.

He laughed his full-belly Burbage laugh, though the way it trailed off hinted at the sorrow behind it.

"We all wear our inky cloaks today," he said, offering me a hand. I didn't take it.

"And yet, we play without him?" I was startled at my own boldness. Burbage smiled ruefully, grabbed my hand, and pulled me up out of Wick's chair.

"There are many shapes of grief, Master Allen" he said, looking into my eyes. "To play is a shape as fitting as any other— more, perhaps, considering the man for whom we grieve."

I glanced back at the script, meticulously annotated in Wick's writing. "I just wish he was still here." I could think of nothing eloquent to say.

"Thou needst not look far for him." Burbage glanced up at the ceiling and back to me. "He shall be always above thee."

He winked. I tried not to roll my teary eyes. Burbage was kind, though, so I smiled back and nodded.

"Good man," Burbage said. "And now the shape our grief must take is rehearsal." He tapped the side of his nose. "The Ghost scenes."

He whisked me out onto the stage: I was suddenly facing the entire company in the yard, who were gazing at me with a mixture of relief and curiosity. Burbage stood by the arches and gave me an encouraging dip of the head. Stanley hadn't moved from his bench. He sat forward, fascinated. Cooke leaned against the front edge of the stage.

"Um, my apologies." I cleared my throat. "My apologies, men, for my absence. I am here today to keep the book for our play—for *Hamlet*. It is with deepest regret that I stand before thee, for I had wished to be standing behind Master Wick quite a bit longer."

My own joke surprised me. The company chuckled, and Cooke grinned up at me adoringly.

"We have some time to rehearse. Shall we review the duel, and the scenes with Master Shakespeare as the Ghost? Haddock, raise the flag—we play today."

👑

A few short hours later, the trumpet blared and the audience cheered. The play would begin.

I sat atop my chair, on the squishy red cushion Cooke had brought for me. Condell waited for my signal. When the cheering subsided ever so slightly, I gave it to him, and then Sly and Heminges directly after.

"Who's there?"

"Nay, answer me. Stand and unfold yourself."

"Long live the king!"

The dialogue snapped back and forth, and I realized I would need to give my cues faster. I had grown slow in the last few weeks of high school *Hamlet*. But I was lucky: Haddock and my crew of stage-keepers knew their stuff, so when I called for the first scene-change cues, they were already waiting behind me with the correct set pieces and props. It was the actors who were still uncertain of the timing. It was just as Wick said: A book-keeper's job is to keep the actors from ruining the play.

In scene two, after setting up the change for scene three, I paused for a moment to hear the non–cue lines. Burbage was being questioned by Condell, now playing Gertrude, about his excessive grieving of his father:

"If it be, why seems it so particular with thee?" Condell's affected high voice carried sincerity and genuine concern for Hamlet.

"'Seems,' madam—nay it is I know not 'seems.'" Burbage's Hamlet had become more bitter. "'Tis not alone my inky cloak, cold mother, nor customary suits of solemn black, nor windy suspiration of forced breath, no, nor the fruitful river in the eye, nor the dejected haviour of the visage, together with all forms, moods, shapes of grief, that can denote me truly."

"There are many shapes of grief," Burbage had told me. I thought about Shakespeare, under the stage, waiting for his next entrance as the Ghost. For the company, this performance was a form of grieving Wick. It struck me that this show—writing it, directing it, acting in it—was a form of grief for Shakespeare. He was mourning his son. That's why *Hamlet* needed to be perfect.

I had Cooke and Tooley stand at the ready earlier than Wick would have. I felt his big magical eye staring down at me. *Can't take any chances,* I explained. *This has to be good. For you, and for Hamnet.*

The Globe's *Hamlet* raced on. *If I were timing this show, I know we'd be going a lot faster than five hours and thirty-four minutes.* At one point, I realized we were skipping some dialogue, which certainly kept me on my toes.

Somewhere during act two, I fell into a trance. I read each line like a typewriter—to the end and back again, quickly, systematically. The poetry wasn't poetry anymore; the script was a manual. I called cues, signaled actors into place, reminded everyone to pick up and put down their props. Haddock managed most of the set changes, and helped with the props too. I was vaguely aware of Cooke's presence—he occasionally hovered behind me. But I didn't want to be distracted; I didn't let myself look at him except to say: "Now, Ophelia, go."

At one point in act three, the cue was between two lines, and I wasn't sure when Burbage should go. Instinctively, I turned over my shoulder to ask Wick—

But he wasn't there. And he wouldn't be there ever again.

No time for tears, although for the first time that day I wished there was. I cued Burbage on my best guess. He entered. The show went on.

Act three, scene four was long, even for the Kings of Snappy Dialogue Delivery. I flipped through the pages calmly as Polonius was stabbed to the right of me behind the center-arch curtain. As I read the next scene to prepare, I could hear Claudius's earlier lines in my head: *My words fly up, my thoughts remain below.* Claudius knew he was going to hell, below, and his empty, insincere words would not get him into heaven. The line rattled around in my brain—

And then it hit me. Burbage's wink, and his words: "He shall be always above thee." It wasn't a reference to heaven in the traditional sense.

Because just as the basement of the Globe was called Hell, the top of the theatre was called the Heavens. And if there was an afterlife, Wick's heaven would be the Heavens of the

Globe. He would be sitting in the attic, watching the plays and the faces of the crowd enjoying his company's work.

My nose began to clog, and new tears formed in my eyes. There was no stopping them this time. I wiped at my face with my sleeve, turned a page, and then panicked: I hadn't cued Shakespeare, and the scene was ending. I looked up: Shakespeare was waiting at the stage-right arch. *He doesn't need my signal.* I watched him enter seamlessly into his own story. I listened to him play the Ghost, and wondered if he was imagining Burbage as his son.

Halfway through the fourth act, I turned away from my script to check that Armin had his gravedigger shovel. As I did, I got caught in Shakespeare's gaze: He was leaning up against the prop table, directly to my left. I had never looked into Shakespeare's eyes for long—I was too intimidated and usually tried to concentrate on his forehead or his nose when he spoke to me. But now I saw that they were round, almost too round to be normal, and deep, too deep, too expansive, too full of *something.* They held too much. Right before he looked away, I briefly saw what I wished I had not seen: pain. Pain and loss.

"Armin," I choked. "Now, go."

Ophelia's funeral took place—Cooke was lowered into his grave. Then the duel was set, and Hamlet and Laertes would fight. Burbage solemnly assured Heminges:

"The readiness is all."

We were almost there, only a few pages not yet played. As we entered the final scene, Haddock approached me:

"Master Allen—"

I appreciated that he had not once that day called me "Miss."

"—I have been thinking . . . shall I light the cannon?"

My stomach gulped. "The cannon? When?" We had never used the cannon for *Hamlet*; we used it mostly for the history plays.

Red-faced, Haddock thumbed at his nose. "At the end. When the prince dies, and the prince o' Norway comes in."

"We needn't go to all that trouble," I assured him, keeping one ear on the dialogue and turning the page.

He nodded and began to walk away, but rushed back over: "But, sir, I have been thinking of it as a salute to Master Wick." The words spilled out of Haddock's mouth.

"A salute?"

"Yea," Haddock said timidly. "As a tribute, sir."

I instinctively looked around the room for someone to ask, *Is this okay?* But there wasn't anyone: I was in charge of the show. It was my job to decide.

I went with my gut.

"If you're going to do it, you better go now," I said. Haddock grinned, grabbed another stage-keeper, and scurried up the ladder at the back.

As we neared Hamlet's death, I had to stop my fingers from reaching forward and tearing pages of the script into bits.

He'll be stuffing the rag into the cannon now. Why did I let him do this? What if the Globe goes up in flames and we all die—the audience, the company, me, Stanley, Shakespeare's family?

Swords clattered. I heard Gertrude tumble down, and Laertes groan. Claudius gurgling his poisonous drink before collapsing. The audience gasped. I could picture Heminges, clutching Burbage as he lay in his arms, sprawled center stage.

"If thou didst ever hold me in thy heart," Burbage sounded pained. "Absent thee from felicity awhile, and in this harsh world draw thy breath in pain, to tell my story."

A violent shiver shook me. On my cue, the stage-keepers, standing at the back of the tiring house, stomped on the floor and banged pewter mugs against each other.

"What warlike noise is this?" Burbage, the dying Hamlet, said his line soft and delirious.

"Young Fortinbras, with conquest come from Poland," Armin, as silly Osric, replied. "To th' ambassadors of England gives this warlike volley."

I signaled for the racket to quiet a little.

"O, I die, Horatio," Burbage's voice was loud, and yet it whispered too. I read his lines as he recited them, and felt them twice over in my heart: "The potent poison quite o'er-crows my spirit. I cannot live to hear the news from England, but I do prophesy th' election lights on Fortinbras: he has my dying voice."

Please be about to light the cannon. Come on, Haddock.

"So tell him, with th' occurents more and less, which have solicited—the rest is silence."

Then there really was silence. My heart raced. No cannon shot, nothing. Sly, playing Fortinbras, stood waiting at the center arch. He looked at me expectantly, and after a few more seconds, I gave up and cued him to go on.

His foot had not set down its step when the cannon shot.

BOOM!

A great blast shook the floor. The audience cried out, in fear and delight. I then cued Sly to enter, and he was met with a cheer. Fortinbras restored order to Denmark, and then it was over.

The dead bodies arose and jogged backstage. I lined them up, cued Armin and his pipe, and ushered them back on for their dancing. It was still unsettling to hear the crowd laugh and clap, moments after the tragedy had devastated them.

I sat back down at my table and ran my fingers lightly down the last page of the script. The paper was bubbled and warped in spots, and it took me a moment to realize that the script was dotted with my tears.

I've ruined your book, Wick.

I couldn't even remember when I had cried. I felt my cheeks—wet and slick. My heart sank into the basement, past the basement, into the center of the earth.

The clapping brought me back to the surface: loud cheers, whoops, thundering applause. Armin started another tune, and they danced again.

Show-offs, I thought, fondly. I could barely remember hating them all a few weeks ago. I guess that's how it works in theatre—the show kind of becomes your family. All sins are forgiven.

I stood, and moved to the far corner of the left arch, and though I knew it was extremely unprofessional, I used one finger to pull aside the curtain.

My company was laughing. Laughing, linked arm in arm, practically throwing each other around the stage. The crowd clapped a rhythm. The men cleared a space on the stage, and Sly did somersaults across, from one column to the other. I laughed out loud, and my hand flew to my mouth. When they finally did their bows, I closed the curtain and quickly sat back down.

That's why they do the dance, I realized. This emotional closure, from the grief of the tragedy to the joy of the dance. It didn't matter how sad the show had been: With the dance at the end, the crowd left bursting with smiles.

The actors poured into the tiring house. Many clapped me on the back and thanked me, and I nodded and smiled at all of them. Cooke didn't approach my desk, and I should have felt more satisfied, but that's never how it works.

Instead, Master Red appeared over me.

"Did you like the show?" I asked.

Stanley just shook his head. Not in the "no" way, but in the "I can't even say anything, this was too amazing" way. I stood up and gave him a hug.

"Mama, we need to go," he whispered in my ear.

Which was totally true. For our body clocks, it was probably four in the morning, and we had the Gretchen run-through the next day. I directed Haddock to hang the costumes, and he obliged. I smiled at him warmly—a silent thanks for the cannon—and he smiled back. He'd make a great book-keeper.

I told Burbage I was needed at home, in the country, right away. He shook my hand firmly.

"Come back quickly, Master Allen." His face was serious. "We need thee to keep the book as soon as is possible."

I didn't know what to say, and I liked Burbage so much, so I promised I'd be back soon. Who knew? Maybe I would be.

I turned to see Cooke and Stanley tiptoeing down the stairs into the basement.

I shook my head. Oh no. He was *not* invited.

I was about to follow and yank Cooke back upstairs when I caught myself. Was I still really mad at Cooke, or was I just holding on to the ghost-feeling of anger? *It wasn't really his fault that my first kiss was like that. He didn't even know it was my first kiss.* I didn't want to feel that coldness inside of me anymore, that awful grudge. It was too painful to push away someone I cared about.

Is this how Lulu felt about me?

Before I started down the stairs, I noticed the light coming through a gap in the curtain. On an impulse, I hurried to the back of the tiring-house, out the side door, and down the stairs into the first-row gallery.

The sun sat low in the sky, making everything and everyone within the Globe glitter. The harsh greens, blues, reds, and golds of the painted wood dazzled my eyes. I sighed. I knew it was the most beautiful theatre I would ever see. The thousands of noisy, smiling Elizabethaners milled about, slowly moving toward the exit in a great tide of people. A family in the yard caught my attention.

At the front of the stage a woman looked around anxiously. She was in her forties, maybe, and her face was pretty. Her outfit pegged her as someone who had been sitting in the gallery—a green silk gown with a high white collar. Although the fabric of the dress was shiny, the cut of the gown was simple, but flattering. Her brown hair was pulled back and up, held in place with a thick, matching green headband. Her hands held two little girls—one on either side. One girl looked about ten or eleven, the other a bit younger, about Abby's age. Both matched their mother's brown hair and simple, elegant clothing. The younger one kept yawning. The mother's nervous energy kept me watching.

Suddenly, Shakespeare, having changed into his shiny deep-blue doublet ensemble, strode to the front of the stage and nimbly leapt down. The two little girls broke into wild grins and attached themselves to his legs. I couldn't hear their happy shouts above the other noises. Shakespeare barely acknowledged them—he absentmindedly patted their heads, but his attention was elsewhere. The woman stepped forward and took his face in her hands. *His wife.* I could barely breathe.

Shakespeare folded his arms around her back, and pressed his chin against her forehead. They stayed that way for a few moments, holding each other at a slight distance, the girls impatiently pulling at their clothes. Finally his wife reached up and tentatively gave him a small kiss. When she pulled back, she was looking up at him. He stared at her, his face expressionless, and then he moved in and wrapped his arms around her waist, pulling her tight against him in one fast motion.

The little girls wiggled their way in between them, giggling. I watched Shakespeare's face as he embraced his wife—he closed his eyes, a tear rolled down his cheek, and yet, the hint of a smile played on his lips.

For the first time since I'd met him, he looked at peace.

A small seed of pride sprouted in my chest. *Brandon may think stage-managing isn't all that hard and doesn't really matter, but I helped this moment happen.*

"Master Allen or whatever!" I looked up. Stanley was poking his head out of the left arch. "We're going!"

I stood up and put my hands on my hips. "Like, you can go without me."

"Just come on! I need my beauty rest."

One last look. The Shakespeares had joined the rest of the crowd and were being swept away, like raindrops in an ocean current.

Time to return to the present.

31

"Gretchen, I respect your opinion," Brandon said, "but I think you're exaggerating."

Gretchen didn't say anything, just raised her eyebrows and sat back in her chair.

I sucked in a breath. It was late. Stanley, Brandon, and I were in Gretchen's office the next night, after the runthrough. Through the frosted-glass window on the door, I could see Cooke's shadow in the hallway outside the office, pacing back and forth. Stanley's arms were crossed over his chest. Brandon's face was still streaked with ghost makeup.

Gretchen had just informed us that our *Hamlet* run time, 5:33:21 tonight, was a *little* too long. And, surprise surprise, she didn't like the no-intermission thing. And she didn't get why some scenes were polished and some were a disaster. She thought the show was discombobulated and the cast was disconnected.

Basically, she didn't like it. And Brandon didn't like that.

"Maybe we should talk about this tomorrow?" I ventured. Tomorrow was our "dark" day, when we had a night off before dress rehearsal. Which, at this point, didn't seem like a great idea, but everyone was exhausted and we all had homework.

"No." Gretchen's large glasses leveled at me. "Because I need you all to be thinking of solutions before your dress rehearsal on Thursday."

She was right. I exhaled and fought the urge to bolt out of the office—I was closest to the door, and I was confident I was faster than all of them.

"We've still got a few days left before the first performance," Brandon asserted, "And there's work to be done, but we're going to put on the show and it's going to be good."

Stanley flicked his hair over his shoulder and shot me a teeny glance of commiseration: *Yeah, right. Am I right?* I kind of admired Brandon for defending the show, but not enough to believe him. Gretchen was spot on—the disapproval and disconnect in the cast was visible onstage. Plus, it was so *long.* . . .

"Brandon." Gretchen leaned forward again and looked at him over the top of her glasses. "You're a student director. It would behoove you to take my criticism and *do something* with it. You're new at this, kiddo."

I could see the word "kiddo" slap Brandon in the face.

Welcome to my life.

"Thank you, I will." He smiled and stood. "But it's late, and I have a test tomorrow."

And with that, he did what I had been longing to do: bolted out the door. Gretchen watched him go, and gestured for me to shut it behind him.

"The design work is lovely, Stanley," she said, handing him a page of notes. "And the tech seems to be fine, Emma." She handed me a page, too. *Gee, thanks.* "But what do you two think of the state of the show?"

Stanley took this opportunity to say what he thought about the state of *Brandon*. "Gretch, he's in denial. Now he's trying to fix things that should've been addressed all along, and he's making everybody crazy. You need to make him do an intermission. And aren't the costumes a total travesty? I told you they were."

Gretchen turned to me. "Do you agree, Emma?"

I was exhausted. I had tried to sleep last night, but by the time Stanley had dropped me off at home my brain had prepared several nightmares of mass graves and smallpox. I kept waking up, sweating and shaking, until I finally pulled a book off the shelf and read until it was an acceptable time to be awake. Then I slept through study hall, before hauling my butt down to the auditorium that afternoon. I didn't know how to deal with my grief over Wick in my own time, so all day I had existed in some kind of bad, fuzzy-brained melancholy.

And yet, there was the jolt of watching our *Hamlet* tonight and realizing what it really lacked: the passionate connection to the material and the commitment that the Chamberlain's Men had. *Hamlet* mattered in 1601. It mattered because the writer and director cared about the play so much that his fire charged his cast, his crew, the audience. *What are we really doing, trying to perform this now?* I had thought, tiredly, watching Josh die in Greg's arms. *What does it mean? We're just faking it. Well, except for Lulu. She truly got Ophelia, but that was a problem in itself.*

"I think . . ." I rubbed my face, smooshing my nose. "I don't know. It's really long, but what can we do about that now? I think we need to support whatever Brandon wants. And just get it over with."

The last part slipped out, and I could see the surprise in Gretchen's magnified eyes.

"I agree that you should support your director, but I think we all know the show is in trouble. Do what you can, both of you. But go get some sleep for now."

With a dramatic sigh, Stanley flung himself out of the office. I got up slowly and put my binder away in my bag. I turned to leave, and shot a defeated smile in Gretchen's direction, not quite looking at her.

"Emma," she said, and I stopped. "Josh told me that his improved performance is thanks to you."

I couldn't help it: I broke out into a grin. I didn't think I had a grin in me. "We worked together on it. He's really dedicated, and he's so enthusiastic. I think he's really getting it now."

Gretchen seemed to size me up and down. "Yes, he seems to be. You've done a great job."

I wanted to twirl in a circle, but I just said:

"Thank you." Thinking it would be good to end this Gretchen interaction on a positive note, I turned to leave, but again she stopped me.

"So why are you calling it quits now?" she asked.

"What?" I almost snapped. I was suddenly *really* tired of this.

"Don't you care about the show anymore?" Her voice was flat, frank.

I kicked my sneaker at the floor. "Of course I care about it. But I'm doing everything right—you said the tech is fine."

"Yes. The tech is fine. It's smooth."

"Right, and that's my job," I said, throwing my backpack over my shoulder. "I'm just the stage manager. It's not my show. I'm just running it."

She eyeballed me again, reminding me of Wick. "Okay," she said. "Good night, Emma." She looked down at her notebook again.

"Um, good night."

She waved a hand at me without looking up. I left the office and slowly pulled the door closed behind me, making the quietest click possible.

I stood with my back against the door. My body wanted to collapse, but I held it together, upright. I closed my eyes.

What did she want from me? I wasn't in a position to do anything other than what I'd already done. And besides, once these performances were over, they weren't going to matter. This wasn't the Globe. Wick and Shakespeare's son had died hundreds of years ago.

A thought nagged at the back of my mind, and as my exhausted, time-addled brain attempted to bring it to the surface, I was suddenly flanked by two grinning boys.

"Emma!" Cooke pulled on the sleeve of my hoodie. "Stanley has bought me the most tremendous dessert." He smiled—stuck in his teeth were the remnants of rainbow gummy candy.

"I took him to the vending machine," Stanley explained. "You should have seen his face when he drank from the water fountain."

"It went up my nostrils!" Cooke cried, his smile reaching from ear to ear.

"Oh, great." I laughed a little. He was really adorable, but I was so tired. "Can we go home now?"

"Yea!" Cooke leapt toward the exit. "In the car!"

"He's a handful," Stanley observed, watching him jig down the hallway. "But unreasonably cute. You're sure he's straight?"

"Pretty sure," I said, watching Cooke do a handstand by the door. "Yeah."

"Seems a waste," Stanley sighed.

"How long is he going to stay here?"

"Dunno." He shrugged. "But Gladys and Herman don't mind. I said he was a student interested in transferring schools. He slept on the couch, and he's really polite. He's a little fascinated by the shower and the toilet, plumbing in general, but I've been able to hide that from them so far."

I knew Cooke deserved to explore our world, just as I had explored his, but part of me wanted him to leave, already. I needed some time to heal from Wick's death, and every time I looked at Cooke I saw the Globe, and the arches, and the desk and Wick's discerning eyes . . .

I also knew he was up to something. He was acting too innocent, not the mischievous Cooke I knew. He had some idea about being back here with me, but he was taking his time. And eating gummy candy.

"Okay," I sighed. "Let's go. We have to be awake for tomorrow."

"At least until the show starts," Stanley nodded, sliding an arm around my shoulders as we went to join Cooke. "After that, nobody would blame us for falling asleep."

I pinched his side and he yelped, and we went out to the car, with Cooke trailing behind, marveling at the streetlamps. I shivered from the cold—somehow, November was almost gone, and holiday lights twinkled in the neighborhood surrounding the theatre. I loved this season, but there wasn't time for celebrating until the show was over—everything outside the auditorium barely existed.

"Mama, I've been thinking." Stanley paused as he opened

his car door. "I think Gretchen is right. I think we can make this performance better."

"I don't know." I watched Cooke inspect a pickup truck bed. "I don't know if I have it in me."

Stanley nodded and leaned his arms on top of his car. "That's fine, honey, you do you. But I had a brain blast about the sound effects . . . and a few other things. Permission to be sneaky?"

I saluted at him. "Permission granted."

"Good." Stanley smiled. "Because I've already started."

"Lovely," I said, not caring enough to be concerned. "Hey, Alex! Let's get going!"

Cooke hopped in the backseat. "Canst thou play the 'radio' again, Master White? I do so love thy music!"

"I'm digging this 'Master' thing." Stanley wiggled his eyebrows at me.

"Stanley, cut it out!"

We danced in the car on the way home.

32

"You." I pulled Stanley by his polo's collar into the booth. "You know I'm going to kill you, right?"

"Are we going to duel right now?" He seemed actually concerned at the prospect.

It was Thursday, the day of our dress rehearsal. I'd spent the day before deliriously trying to do as much homework as possible. So much for a rest.

Stanley, evidently, had spent our night off working double time. I had walked into the auditorium to prep for dress rehearsal, and found he had implemented one of his "sneaky" design surprises: fake red-marble columns. They weren't as towering as the ones at the Globe, but they were suddenly *there*, as a pretty big last-minute addition to the set. Turns out he'd been working on them since we came back through the trapdoor, and I had to admit, they were beautifully done: They looked uncannily like the pillars from the Globe. I was almost suspicious he had somehow stolen them, and then I remembered: The pictures from his phone. Oh, and his own personal design consultant, Cooke. The paint job was accurate for a reason.

"How could you put those in without talking to me?!" I fumed. "They throw off all of the blocking!"

"We agreed I'd be sneaky and make the show better!" Stanley yelped and detached my grip from his shirt. "Zoe and I worked on those columns for two days straight, and they look fabulous!"

Stanley's idea of a better show was different from mine. Mine involved actors not bumping into things.

Brandon, unfortunately, loved the pillars.

"Yes!" he had jumped up onto the stage. "This is exactly what our show needs!"

Right. Because huge columns are going to fix all of our timing problems!

To be fair, the pillars really did add that extra *oomph* to the set, and that was great and all, but as I predicted, the actors were pretty confused by their sudden appearance. But Brandon and Stanley couldn't shut up about their *authenticity*, so, despite my protests, the columns stayed. There was nothing I could do.

With that as our beginning, the dress-rehearsal run really didn't stand a chance. Rosie walked straight into a pillar in the opening scene on the battlements. Josh forgot his lines in the middle of three of his five biggest soliloquies, and I had to prompt him, which wasn't usually the protocol, but I let him stand around, helpless, for thirty seconds before I snapped on the God Mic. Lulu tripped over her dress in her madness scene, and Kelly got up too early at the end, before Fortinbras had entered, realized what she had done, and then clasped her throat and died. Again.

But it wasn't just the actors—everyone was off. Lily was late on most of the sound cues, and Yohan's headset batteries died, and without my voice in his head, he threw off the crew's timing on three set changes, which wasn't totally his fault—I should have checked in with him.

Techie rule #1: You always need more batteries.

At the end of the night, notes took forever. Afterward, I promised my traumatized crew I would buy fresh batteries for all the mics and headsets.

Brandon's end-of-the-night speech was stern, discouraging, and, quite frankly, unhelpful.

"We need to pull it together!" He seemed to be trying to shame every single cast member with eye contact. "What happened tonight wasn't my *Hamlet*. We can't show that to an audience. Come back tomorrow, directly after school, and be ready to do this one thousand times better."

How are they supposed to be a thousand times better without any encouragement?

When it was my turn to speak, I told them it was always the same—shows really didn't come together till opening night.

Not entirely true in every case, but we'll run with it, I added silently.

I told them that, tomorrow, having an audience would get them psyched. I told them they were all doing a great job.

Then I dismissed them. My words couldn't make it through with their ears full of cotton and criticism, anyway. I watched the actors heave great sighs and, in the case of few, cry a little, on their way out. I thought of the lively relationship between Shakespeare and his cast—how he corrected them, drilled them, drove them insane—but how when he joked, paired with Burbage's smiles and calm attitude, the cast seemed more driven. Why couldn't Brandon be like that?

Stanley and I were discussing his ideas for fixing the sound effects when Josh approached me.

"Emma, I'm so sorry about the lines tonight." He looked it. "Thanks for bailing me out. That won't happen tomorrow, I promise."

"Hey, that's okay." I smiled at him, resisting the urge to touch his hand. "You had a lot to deal with. And everyone knows a bad dress rehearsal means a good opening night."

"Really?" He lit up. "Guess we're gonna rock it, then."

"Definitely," I said. "Just make sure to do some reviewing tonight."

He looked bashful. "Good idea, yeah. I will." He paused, then continued: "When I froze during 'To be or not to be,' it was 'cause this bug kept flying into one of the side lights."

I laughed. He let out a breath of laughter, too.

"It was just so futile, you know?" He was grinning now. "And the timing was so perfect."

"To bee, or not to bee!" I offered. He cracked up, and made one of his hands the light and the other the bug, and pantomimed it flying into the light over and over,

"Buzz, buzz, buzzzzzzap!"

"Josh, you ready?" Brandon called from the back of the auditorium.

"Yeah!" he turned back to me. "I'll review tonight, promise."

"Okay. Have a good night!"

What was really going on between those two?

He nodded and waved a hand at Stanley and Lulu before walking toward Brandon. I didn't know what to think—on the one hand, I trusted Stanley's ability to discern whether Josh was gay or not. On the other, why was he spending so much time with Brandon? Didn't he want to ride home with us, with me?

On his way up the aisle, Josh bumped into Cooke, who was careening down. They smiled, shook hands, and then Cooke continued down toward us.

"Friends, the things I have seen tonight!" Cooke was breathless. He had watched the show from the center orchestra, and then waited patiently through the notes. "'Twas most fantastical, as something from my dreams."

"At least Alex liked it," Lulu grumbled. She bought the same lie Stanley's parents, and the school, had. Cooke had shadowed Stanley during the school day.

"Did you?" I said, surprised.

"If thou wishest me to be honest." Cooke screwed up his face, like being dishonest would be physically uncomfortable. "A mixture of utter awe and sincere distaste swirls in my chest."

"How about don't be honest, then?" Lulu snapped.

"Very well," Cooke agreed quickly.

I pulled her in for a hug: "You were great, sweetie."

"Truly," Cooke assured her. "To see a truly feminine Ophelia was breathtaking."

Horns grew out of Lulu's head.

"Alex?" I whispered, and then lifted a pointer finger to my lips: *Shhhhh.* He got it. "Why don't we all head out?" I suggested. "We've had enough theatre for one day."

"Speak for yourself, Mama," Stanley said wistfully, as we exited out the side door. "I've never had 'enough' theatre."

33

"Just a quick update," Lulu said, standing in the doorway of the tech booth. "Our director is still not here. Can we panic now?"

I sucked in a breath. It was opening-performance day, and we had just spent the last two hours texting, e-mailing, and calling Brandon with no response. Stanley had even driven to his house, but the place had been dark. Where *was* he? Was he okay? And if he was . . . how was he not *here*?

"We still have"—I checked my phone—"an hour and fifty-three."

"The parent-ushers are going to be here soon," Stanley reminded me. "And we'll have an audience waiting outside by seven."

I dropped my head and pinched the skin between my eyes. Out on the stage, the cast dutifully ran through their lines as I'd asked them to do. They had no idea that Lulu, Stanley, Yohan, Lily, Cooke, and I were running around in a panic trying to save all of our butts. At this point, I didn't care if the show was good, but I did care if there *was* a show.

"Hi, kids."

Gretchen, wearing her formal black velvet turtleneck, appeared next to Lulu. I felt a wave of relief wash over me: There was an adult here to save us.

"I'm sorry, I just got Yohan's messages. Has our director shown up yet?"

"No," I told her, "he hasn't, and he won't answer his phone."

"And what do you want to do?" She was looking at me, but her face was blank.

In that moment, I wanted to *scream* at her. My anxiety had been peaking, and then it took a sharp left and turned into anger. *What do I want to do? I want to grieve for my dead friend. I want to ditch this stupid high school production. I want to go home and crawl under the covers and never come out.*

I want you to fix this.

I looked at Stanley, then back at Gretchen, then back to the auditorium, as if someone else would materialize there who could make these kind of decisions. It didn't feel fair that the show was landing on my inexperienced shoulders.

"I—I don't know," I said finally. "I don't know what to do."

Gretchen sighed. "You're in a tight spot. If you want me to cancel the show, I will, but I think we can figure this out."

Cooke cleared his throat in the corner. Everyone stopped and turned to stare. "If anyone can fix the play, 'tis Emma. I've seen her conquer before."

His eyes twinkled. *Finally, a little support.*

"Who are you?" Gretchen asked, confused.

"Friend from out of town." Stanley nodded at me.

"Okay." I let out a huge breath. "I was thinking, worse comes to worst, I could read the Ghost's lines over the God

Mic. Not ideal, and we'd have to figure out how to coordinate that with the sound effects—"

"Emma?" Josh appeared behind Gretchen. "Oh, hi, Gretchen. Um, Emma? Could I speak to you in private for a minute?"

He looked strangely pale, but I was in the middle of a crisis. "In a few minutes, okay, Josh? I'm sorry. I'm trying to figure out something with Gretchen."

"Yeah, yeah, of course, no worries." Josh shook his head and backed out of sight, and about three seconds later I heard a heave, and then the sound of vomit hitting the carpet. Everyone in the booth froze.

Stanley seized the opportunity of silence.

"Can we panic *now?*"

Gretchen took Josh to the bathroom, and Yohan got Janitor Kyle, and that mess was taken care of.

But the mess that was our show was just expanding, and somehow that was my responsibility.

"How's he doing?" I called through the door of the bathroom. Gretchen stepped into the hallway.

"Not great." She sighed. "He's thrown up twice more. I think it must be a stomach bug."

"Should I check on him?" I asked dubiously.

"Why don't you stay with him while I grab him some stuff from my office?"

I must've looked terrified, because she patted my shoulder and said: "If he throws up again, just try to remember what it's like when *you're* throwing up, and what you want for support. It'll be fine."

I nodded, faintly, and she disappeared down the hall. I stared at the doorknob.

What if I just wait out here? What if he doesn't want me to see him sick?

I shook my head. I knew if the situation were reversed, he would be in there with me. I opened the door and found him slumped up against a stall wall. His face was a mixture of yellow, green, and gray. I wasn't sure what to say, and the only idea that kept coming up in my mind was: *Hey! Did you know Shakespeare invented the word "puking"?*

"Hey." Josh jutted out his chin at me and smiled. "Sorry I'm gross."

I tried not to laugh, but failed, and my sneakers compelled me forward—I sat down against the opposite wall.

"I'm sorry, too." I hugged my knees. "Gretchen says she thinks you have a stomach bug?"

He closed his eyes and sighed: "No, I don't think it's that."

"Food poisoning?" I ventured. "How many Fruit Roll-Ups have you had today?"

He laughed. "I've hardly eaten anything today. Definitely not food poisoning."

"So?"

He opened his eyes—his bloodshot, apologetic brown eyes. "It's nerves. All week, I've felt this thing building inside me—like a slow volcano of panic."

He stopped to rub his stomach. Whatever he was feeling seemed to pass, and he looked at me again.

"This is like the homecoming game, when a college scout is watching, and, like, the SATs, all combined. You know?"

I'd never been so panicked that I'd thrown up, but I could imagine what it might be like.

"I'm really sorry you're feeling like this."

He just nodded and closed his eyes again. Quick phone check: We had an hour and a half, and he looked worse than ever. Gretchen came back in.

"How's Sicky doing?"

"He hasn't thrown up again," I said cheerfully.

"Yet," Josh groaned.

"I brought water and a ginger ale," Gretchen said, "and these." She palmed two white pills. "Anti-nausea. For when you're done."

He nodded, eyes still closed. I stood up and pulled Gretchen over to the sinks, out of his eyesight.

"I think we need to cancel," I said. "He's not getting better, and that means we have no Hamlet and no Ghost—at least not one who can be on stage."

Gretchen bit her tongue, looked back at Josh, and then at me: "All right, it's your call. We'll cancel." She didn't seem pleased, but she couldn't really argue with me at this point.

"No!"

We both peeked back over at Josh.

"You can't . . . you can't cancel the show." Josh had crawled over to the toilet and was hovered over the bowl. Gretchen immediately went to him and began rubbing his back, like my parents used to do for me when I was throwing up as a kid. It was so hard to see him like that, but I forced myself to not look away.

"You can't go on, Josh, I'm sorry." I felt thoroughly defeated. At this point, everything was stacked against us.

"No, I can't." He paused for a few deep breaths. "But this is our show, Emma. The cast—they don't deserve this. The show can't stop because Brandon's a flake and I'm a nervous idiot."

Josh's voice cracked, and he finished his speech with a wince. Gretchen stared at me pointedly, and I gaped back at her.

Was she serious? We were going to listen to a puking soccer goalie right now?

"Look," I said, my voice thin, "even if we wanted the show to go on tonight, there's no show. We don't have a Ghost. Or a Hamlet."

As if to prove my point, Josh finally heaved again. I looked away—from the sound of it, not much had actually come up. When he was done he sat back, next to Gretchen, against the wall. She handed him toilet paper, and he wiped at his mouth, his motions quick and efficient. He took a sip of the water and then looked up at me.

"You're wrong. We do have a Hamlet."

It took me approximately six seconds to get it, but when I did, I felt my jaw drop.

"She can do this—you know she can. But you're running out of time, and I need to puke again. So go make it happen."

I backed up slowly, the reality of what I was about to do sinking in.

Even now, something about Hamlet must still matter, or why am I doing this?

My sneakers squeaked as I tore down the hallway.

34

Gretchen ran Josh home. After relaying my plans to Stanley, I started breaking the news. To Lulu's credit, her face didn't light up with the least bit of glee when I told her Josh was sick from nerves, couldn't go on, and she would have to play Hamlet.

"All right, whatever you need." She squeezed my arm a little too hard—her excitement couldn't be completely contained. "But who's going to play Ophelia?"

I glanced at the stage, where a fair, delicate boy with dark hair was wandering around, staring up at the lights in awe.

"I've got someone in mind," I said.

After a quick word with Cooke, I gathered everyone on the stage once more and asked Stanley for a little light. With everyone looking at me like this, I suddenly felt nervous about my decisions.

What if they revolt?

"Hey, everyone."

The worried chatter subsided.

"I have some bad news," I said. "But it's all going to be okay."

Silence. Dubious looks. Raw panic in some faces.

"Josh is sick, and Brandon is MIA."

Amelia gasped, and Greg looked like he was going to cry. The freshmen clung to each other.

"But it's fine! We're going to be *fine,* all right? Lulu knows Josh's lines, and she's going to be great."

A collective "Oooh."

"As for Ophelia, luckily, we have someone here who happens to know the part. Maybe you've already met him, but this is my friend Alex."

Cooke bounded out of the stage-right wing in a suit and tie. Stanley had clearly dressed him up. "Friends, 'tis such an honor to be part of thy fantastical, strange *Hamlet—*" he began, but I quickly shushed him and made him sit down with everyone else.

"So . . ." Kelly looked from Lulu to Alex. "Hamlet's a girl, and Ophelia's a guy."

"Yes," I said, inwardly biting my nails. The cast digested this information for a moment before Kelly spoke again.

"All right, I can get on board with that. But who's gonna play Ghostie?"

The trapdoor hovered in front of me, and for a moment, I thought about jumping through it and bringing Shakespeare back to my high school auditorium.

I did it for him, didn't I?

But there would be no way to explain an unfamiliar older man in our high school cast.

If only we had our own Shakespeare, someone who knew the plays so well they could step into any role.

I broke my gaze from the trapdoor and saw Gretchen entering at the back of the auditorium. If I hadn't looked up then, I wouldn't have noticed her: She had closed the door behind her without so much as a click.

"I'll take care of it," I said quickly. "Now, two more changes. First—our new Hamlet and Ophelia won't fit into the costumes, so we're gonna cut the costumes entirely. Everybody just wear your street clothes. And we'll be adding an intermission after the player scene."

This new information seemed to please some (Kelly in particular), and terrify others. Too many changes too fast.

"Please go review your parts." I began to dismiss them. "Lulu, you need to run the duel with Evan, and Alex, you and I will need to go over your blocking. We have half an hour till house opens."

I thought that would prompt them all to leave, but instead they stayed where they were, huddled onstage.

"Um . . ." I searched for the words that would restore their humanity, so I would have a cast of people, not frightened gargoyles. "Like I said, this is all going to be *fine*. We're going to get through this together."

"But . . ." Rosie spoke up. "What if the whole thing falls apart?"

The other freshmen nodded on cue, and even the upperclassmen looked up at me fearfully.

"What if the auditorium burns down?" I replied evenly, though my hands were shaking so hard I had to clasp them together. "It's just not going to. It's not. We're not going to fall apart; we're going to do this. Now, go."

This time they all stood and hurried backstage, whispering as they went. I could pick out a few sentences: "What if Brandon shows up and we're not wearing costumes?" "First freakin' *columns*, and now this?" "Where is that Alex kid from? Such a weird accent." "Do you think I should tell my mom not to come tonight?" I couldn't blame them—only when we finished the show safe and sound would they actually believe me.

I barely believed me.

As I jumped down from the stage, I heard Yohan mutter to one of the crew members: "This is going to be such crap."

I froze for a second, as my insides began their usual twist, before forcing myself up the aisle toward Gretchen.

"What do you need me to do, Emma?" she asked when I approached her at the top of the auditorium.

"Are the ushers here? And the ticket people?" We had parents and other students volunteer to take tickets and hand out programs.

"Yes, they're setting up."

"Can you tell them there's going to be an intermission, about two-and-a-half hours in?"

She smiled, eyes twinkling. "I'll tell them."

"And one more thing." I grabbed an extra script out of my bag and handed it to her. "I need you to play the Ghost."

"Oh, Emma, no, I'm not—"

"You asked what I need." I could feel the breakdown coming. "I need your help."

She sighed and opened the script. She stopped a few scenes in, scanning a page. "Swear to me!" she said, making her voice deep and gruff.

"Yeah, exactly."

"All right, just for tonight. I'll be back in a minute, and you can run me through the blocking."

I watched her disappear through the big double doors, into the lobby, and then went into the booth to grab my binder—I had twenty minutes to show both Gretchen and Cooke their blocking.

I squatted down and reached for my binder. It had fallen on the floor, under the light board. I got down in the dark under the long shelf, and all of a sudden I found myself curled up among the power strips and extension cords, hands shaking, knees knocking. I forced myself to hug my legs tight to my chest.

My whole being felt pressured—one touch, and I could shatter into a million pieces. And at the same time, I felt completely detached, like none of this was real, and if I closed my eyes and reopened them, I would realize I had been asleep the whole time.

My phone blinked warnings at me:

Nineteen minutes . . . Eighteen minutes . . . This is a nightmare. . . .

"Mama? Get out from under there." I peeked up. Stanley was holding out a can of some kind of beverage. "It looks like alien pee, but it's got enough caffeine to get us through."

"Stanley, I'm . . . scared."

His beady eyes softened; he set down a six pack of the drinks and gently pulled me out from under the shelf.

"Don't forget, I've seen what you can do, Mama," he said. "And you're not doing it alone. We're here."

Lily popped out from behind Stanley and waved at me.

"Now give me your binder. I'll run Gretch through her blocking, and you take care of Alex."

I handed him my binder, and he shoved a drink into my hand.

"Thanks." I felt my lip quivering, although I wasn't sure which emotion was causing it to do so. "Let's do this."

Twenty minutes later, Lulu texted me to come backstage. The audience had been steadily filling in. We had an almost-full house now, masses of heavy coats and hats piled all over the seats. Ashlee, Ashley, and Jennifer were sitting in the front row.

If it's terrible, at least they have to sit through it, I noted as I made my way down to the lower backstage area outside the dressing rooms.

"There she is!" Lulu smiled radiantly. "Come here, Emma, next to me."

The whole cast and crew were standing in one big circle, hands joined. I ducked self-consciously under arms and ran through the circle to Lulu. She scooted me in between her and Cooke. He took my hand, and my whole arm prickled. *Not the time, arm, thanks.* I looked around the circle: They were all in their street clothes. Kelly wore a flattering dark green top, with nice jeans. *Much better.* Rosencrantz and Guildenstern wore band T-shirts and slouchy pants. Claudius had on a surfer hoodie. Lulu wore a faded red T-shirt, jeans, and her sneakers. Nobody looked like they were about to walk out onstage, except for Cooke, who was gorgeous in his sleek black suit.

"Now that we're all here," Lulu said, holding up her hands in mine and Evan's, "I just want to say that I know this isn't the show we rehearsed, but it's still our show. Brandon and Josh may not be here, but it's their show, too, and in their honor, we're gonna rock it so hard core!"

Greg whooped, and everyone else joined in with a solid cheer.

"Let's make this the best five hours anyone has ever spent in our auditorium!" she cried.

Another big laugh, because no one had ever done a play this long in BHS history.

"Now, for the squeeze," she said, and held up her hand in Evan's. "For those of you who have never done this before, we're going to close our eyes. I'm going to squeeze Evan's hand, and then Emma's. When you get the squeeze, you pass it on. Ready?"

Victoria had done this for *Midsummer*, but I had completely forgotten about it, and was glad Lulu had remembered. We closed our eyes, everyone giggling. I got the squeeze and passed it to Cooke. I pictured it being passed around, a little energy flowing from one person to another. Cooke's hand squeezed mine, and I passed it to Lulu, and then I realized Cooke hadn't stopped squeezing. My hand was firmly caught in his small grasp, his powdery-smooth fingers. I took a deep breath, and then did the same to Lulu, held her hand tightly, pouring all the energy I could into her. The group fell silent; curious, I opened one eye and saw that everyone was squeezing, holding on to each other for dear life.

I didn't want to break the spell, but I had a feeling we were cutting it close. I took my hand from Cooke's, wiped it on my black jeans, and pulled my phone from my pocket: *Four minutes!*

"All right, places, everyone!" I shouted as I took off up the stairs, two at a time. "And break legs!"

I ran into Gretchen on the stairwell—

"Emma, so I'm entering left, and exiting right?"

"Right," I confirmed.

"And I leave through the trapdoor—"

"After the first scene with Hamlet. Yohan will be helping you down the ladder. Then you hang out under the stage for 'Swear.'"

She marked her script. "Got it."

I turned to go, and she called after me: "Break a leg, kiddo!"

Fumbling up the last step, I nearly did. As I tripped forward, Cooke appeared just in time and caught me by the elbows. He stood me up, grinning his elf-like grin at me.

"Thank you." He really looked too good. His dark hair and dark suit made his pale skin seem more luminous.

"Master Allen, remind me, I enter . . . ?" He held out his script.

"Here." My hands reached out automatically, starring his cue with my pencil.

"Cool. Thanks, dude."

I laughed, and before I could say another word, he jumped away, disappearing through the door into the wing.

I burst into the auditorium and shuffled up the right aisle—the house was completely packed. I closed the booth door behind me, and Stanley shoved another drink into my hands.

"Thanks. We ready? Lily?"

"Ready!"

"On your cue, Mama Stage Manager."

I laid out my binder and flicked on the desk light. I grabbed my headset and wedged it on comfortably. I had nothing to do now but start the show.

"We're at places," I spoke into the mouthpiece softly.

"Copy that. Ready when you are," Yohan's voice crackled.

I looked at the stage—two columns at the front and three arches at the back, but otherwise empty. Stanley's fake sunlight projected an early-afternoon glare. If I squinted, I could almost see the groundlings crowding the front of the stage. If I squinted my ears, I could almost hear the trumpets blaring.

The audience was still chattering, waiting for the house-lights to go down.

Well, that's not happening.

I pressed the God Mic button.

"Good evening, and thank you for, um, joining us for the BHS drama club's production of William Shakespeare's *Hamlet*."

Stanley snickered, and I punched him.

"Tonight, the role of the Ghost will be played by Gretchen Terry, the role of Ophelia will be played by Alexander Cooke, and the role of Hamlet will be played by Lulu Parks."

From our position in the booth, I could hear the audience reacting—a few gasps, and some heavy tittering. I soldiered on.

"There will be one fifteen-minute intermission halfway through the play. Thank you, and we hope you enjoy the show."

I switched off the God Mic, glanced at Lily, who nodded, and Stanley, whose look said *Come on, already.*

"Sound cue one, go," I whispered.

Then trumpets *actually* blared. I startled, and looked sharply over at Stanley. He smiled innocently.

"Actual sound cue one, go," he whispered to Lily. The trumpets faded, and howling noises and tin rattling played over the speakers. The audience settled and turned their attention to the stage.

"Yohan, cue Bernardo and Francisco."

Two shivering guards, Rosie in a plaid dress and Peter in sweatpants, took their places onstage, carrying spears.

"Who's there?" Rosie called into the audience.

"Well, we're screwed now," Stanley murmured. "We've started and we can't stop."

Greg entered, in his stripy polo shirt, with Amelia, carrying a spear, wearing a plaid skirt, tights, and heels.

"Sound cue two, go."

Gretchen made her first entrance, from stage left, in her black velvet turtleneck. Greg, Rosie, and Amelia all cowered into the downstage-right corner. Stanley burst out laughing.

"Oh man, oh man, this just got so good."

I hoped he was right, or we had a painful five hours ahead of us.

35

The first act was weird. I mean, to be expected, because the whole cast had to adjust to a different Hamlet and a stranger as Ophelia. I had been right: The adrenaline of live performance helped them pick up the pace, and the dialogue was a little speedier. But it was definitely jarring at times: There wasn't a real sense of ease onstage, except for Lulu and Gretchen, who seemed to be having a wonderful time.

"Revenge his foul and most unnatural murder!" Gretchen cried at Lulu, who looked terrified—and it may not have been acting. Gretchen was a formidable Ghost.

"You know," Stanley said, pressing the "Go" button for the next slow, slightly-sinking-sun cue, "something about the no-costumes thing is really working."

I watched Gretchen, in her turtleneck, with Lulu, her silvery blond bob bouncing as she paced in her shiny sneakers.

"I think you're right," I murmured. "Although I don't quite know what it is."

I remembered the extravagant costumes at the Globe, and how the actors' larger-than-life performances were enhanced by the bustles, the beading, the details of the gorgeous clothes.

"Maybe— Sound cue nine, go!" I interrupted myself.

More wind howling.

"Maybe those big costumes kind of overshadowed their performances?" I mused. "They're only high school actors. Maybe the big costumes were too much, and we can see their performances better now."

"Mmmm." Stanley nodded. "That might be it." He paused, and then said, "You're such a smarty-pants, Mama."

I didn't look at him, but I smiled into my headset.

"Yohan, ready for set change three, please."

"We're ready." Gretchen exited down through the trap-door, holding out one hand:

"Adieu, adieu, adieu. Remember me!"

Lulu stood downstage left, staring after her. As soon as Gretchen was through the floor and out of sight, Lulu whipped around to face the audience, her look fervent, but her voice soft:

". . . Remember thee? Ay, thou poor ghost, whiles memory holds a seat in this distracted globe." She looked back at where Gretchen had stood. "Remember thee?"

There was no denying it: Lulu's Hamlet was beautiful. When it was just her onstage, the awkwardness of the other scenes faded away, and I felt rapt in her performance. She was more polished than Josh, and when she said Shakespeare's words, they carried the emotion, but they also made more sense. The meanings were clearer when she spoke them. Like Burbage.

And yet, I couldn't quite say I liked her better than Josh. Her presence onstage was certainly different. She was completely comfortable up there, while Josh was a nervous ball of energy. That had made his Hamlet more fearful, more jittery, which to me had made sense in its own way. Hamlet isn't comfortable.

Act two kicked off with smooth cues. No batteries had died yet, so the tech was running well, but it felt good to know the plots were pinned up in the wings, just in case. I watched Cooke fly onto the stage, into Grant's/Polonius's arms.

"How now, Ophelia, what's the matter?"

"O my lord, my lord, I have been so affrighted!"

Grant's face wavered for a split second, like he was about to laugh at the guy clutching to him. It was a good thing Cooke wasn't doing his official Ophelia voice, or Grant would have been rolling on the floor. The scene continued with no laughter, from Grant or the audience. I was very grateful.

"We're getting there." Stanley turned a page as we entered act three. I nodded, but I couldn't relax yet—we still had "Get thee to a nunnery" and the player scene before the intermission.

"I love my design. I just wish"—he sighed as Lulu came down center—"that she had a spotlight for this one speech."

Lulu held one hand in the other, and then looked up, directly into the audience: "To be, or not to be—that is the question."

"Brrrrrugh!" Stanley shuddered. I silently agreed, as chills went up and down the backs of my arms.

"Whether 'tis nobler in the mind to suffer the slings and arrows of outrageous fortune, or to take arms against a sea of troubles, and by opposing end them."

She took the small knife from her pocket and ran her fingertips along the edge.

". . . to die: to sleep—no more, and by a sleep to say we end the heartache and the thousand natural shocks that flesh is heir to . . . "

She put the knife back in her pocket and sat on the ground, cross-legged, and spoke to the first row of seating.

". . . to die: to sleep—to sleep, perchance to dream—ay, there's the rub, for in that sleep of death what dreams may come when we have shuffled off this mortal coil must give us pause . . ."

She herself paused, and brushed her bob back out of her face.

". . . there's the respect that makes calamity of so long life."

I slipped one ear out of my headphones and listened through the sliding window crack—in the four-hundred-seat auditorium, not one person made a noise. They were captivated. My chest began to fill up with mushy pride, and it felt like all my limbs might pop off. Just as I couldn't feel any more—

"Good my lord, how does your honor for this many a day?"

Cooke entered, hesitant, and Lulu scrambled up. He handed her the letters that Hamlet had given Ophelia. As their dialogue went on, my brain almost broke—to hear Hamlet's lines coming from a woman, and Ophelia's lines from a guy . . . not a guy playing a woman, but a *guy*. It changed the whole dynamic of the scene. It felt so backward, but so right. Lulu's Hamlet was sensitive, rash—and Cooke's Ophelia was strong, but confused and hurt. Their parts seemed to blur.

These lines could be said by anyone, whatever their gender.

When Lulu screamed at Cooke and he drew back, my heart stopped. She stormed offstage, and Cooke collapsed on the ground, shaking.

"O, what a noble mind is here o'erthrown!"

When the scene was over, and Kelly, Evan, and Grant ushered him offstage, the audience actually clapped.

"Damn," Stanley whistled.

"That was really good."

Lily's small voice startled us both, and we turned around and stared at her. She ducked her face into her binder.

"Yeah, it really was," I agreed, grinning. "Sound cue twelve, go."

The player scene was a bit of a mess. People dropped lines, and because of that it slogged on a bit. Things picked up when Claudius bolted off into the right wing, and everyone started yelling and exiting at once. The whole cast cleared the stage, and it was time for intermission. Unfortunately, there was no cue for this, because the houselights had remained up for the performance. The audience didn't move and started to whisper in their seats. Stanley gestured at them violently.

"What the hell are you doing? Leave!"

I was glad the sliding window was mostly closed. I God Mic'ed it: **"Hello. There will now be a fifteen-minute intermission."**

I flicked it off. The fog was lifted, and everyone began to stand and stretch.

"Was the 'hello' necessary?" Stanley hopped off his stool.

"I got them up, didn't I? So shut up."

"Oooh, a sassy stage manager."

I put Yohan in charge of giving the actors their intermission-countdown cues. We filed out into the auditorium. Lily went to the lobby; Stanley made for the bathroom. I checked my phone, but had no texts from Josh. Was he still throwing up?

I meandered down the right aisle toward the backstage entrance, smiling and nodding at various teachers and classmates, not really seeing anyone. As I passed the second block of seating, a hand reached out and grabbed mine. I spun around, instinctively pulling my hand back into my chest.

"Emma."

I couldn't believe it: curly black hair, a familiar black leather jacket, and an orange messenger bag under his feet.

"Brandon?" I nearly shrieked.

36

My whole body tensed, and I felt the urge to smack him across the face. Instead, my hand gripped my phone so tight I thought I might break it into bits.

"Where have you *been?*"

"Can we go talk somewhere?"

"Okay," I said, "but you get five minutes—I want to talk to the cast before the second half."

He stood and gestured up the aisle. I tried not to stomp in front of him. We walked to the top of the auditorium, through the lobby, and into the quieter hallway outside the cafeteria. He paced back and forth, avoiding my gaze. I crossed my arms and waited. When he didn't say anything for ten seconds, I gave up.

"Brandon, I've got a show to run, so—"

"I'm so sorry." He stopped mid-pace, and ran his hands up and down his face. "I'm sorry I—"

"Didn't show up and abandoned our production?" I finished for him. *And abandoned me?*

"For that," Brandon agreed. "And for everything. I feel like I've screwed this up from the very beginning."

I dropped my gaze to the floor and didn't say anything.

"First, I should have, um"—he cleared his throat—"I should have listened to Gretchen and cast Lulu as Hamlet."

"Gretchen wanted Lulu to play Hamlet?"

"I just . . ." He covered his mouth with one hand, then brought it down, and leveled his eyes at me. "I liked Josh. Like, *liked* him."

I fought the urge to scream *Oh my God!*

"And I thought he might be good as Hamlet, too."

"He *was*," I snapped. "He is."

Brandon nodded slowly. "But not as good as Lulu. Definitely not at auditions. It was a mistake to cast him. But it wasn't only that I liked him. . . . I thought if I could pull it off, casting him, and making him good, then I would be this great director. I was going to write about it in my college essay."

So Stanley was right: Brandon was gay . . . and liked Josh. But he was also kind of using Josh?

"But that wasn't me." He pulled at his curls despairingly. "I'm not the one who made him good. You are."

Suddenly, I was on the defensive. "What? How did you— Did Gretchen . . . ?"

"Josh." Brandon shrugged. "Last night I gave him a ride home, and I told him how proud I was that he had come so far. I kept complimenting him . . . and then he finally told me it was you—that you had worked with him and made him better. And I realized I've done nothing right for this show, nothing at all."

My head seemed to float up to the top of the hallway. Had Brandon not come tonight because I helped Josh? Had I made all of this happen?

"Brandon, I'm sorry I didn't tell you, but I really can't deal with this right now," I said simply.

"Look, I know," Brandon stepped forward. "I know you have to go. But I wanted to apologize for messing up this whole thing for my own selfish gain. I woke up this morning and I just couldn't, I couldn't . . ."

He sighed, reached into his pocket, and pulled out a letter and handed it to me. The heading was so loud my eyes bugged out of my head.

Congratulations, Mr. Aiello . . .

"You got accepted to *Stanford?*"

"It came this afternoon. My parents sent my application in early decision without telling me." Brandon took the letter back and stared at it.

"Congratulations?" I said.

"Thanks." He laughed wryly. "And now I'm going to spend my entire life behind a computer. Which is just as well, because I suck at theatre anyway."

On instinct, I protested. "No, you don't—"

Brandon held up a hand and shook his head, silencing me. He folded up the letter. *He must've brought that with him as a prop.* I realized. *Always performing.*

"Anyway," he continued, "I freaked. I couldn't deal with any of it. I took my parents' car and I just drove. . . . By the time I realized what I had done, and where I was, it was too late to get back in time. That's my excuse. It's lame. I'm really sorry, Emma."

I still liked the sound of my name in his brisk, warm voice. But now, all I could do was pity him. He was trapped in so many ways. No wonder directing was hard for him. Ditching was still a messed-up thing to do, but . . .

"You don't suck at theatre," I said softly. "You're brilliant. You're a brilliant actor." In a fit of boldness, I grabbed the letter out of his hands and ripped it down the middle.

"Hey!" he yelped.

"If you don't want to go to Stanford, don't go. You'll figure something out." I handed him the ripped halves, cringing slightly at my own audacity. "But this *Hamlet* isn't horrible, it's pretty all right, and it wouldn't have even happened at all if you hadn't had the guts to do it."

He stared at the ripped-up paper and didn't say anything.

"And I have to go run it now," I said. I paused at the entrance to the auditorium lobby. "And you're wrong. It wasn't me that made Josh good. Casting him wasn't a mistake."

He looked up and smiled with one side of his mouth, one dimple forming in his left cheek.

"So are you coming?" I said impatiently. "I think Gretchen could use a sub for the second half."

Without a word, Brandon darted forward through the lobby and into the auditorium. I paused in the lobby for a moment, where the audience was crowded, buying baked goods and roses, and chatting.

"Honey, should we call the sitter?" I heard a woman ask her husband. "We're only halfway through."

"Dear God." The husband sighed. "Yeah, I'll give 'em a call."

Clearly, people are enjoying this. Fantastic.

Time check: eight minutes. I jogged down the center aisle. Just before I went backstage, I thought I saw a familiar head of short, shiny black hair moving through the crowd, and a wave of déjà vu flooded over me—my skin felt prickly.

Hallucinating now, Emma? Add that to your party tricks.

I shook my head and shut the girls' dressing room door behind me. Lulu was refreshing her shiny pink lip gloss.

"You're doing awesome, sweetie." I smiled at her.

"Thanks, babe! Is it going okay? How's the audience liking it?"

Kelly and the other girls all turned toward me, eager for the news.

"Great, great, it's great. Break a leg for round two!" I ducked back out again before anyone asked me anything too specific.

I headed into the wings. Yohan gave me a good report, and then went downstairs to give the actors five. I said a few encouraging words to my crew, and was about to go back to the booth when I saw Cooke, sitting on one of the thrones, studying his script.

"Hey, Ophelia!" I called back. "You ready to go crazy?"

He smiled and pushed himself up out of the throne. "O yes. 'Tis a simple thing, with all my practice." He fluttered up to me and took a step too close—right up against my face. "Tormented by a fickle love."

"Hamlet's a mystery," I agreed, my heel reaching back, ready to pull away if I needed to.

"A great one." Cooke's eyelashes batted at me. Had someone given him mascara? Goose bumps crawled up the backs of my arms. "'Tis a shame he never reveals to Ophelia the truth of how he feels."

"Maybe he doesn't know what he feels," I offered. Then I spun around and fled. In the stairwell, my stomach dipped: *Whoosh.* Too many feelings, no clue what to do with them.

The crowd was starting to settle back into their seats— the soccer girls' seats were empty. Not surprising. From the booth, I could see the audience was noticeably thinner, but we still had well over half the house. Victory!

"All right, here we go: 'I like him not, nor stands it safe with us to let his madness range,'" I whispered into the mouthpiece.

"Here comes the madness!" Yohan crackled back over the headset.

"Too appropriate." Stanley shook his head.

And we began again. The end of act three passed quickly: Brandon's sudden appearance as the Ghost, in his leather jacket, was pretty weird, but no weirder than the rest of the casting changes that night. His scene was appropriately frightening and tense. Brandon and Lulu still had excellent acting chemistry.

Polonius was stabbed, and Lulu had to drag Grant's decidedly larger body offstage, which was a struggle. She got some good laughs when she played it up, though. The audience seemed to be holding on for her performance.

Act four slowed down when Lulu was sent off to be murdered by pirates. I was afraid of losing more audience members, when Cooke's madness scene began. He entered from stage left, his jacket and shoes off, his tie undone. In my peripheral vision, I could see Stanley sit up straight and lean forward, and I realized Lily and I were doing the same thing.

This was gonna be good.

"How now, Ophelia?" Kelly asked gently.

"How should I your true love know from another one?" Cooke sang, staring off into space. He stepped forward and twirled around, his socks making for quick turns as he spun toward the front of the stage. It looked like he would fall over the edge and right into the audience—the rest of the cast onstage all reached forward at once to try and grab him—but at the last minute, he stopped on his toes, dropped onto his knees, and somersaulted into Kelly's legs, crying.

"He is dead and gone, lady, he is dead and gone."

Kelly nervously tried to pry him from her. "Nay, but Ophelia—"

Cooke huddled into a ball at her feet and hugged his knees into his chest. "Pray you mark. White his shroud as the mountain snow—"

He looked like a little kid cowering at his mom's side when he's seen something scary.

"He would totally get us through to finals in the drama festival," Stanley said. "Think we can convince him to stay?"

"We'd have to pay him, probably, since he's a professional." I turned the page. "But I think he's used to, like . . . a dollar a week, maybe?"

"And will 'a not come again?" Cooke had rolled up his sleeves, all disheveled, and was pleading to Claudius. "And will 'a not come again? No, no, he is dead, go to thy death-bed. He never will come again."

Cooke collapsed. Evan's Laertes, true to his blocking, scooped Ophelia up in his arms. With Lulu, it had seemed cheesy and over-the-top, but now it was touching in a way I hadn't seen—usually there wasn't such sweet affection between two guys onstage. My heart warmed, but the minute Cooke was offstage, it sank.

He's going to die now, he will not come again.

My eyes burned, and I blinked at my script—for a second, my writing seemed to be Wick's, all inky and flourishing. When I blinked again, it was just my plain penciled directions.

I felt Stanley staring at me. It was a huge relief when Lulu, now wearing a soft gray zip-up sweater, returned to the stage with Greg for the funeral scene at the beginning of act five.

"Alas, poor Yorick!" She held up our decidedly plastic skull. "I knew him, Horatio."

When they started lowering Cooke's body on the stretcher into the trapdoor/grave, I punched Stanley in the shoulder affectionately. It did look really cool, but as I watched the stretcher disappear, a bolt of panic struck me.

"Hey, Yohan," I hissed into the mouthpiece. "Everyone's in place, right?"

"Four people are catching him on the other side. I got this."

"Thanks. Just double-checking."

As the cast gathered onstage for the last scene—the duel— the *Hamlet* I had once imagined flashed in my mind, and the memories played: the calmness I had felt, the readiness for everything that was coming, accepting my own fate. Horatio and Hamlet met center stage, the whistle blew, Hamlet lunged forward—

But this time I didn't fall through the hole. This time the swords struck.

Lulu was a less convincing dueler than Josh, but it went all right. She and Evan almost stabbed each other a couple times in the wrong places, but it was okay—these weren't real swords, as Cooke had pointed out to me, smugly, during rehearsal.

Down went Gertrude, Laertes, Claudius. The rest of the cast deserted, leaving just Greg onstage, Lulu staggering toward him.

"As th'art a man, give me the cup."

Greg passed Lulu the poisoned cup, she sipped, and then

she crumpled into his arms. When she fell, I almost cried out, but caught myself. Greg lowered her down and sat, cradling her. She clutched one of his arms.

"If thou didst ever hold me in thy heart . . ." She winced in pain, and my heart beat forcefully in my chest. "Absent thee from felicity awhile, and in this harsh world draw thy breath in pain, to tell my story."

She seemed so weak, so faint, so defeated. I willed my eyes to stay dry—it was one thing to cry for Hamlet, but I felt like my tears were coming for the death of Lulu instead.

"O, I die, Horatio," she panted. "The potent poison quite o'ercrows my spirit. I cannot live to hear the news from England, but I do prophesy th' election lights on Fortinbras: he has my dying voice."

Greg nodded, and tenderly brushed Lulu's hair off her face. *Nice, Greg.* She closed her eyes for her next line:

"So tell him, with th' occurents, more and less, which have solicited—"

She stopped and opened her eyes again, wide, and stared up into the light overheard, before delivering her last line, softly, peacefully:

"The rest is silence."

Her eyes closed again, and her body went limp. I barely remembered to cue Lily for the Fortinbras sounds.

Trumpets blared, and a cannon fired.

Stanley reached over and held my hand. We tilted our heads together and watched as Fortinbras burst onto the stage. Greg carefully laid Lulu's body on the ground, her hair splaying like a silver halo.

Then finally, with a tap of Stanley's finger, the lights went out.

37

There was a lot of applause.

"This five-hour nightmare is over!" Stanley narrated, clapping along with them. "We couldn't be happier to be finished watching this satanic show!"

I checked my phone: 5:16:03. Our fastest time, by far. I was content with that.

Even if they were clapping out of relief, they gave us a standing ovation for the full-cast bow, and Lulu and Cooke got a lot of whistles and cheers for their encore individual bows. After her last bow, Lulu gestured to the lighting booth, and Stanley, Lily, and I all gave a little wave.

Then I whispered to Lily: "Sound cue forty-three, go."

She pressed the button, and a dance-party beat started blasting through the speakers. The cast froze, but quickly recovered, and everyone started dancing—even Cooke, although his jigging looked pretty odd next to everyone else's booty-shaking, erratic jumping, and air guitars. The audience stood and clapped with the beat, and after a while I cued Lily to start the fade out—as the music got softer, the cast danced their way offstage. I could see laughing faces as the audience stood up from their seats.

That totally kind of worked.

Stanley switched the houselights back on and brought down the stage lights. Lily reset her soundboard, gave both me and Stanley a quick hug, and then sprinted out of the booth to go say hi to friends. I flipped my binder back to the beginning and turned off my headset. Stanley opened the door for me, and we both stepped out into the auditorium—the roar of the audience post-performance had already started. It sounded *mostly* positive.

"I'll catch up to you in a minute?" Stanley called. I could see Gladys and Herman waiting for him in the corner, with flowers. I gave him a thumbs-up.

I zigzagged through the crowd on my way backstage. Nobody even noticed me. They were all crowding at the side entrance, waiting for the actors to come up.

I avoided that entrance and hopped up onto the stage to go through the wings, smiling at my crew and congratulating them as I went. I remembered how important it had been when Janet did that for me.

"Way to go, Sara. Thanks so much, Vera, Ellie, Willson. We'll do notes tomorrow."

I headed down into the dressing room and was immediately slammed up into the wall by a hug from Kelly.

"Thanks so much, Emma." She smiled into my face, practically biting my cheek. "I'm so glad it wasn't a disaster."

"No problem." I extracted myself. "Me too! You were great."

She bounced past me to the exit, and I could hear a big cheer when she emerged into the auditorium.

It turned out quite a lot of the cast were grateful for the show not being a disaster, and I was hugged more times in two minutes than I had ever been hugged. Well, since that day I had assisted the winning goal last fall. I told everyone how great they were, and I could tell from their smiles that they believed it. I gently opened the door to the girls' dressing room and found Lulu in there, alone, sitting with her feet up on the counter, holding a small piece of pink paper with a rose attached—one of those notes that friends and families can send backstage.

"Hey, Hamlet!" I said, scurrying over and wrapping my arms around her shoulders. "You were outstanding, as usual. Did you have a good time?"

"Oh, yeah." She smiled. "But if I'm being honest, playing opposite Alex gave me some ideas to try for Ophelia. I'm really looking forward to tomorrow night."

The small amount of worry I'd had about her relinquishing the part back to Josh dissolved. If we could even get Josh back onstage.

"That's so great!" I squeezed her, planted a kiss on her cheek, and then peeked over her shoulder. "You got a rose! Was Chip here tonight?"

She didn't say anything. My eyes focused on the note. The card read:

You are incredible. I'll be waiting afterward.

—M

A flashback: the shiny-black-haired head I saw in the crowd earlier. So it was Megan. My best friend's loud, colorful girlfriend.

"She's here!" I cried, thrilled. But Lulu was still silent. I knelt beside her chair and looked up at her. "Honey, are you okay?"

"Did you see my parents out there?" she whispered.

I shook my head. "I can't say for sure, though; I haven't really been paying attention."

Lulu tapped the head of the rose on the counter and sighed.

"I don't know what to do," she said finally. "I mean, it's *Megan*, but . . . if I do this here, at school, it's really going to change everything."

I reached up and ran my fingers through her hair. "Everything's already changed," I pointed out. "And you're okay."

Her mouth bent into a pre-sobbing frown, and she scrunched down into my shoulder. "I don't know if I'm okay."

I felt light-headed. "You just played the hardest part in Shakespeare," I reminded her. "You're more than okay, you're incredible."

She sniffled a little.

"And I love you, and I always will, no matter how many times you change everything."

She clung to me tighter, but her breath began to sound normal, less wet.

"And you've got a girl out there who loves you." My voice shook. "And she just survived a five-hour high school Shakespeare production to see you."

She laughed and straightened up, wiping at her eyes. "You're right, you're right. Okay, babe. How do I look?"

Puffy, red eyes. Sleek bob turned tousled and slightly greasy. A few zits breaking out along her jawline. Clothes crumpled from dying onstage. But I knew it didn't matter.

"Perfect. Go get her."

She smiled so wide it split her face. She hugged me, applied another coat of lip gloss (while I laughed), and then tore out of the dressing room. I followed her into the tiled hallway with the sterile fluorescent lighting, our sneakers slapping the linoleum. The doors to the auditorium entrance burst open at her touch, and another huge round of applause for Lulu began. She bowed her head a little, and whispered a few thank-yous, but her eyes were searching.

"Lulu, the stage!" I pointed.

She turned. Megan sat on the edge, swinging her feet, a glittery hair clip holding back her bangs. She had my same sneakers, but in red, and wore a matching bright-red, flouncy dress with a blue cardigan. Her tan, heart-shaped face looked nervous and hopeful, and she held a bouquet of yellow roses.

When she saw Lulu, she threw the flowers down and launched herself into Lulu's arms. Lulu burst into tears, and kept alternating between holding Megan's head to her chest and pulling back so she could look at her. Finally, they shared one soft kiss. And this time, my stomach didn't squeeze—my heart melted, and I felt a teeny pang of envy. But mostly the melting of the heart. For the first time in months, my best friend was safe and happy.

The crowd of families watching seemed a little confused, but no one said anything. Just then, Greg came out from behind the doors:

"TA-DA! I know, I was *amazing!*"

And everyone's attention shifted to him.

I wandered up into the aisle and found a surprise waiting by the booth: my parents.

"There she is!" Dad cried.

"We didn't know if you wanted flowers, so Abby suggested we get you donuts," Mom handed me a box. "There's enough for Lulu and Stanley, too."

"Abby is the greatest child alive." I opened the box and stuffed half a donut in my mouth. "What did you think of the show?"

"It's quite long, isn't it?" Dad observed. "And strange choice to make Hamlet a woman. But I thought it worked out all right."

My mom rolled her eyes and patted his shoulder: "Lulu was fabulous, as was that boy playing Ophelia . . . Who's he?"

"Alex." I stuffed the other half of the donut in. "He's a friend."

"A friend?" Mom looked at me pointedly, and I ignored her, because donuts. "Between Brandon, Stanley, and Alex, you sure do have a lot of—"

"Josh?" I gaped. Standing behind my parents, staring into space, was Josh. He had changed into a new set of his usual button-up and khakis. The button-up was light green. He wasn't green in the face anymore, though.

"Oh, yeah, hi!" He smiled. "Sorry, I didn't mean to interrupt."

"You didn't," Mom said kindly.

She and Dad introduced themselves, making big eyes at me in a completely subtle manner.

"Well, we better go find Lulu. We'll see you at home, kiddo," Dad said. "You must have a lot of work to do to pack it up."

"Yeah," I muttered. "Yeah, I do, actually. Stanley'll give me a ride."

They both gave me a hug, and then Josh and I were alone.

"Are you feeling better?" I asked.

"Yeah, much, thanks. He smiled and scratched the back of his head. "I made it back for the second half."

"Oh! Cool! What did you think?" I leaned up against the booth wall, certain I was going to pass out any second.

"I think . . ." Josh scuffed the ground with his shoe, and then mimed juggling a soccer ball. He was stalling. "I think Lulu's a lot better than I am. And that Alex kid is, like, amazing."

"He's had a lot of practice." I shrugged. "But Lulu isn't—"

"No, it's okay, she totally is." He smiled, but I knew him well enough at this point to know it wasn't a *real* Josh smile. Those included crinkles around his eyes, and they made you feel as good as cookie dough tastes. "I think I should back out. For tomorrow and Sunday. And next weekend. What if I puke again? And she's so much better."

I reached forward, instinctively, and took his hand. If I hadn't been so tired, I never would have had the nerve. "No, she's not better. She's just different. You're an actor too, Josh, and I know you're going to be an awesome Hamlet tomorrow."

His hand was larger than Cooke's—his fingers were long and spidery, as a good goalie's should be. His large brown eyes met mine, shining.

"Really?"

"Really. You're gonna rock it."

I squeezed his hand again and then let go, suddenly self-conscious of who might be around watching. He didn't seem fazed by it.

"All right, well, I believe you, then. I'll try to, anyway." He smiled, this time with crinkly eyes. I cookie-doughed. "Do you think you could help me run lines tomorrow morning?"

"Sure!" I chirped, with every ounce of energy I had left in me. "But . . . I should probably check the booth now and start the wrap-up. I need sleep worse than Lady Macbeth."

He chuckled. "You do that. I'll see you tomorrow."

"Great."

"I'll text you."

"Great!"

I opened the booth door, and then felt a finger tap my shoulder. I turned—Josh was still there.

"Oh, hi," I said.

"Look, before I go, I just have a question."

"Go for it." *And make it quick before I faint.*

"Is that Alex guy your boyfriend?"

I blinked. *What what what what?!* I sputtered internally. Outwardly, I calmly, nonchalantly croaked, "Um, no, no, uh, no. He's not."

I expected some sort of dramatic reaction, or an explanation, but Josh just nodded solemnly. "Okay. Well, see you tomorrow!"

"Tomorrow!" I repeated after him to his back as he walked away. I was going to need Stanley's and Lulu's opinions on that.

I was back in the peace of the lighting booth for five seconds before Gretchen appeared in the doorway, in her shiny turtleneck. *Seriously?* Why was I suddenly so popular?!

"You ran a great show, Emma. All of it."

"Thank you," I said, feeling like my eyeballs were going to dissolve.

"I talked to Brandon—I'm going to meet with him and his parents to talk about his future."

"That's great." The words came out flat, but I meant them.

"I think you should be the assistant director next year," she said thoughtfully. "You're more than ready to try something like that, if you'd like to."

"Oh," I said.

"Would you like to?"

"Yeah, I would."

"Good. By the way—I don't think I ever told you, but I like the hair."

I stared at her blankly. She smiled and tapped the doorway before finally leaving me alone. I closed the door, and then let myself fall to my knees, then onto my back. I waited for it.

The rush came. Everything ran through me all at once, the past week hitting me in the chest like a bag of bricks. I lay on the lighting booth floor and stared up at the ceiling, pretending the cables and flickering wires were stars. It was all too much, and I almost wanted it to stop, but *none of it can, because this is* Hamlet, *and* Hamlet *never ends.*

"On her headstone it reads: 'Here lies't a beautiful bookkeeper, who could travel through time; she died from fizzy drinks.'"

I lifted my head slightly. Cooke was staring down at me, among the drink cans littering the floor of the lighting booth. I giggled. It hurt my throat. Every part of me was tired.

"Emma . . . I want thee to come back with me." Cooke stood in the doorway, all pretty and delicate, leaning elegantly on the frame in his black suit. "Thou art the most lovely bookkeeper the Globe shall ever have, and from what I have seen tonight—the most gifted."

Ahhh. So that's what he wants.

"No," I sighed, and stood up, my muscles screaming from the effort. "I can't go back with you. I'm too sleepy."

He laughed: "I fear I am still paying for that kiss."

"Yea, thou art," I said, though it wasn't entirely true. With everything going on, I had completely forgotten about Prudence. "That was my first-ever kiss, you know."

"In sooth?" His blue eyes widened to the point of absurdity. "Why didst thou not tell me?"

I shrugged. "Either way, I feel like thou weren't a buttface."

He *really* laughed: "A buttface! I shall tell that one to Master Shakespeare."

I smiled, tight-lipped, and went to spin away, but he placed a hand on my shoulder to keep me from turning. He was no longer laughing. His face was suddenly serious, but soft, the place between his eyes smooth.

"Dearest Emma, please accept my humblest apologies for a most vile first-ever kiss. Wilt thou allow me to correct it?"

I froze. "How?"

He smiled with his pink lips and took a step toward me, but stopped.

He was waiting for me. But did I want this?

I searched in my heart again. It was so full I couldn't sort through it—two *Hamlets*, three Hamlets, two Ophelias, Lulu, Josh, Brandon, Stanley, Gretchen, Burbage, Shakespeare, his wife, his daughters, his son, Wick—

What does all of this mean? What does all of this struggle have to do with theatre?

I could feel my brain beginning to shut down. I tried to fight it with one last question:

What does it all have to do with Hamlet?

I wasn't sure. But under the singing stars, I kissed him for about three minutes straight.

Epilogue

"Emma, Lulu!" Greg opened the door just as I was about to ring the bell. "And Megan, right?"

"Hey, Greg!" I smiled. "Thanks again for having the cast party here."

"No problem." Greg ushered us inside. "Just don't touch any of the furniture, don't look in my refrigerator, and you're not allowed to use the bathroom."

I laughed. "Wouldn't dream of it."

"Almost everyone's already here." Greg led us through the hallway. "Down in the basement."

He opened a white door—light-tan-carpeted stairs, pop music drifting up from below. It looked a little dark, and I paused at the head of the stairway. Me and stairs weren't a good combination, especially right now, with my ankle in a cast. And basements weren't exactly my thing.

Not post-seventeenth-century basements, anyway.

"Emma, let me take that." Megan whisked the tray of cupcakes out of my hands.

"Babe, come on." Lulu took my hand and eased me down the stairs. I cherished the brief moment of being hers. In the last week, I it had kind of felt like Lulu and Megan were the sickeningly sweet romantic couple in a Shakespeare comedy, and I was a minor character.

Once we'd arrived at the bottom, I realized the basement was actually pretty bright: The walls were light moss green and Greg (or Greg's parents) had strung white lights everywhere. It looked like a sparkly woodland den.

All three of us ditched our coats in the coat pile. I was wearing a new purple dress, with a high, flattering collar, black tights, and one black high-top sneaker. I'd even worn dangly silver earrings and spiked my hair up. A complete turnaround from the mess I had been during strike—the take-down of the set and cleanup of the theatre that afternoon.

I spotted Stanley in the corner, in a magenta button-up and black dress pants, hair extra shiny and falling around his shoulders. As I approached through the buzzing crowd, I saw he was with Brandon, who wore his usual black leather jacket.

"Mama!" Stanley grabbed my hand and spun me around awkwardly. "You look adorable."

"Really cute." Brandon smiled in agreement, dimples flashing. I waited for my stomach to flip—but nothing. *Maybe I'm officially cured?*

"Thanks! You both look cute, too."

"Where's Lu?"

"Snack table."

We both looked over the top of the crowd and saw the couple feeding each other cheese puffs.

"Revolting," Stanley observed. "It's a good thing she's done playing Ophelia. She is far too disgustingly blissful to do it now."

"Don't be cynical," Brandon chided. "They're brave."

He was right—they were pretty out there for the world to see. Megan had been to every performance of *Hamlet*, finishing off with our matinee this afternoon. I couldn't imagine the kind of devotion it took to sit through six five-hour *Hamlets*. I could barely do it myself.

It was a good run, though, and there was already a hole beginning to widen in my heart where the BHS *Hamlet* would burrow—I would miss it more than any show I'd worked on.

Well, almost any show . . .

Stanley poked me in the stomach. "Did you bring Alex?"

I shook my head. I still hadn't told Stanley the truth about the trapdoor.

After that first performance, Cooke needed to get back to the Globe, and I needed to prepare my actual cast for their first real show. I hadn't even come out of Hell when I'd dropped him off, I had just wanted to make sure he got through safely. Before I left again, when we were down in the Globe's basement together, I had kissed him one more time. It was soft and long, but close-lipped, and I felt something sad in it. I didn't know what that was until the next day, when I tried to go through the trapdoor to check on everyone and the book-keeper situation.

I'd fallen through the hole fast, too fast, and landed on the gymnastics mat that Gretchen and I had moved into the Black Box. It was bright red and clean, not a piece of straw in sight.

It was also not as puffy as the Globe's mat, because people weren't actually supposed to fall onto it: They were supposed to climb down the ladder, with assistance. It was there just as a buffer in case someone tripped on their way down.

Hence the cast I now sported on my ankle. It wasn't broken, just sprained, and, luckily, no one really questioned my story about tripping down the stairs—it was way too likely.

I hadn't tried to go back since. I already missed Cooke so much: his laugh, his enthusiasm, his way with words. But I told myself it never would've worked out between us—he was kind of already dead, after all.

Stanley nudged. "Go get punch."

"What?"

My gaze followed his finger to the punch bowl: Josh, pouring himself a glass *very slowly*, glancing around the room. He was wearing a deliberately faded red button-up with the sleeves rolled up, fitted jeans, and his brown belt. His sandy-blond hair was even longer now, perfectly messy. He looked way too hot.

I eyed Brandon, who I could tell was thinking the same thing. He noticed me and smiled.

"Oh, all yours," he said, good-naturedly.

What universe is this again?

"Go!" Stanley shoved me in the direction of the punch bowl, and I stumbled forward. I almost turned back to say something snarky, but I was already a few feet closer, so I soldiered on.

I clunked quietly toward Josh and slid along the edge of the table till we were almost touching.

"Hey," I said. He nearly spit his punch back into his cup.

"Emma!" He fought back a choke. "I didn't see you. Or hear you."

"Techie powers." I smiled. "Sorry, didn't mean to scare you."

"You scare me all the time." He hunched over a bit, toward me. "You're the scariest person I know."

"I bet you say that to all the stage managers." I grinned.

Whoa. Was that just flirting? Did flirting come out of my mouth? Who authorized that?

"No." Josh smiled, his eyes crinkling at the corners. "I don't."

I gulped, and quickly backtracked. "So, it's over, huh? Back to real life. Soccer and all that."

He nodded while pouring another cup of punch. "Yeah— track team for the winter. And I can't sing to save my life, so the spring musical's out."

"And you'll be so busy senior year . . ." I trailed off, not really wanting to say it.

"Oh, I'll definitely audition for next year's Shakespeare." He handed me a cup of punch. "Though I doubt I'll get cast— there's a rumor Lulu's applying to direct."

If she was still living in the state by then.

I cradled the cup in my hand and tried to play it cool: Excitement buzzed in my ears. The thought of never working on Shakespeare with Josh again had been so bleak I had barely let myself feel anything about it. We had met last Saturday morning, the day after opening night, the day of his first show as Hamlet. We'd gotten breakfast at Outerspace, and I'd made him recite his five big soliloquies *before* his first sip of coffee. He'd nailed them all, word for word, and we'd spent the rest of the morning just hanging out. I figured the more relaxed I could get him, the better his performance would be.

He was good. Nervous, sure, but because he bounced all over the stage, his Hamlet was someone I could relate to. Not calm, easing from one speech to the next, but always on edge. And he never threw up again (not that he told me, anyway). He'd made it through all five shows, and I was so proud after our last show that I had wanted to throw my arms around his chest, smooshing my face into his neck and—

"Well, if you work hard all year," I said, "you may have a shot at getting a part in Lulu's chorus."

"Sounds like I'll need some help preparing my audition," he said thoughtfully.

"Probably," I agreed, looking down. "Gretchen should be able to get you ready in time."

"I wasn't thinking of Gretchen."

"I don't know why." I sipped my punch. "She's the best at Shakespeare."

"One of the best." His voice was closer.

I looked up: brown eyes close to mine, and full.

"Wanna dance?"

I was suddenly aware of the music: It was kind of slow, and sweet, and mushy. I glanced around the room. Everyone had awkwardly cleared to the sides. *Theatre kids: We know how to ask each other to dance.*

"I don't think people are dancing," I observed.

"They will if I start it." Josh set his punch down. "I don't know if you know this, but I'm really popular."

I feigned outrage. "How could you hide that from me?"

"I've never hidden anything from you." He shook his head as I let him take my punch and set it down. "You just haven't been paying attention."

"Grrrhlugh," I replied, stunned. Josh was getting more dramatic by the second, like Hamlet had rubbed off on him.

"So, wanna dance?"

I wasn't sure I could handle the whole cast and crew watching me dance with Josh, especially with my stupid ankle. I stalled, but then Megan led Lulu out onto the dance floor and wrapped her arms around her. The cast and crew began to giggle, whispering, and without thinking, I grabbed Josh and pulled him out there, too, tentatively resting my wrists on his collarbone. I stared at his chest—he was so tall—and then his long arms were pulling me in, just a little.

I glanced around the room and took note of the looks and the murmuring. I felt myself start to blush, but then I looked up: Josh's smile was manic. His eyes squinted, they were so crinkly. I smiled back, realizing at that moment I didn't really care that people were noticing us: I just cared about his smile and how it all felt. In a fit of boldness, I leaned my head against his shoulder, closing the distance between us.

Whoosh. My whole body sparkled, from head to toe, like nothing I'd ever felt before. Not when Brandon winked at me, not even when Cooke kissed me. Suddenly I was shaking, too, but it wasn't anxious shaking—it felt like I just couldn't contain all the feeling and it was trying to burst out.

"Hey, you okay?" Josh whispered, causing my ear to fall off from tingling, and sending small fireworks shooting out the top of my head. He was obviously concerned that the person he was dancing with was, you know, trembling a whole bunch.

"Yeah," I looked up at him. "I'm just . . . um . . ."

His eyes shone down at me, and I sighed and put my head back on his shoulder.

"I'm just happy."

I took a breath and told myself to try to relax. The trembling gradually subsided as we swayed (we didn't move much, because of my ankle).

After another chorus, Josh pulled back, just a little, and seemed to eye the top of my head.

"Are you going to grow your hair out again?"

"I don't know." I laughed. "Why?"

"I just wondered," he whispered. "I liked your long hair, but I like this too. I like being able to see your face."

I leaned my head back onto his shoulder. I wasn't sure yet what I could say, what all of this was. He seemed content with my silence, though: the soft swaying and the tiny trembles left in my arms.

One thing I was sure of: *The hair is definitely working.*

The shaking finally stopped altogether just as the song was ending. I looked around and realized Josh had been right: Almost everyone had followed us out onto the dance floor.

Kelly and Greg?? Should have seen that one coming.

The last note of the song startled me, and I sprang clumsily backward, off him. He stood in front of me, bemused, as the next song, a fast song, began.

"I'll grab some snacks. We should go hang out with Stanley."

"Sounds like a plan." Josh jogged over to Stanley and Brandon, now with the Megan-Lulu conglomerate. I grabbed a plate of cookies and hobbled over to join them.

"Do a comedy." Brandon was pointing at Lulu. "Trust me. Do. A. Comedy."

Stanley smirked. "Take his word for it."

"I really love *Twelfth Night*." Lulu smiled. Megan pulled her closer, if that was possible. "But I'm still mulling it over."

"Really?" Josh stole the plate from me and engulfed two cookies at once. "I would've pegged you as a tragedy kind of girl."

Lulu narrowed her eyes. "Okay, Hamlet, which one?"

"Romeo and Juliet," he answered immediately.

Everyone stared at him. I smiled and munched smugly on a cookie.

"I mean, right?" he said, startled by the group's looks. "It's perfect for you."

"Totally!" Megan nodded, her green eyes wide. "Lu, he's right—you'd be perfect at that. You are perfect, by the way."

"Awww, Megs—"

"Enough," Stanley groaned. "I literally will pour the punch bowl over your heads."

They both giggled, and then whispered and snuck away. I wondered if Greg anticipated people making out in his closet.

"Anywho—what are you two going to do without us next year?" Stanley put an arm around Brandon and looked fondly at Josh and me.

"I was thinking I'd try designing," Josh said, deadpan. "It doesn't look that hard."

"He's kidding," I rushed in, responding to Stanley's fireball eyes.

"Oh, yeah, really kidding," Josh assured him. "But I guess Emma'll be assistant directing. So we'll definitely miss you both, but we can't really go wrong with her in charge, can we?" He slung an arm over my shoulders.

"No, you can't." Brandon smiled, a little sadly, but still with dimples. "She's the greatest."

"Kind of bossy." Stanley wrinkled his nose.

"Hey!"

"I like bossy," Josh quipped.

"We know!" Stanley groaned.

"So next year, what part do you want?" I looked up at Josh.

"I was thinking Juliet," he said. "Romeo's pretty stupid."

"That's so true." Brandon nodded. "But Juliet is so dramatic. . . ."

"At least she's actually in love. Romeo was into Rosaline, and then suddenly he's into Juliet?" Josh rolled his eyes.

"You're both wrong," Stanley protested. "The best role is clearly Tybalt. What a fiery little bitchcake."

"Mercutio has the best death," I offered.

"How can you say that when Juliet *stabs herself* for the sake of her *love?*" Josh demanded. "What could be more hard core than that?"

I laughed. I couldn't believe how passionate Josh was getting, and I loved how the spell of getting-along-ness was still lingering over us, even though the show was over.

I looked up: The twinkling lights above our heads caught my gaze and held it. Then everything turned fuzzy and bright, and I felt myself slip into daydreams about doing *Romeo and Juliet* next year: handing off the stage managing to Yohan, sitting in on auditions, offering opinions, blocking a scene of my own . . .

The fuzzy brightness got brighter and brighter until it looked like the sun, and when it got so bright I couldn't stare at it any longer, I winced and looked away. Suddenly, I realized I was standing on the edge of the stage, in the painted wooden O. I turned around, and there was Cooke, in his blue dress, standing up in the gallery above the arches, reaching down toward me, smiling his mischievous smile.

"Romeo, Romeo, wherefore art thou Romeo?"

I blinked, and I was back in Greg's basement, with Josh's arm around me.

"What do you think, Emma? Is it primarily about the foolishness of love, or feuding?" Brandon was looking at me earnestly.

"Love!" I said firmly, and then, aware of Josh's arm around me, tried not to blush. "Definitely about love. The feuding wouldn't have stopped without it."

"That's deep, Mama." Stanley sipped his punch. "But I bet Lu is all about the feuding."

"It's really about both though, isn't it?" Josh took his arm from around my shoulder to scratch the back of his head. I felt cold, disappointed for a brief second, but then felt his hand slip around my waist.

Whoosh. Sparkles. Teeny cannons firing.

His question launched a whole other tirade of opinions. I smiled and felt that happy glow begin in my chest. Because I had this, sure, and this was great. But that vision of the Globe, and Cooke—someday, I knew I would be ready to return. It wasn't over; it hadn't ended yet.

I hoped it never would.

WHAT MAY HAVE HAPPENED:
A Note on *Saving Hamlet*'s Historical Accuracy

Aristotle, in his dramatic philosophy, *Poetics*, says that history relates "what happened," while poetry (or works of fiction) relate "what may happen."

Shakespeare blended the two. He knew that successful plays drew on society's knowledge, and some of the most popular stories in his time were histories. Shakespeare took these stories, and sometimes other writer's renditions of these stories, and added his own insight to the plot and characters. He took what Aristotle calls "the particular" and added to it what he felt were "universal" characters and moments for his audience. Much of what Shakespeare wrote, we would now call historical fiction.

I found this fact very comforting while working on *Saving Hamlet*. I wanted to take Shakespeare and London's history, bring it alive, and make it relevant to our world today. The settings and history in this book are as accurate as I felt was possible. My theatre and history professor, Paul Nelsen, often answered my Shakespeare history questions with, "The truth is, we really don't know." I got used to filling in gaps of knowledge to suit Emma's story. Do I know if they used goat's blood at the Globe for battle scenes? No, not for sure—it's an idea some Shakespeare scholars speculate about. Were the shareholders called "the shareholders" back in 1601? Probably not, but adding those details made it easier to tell the story.

Between the second and third drafts of writing *Saving Hamlet*, I took a trip to London. My college, Marlboro College, sent me abroad with Paul to do historical research for my senior thesis. It was a transformative trip—I stood in the re-created playhouse, Shakespeare's Globe, feeling dust dance around me, light pouring in over the top of the theatre. We also visited the original site of the actual Globe, and I could almost feel ghosts brushing by me on the way into the playhouse. For me, nothing has ever felt closer to magic than Shakespeare and this history. I will forever be thankful to Marlboro College and Paul Nelsen for funding this first trip to London.

Additionally, I owe a great debt to the following books and resources, and highly recommend them:

King of Shadows by Susan Cooper

The Historian's Craft by Marc Bloch

Playgoing in Shakespeare's London and *The Shakespearean Stage, 1574–1642* by Andrew Gurr

Rebuilding Shakespeare's Globe by Andrew Gurr with John Orrell

Shakespeare in Love directed by John Madden

The Time Traveller's Guide to Elizabethan England by Ian Mortimer

1599: A Year in the Life of William Shakespeare by James Shapiro

Rehearsal from Shakespeare to Sheridan by Tiffany Stern

Hamlet: Arden Shakespeare Third Series edited by Neil Taylor and Ann Thompson

http://www.opensourceshakespeare.org/

And yes, wikipedia.org.

As well as many other wonderful books and resources! You can find a complete list of recommendations on my website.

I hope this history resonated with you as it has with me—and that you found this time period thrilling through Emma's eyes. If I could travel back in time, the Globe is where I would go. I would hide backstage and breathe in all the horrible smells and watch the real live magic being created before me.

Thank you for reading!

—Molly

Acknowledgments

If I were to divide my kingdom, I would give a part to thee.
I have a feeling with subsequent novels, this list might not be quite as long. But many people helped me to write and publish my first book, so this is a long list. I am so, so grateful. Thank you, Mom, Vicki Booth, for homeschooling me. Thank you, Dad, Robert Booth, for understanding and encouraging my love of literature. Thank you, Gus, for your writing buddyship and generosity. Thank you, Nellie, for being there in the middle of the night. Thank you, Tory, for your wit, strength, and friendship. Thank you, Jenny, for being you. And for being a potato.

My agent, Alex Slater: We would not be here if you hadn't read my book, all original 100,000 words of it. Thank you to everyone at Trident Media Group. My editor, Kieran Viola: You got the book from day one, and then helped shaped Emma's story with such care. Thank you and everyone at Hyperion. Thank you, Tyler Nevins and Red Hansen, for designing and creating my dream book cover, and Celia Blue Johnson for sending me to Alex.

Thank you, Marlboro College and Bunker Hill Community College.

T. Wilson, for imagining this book with me and coming up with the title. Paul Nelsen, for taking me to Shakespeare's London. Michelle Terry, for your kindness, enthusiasm, and sneaking skills. Geraldine Pittman de Batlle, for your faith in me, and for letting me pause my paper to write this book. Brian Mooney and Vaune Trachtman, for never-ending support and thoughtful advice. Julia Perlowski, for the best thesis examination a girl could ask for. Lucius Salisbury, for introducing me to Shakespeare's plays with such joy and excitement.

I worked in community theatres for a long time, and I would not have been able to write this book without the great people who took me on. Thank you, Ginny Morton and John Fogle. And big thanks to the original Boston Children's Theatre for my best high school theatre experiences, directed so passionately by Patricia Gleeson and Sara Buswell.

Thank you, Sarah Pichler, for asking to read this book. It was a privilege to share it with you.

Emily Cox, Elisabeth Joffe, Rosie Kahan, Megan Reed, and Ellie Roark: Where would I be without you? Definitely crying in my dorm room. Lindsay Coffin: Remember when you titled all of your Shakespeare papers with Arcade Fire songs? Will Hernandez: Dude, you're the best. Sam Stratton: Let's write Charnolia Sil's memoirs. Steve Vieira: All of those inappropriate hangman games during rehearsals.

Thank you to the many, many authors and scholars who write wonderful things about Shakespeare and writing. Thank you to the students and directors putting on Shakespeare plays.

Thank you, readers!!

Thank you to the Chamberlain's Men and the stage-keepers!

Lastly, and least of all interested in this book, thank you, Harriet.